The Bride Wore Denim

The Bride Wore Denim

A Seven Brides for Seven Cowboys Novel

LIZBETH SELVIG

AVONIMPULSE
An Imprint of HarperCollinsPublishers

Excerpt from *The Bride Wore Red Boots* copyright © 2015 by Lizbeth Selvig
Excerpt from *Chasing Jillian* copyright © 2015 by Julie Revell Benjamin.
Excerpt from *Easy Target* copyright © 2015 by Kay Thomas.
Excerpt from *Dirty Thoughts* copyright © 2015 by Megan Erickson.
Excerpt from *Last First Kiss* copyright © 2015 by Lia Riley.

EPub Edition JULY 2015 ISBN: 9780062413925

Print Edition ISBN: 9780062413932

AM 10 9 8 7 6 5 4 3 2 1

To the brides from my family who came before me:
Two great-grandmothers who left their homes
and crossed an ocean on their own
to find their happily-ever-afters;
two grandmothers who married the men of
their dreams and then pulled with them
through hardships I can't imagine to
live their happily-ever-afters;
and finally to my mother who is the most incredibly
faithful bride still after sixty-plus years
of happily-ever-after marriage.
Thank you all for giving me my belief in romance.

Acknowledgments

THIS BOOK BEGINS a new series of stories, and I would not be writing them without the push and inspiration from Jennifer Bernard, who reminded me that no little helpful fairies were going to come and give me the concept for a new set of books; I had to use my own brain!

A hundred hugs and thank-yous go big time to my fantastic, beautiful agent Elizabeth Winick Rubinstein, who brainstormed during long conversations and caught all the perfect idea nuggets I let fall, then helped me weave them into the Seven Brides for Seven Cowboys concept.

My critique partners, Ellen Lindseth (who talks me expertly off of ledges quite regularly), Nancy Holland (who is willing to argue with me until I relent—although she doesn't know I do), and Naomi Stone (who almost always sees the meaning in what I write and doesn't let me leave a crit session depressed). They all refuse to let me coast, despite my whining.

Thanks to Avon Books editorial assistant Gabrielle Keck, who got me through the beginnings of starting the book, and who found lots of great things to fix.

Most of all I thank my brilliant, kind, encouraging editor Tessa Woodward, who knew exactly how to fix all the broken pieces of the original draft and made me feel like it was never my fault they needed fixing! This story rocks because of her!

Thank you, too, to Adam Muhlig and his wife, Ellie, who went to their ranching family and asked research questions on my behalf. Ellie's uncle Steve Gruy and cousin Alberto Muzquiz of Rancho Solo in Hebbronville, Texas, offered me wonderful details about the business of running a large cattle ranch—and promised more when I need it. I am very grateful!

Chapter One

THANK GOD FOR the chickens. *They* knew how to liven up a funeral.

Harper Crockett crouched against the rain-soaked wall of her father's extravagant chicken coop and laughed until she cried. This time, however, the tears weren't for the man who'd built the Henhouse Hilton—as she and her sisters had christened the porch-fronted coop that rivaled most human homes—they were for the eight multicolored, escaped fowl that careened around the yard like over-caffeinated bees.

The very idea of a chicken stampede on one of Wyoming's largest cattle ranches was enough to ease her sorrow, even today.

She glanced toward the back porch of her parents' huge log home several hundred yards away to make sure she was still alone, and she wiped the tears and the rain from her eyes. "I know you probably aren't liking this,

Dad," she said, aiming her words at the sopping chickens. "Chaos instead of order."

Chaos had never been acceptable to Samuel Crockett.

A *bock-bocking* Welsummer rooster, gorgeous with its burnt-orange-and-blue body and iridescent green tail, powered past, close enough for an ambush. Harper sprang and nabbed the affronted bird around its thick, shiny body. "Gotcha," she said as its feathers soaked her sweater. "Back to the pen for you."

The rest of the chickens squawked in alarm at the apprehension and arrest of one of their own. They scattered again, scolding and flapping.

Yeah, she thought as she deposited the rooster back in the chicken yard, her father had no choice but to glower at the bedlam from heaven. He was the one who'd left the dang birds behind.

As the hens fussed, Harper assessed the little flock made up of her father's favorite breeds—all chosen for their easygoing temperaments: friendly, buff-colored Cochins; smart, docile, black-and-white Plymouth Rocks; and sweet, shy, black Australorps. What a little freedom and gang mentality could do, she mused, plotting her next capture. They'd turned into a band of egg-laying gangsters, helping each other escape the law.

Despite there being seven chickens still left to corral, Harper reveled in sharing their attempted run for freedom with nobody. She brushed ineffectually at the mud on her soggy blue-and-brown broom skirt—hippie clothing in the words of her sisters—and the stains on her favorite, crocheted summer sweater. It would have been much smarter to recruit help. Any number of kids bored with funereal reminiscing would have gladly volunteered. Her sisters—Joely and the triplets, if not Amelia—might have as well. The wrangling would have been done in minutes.

Something about handling this alone, however, fed her need to dredge whatever good memories she could from the day. She'd chased an awful lot of chickens throughout her youth. The memories served her sadness, and she didn't want to share them.

Another lucky grab garnered a little Australorp who was returned, protesting, to the yard. Glancing around once more to check the rainy yard, Harper squatted back under the eaves of the ostentatious yellow chicken mansion and let the half dozen birds settle. These were not her mother's pets. These were her father's "girls"—creatures who'd sometimes received more warmth than the human females he'd raised.

Good memories tried to flee in the wake of her petty thoughts, and she grabbed them back. Of course her father had loved his daughters. He'd just never been good at showing it. There'd been plenty of good times.

Rain pittered in a slow, steady rhythm over the lawn and against the coop's gingerbread scrollwork. It pattered into the genuine, petunia-filled, window boxes on their actual multipaned windows. Inside, the chickens enjoyed oak-trimmed nesting boxes, two flights of ladders, and chicken-themed artwork. Behind their over-the-top manse stretched half an acre of safely fenced running yard, which was trimmed with white picket fencing. Why the idiot birds were shunning such luxury to go AWOL out here in the rain was beyond Harper—even if they had found the gate improperly latched.

Wiping rain from her face again, she concentrated like a cat stalking canaries. Chicken wrangling was rarely about mad chasing and much more about patience. She made three more successful captures and then smiled evilly at the remaining three criminals who eyed her with concern. "Give yourselves up, you dirty birds. Your time on the lam is finished."

She swooped toward a fluffy Cochin, a chicken breed normally known for its lazy friendliness, and the fat creature shocked her by feinting and then dodging. For the first time in the hunt, Harper missed her chicken. A resulting belly flop onto the grass forced a startled grunt from her throat, and she slid four inches through a puddle. Before she could let loose the mild curse that bubbled up to her tongue, the mortifying sound of clapping echoed through the rain.

"I definitely give that a nine-point-five."

A hot flash of awareness blazed through her stomach, leaving behind unwanted flutters, and she closed her eyes, fighting back embarrassment. Her voice was still missing when a large, sinewy male hand appeared in front of her, accompanied by rich, baritone laugher. She groaned and reached for his fingers.

"Hello, Cole," she said, resignation forcing her vocal chords to work as she let him help her gently but unceremoniously to her feet.

Cole Wainwright stood before her, the knot of his tie pulled three inches down his white shirt front, the two buttons above it spread open. That left the tanned, corded skin of his neck at Harper's eye level. She swallowed hard. His brown-black hair was spiked and mussed, as if he'd awoken, and his eyes sparkled in the rain like blue diamonds. She took a step back.

"Hullo, you," he replied.

His pirate's grin, wide and warm and charming, hadn't changed since they'd been kids. It had been dorky when he'd been ten and she eight and they, together with Harper's five sisters, had played at being the only pirates who'd sought treasure on horseback rather than from a ship's deck. Then she'd turned twelve and one day found she would have rather been a captured princess than one of the crew. Because that smile had no longer been dorky. It had been a nice fantasy—but Amelia had always made herself the pirate's princess. The highest Harper could rise was to being the round butterball of a maid servant.

Cole's family had owned Paradise's neighboring ranch the Double Diamond. The Crockett daughters and the Wainwright son had all stayed friends through high school, even though Cole had chosen Amelia for, first, the homecoming dance, then Snow Ball, and finally prom. Once the years of exploring their adjoining land on horseback and hanging out being ranch kids had ended, Cole and Amelia had quickly become The Super Couple—gorgeous on gorgeous. Harper had let her secret Cole fantasies fade away, finished high school, gone off to her wild and failed college years, and kept track of Cole and Amelia only the rare holidays they all visited

Paradise Ranch at the same time—like last Christmas when she'd spoken to Cole one-on-one for the first time in years.

His relationship with Amelia had been complicated. Dating for two years after graduation, staying apart for another three years, getting back together so that the family had, for a long time, considered Cole and Amelia all but married. Then, unexpectedly three years ago, the Super Couple had broken up—amicably but permanently, they'd insisted, even though some people still believed, even hoped, they'd reunite.

They hadn't. It didn't look as if they would. But everyone was still friends.

Except for the eighteen months after Harper's father had purchased the Double Diamond. Cole and Mia had broken up, and Cole had disappeared without a trace.

Eventually he'd come back, and the past two winters he'd worked for Sam Crockett on Paradise. Everyone said he was fine.

"Earth to Harpo."

His hand waved in front of her face. She shook her head, and suddenly she was staring at him, having missed every word he'd said. And there were flutters, deep and unmistakably caused by his proximity.

She blinked. "Oh! I'm sorry. What were you saying?"

He laughed again. "Are you all right?"

No. No, no, no. This was unacceptable. As happy as she was to see him, these were not the memories she'd been after. This was not a reaction she wanted—this electric anticipation that had been thrumming through her body ever since he'd walked into the church that morning almost late for the service.

"I'm fine."

"You still do it." He peered at her, grinning again.

"Do what?"

"Go off into that little artist's daze. I always wondered what you were seeing while you were in those trances. Usually you'd disappear after one of them, and we'd find you in some corner painting or drawing. But you weren't big on showing me your work. I was left thinking you'd gotten some great vision or prophecy. Like now."

She nearly choked on her laughter. "I do not do that! And believe me, I was having no visions of any kind. I was seeing three chickens laughing at me, so I was plotting revenge."

That was a lie, but he didn't need to know it.

"Well, you *did* go into trances, but who am I to argue? If this was only revenge plotting, I think you're justified. You are kind of a mud ball, aren't you?"

His familiar, mischievous voice finally calmed her, sent her gaze downward to survey the damage to her only dressy clothes, and, most importantly, made her think the whole episode including the wet clothing, was funny. She lifted her eyes.

"I dunno. I think mud is the new chic."

"Aw, Harpo, if mud is in, then you look fantastic." He hesitated and studied her, his bright blue eyes as warm as his smile. "You look pretty fantastic even if mud isn't a fashion statement."

She lifted her face to the sky, letting the rain that was starting to slow into huge drops burst like little water balloons on her cheeks, keeping the heat in them from showing.

"Yeah? Well, thank you, my old silver-tongued friend. But you know you're going to look equally fantastic if you stay out here much longer."

Without thinking, she brushed raindrops off the shoulders of his shirt, skimming their broad expanse twice with cupped fingers. Then she flicked drops from his hair. The tousled, just-out-of-bed look was beginning to flatten like the chickens' wet feathers.

He stared at her, and she jerked her hand away, dismayed by her bold touches.

"You should get back inside," she said. "I was on my way to the barn to find Joely, but the chickens' gate got unlatched. I had to side track. I'll get these last three chickens and join you."

"I'll help. It'll go faster."

"That's silly. You'll only get muddy, too."

"No, just wet. Because unlike you, I'm good at this."

"Oh, wow. There was a gauntlet hitting the lawn with a giant, rippling splash."

He grinned. She returned it.

"He who returns the most remaining chickens to the yard, gets to…" Cole made a show of thinking up the prize. "Put anything he wants on a piece of Melanie's lefse and make the loser eat it."

"Oh my gosh, what are you? Ten?" She sputtered with more laughter.

Melanie Thorson, the Southern belle wife of Paradise Ranch's foreman who was, in contrast, a first-generation Norwegian-American through and through, had learned to make the best lefse this side of Oslo. The trouble was, a mean person could stuff it with anything from cinnamon sugar to pickled herring.

"Deal or no deal?" Cole asked, his handsome nose now dripping water.

"Oh, it's a deal. But I warn you, the winner? *She* is going to come up with something really disgusting."

"Dream on. One, two, three, go. Catch one if you can, Harpo."

The three chickens had huddled for safety and shelter beneath a huge linden tree, but the instant Harper and Cole took off, the birds clucked into panic mode and went three different directions like possessed bobblehead dolls. Harper went after the Cochin that had left her in the grass and caught her in seconds.

"Hah!" She held up the chicken in triumph, only to see Cole with a flapping Plymouth Rock hen.

"Lucky," he called.

"You keep thinking that," she replied.

They reincarcerated the two chickens and turned to the last escapee. This hen, Harper knew, was the oldest chicken in the flock, the only Rhode Island Red, a hen that had been around at least five or six years. She was wily and stubborn and laid a lot of eggs.

"Roxie Red," Harper said, in the same tone she might have said "Lizzie Borden."

"They all have names, don't they?" Cole asked.

"He always named them, but I don't know what they are. Who can tell them apart? She stands out, the old, cranky biddy."

"Don't you worry your head," he teased. "Let me take care of her."

"Not on your life."

The ridiculousness of their impromptu game felt a little disrespectful given the reason she and Cole were really here, but Harper couldn't rein in the streak of temporary insanity she'd obviously caught from the chickens. At last she'd found the release—the relief—she'd wanted.

They chased the crafty old hen for five full minutes, cutting each other off, herding her into corners, cooing softly but then charging when she dodged and bobbed like a running back. Harper swore the old girl was having as much fun as they were. At last she managed to streak ahead of Cole and reach Roxie as the hen made it to the rabbit fencing around her mother and grandmother's huge vegetable garden behind the coop.

"Gotcha!" She sprang forward, but she tripped and landed on Cole's arm. His hand covered hers as both of them grasped simultaneously for the scolding Roxie.

"Get away from my bird!" Harper shot Cole a withering look.

"Hands off *my* chicken." His voice was high-pitched with mirth.

Roxie flapped easily away, and Harper dissolved into laughter, splayed once again face down on the ground. She lifted her head to find Cole flat on his back gasping for air. He reached across her back, grabbed her arm, and rolled her over, until she, too, lay on her back, her head cradled on his shoulder.

Her first shivering instinct was to leap away, but his laughter held her in place—rumbly and comforting beneath her.

"Remember when we used to do shit like this all the time?" he asked.

"Again," she said, firming her voice so it didn't match her wayward, quivering insides, "when we were ten."

"It's really good to see you, Harpo."

"Yeah." She closed her eyes while the rain splashed her face again, definitely feeling closer to ten than her sometimes ancient-seeming thirty.

They lay a moment longer, letting their laughter ebb, but then, with her heart pounding, Harper came to her senses and scrambled to her feet. It had to be the raw, see-saw emotions of the day causing this unwarranted reaction to him. Her friendship with Cole went back too far for her to allow some rogue attraction to take root. He and Amelia might be ex-lovers, but there was a code between sisters you didn't break.

She held out her hand this time, and he took it. Once he was standing, she dropped the contact.

"I declare this a tie," she said. "I propose we work together to get the chicken and neither of us has to eat lefse."

"We call it a tie. I'll help you catch the chicken. We both eat lefse," he said, making a counteroffer.

"Oh, fine."

Once they weren't sabotaging each other, they cornered Roxie and had her in custody within two minutes.

Since Harper was the dirtiest—and she was extremely dirty—she carried the ticked-off chicken to the coop. Once she'd double-checked the gate, she sagged against it, wet to the skin and slightly chilled from the breeze, despite it being August.

"Thank you," she said, as her adrenaline drained away and took her energy with it. "I'm sorry you got caught up in the rodeo."

"Don't be. The company inside was...frankly, not this much fun."

"I never asked why you came out here in the first place."

He gave a quick frown, an attractive wrinkle forming between his brows. He'd changed over the past decade. All signs of the cute-faced boy and young man he'd been had disappeared beneath the angles and planes of a stunning adult-male face.

"Oh yeah, I guess I did have an official mission," he said. "Joely got back from the barn fifteen minutes ago, and we wondered where you ended up. Your grandmother has called an all-hands meeting."

"Grandma Sadie?" She shouldn't have been surprised. Sadie Crockett had to be the only nonagenarian who could still command her family like a naval admiral. "What's our matriarch got under her bonnet now? Another private prayer meeting? A final eulogy? Can't be about the will; that isn't a secret."

"I don't know," Cole said. "The only thing she told me was that attendance isn't optional."

"Crazy old lady," Harper said fondly, feeling the mood start to slide.

Grandma Sadie wasn't even a little crazy. She was still sharp as a pinprick, and if she wanted a meeting, she had all the moral authority in the world. At ninety-four she had buried a son.

As Harper and her sisters had buried a father.

As their mother had buried a husband.

And not one of them understood how Samuel Crockett could be dead. In the space of a finger snap, the hurricane that had been his big, intense life had gone aground and dissipated long before any expert had predicted or expected.

She tried to cling to the silliness of the chicken chase, but it was fully gone. A tear escaped, and she swiped it away before it could traverse her cheek. They'd all cried plenty in the past days. Wasn't that enough of a tribute to the man who'd inspired awe, respect, sometimes even adulation, but never warm, schmaltzy emotion?

Cole's arm came around her, and he pulled her close. She felt his kiss on the top of her head.

"Look." He pointed across the yard, past the working heart of Paradise Ranch with its barns, sheds, and cattle pens, to the view of Grand Teton National Park sixty-five miles away. In the deep purple sky over the mountains, one fat sunbeam had beaten back the rain clouds to create a brilliant rainbow. "I think that came out for you," he said. "You've always known how to pull hope out of a rain cloud."

How did he know to say something that would soothe her so perfectly?

"If only my father had shown me a fraction of that kind of insight. After all these years—that was really nice of you to say."

"You weren't big on letting us see your work when we were younger, but I still caught wisps of your talent. We all did. I know you still have it."

She wanted to tell him then. She'd promised herself not to say anything to anyone about her news until after the funeral. This was not about her and her dreams—this was about her father and the end of his. She stared at the sky and, in her mind, mixed the oil colors that would approximate its vivid beauty on canvas.

Her fingers itched for her brushes. Her head and heart longed for a secluded room and an easel. But she hadn't brought any supplies with her from Chicago. She'd contented herself with a sketchbook and case of pencils. This trip was not about escape, and a good daughter wouldn't keep wishing for it. Then again, when had she ever been the good daughter?

The rainbow intensified. Cole held her more tightly. The rain slowed further, and after a few more moments, she realized it had stopped altogether.

"I guess we should go in. I volunteered to find Joely for purely selfish reasons—I wanted to get away."

"There's nothing wrong with that."

"I should be in with the rest of the family. It seems better if I don't spend too much time with Mia, and I was one step from having to organize food with her. Not a good plan."

"Your Mia? Dr. Amelia Crockett, the very one who keeps all order and makes all peace? Why would you need to keep your distance from your sister?"

"Amelia moved out a dozen years ago and has never looked back. We haven't lived together in all that time. But to her, I'm still the hippie screw-up, the sister who couldn't be organized if her life depended on it. She's a lot like Dad. I get tired of her telling me what to do as if I don't understand the world." She laughed humorlessly. "She was always the border collie, and I was the sheep she couldn't get into the pen."

"I miss the border collies," he said. "Loved the ones we had. But Mia is no border collie, Harpo. She doesn't care where the sheep go—she's only worried about her own destination. She's more like a bloodhound."

"I disagree. Mia could organize squirrels to line dance if she wanted to. Sorry. I'm speaking ill of your ex."

Harper hoped no old bitterness bled through the words. Childhood pettiness had no place in their lives anymore, especially at a time like this.

"I love Mia," he said, "and I'm sorry things are strained between you. But 'ex' is the operative word here, so I'm not necessarily on her side. I think this is a hard time, and you sisters haven't been around each other enough to smooth things over. Give it time."

"Okay, enough of the sensitive cowboy."

That was another thing she was remembering about Cole. For a ranch-loving cowboy, he'd always been accused of having a streak of insight and chivalry in him that most macho guys lacked. The soul of a cowboy poet. It was why he'd once juxtaposed so well with the straight-shooting, ultra-efficient Amelia.

"Hey, I'm no cowboy anymore. At least not most of the time."

"Oh yeah," she said, glad to leave talk and thoughts of Mia behind. "You have some sort of mechanic's job now."

"I work for a company that contracts out big-machinery mechanics to anyone who needs them. It's not a bad fit for me during the summer. I always liked working on the equipment around here and home. I'm staying on here through the winter now, though. I left the other job early when I heard about your dad. Leif and Bjorn will need all the help they can get, and I was coming back in three weeks at the beginning of September anyhow."

Her heart squeezed at the mention of Leif and Bjorn Thorson. Leif had been her father's right-hand man for forty years. His son, Bjorn, was now the best foreman any ranch owner could ask for. They were devastated by the loss of their tough, savvy boss. Harper felt worse for them than she did for herself.

"You're a good guy, Cole. It can't be easy for you to come back since the Double Diamond was sold."

He shook his head. "I was really angry at first. But not at your father like you might think. He did my dad a favor by buying him out so we didn't have to sell to developers. But I was furious at my father for giving up. For selling off our legacy."

"And still, you came back to work for the enemy."

"I got over it. I understand what happened to the Double Diamond, and my father made the only choice he could. But I won't lie. I'm not letting it out of my sight, and I'll stick around until I can get it back. I'm damn close, Harpo. I'd almost convinced Sam he didn't really want to keep that little piece of property."

"It is a gorgeous hunk of land."

"The Double Di was in my family as long as Paradise has been in yours. I'd like to be the one to restore the legacy."

"Ironic."

"What is?"

"Out of four tries and six children, my dad didn't get a son—or even a daughter—who wants this place as much as your father's one child wants his. You lost yours to our passel of ingrates."

"I wasn't going to say it."

"Hey." She frowned. "You're not supposed to agree with me."

"Hey." He echoed her. "This is an astounding legacy you girls walked away from."

She felt the slight, sudden tension. "C'mon, Cole. You know how he was. It was impossible to fall in love with a place that was run like a cross between boarding school and a tough-love boot camp for delinquents."

"I do admit, your father was the nicest asshole I've ever known."

The accurate oxymoron drew rueful laughter from Harper, and the tension dissipated. "Yeah. And nobody said that out loud at the service did they?"

"Funerals aren't for honesty. You know that. And Sam was a good man. He wasn't cruel."

"Just obsessed," she said.

"Exacting. Demanding." He nodded.

"Arrogant." Harper sighed. "He chose Amelia to take over, but in truth I think he had his best chance at an heir with Raquel. He lost her when the other two triplets left. She wasn't about to stay here alone. Besides, my father's hired workers always did better dealing with his rigidness than we did."

"If you did your job around him, showed a little initiative, based on his standards, of course, he left you alone," Cole said. "On the other hand, look what he built because of those standards. This place is spectacular. The man was brilliant."

"He was that."

She looked up, surprised to see they'd left the chicken coop and nearly reached the long, triple-level back deck of the big log ranch house, surrounded by its trellises of stunning blue and lavender morning glories—her mother's favorite flowers. The chickens might have the Hilton because of her father, but the family had this warm, wonderful place, Rosecroft, because of their mother. Bella Crockett had designed and decorated the big house, planning its charm from the ground up, including the name because she'd fallen in love with the tradition of naming homes during a trip to Scotland in her youth. It was the one place on Paradise Ranch Harper always missed.

To her surprise, Cole picked up her hand and squeezed it between both of his. He'd held it plenty of times in their lives—after she'd been teased on the school bus, the first time she'd been bucked off a horse—but the strong, long-fingered, broad-nailed hand engulfing hers caused as much trembling as it did comfort. "The bottom line is Sam Crockett left us too soon."

"Not that long ago, sixty-eight would have been *old*," she murmured.

"He might have been an ass once in a while, but your father was not old."

She nodded and sighed. "I figured he'd live forever."

They both hesitated, as if heading up to the back door was something neither of them wanted.

"I hear you're not staying long," he said. "That's too bad. Are you sure you don't want to hang around another week or so? Take some rides around the old place, for the heck of it?"

She debated only a moment before lifting her eyes to his, a slow burn of excitement taking the place of heavy sadness. "Can I swear you to secrecy?"

"Ah, intrigue. Sure." He crossed his heart, eyes sparkling.

"Tristan, you remember me talking about him? He booked me a gallery showing."

The genuine pleasure in Cole's eyes thrilled her. "Seriously?"

She nodded, and before she could elaborate he crushed her into a bear hug and twirled her in place hard enough to swirl her wet skirt in a dripping circle.

"Tristan. He was that hippie-assed boyfriend of yours, right? The one who promised to make you famous?"

Tristan Carmichael was her de facto manager—a fellow artist with far more connections than Harper would ever have. He'd been a…What? A lover for a while.

But a boyfriend? She laughed. "He's definitely not my boyfriend."

"Not what I heard."

She frowned at his teasing and finger-flicked him on the shoulder. He laughed and set her down. "The point is, Tristan found a small, classy private gallery and gave them three of my paintings. The owner loved them, sold one the day he put it on display, and he agreed to host a full show. It's scheduled to open a week from tomorrow." Her words came in a rush now. "The gallery is called Crucible—it's on the lakefront in Chicago—and I have a million things to do to get ready…"

He bent. To the shock of her entire body, he slipped a kiss onto her mouth, and she froze. Wrong. This was very wrong. But the kiss fit as if it had been custom made for her lips. Sparklers zipped to life deep inside her belly, and she closed her eyes when she should have pulled away. Whatever scent or aftershave it was that made him smell like a spicy movie star turned her knees to rubber, and she couldn't stop drinking it in.

As kisses went, it was simple. No tongue, no sound. He opened and closed his mouth so lightly on her bottom lip she should barely have felt the butterfly touch, yet shivers rolled down her neck and across her shoulders like explosions.

This was insane.

She gasped and pulled away, avoiding his eyes. "Cole, no. We can't…"

"I'm sorry," he said.

"Mia is—"

"No longer anything except a friend." He turned her face gently with one finger, so she had to meet his smiling eyes. "But still, I know that was too quick. I didn't mean to make you uncomfortable. Especially if there's anyone else—I didn't even ask. I honestly just got excited for you."

Mia was more than his friend. She was and always would be his ex-girlfriend, lover, almost fiancée. No matter how strained her relationship with her sister might be, Harper would never do the stealing thing. The comparison thing.

"There's no one else."

She stared, dumbstruck at herself. That wasn't what she'd intended to say.

"Well, then. That's good." He let her go. "And for the record? It was a good kiss."

It definitely had been that.

"And congratulations on the art showing. I know this is your dream."

"Uh…" She scrambled to regain her composure. "It is. But don't tell anyone."

"Why would you keep it a secret?"

"I didn't feel right celebrating it before Dad's funeral. Tomorrow is soon enough."

"Okay. But then you're shouting it from the rooftop."

Her composure wouldn't quite cooperate by fully returning, but Cole looked down at their clothing and made a face that at least dispelled her awkwardness.

"We'd better go in. I've pushed the limits of your grandmother's timeline. I was supposed to have you back ten minutes ago. She didn't seem much inclined to be patient."

"Grandma gets what she wants, that's for sure. But I'm sure it's something simple like what to do with all the flowers. It has to be."

She looked to him for confirmation, but a surprising shadow of concern crossed his eyes. "I don't know," he said. "In all honesty I got out of the house to procrastinate, too. I had the weird feeling this meeting might be something we all wish it weren't."

Chapter Two

THEY HADN'T BEEN in the house ten seconds before they were accosted by Amelia, a wineglass and a dishtowel clutched in her hands, her long brown hair spilling from a bun-like thing on the top of her head. Cole knew the harried look—the one she wore whenever she took on too many tasks at once.

"Where in the world were you two?" Mia scolded like the chickens he and Harper had just corralled.

"Relax, it's okay," he said. "Got into some chicken wrangling. Harpo saved the day and rescued a bunch of escapees."

"Oh, for the love…" Mia shook her head. "Mother let some of the little kids go see the chickens. They probably left the gate unlatched. I told her—"

"Mia, don't worry," Harper said softly. "They're all back where they belong. No need to say anything about it. I'll go change as quickly as I can."

"Fine. Yes, go, go, hurry." Mia swapped her annoyance for bustling marching orders. "Grandma and Mother are already waiting in the study."

"Do you have anything to change into?" Harper looked at him. "I can probably find you something of…Dad's." Her voice caught.

Warmth at her emotional offer spread through his chest. "It's okay. I'm staying in the guest room for now. My things are there. Thanks, Harpo."

She nodded; gave a quick, sad smile to her sister; and headed out of the kitchen. Mia sighed and shook her head.

"You picked a brilliant time to jump into champion mode, Cole. Honestly, she was really chasing chickens?" She turned with a scowl, set the wineglass on the counter, and hung the towel neatly on a holder. "You didn't have to fall into her crazy, you know."

"In fact she told me to go in and not get wet, but I ignored her. Look, Harper isn't crazy, she's fine. She used this as a little bit of therapy, I think. Be nice now."

"Sure, she's fine. *Harper* is always fine." For the first time, bitterness crept into Mia's voice—an echo of what he'd heard earlier in Harper's. "It doesn't surprise me a bit that she disappeared to drench herself in the rain with chickens. It's typical, actually. She'll say it inspired her. She'll probably wander off now and paint them, complete with her wacka-doodle colors to 'express the emotion.'" The prickles in her voice made him turn to her with gentle chastisement.

"Let me say it again. Be charitable, Mia. Nobody is doing well today. Pretty much anything goes for crazy emotions, don't you think?"

She immediately bowed her head and covered her eyes with one hand. "You're right," she said. "I'm sorry."

"Don't be. You're allowed the emotions, too." He reached for her hand and squeezed it.

She allowed the tiniest uptick of a smile. "Kind as always. It's good to see you again, Cole. I'm sorry we haven't had much time to catch up."

"We will," he replied. "Everything's good in New York?"

"It is. I applied for a new job in the hospital—chief resident in pediatrics. I've been working on pediatric surgery rotations, and the last step in certification is to hold a position of leadership. If I'm lucky I'll have my certification this time next year."

"Pediatric as well as general surgery. Impressive goals, as usual. Will we have to call you Dr. Dr. Crockett?"

"Sure. I'm that arrogant." She actually smiled. "Don't be ridiculous. Now go. Get cleaned up. You look like you've been mud wrestling."

He looked to where Harper's swinging black braid was disappearing through the dining room attached to the kitchen. He didn't know what had happened to him outside, but whatever it was, he wished he could re-create that chicken dive and have Harper's head wind up cushioned against his arm for a little while longer. It wasn't mud *wrestling*—but getting down and dirty with her again…He turned back to Mia.

"I'm happy for you," he said. "Good luck with the job. When do you find out?"

"A couple of months yet. The beginning of November. It sounds a little puffed up, I know, but I'm fairly confident."

"I'm sure you have every reason—as usual. See you in a few minutes."

He was lucky. Rarely could a person spend six years dating someone, mutually and completely agree to separate, and remain genuine friends. He loved Mia, but they'd accepted long ago they'd never really been *in* love. It would take the family even longer than the two years that had already passed to believe they'd never get back together.

As he went through the huge dining room and the smaller sunken living room—smaller but still spacious enough to host a presidential reception—Cole smiled at Bjorn and Melanie Thorson and two of their kids, and a remaining handful of Bella's relatives who were staying in the tiny nearby town of Wolf Paw Pass. Rosecroft could have been an ostentatious monstrosity, with its nine bedrooms and five bathrooms and all this space on the main floor, but despite the size it embraced its people like a much smaller cottage. Bella had always seen to the friendliness of her home. The furniture was upholstered in reds, maroons, and subtle oranges—and their conversational groupings on thick, pale blue area rugs made the space warm as a sunset.

He climbed the wide wooden stairway to the second floor and followed the airy hallway to his temporary room at the end of the house. Each of the girls still had her own bedroom, despite the fact that the triplets had moved out five years ago and none of the sisters had lived here since each had left for college.

The guest room was simply decorated in blue and white, with a view toward the mountains, an attached bathroom, and shelves filled with books of every genre. The walls were decorated with photographs of Paradise Ranch—amazing images he knew had come from Harper's camera. The girl was artistic in more ways than painting.

Harper.

He stood by the bed and shucked off his soaking shirt, glad to have the cold, mucky fabric off his body. His mind moved from his moment in the mud with his old best friend, to that unplanned kiss they'd shared.

Absolutely unplanned.

In all truth, he couldn't say he'd never imagined kissing her. Seeds of feelings for Harper that were more than friendship had been germinating longer than he'd ever admit out loud, but she'd never seemed interested—and Mia had. He couldn't explain what had made those feelings sprout today after so many dormant years. Sure, he'd spent a lot of time talking to Harper the past Christmas, for the first time in years. And, yes, after that, he'd found himself unable to stop wondering about her: how her painting was progressing or how the community education classes she taught were going. But those thoughts weren't attraction—he'd simply rekindled the friendship they'd always had.

Seeing her today, however, all the latent thoughts he'd once had about her had risen out of hiding and boiled over: how unique among the six sisters she was; how soft-spoken she could be until her adamant, highly opinionated side would burst through; how sweetly curvy and feminine, like her Grandma Sadie, she'd always been, compared to the other five who'd gotten their mother's taller, slighter build. Twenty minutes ago, wet and bedraggled and stubbornly determined to catch the damn chickens, she'd suddenly struck him as fifties-movie-starlet sexy. And stoic. And vulnerable. It had always been rare to glimpse Harper Crockett being vulnerable. She knew how to bury that weakness. In a way, Sam Crockett had taught that to all his girls. But Cole had fallen into, what had Mia called it? Champion mode.

Ridiculous. Harper might need, even appreciate, a shoulder to lean on, but she was no damsel in distress. She didn't need a champion. God knew he didn't need the complication of an attraction to her.

His dress pants came off, and he dragged on dry jeans.

Starting anything with Harper would be a fool's pursuit. He had a plan, and it would not work with a long-distance relationship or a woman, however much he admired her and found her sexier than hell, who'd made it clear years ago that she wanted no part of ranch life. He'd told her already—he was going to get the Double Diamond back. It wasn't an idle wish.

He was it. The last of his line. Poor health had robbed his mother of having more children. His father had been robbed of passing the Double Di down to his only son by timing and economy. Now all Cole had was his own brand of stubborn determination. He'd worked his ass off the past three summers, making great money in North Dakota, riding the oil-rich economy as a mechanic. He'd learned to repair everything from transport vehicles to parts of oil wells. He'd come back to Paradise in the winter, when the demand for manpower in North Dakota waned, and it was hard for Sam and Leif to keep help on the ranch for the harsh winters. He didn't know how much longer the work in North Dakota would last, since oil prices were falling. But it didn't matter. He was close— within a year or two of having enough money to buy his property back from Paradise.

And once he did, he wanted to make sure it wouldn't leave his family again. He wanted a wife someday, one who'd love the land as much as he did. And he wanted kids. A passel of them, like Sam had raised.

Girls. Boys. He didn't care. The difference would be, they wouldn't want to leave.

So maybe the last parts of his dream were still in the wishing phase. It didn't make them any less real.

He still had no right to push anything with Harper— it wasn't fair to either of them. No matter that the kiss had been more than fun. It had scared him with its honest intensity. And Harper had shied from it like a day-old foal. He didn't blame her. At the very least, he could admit that a day like today was not the best time to mess with the shaky status quo. Everyone's heart was broken— his included. He hadn't lied. He'd believed Sam Crockett would live forever. He'd liked the man despite his iron will and unbending vision.

And his death was going to throw a wrench into Cole's goals. Sam alone had known the details of a potential sale.

He pulled on his favorite old V-neck sweater, ignoring the fraying cuffs and the slightly stretched-out hem. He didn't need to be formal anymore. He pulled on clean socks and his worn boots, then longingly eyed his everyday Stetson sitting on the small desk by the window. He wished he could wear it—it always made him feel complete. On the job in the Midwest, they'd called him Cowboy, and it had made him unique. Here, it was who he was.

He didn't want to go to the meeting Sadie had called. But she'd specifically asked for him and for Leif to attend. He couldn't imagine what it was about, but he closed the bedroom door behind him and made his way down the stairs.

HARPER HESITATED AT the door to her father's office, trying for the hundredth time to imagine what this meeting was about. She'd changed into jeans, a comfortable tank top, and a thigh-length, loose-knit cardigan that was her favorite "curl-up and get warm" sweater. Her well-loved Uggs would assure that Mia continued picking on her clothing, but she was beyond caring. Too many emotions took precedence over whether her sister thought she dressed like a crazy artist. Like what would Mia think if she knew Harper had just kissed her ex-lover? Did *that* matter?

With a deep breath, she entered the room and was swept away from every emotion but the conflicting ones over her father. She might have had her issues with him, but this room embodied everything Samuel Crockett had been—good and bad.

The office walls were navy blue, the masculine darkness offset by a lighter patterned area rug on the pine floor in blues and creams. The chairs and sofa were burgundy leather, the desk a massive cherry piece handed down from Sam's father, Sebastian. Her father's signature pipe tobacco, dark and spicy, had permeated the furniture and fabrics and hung in the air—as if his spirt stood watching in the background. An oil painting of him with his favorite horse, Smokey Jasper, hung in a row with portraits of Harper's other Crockett relatives: Benjamin, her uncle, who'd died in Vietnam; her grandfather Sebastian, who'd been Sadie's husband; and her great-grandfather Eli, who'd homesteaded the ranch in 1916. All the men looked alike—tall, broad-shouldered, sandy-haired, intense-eyed.

Harper turned from the memories and faced the living people in the room. Cole wasn't there yet, but her mother, tall and regally beautiful in a soft gray dress, smiled with stoic, buried grief. Beside her, leaning heavily on the black-and-red flowered cane, stood stooped-but-indomitable Grandma Sadie.

Brilliant, organized, no-nonsense Amelia held a deep discussion with Bjorn. The triplets, Raquel, Kelly, and Grace, her adorable, accomplished baby sisters named for their father's favorite two movie stars, sat in front of their grandmother. And then there was Joely, standing like a sunbeam in the middle of the room—the only sister with their father's light, honey-colored hair, and the one who could have worn puce- and mustard-colored pajamas to a state dinner and pulled them off. If Mia was brilliant and no-nonsense, Joely was her opposite—social and popular.

The homecoming queen, the rodeo queen, and, six years ago, Miss Wyoming, she'd been the first and only sister to marry. That had been four years ago, and Joely was still, and probably always would be, beauty queen stunning.

The sisters represented the entire breadth of the country now. Harper liked her crazy life in Chicago with her painting and teaching. Mia had her surgical practice in New York and seemed to love it there. Joely lived in California with her husband, Tim, and the triplets were in Denver with their very successful organic coffee shop and restaurant called Triple Bean.

Each of them had found success in her own right. Just not at ranching—to their father's now-permanent sorrow.

"You okay, little Harpo?"

She looked into Leif's familiar old face and tears finally threatened. By "little" he meant, of course, to invoke the spirit of the Harper he'd watched grow up. With all the surreal emotions sitting on her heart, today she felt just shy of ancient.

She accepted his hug, feeling a touch of desperation in the old cowboy's embrace. He'd been hired for this job by Sebastian practically upon getting of the boat from Norway almost fifty years earlier. Now he was a true American cowboy—right down to his handlebar mustache and bowlegs.

"I'm okay, Leif, but how about you?"

"It's hard. Didn't think I'd outlive two Crockett bosses. But we'll go on."

Her mother appeared quietly beside them and rested her hand on Leif's arm. "Yes, we will. Hello, sweetheart," she said, turning to Harper.

"Oh, Mama." Harper kissed her cheek. "Is this meeting something you have to do now? It's not too hard on you?"

She smiled, a wounded half-lift at the corner of her mouth. "Sadie is adamant that we tell you girls how your dad left things, and the triplets have to leave tomorrow. No, I don't want to do this, but we have to. It's all right."

"It doesn't sound like you have good news."

Her mother cupped her cheek. "Not the best. Come sit down and you'll see."

A boulder dropped into the pit of Harper's stomach.

"Ah, there's our boy." Her mother turned Harper to face the door.

Cole stood just inside the room. The sound around her seemed to fuzz in her ears, and all Harper could discern was her own thumping heart. The sensation lasted only a few beats before she shook it off; still, he was a sight for sad eyes. The dress shirt and loose tie were gone. In their place was a softly worn gray sweater that hugged his frame the way Harper would have like to. It showed off his strong, muscled chest and shoulders and his tapered waist and hips. Below that, his long, denim-clad legs led her to the toes of his cowboy boots, which looked as worn and as comfortable as her suede Uggs.

He reached her with an unhidden smile and followed her to an armchair, indicating without words she should sit. He perched beside her, and without a single touch he eased the anxiety churning inside.

Grandma Sadie rapped on the desk with the handle of her cane and the talking ceased immediately. All eyes turned to their matriarch like subjects to a queen.

"I know you're all displeased with me for pulling you away from guests and food and chickens and whatnot." Sadie's voice, naturally forceful, had mellowed with age. Harper took in her wizened grandmother's snow white hair and naturally pleasant features, and she caught a knowing little smile at the word *chicken*. "I'm sorry for that, but even though this is one of the hardest days of my life, of all our lives, the rest of the world doesn't stop. And business must be discussed."

"You don't need to do this." Her mother's soft voice juxtaposed with Grandma's slight rasp. "I can handle—"

"Isabella, you sit now and let the children comfort you. I don't have much left to do on this earth, but I can still act the part of the testy old matriarch. Your time will come quite soon enough."

"Don't say that, Grandma," Kelly said. "Today we need to think you're staying with us forever."

"Hush, child. I appreciate the sentiment, but that's far from the point. I have called you all here today because you're entitled to know the state of the ranch your father left to you, and the struggle your mother has in front of her. Let me say right up front that Bella has my highest respect. If my Sam was the backbone and heart of Paradise Ranch, she's been the blood. And Leif and Bjorn have been the muscle and bone."

Sadie's pale eyes slid around the room, missing nothing, hiding nothing.

"The rest of you," she continued, "have fallen far short over the past decade. And we are about to pay the piper."

A punch to Harper's heart was echoed by the collective gasp around the room. A quick glance proved that everyone felt the sting of the blunt criticism.

"Oh, Sadie, come now—" Her mother stood.

"No, Bella." Grandma Sadie put up a hand. "This is not the time for pussyfooting. Paradise is in trouble, and the girls need to know it."

"Trouble?" Harper blurted out the word. "What possible kind of trouble? I don't understand."

"That is true. You could not understand."

She took in her sisters' faces; each one looked like someone had slapped her puppy. Harper couldn't deny the sense of guilt building inside, but there was no point in acting wounded now. They'd all made choices.

"Then it is good you called us here. Sounds like we need…enlightenment."

Cole rested a hand on her shoulder and gave her a thumbs-up.

"Thank you," Sadie said. "Enlightenment is a good word. Something neither I nor your mother could ever get your father to embrace. He insisted the problems no longer concerned you girls. He was not going to use the threat of financial deterioration to guilt you into coming home. I, however, have no such compunction. I'm very old. Too old to mince words. Paradise Ranch is, for all intents and purposes, nearly out of money. And everybody in this room needs to think about what's going to happen next."

Another round of gasps and murmurs spilled through the office. Out of money? Harper's jaw slackened. Only three faces besides Grandma Sadie's registered no shock—her mother's, Leif's, and Bjorn's. It wasn't at all clear yet how long this had been brewing, but obviously the topic was not new to the family leaders.

"All right," Harper said, since even super-practical Mia was still staring dumbly. "What exactly do we need to know?"

"To start with, you all need to understand that the cost of every single basic need on this ranch has skyrocketed in the past decade: fuel, feed, equipment repair, wages, transportation, veterinary care. Everything."

"But hasn't the price of beef gone up as well?" Cole asked. "The cattle industry is in a boom period—aren't the rising costs covered?"

"Cattle ranchers across the country took a big hit several years ago when that wasn't the case. Ranchers were forced to diversify to survive."

A sudden spark of angry understanding ran through Harper's body and she stood. "You mean they're calling in the oil and gas companies."

"That's always been an important option. It's long-term security if there's oil on the land," Amelia said.

"It's no option." Harper tried hard to tamp down the surge of annoyance that rose like one of the oil wells they obliquely discussed. "How could you forget what happened to Martin Buckner?"

"You've always blown that out of proportion, Harper," Mia said.

"And you never saw it for yourself." Harper held back her anger with effort.

None of the others had seen the devastation that day. Harper had been eight, and she still didn't know why she'd been with her father the day he'd gone to help Mr. Buckner, a neighboring rancher, with some equipment problems. She'd been in a barn with the Buckners' kids when she'd heard the explosion. She rushed out with everyone else to see the oil geyser—something she'd been told over and over was so rare as to be nonexistent with modern wells. Not only had the chaos that had followed scared the devil out of her, but the revolting mess left by the oil, spread over acres, had also made her extract a promise from her father. He'd never let that happen to Paradise Ranch.

She'd made it clear from that young age on that if she ever ran a ranch, it would be different. To the endless teasing of family and friends, she'd thrown herself into learning about the environmentally green side of life. She'd forced her mother to recycle and her siblings to conserve water and her father to treat his cattle and all animals with the least amount of chemicals and pharmaceuticals he'd agree to. They indulged her to a point, but she'd been the tree-hugging, weirdo hippie Wyomingite ever since.

The epithets had long since ceased to bother her.

"If we're in trouble, we need to consider everything," Mia said.

"We?" Harper replied. "Who is 'we'? Grandma's right, none of us has been here recently. There's no 'we.'"

"Harper, your father took your oil concerns seriously," her grandmother said. "He wasn't one of the landowners who looked into drilling. But because of that, he made some other investments that didn't work out as well."

Surprise didn't begin to describe Harper's reaction to such news. When had her father ever listened to her?

"Fine," Mia said. "But we have fifty-thousand acres. We've always been able to run enough cattle to do well."

"It's been a slow, steady decline," their mother said. "In the past six years, your dad had to reduce herd sizes in order to let some workers go and pay off immediate debts. Leif is looking at only three extra hands this winter, including himself—and we're running only thirty-five hundred head."

"Really? That few men?" Cole asked. "Down from eight last winter. How are beef prices?"

"They're good," Bjorn replied. "But building back up is taking a very long time, and the costs per cow have skyrocketed. If we could get ourselves up to eight thousand head and hire back some hands, we'd have a chance. The problem is the debt load. Sam invested in a couple of businesses that didn't pan out."

With a gush like a broken dam, Harper and her sisters surged into speech at the same moment. Her head spun in the chaos, mostly because she couldn't comprehend how a ranch with a helmsman as adept as she'd always heard Sam Crockett had been, could fall into such disastrous straits. She took out her frustration in the form of questions right along with the others, and it took Sadie with the help of Leif long moments to quiet them.

"We will have time for all these questions," her grandmother said. "But the reasons for the problems on the ranch are not our first priority. The important issue is that your mother cannot run Paradise alone."

"I don't *want* to run it alone," her mother said, clarifying the point. "Not without your father."

"You're smart enough to run anything, Mama," Grace said.

"Thank you, sweetheart. But it has nothing to do with intelligence. Paradise Ranch is not my legacy."

"And that's why I insisted we call this meeting," Sadie continued. "It is not my legacy either, although it certainly has fallen to the women to figure things out. It is *your* legacy, girls." She sent her piercing gaze once again over her granddaughters. "Your father left the ranch entirely to you six, and your mother. There are not too many options inherent in that bequeathal. In fact, you really only have two choices: one of you, or more than one of you, take over for your father, or you sell Paradise."

"What?"

"What?"

"No way!"

The triplets' exclamations emerged simultaneously. Harper shook her head at them—they had their own idiosyncrasies, she thought. The three had thoroughly distinct personalities, but they were still connected by the mysterious, slightly eerie thread that often made them seem like one conglomerate person.

"We're not here to make that decision at this moment." Her mother spoke quietly. "That needs very careful thought and discussion." She roamed the room with her eyes. "Or maybe not. You all have such full and busy lives built far from Wyoming."

It was telling, Cole thought, that nobody contradicted her.

"We can get through the next month or two talking about the options," she continued. "But it's the end of August, and starting next month, the cattle must be brought from the high range to winter-over. Then starts the pregnancy testing, shipping, weaning, fence riding, equipment repair…"

"COLE, YOU COULD do it. You could take it over." Grace spoke for the first time, her voice as quiet and calm as her name.

Harper looked at Cole. His eyes had gone wide and his mouth opened and closed without a sound. Finally he managed a choked, "Excuse me?"

"You could." Grace smiled almost beatifically. She was the Crockett who most perfectly reflected her name—ever kind and gracious. "You know this place far better than we do anymore. We could hire you to be the…what?" She looked around as if for suggestions. "The manager, the CEO…" She shrugged. "Heck, the King of Paradise."

"That sounds vaguely blasphemous." Raquel smiled, albeit a little wanly, and crossed her legs, showing off the rich, polished brown leather of cowboy boots beneath her long jewel-toned skirt. She was the rough-and-tumble compared to Grace's feminine-and-refined. The three oldest girls had done plenty of exploring and tree-climbing and falling out of trees as kids, but Raquel had taken "tomboy" to a whole new level. She'd found the caves in the hills and collected the snakes and frogs. She'd never wanted to be the pirate princess. And she had a logic and thought process definitely inherited from their father. She was the closest Sam had come to having a son. If she'd had the will, Harper thought Raquel would have been the best choice of all to take over the ranch.

"No, ladies, it's not me you want," Cole said. "I've told your mama many times that running the Paradise isn't in my blood. And I'm not here year 'round. I'm willing to help however I can, though. You know I have a vested interest in this place."

"Are you still trying to buy your father's section back?" Raquel asked.

"I am. No apologies."

"You shouldn't apologize. I admire you for working toward that." She rubbed her forehead. "What about the rest of us? I feel awful now that Kelly and Grace and I have to bug out tomorrow. But our new location opens the day after that, and there's nothing we can do at this late date. I guess that means, though, that we're not the choices for new CEOs either."

All three triplets wore expressions mixing regret with torn emotions. It was hard to begrudge them their conflicted feelings. They'd opened Triple Bean while they'd all still been in college. Between Kelly's culinary arts degree, Raquel's business degree, and Grace's art and psychology double major, the little college endeavor had turned into a super-successful Denver business. They were opening a second branch of Triple Bean only a few years after graduation, and as far as Harper was concerned, the sky was going to be the limit for the three of them.

"Don't you dare feel awful about anything," Harper said. "You need to go back and make that new store a wonderful second success." She took a deep breath and forged ahead. "I wasn't going to say anything today, but I have to leave by the end of the week myself. I, ah, have a gallery showing of my paintings the following Friday. My first one. I promised to be around for the week in order to help with the preshow work. I'm sorry the timing is poor."

With a squeal Kelly jumped from her chair and crossed the five feet to Harper's chair. Ignoring Cole still on the arm, she grabbed Harper in a fierce hug. "Oh my gosh, that's the most wonderful thing! I'm thrilled for you, Harpo."

"Can it be rescheduled?" Amelia asked, out of the blue.

The room, which had started to buzz again, went still.

Harper closed her eyes and tried to call up her yoga Ujjayi breathing. "I probably should want to reschedule, Mia, but this show took years to get, and for me to renege at this point would screw my reputation, which isn't all that big to begin with. I probably should love my father's memory a little more, huh?"

"Oh, for God's sake, Harper. That isn't what I meant."

"Are *you* going to stay?" Harper asked.

"I have surgeries scheduled nonstop next week."

"And can *they* be postponed?"

"All right," Cole said. "That's enough for now. Mia, we're not in crisis this second. I think something your sister has waited for most of her life can take precedence."

"I'm sorry," Mia replied. "We're all in shock, and I thought maybe she was looking for an excuse to get out of her commitment. It wasn't meant to be a slam."

"You're right," Harper said, reluctant to say much. "We have no idea about each other's lives or priorities anymore. We had a bomb dropped on us after we'd already been through a disaster, and it's hard not to get defensive. We should be more careful of each other's fragile spirits right now."

"Fragile spirits? If that wasn't spoken like the gypsy artist you've always been."

Anger flared again. "Is this your normal bedside manner?"

"Girls, that's enough," Bella said. "It's time to put the big differences among you aside. You've always been six unique people, and that's why you're all creative and have found your own ways. Try to celebrate that."

"No." Grandma Sadie held up her hand. "I have to disagree, Isabella. It's not time to coddle each other; it's time for some ruthless honesty. I say it again. I'm a very old woman, and I remember back before what you young people call political correctness took over. We didn't have time to say things we didn't mean. Nor do we now, because the decision that must be made is going to change lives, mark my words. I'm not telling you what that decision should be, but it has to be made without the burden of secrets and hard feelings, or it's going to ruin lives."

"You," she fixed her stare on Amelia, "are a wonderful doctor. Most commendable. You *must* figure out what's important to you here, if anything is. There are no wrong choices, but you can't not make a choice.

"You," she turned next to Harper, "have always had a free spirit. I envy you, but live your dream and stop defending it as if it needs defending.

"Joely, you seem the most wounded by this. I know you think we don't notice, but if there's something wrong, you need to learn to tell your family.

"You three…" For the first time, Sadie's tired-but-firm mouth softened into a smile that actually looked like a grandmother's rather than an ancient, exasperated monarch's. "Our little caboose babies, as my mother used to call the youngest children. You're making your ways, too, very impressively. I'm sorry this is being forced on your young shoulders.

"Finally, you, Cole Wainwright, the prodigal son. This ranch is not your responsibility, as you've so adamantly insisted. And you say you know where you're headed. Make sure that's truly where you want to go."

As all the pronouncements settled on their recipients, Grandma Sadie took in the uneasy quiet without apology. "That was too many words for me to say and too many for you to hear. My part in this is over, and my purpose has been served. I will accept whatever decisions are made, but you had to know the problems are here to be dealt with. I'm tired. I'm going upstairs to my bedroom, and I'm going to weep again for my son. But lest you think the last tough-minded Crockett is gone, think again. You are each more like your father than you'll ever admit."

Sadie eased her way slowly from behind Sam's desk, leaning heavily on her cane. For all her forceful words, she suddenly did look tired and a little frail, stooped in her plain black dress, snowy pearls stark against her chest, and her thick white curls starting to relax from the long, sad, rainy day. Leif and Bjorn followed her through the room, each on an arm. She stopped in front of Harper and placed a warm, gnarled hand on her cheek.

"My sweet Harper Lee. Find your common ground with Amelia. You two are the keys."

For the first time, Harper felt the full force of guilt, resentment, and sorrow. She kissed her grandmother and offered a hug, which the old woman accepted. "I don't think we can be as wise and tough as you are, Gram," Harper said. "I'm certainly not."

"Well, you have to start thinking differently. If anyone can change the course of her long-held ideas, it's you. You have the imagination for it."

Once Sadie was gone, the room burst into noise again, but Harper had no heart for the arguments and questions. Her mother sat quietly at the desk, her face a mask of endurance, while her girls talked around each other like traders on the stock exchange. After five minutes, Harper could stand it no longer. She moved to the front edge of the desk, sat on its gleaming surface, and placed two fingers in her mouth. She let loose a window-rattling whistle.

"Excuse me?" Amelia's brows furrowed at the interruption.

"Sorry," Harper said, smiling despite the tension. "A ten-year-old community ed art student taught me how to do that. I think we need to stop and all take time to think. This moment isn't the time to make a decision. The movie stars have to leave, but Mia, Joely, and I have five days yet, which gives us time to look at all the options, and we can keep in touch with Kel, Rocky, and Gracie." She twisted to look behind herself. "Is that okay with you, Mama?"

"It sounds perfect," she replied.

"We'll make something work out," Joely said. "There are six of us. We can keep Paradise. We'll figure it out."

That's when Amelia stood. With a calm that almost chilled the room, she stared at the group. "For once I agree with Harper," she said at last. "This is the wrong time to be making maudlin promises."

"Aw, c'mon, Mia." Grace looked up. "This is a maudlin day. An awful day. We can't be logical and detached either. Doesn't the thought of losing Paradise double the pain of losing Dad?"

"On the contrary." Amelia's voice remained calm. "It should be clearer than ever. Paradise Ranch drove us all away, and it killed our father, just as it killed his father. I, for one, don't intend to let it kill any more of us."

"That's ridiculous!" Joely turned from the huddle. "Dad loved this place."

"Dad sacrificed everything to this place, including his family."

"That isn't true, Amelia," their mother said, with the same quiet intensity her daughter exuded.

"It is true, Mother. Don't get me wrong, growing up on a ranch was the most phenomenal life training a girl could ask for. But it's a driven and unforgiving lifestyle. The new grave at the church cemetery proves that."

"That's the grief talking. You don't mean this." Harper started toward Mia.

"Don't tell me that it's grief." Mia glared and backed toward the office door. "You think we all need to dwell on this for five days? I say you're wrong. Sell this place, take the money, and let someone else die of a heart attack ten years from now."

"Mia, stop," Raquel said sharply. "That's not a sensible argument."

"Life and death isn't sensible?" She looked at each person in turn, ending with Harper. "Sell Paradise Ranch."

Harper stared at the door after her sister had powered through it and gazed anxiously around the room. Every person left looked as if a knife had been thrust into her or his heart.

Chapter Three

SKYLAR THORSON SAT in the rough mounds of scree and stumpy, weedy alpine grass at the base of her favorite mountain, a sketch pad at her feet and an ancient Minolta 35-millimeter camera in her lap. Wolf Paw Peak wasn't a true mountain, just one of a handful of random foothills rising from the plains south of the Teton Range, which anyone on Paradise Ranch could see any time they looked to the northwest. But Wolf Paw's unique shape, like the head and front leg of a wolf rising from its den according to Indian legend, stood fully on Paradise land and always made Skylar feel safe. Safe and lucky to live within riding distance of its wild slopes, which rose a little over three thousand feet into the Wyoming sky. Although she'd reached its summit twice in the company of her older brother, Marcus, she was forbidden to climb it alone, which pissed her off because she was fourteen and totally capable.

She'd nearly defied the rule this morning. After Mr. Crockett's funeral yesterday, the last thing she'd wanted was to hang around while her Grandpa Leif, her parents, and all of Mr. Crockett's daughters came down to the barns and kept talking about him and starting to cry. She was done crying. Her mother, who was normally really strict for a homeschool teacher, had given her and her two brothers another free day from lessons, so she'd taken Bungu out and come here to escape.

Mr. Crockett was gone, and he'd been her friend— even though everyone else except her grandfather thought he was hard and even a little bit mean. He'd never been mean to her. When she'd been little, he'd always pulled out a hidden candy bar when he'd come to visit. As she'd gotten older, he'd taught her how to swing a lariat the old-fashioned way. When she'd decided she liked photography, he'd given her the old camera.

Her parents thought all the developing was too expensive and she should save her money for a digital camera. She didn't want one. Like she didn't want a digital watch. Like she didn't want to be around mourners for Mr. Crockett. So, she'd almost decided to climb her mountain to be sad and grieve in her own way. But she wasn't stupid. It would be dangerous to start the trek after all the rain they'd had yesterday. Besides, she wasn't in the mood to get yelled at for getting in trouble. And she'd be in trouble if she climbed Wolf Paw on her own.

Glancing to her right, she watched Bungu grazing contentedly where she'd hobbled him, the white coloring with its black spots shone stark and beautiful on his broad Appaloosa rump against the rest of his black coat. She wasn't supposed to ride him out alone either—he was only four and still green to field and trail work. But she'd raised him from a foal and knew him better than she knew anyone or anything else on the ranch. She wasn't about to listen to her worrywart parents. Besides, she'd been riding horses since the age of three.

She looked back down at her sketchbook and assessed the pencil drawing she'd made of Bungu beneath the cloudy sky. Earlier there'd been a rainbow, and she'd captured it with the camera. She could finish her drawing and put in the color at home after she got the film developed. Maybe her dad would be willing to take her into Wolf Paw Pass tonight after work. It was one of the only advantages to being homeschooled—she could do homework anytime. Pretty much everything else about it, she hated.

On the other hand, she'd heard her father talking to Grandpa Leif that morning. The ranch, the only home she'd ever known, was in some kind of trouble. The Crocketts might decide to sell, and the ranch families might be forced to move. Maybe she'd get a chance to go to a regular school.

The thought was clinical and calm. The roiling in her stomach over the thought of leaving Paradise Ranch was not. She made a few swipes with her pencil on the preliminary drawing. Her family had worked with the Crocketts for two generations. How could anything happen to this place she loved?

Bungu's sudden, shrill whinny catapulted Skylar to her feet and nearly sent her into respiratory failure. Her horse stood alert, ears pricked to statue-perfect points, every muscle coiled, eyes fixed on the trees along the trail. Skylar searched desperately for a place to hide, unable to imagine who but trespassers would be all the way out here on a day like this. She shrank into the closest hillock and tried to edge toward her horse.

She didn't make it.

The pretty sorrel quarter horse Skylar recognized as Chevy appeared around a copse of scrub pine and replied to Bungu's ringing call with one of his own. The woman on his back reached forward to stroke his neck, and Skylar recognized her, too.

"Oh!" Harper Crockett pulled up quickly when she spotted Skylar. Her flushed face and rounded eyes proved she hadn't come looking for anyone. "Hello there. I…sorry, didn't mean to scare your horse."

"He's not afraid." Skylar couldn't keep the defiance out of her voice. "He's the bravest horse I've ever known."

Harper looked like she could maybe laugh, and Skylar found resentment rising along with her other emotions. She wondered if "Miss Harper," as Mama had always required her to say, even remembered her. All the Crockett ladies had been "Miss." Except Mrs. Crockett. She was Mrs. Crockett. But she and *Harper*—she thought with purposeful disrespect—hadn't seen each other since Skylar had been five.

"It's a good thing to have that trust in your horse up here in the high country. Do you ride here often?"

"All the time." Skylar stared at her, waiting.

"Do I…know you?"

She *didn't* remember. For some reason that only depressed Skylar further. She shrugged. "I know you."

"You actually live here, then? Wait. No, you can't be. Bjorn's daughter?"

"Yeah."

"Skylar?"

"Yes." Stupid relief and a little happiness flooded through her.

"Oh my gosh, sweetie, how is this possible? You're all grown up."

A fragment of defensiveness melted. Nobody called her a grown-up. "Kind of. I guess."

"Oh, you have. I remember babysitting you. But not very many times, I don't think, because I left for college. I think maybe Joely took care of you more often."

Skylar nodded. "I saw her today. She's still, like, gorgeous. I think my grandpa said she was a model or something."

"She is definitely still beautiful," Harper replied. "She modeled for about a year. Then she got married and moved to California."

"Does she have kids?"

"No. Not yet."

"Do you?"

Harper laughed. "Nope. I'm a long way from that. How 'bout you?"

Her eyes twinkled in fun. Skylar felt a smile beg to be set free, and although she really, really didn't want it to, it slipped onto her lips. "I'm a long ways from that, too."

"Thank heavens. You're not *that* grown up yet."

"Besides. Don't you need, like, a guy first?"

This time Harper snorted. "Uh…yes, ma'am. Do we know each other well enough to be moving in this direction?"

In Skylar's experience you could say almost anything on the ranch. Guys talked about girls and sex and cow sex and food and politics and pretty much everything else. She heard a lot the adults didn't think she heard.

She shrugged. "I don't care. I don't have a boyfriend; that's no secret. The only person around here who's cute enough to be a boyfriend is Cole." She saw Harper's features fold immediately into a frown. "Cole Wainwright, I mean. Do you know who he is? He's hot."

"Oh, believe me, I know him. We've been friends most of our lives. He's a very nice guy."

"My grandpa says the ranch runs smoother when Cole comes back every year."

Harper moved Chevy two steps closer and leaned forward over the saddle horn. "What are you working on? I don't mean to pry, but it looks like you're sketching, and I'm kind of an art fanatic."

Everyone said Harper was some kind of new-age, liberal hippie who lived in communes, protested things, and thought she was an artist. Skylar studied her fully for the first time. She sure didn't look like any hippie she seen in books. She looked like a normal person in jeans and a cool, worn jean jacket and cowboy boots. In her own way, she was prettier even than Miss Joely. She took a deep, rebellious breath. Than *Joely*. No "Miss." This wasn't her mom's freakin' South Carolina.

"I like to draw my horse. Sometimes I start the drawing then take pictures and finish it at home."

"Could I...see your drawing?" She seemed a little embarrassed to be asking. "You don't have to. I know drawings can be private."

Skylar shrugged, surprised again. Nobody ever really looked at her drawings. "Yes, very nice," they always said, and that was about it. "I don't care. You can."

Harper straightened in the saddle and swung down, completely unlike a city-girl hippie. She held Chevy's reins casually as she dug in a worn leather saddle bag, produced a notebook of some kind, and then flung the ends of the reins around a short, thick-branched bush.

"Turnabout is fair play. I'll show you mine, too," she said.

To Skylar's astonishment, the notebook was a sketchpad, similar to her own. She handed hers to Harper first and took the one offered to her without opening it. Instead, she watched Harper flip pages. Suddenly, desperately, she wished she hadn't agreed to give it to her.

Harper's face didn't change, although her frown disappeared. She studied each page for a long time, as if she were looking at every line or...or for mistakes. To protect herself from the sudden urge to grab the book away, she opened Harper's. With one glance at the first drawing, she had to swallow hard to keep from totally throwing up. It was just a flower, in pencil like her own sketches, but it looked like Harper had picked it out of the field and pressed it into the book. An actual photograph couldn't have looked any more real.

She flipped the page, spiral-bound at the top, and stared at the next drawings—three small studies of a stalk of wheat with grass stems blowing around it. Every little kernel of bran on the wheat head was perfect.

Humiliation burned through her like a grass fire. If Harper didn't laugh her head off at the drawings in Skylar's book, it was because she was the nicest person in the world. With a sick fluttering in her stomach, she turned to another picture and then another. The horse barn. A bird feeder. A chicken. Skylar sighed. Even the quick line drawings were perfect. She turned the page a final time and gasped. She'd been so dumb. She'd asked if Harper knew Cole Wainwright, and there he was on the page. The sketch was simple, but there was no doubt whatsoever who it was.

"Ahhh, you found Cole." Harper smiled. "I did that for him to go with one I drew when we were kids. It's not quite finished."

"Oh. Sure. That's cool."

Skylar's chest tightened, and she looked at the picture rather than face Harper. She didn't tell anybody about her fantasy crush for Cole. He wasn't around much in the summer, but every winter he came back—just as nice as Mr. Crockett had been, but much, much younger. And hot. But it was her deepest secret.

"Wow." Harper had stopped at one of Skylar's drawings. "This is amazing."

She turned the pad around so Skylar could see which page. It was a close-up of Bungu's ear and eye. "I sketched it from a photo."

"It's really good. You have a lovely touch with your pencils."

"Not as good as yours." Skylar exchanged sketchpads with her.

"They aren't supposed to be like mine. They're yours. They're wonderful. I hope you keep it up."

Skylar didn't know how to respond. Definitely nobody had ever called her drawings wonderful. She managed a blown-away "thank you," and Harper saved her from having to say anything more intelligent by noticing the camera.

"That's an old beauty." She pointed. "A thirty-five-millimeter Minolta? My dad used to have a camera like that. I played with it when I was younger than you are."

"It is your dad's," Skylar said without preamble and without really thinking. She swore Harper's face went a little bit white.

"What do you mean it's my dad's?"

"He, um, gave it to me. He taught me how to use it and where to send the film to get it developed."

"*My* father?"

Skylar nodded.

"When did he do this?"

The joyful twinkle and flowing compliments had disappeared. Harper suddenly looked more suspicious than friendly, and Skylar stepped back one involuntary step. "About two years ago. I don't know."

"Why would he do that? He loved that camera."

"I don't know. He…he said it would teach me how to take good pictures. He said I had…" She lowered her head, thoroughly embarrassed.

"Had what?" Harper's voice gentled again.

"Talent."

Harper surprised her again with a harsh burst of laughter. "Seriously? *My* father told someone she had talent? You're sure?"

Skylar didn't understand at all and didn't say a word. Harper's change of mood made no sense.

"I'm sorry," Harper said again. "I guess this is a little weird for me. My father is gone, and I'm finding out all kinds of thing I never knew about him." She straightened. "I'm glad his camera is in good hands. You take care of it."

"O-okay."

"So, it was great seeing you, Skylar. I'm sure we'll meet again. Time for me to head on. You be careful up here in the foothills."

Just like that, because of the camera, someone Skylar thought might be a little different from the others on Paradise Ranch, turned cool and standoffish. It was almost like she hadn't believed Mr. Crockett had really given away the camera. Resentment swelled up again. It was pretty typical for people to change their opinions of her, but this was even faster than usual.

"I will," she said. "I've lived here my whole life."

For an instant she thought Harper might say something more, or apologize or something, but she gathered up Chevy's reins, and mounted smooth as any cowboy on the place.

"Good." She smiled, but not like she had when they'd first met. "I'll see you around, okay?"

She was moving before Skylar could reply. After she'd disappeared down the trail, Skylar fought with tears for one brief moment before anger replaced her hurt feelings.

"Whatever," she said to no one.

CHEVY PICKED HIS way along the rocky trail without help from Harper. With only a steadying hand on the reins, she let the gelding have his head. The farther she got from her encounter with the girl, the stronger her mortification grew. The meeting had turned Harper into a bigger mess than she'd been at the funeral, and she'd been unconscionably rude.

But her father's camera? He'd nearly had apoplectic attacks if she or her sisters had touched it. Then he'd turned around and given it to a teenager he barely knew? Harper couldn't deny the pain of betrayal squeezing her heart. So long. So *long* she'd prayed for his acceptance. Apparently young Skylar Thorson naturally possessed the key to getting that rare commodity.

The first tear traced down her cheek. It wasn't Skylar's fault, but envy blazed through Harper as if she were a child again, burning through her rational thinking and heading straight for the tinder that was her grief. None of this was fair. It hadn't been fair from that night when, at age ten, she'd refused to help feed the horses until she'd finished her painting. Without any warning or second chance, Dad had hidden her pad of heavy canvas paper and starter set of brushes in his study and locked her easel in a closet where she would not have access to it until she'd learned to straighten out her priorities.

The moment still loomed as pivotal. It had started Harper on the path of hiding her work and sneaking away to draw. It had pushed her away from the ranch as soon as she was old enough to go to college, but she had been too young to know how to handle the freedom she'd never had under her father's thumb. She'd made terrible choices about friends and school and her life for the first years of independence. Choices so stupid that she'd been kicked out of art school. Evicted from apartments. Fired from jobs. It had taken four more years of intermittent counseling and Tristan Carmichael's constant "believe in yourself" mentoring to turn her into the artist she'd always wanted to be. Nonetheless, she still considered herself more of a failure at life than she ever wanted her good, God-fearing family to know.

She'd made a terrible choice again. A very selfish one. She'd seen Skylar's face at the end of the camera discussion. Clearly confused and wounded, the girl had drawn up the protective wall of suspicion and attitude that had temporarily fallen away as she'd shared her drawings.

Harper knew how fragile an artist's ego and confidence were. The girl had to have been hungry for feedback, or she wouldn't have trusted Harper to look at the sketches. And she was surprisingly good, with an innate understanding of shading and texture. Given some instruction her talent could become something special.

There was no excuse for Harper's pettiness.

And yet. The thought of pretty, young Skylar with her wide, blue eyes and spikey, strawberry blonde hair having possession of that Minolta created stupid and unreasonable feelings.

"Please, please." She raised her eyes to the cloudy heavens. "Let this be because my system is out of whack from all this emotion." She didn't want to be known as the jealous diva sister. The inner demons she already owned were enough to handle.

"I should go back," she said aloud. Chevy flicked his ears back, awaiting further instruction.

She picked up her slack reins, but before she could start the turn to head back, Chevy halted with a forceful hoof plant and wheeled all by himself. She kept him from bolting, holding him steady with her legs, and coaxed him back in the direction they'd been traveling. He sidestepped and let out a powerful whinny, but he moved forward.

"What is it, boy?" she asked. "Another rider?" She stroked his neck. He was only five—new to the ranch Rico, one of the ranch hands, had told her at the barn—so given his inexperience it was good behavior for him to trust her. Still, she had to continually persuade him to move down the gently sloping hill on the scree-and-dirt path that skirted the wide base of Wolf Paw Peak.

Before they reached the back side of the mountain, a rumble of engines grinding over uneven terrain confused her. When Chevy rounded a last bend, Harper stared across the green-and-yellow expanse of valley floor spreading between Paradise and the Teton Range sixty-five miles north, and her mouth popped open in shock. Two hundred yards away, a small fleet of four white vehicles trundled toward her. Chevy snorted and danced sideways.

Mystified, and more than a little uneasy, she tried to imagine how the mini convoy had gotten onto such remote Paradise land. This was one of the prime grazing areas—although she saw no cattle today—usually accessible only by horseback. As they drew closer she recognized a familiar logo on each vehicle door. Curled blue waves under a three-peaked purple mountain, set against a golden yellow sun: the ubiquitous symbol of Mountain Pacific Oil.

The two pickup trucks, a van, and a Jeep stopped before they reached Harper. Two people emerged from each and, clearly unaware of her presence, moved to stand in one group. As a collective they turned slightly away from her, and the man at the front of the clump pointed. She could hear their voices but couldn't make out the words.

With a squeeze of her calves, Harper moved Chevy forward again, annoyance growing out of her curiosity. A proprietary aura emanated from the group, and along with her natural prejudice against oil people, it blew away all nervousness that had taken shallow root in her gut. They didn't notice her until she'd ridden to within fifty feet and could see all eight people, including three women, clearly. Coordinated and hyper-neat, they wore navy slacks and company polo shirts in blue and purple, with the logo embroidered on each breast pocket. When they saw her, they smiled in unison like a team of robotic cable TV techs.

"Hello there!" One of the women, brandishing a clipboard and adjusting expensive-looking aviator sunglasses, approached with a widening smile. "I'm Magdalen Pearce, senior technology analyst for Mountain Pacific Oil." She craned her neck to look around Harper as if expecting someone to be behind her. "Are you here with Sam Crockett?"

Harper's stomach lurched and then throbbed, as if she'd been punched. For long seconds she literally could not speak. Finally, she swallowed away the tightness in her throat.

"Is this some kind of joke? What are you doing here? How did you get here?"

Magdalen Pearce looked genuinely confused by the questions. "I'm sorry, I don't understand," she said. "We had an appointment to meet Samuel Crockett here about an hour ago. We drove in on the east road, exactly as he directed, and have been surveying the area while we waited. I know he's a busy man; we weren't terribly concerned that he's been detained."

Harper had no idea where to begin or how to tell this woman she had to be mistaken. There was no "east road." Her father couldn't have made an appointment with these people from beyond the grave.

Her heart pounded with awful realization. He certainly could have. He'd only been dead five days. Nobody had expected to find strong, Wyoming-steeled Sam Crockett collapsed in the barn on Thursday morning. Still, he'd have told his wife about meeting with an *oil company*. Certainly she'd looked at his calendar after he'd died. Harper wanted to rail at the intruders, but deep in her sorrow-filled, and now confused, heart she knew that wasn't fair. Slowly she dismounted, her legs starting to stiffen from two hours in the saddle after two years out of it. She'd ridden her entire childhood but had only found time to ride once in a while on her rare visits home.

Corralling her drifting thoughts and focusing on the group of polo-shirted people, she held out her hand to the woman. The handshake was as tight and businesslike as Harper had expected.

"I'm Harper Crockett, Sam's daughter."

"How good of you to come," Magdalen Pearce said.

"I'm afraid I have very bad news. My father passed away last week—unexpectedly."

"Oh, dear heavens, I'm terribly sorry. What happened?"

The woman seemed utterly sincere. There wasn't any reason to take offense or umbrage to her question, but Harper's blood started a slow simmer, and she stared at the entourage trying to figure out why.

"A heart attack," she said simply. "I'm also afraid he didn't tell anyone about a meeting with you. Or, if he did, it was totally forgotten."

"Certainly understandable," Ms. Pearce said.

"I happen to be out here today, otherwise nobody would have met you. I'm sorry you made the trip for nothing." No, she really wasn't.

"It doesn't need to be for nothing. Ms. Crockett." One of the men, fiftyish and squat as a fire hydrant, spoke. "We could finish our survey and simply send the report to whoever is in charge. We can speak at a more convenient time."

At the man's suggestion, Magdalene Pearce eyes took on a sheen of excitement, erasing all the sympathy she'd just displayed.

Or maybe Harper was making that up. Maybe she was too numb to read emotions accurately. Anger was definitely flaring a little bit too easily today. Still, she shook her head firmly. "No. In all honesty, I can't tell you exactly who's in charge at the moment. I have as much authority to speak for the family as anyone, however, and I can tell you that we aren't interested in gas and oil exploration on Paradise Ranch."

"With all due respect," Magdalene said. "Your father was extremely interested."

"I doubt that. He was pretty proud of the pristine land he owned."

"I could show you the preliminary documents he signed, allowing us to start some field testing."

Harper breathed slowly and clutched Chevy's reins, her knuckles straining white beneath her skin. Confusion and disbelief assailed her more than anger, but still she controlled her temper with effort.

"Please understand. I don't want to discuss this now, and I don't want you to conduct any kind of surveys or tests on my property until I have a chance to talk to my family. Once I have, I'll get back to you if need be. If one of you has a card?"

Three cards appeared almost before she finished asking. She took them without so much as a glance.

"Please do call us as soon as possible," Magdalene said. "We're very eager to follow up on some initial findings. I think your family might be sitting on a black gold mine."

She smiled as if she considered herself a modern-day fairy godmother and thought Harper should shower her with thanks for the chance to go to the ball.

Harper pushed back angrily at her grandmother's voice from hours earlier, warning them about the ranch's dire straits. The truth couldn't stave off her astonishment over this blatant display of greed.

"You did hear me?" she asked. "We buried my father yesterday. This haste feels more than a little disrespectful. I'd like to ask you to leave now and let us deal with some other issues first. If we're still interested, we'll be in touch."

She had no intention of mentioning she hadn't lived at Paradise for eight years. As far as these people were concerned, she wanted them to believe she had every moral right to take charge of their current situation.

Magdalene Pearce opened her mouth, but she got cut off by fireplug man, who reached around her and held out *his* hand. "I'm sorry, Ms. Crockett. Of course, we'll leave immediately. I think we're all as shocked as you, and your family must be and are scrambling for the right words."

She knew why *he* was on the team.

"Thank you, Mr...."

"Brian Baumgartner. Another analyst. I'll look forward to hearing from someone in your family whenever the time is right."

Brian Baumgartner had just saved his company's hide. Harper didn't see his female colleague's lustful light of black gold fever in his kind smile. Instead he carried an air of wisdom that let her trust his promise they'd leave.

"It was lovely to meet you." Magdalen Pearce's material-girl fire had died down again, too, and her sincere voice returned. "Truly, our deepest condolences on your father's passing."

Passing? That was too soft. A church word. One she'd used herself earlier to soften the blow of reality: death. On her father's *death*. And *dead* meant he was so permanently gone that she couldn't go riding back to him and find out what on earth he'd been thinking. Consorting with an oil company, giving away an heirloom camera, leaving the ranch in jeopardy. Being the nicest asshole anyone had ever known.

Cole. She could run to him. He might know—

You don't know him anymore. Why would you even think that?

"Thank you."

She managed to choke out the required words without tears, but they ripped through her throat, leaving it aching to cry for a father who, even from the grave, had managed to betray her and turn her world into a distorted painting she didn't recognize.

Chapter Four

"WHO IS THE man we buried yesterday? Nobody I remember."

Cole listened to Harper's sharp words slice incongruously through a thick sadness she'd worn like false skin ever since returning from her half-day ride. Her family, truncated and skeletal now that the triplets had left for Denver, took up five puny spaces at the end of the massive dining table built thirty years earlier by Sebastian Crockett, who, he'd heard many times, fully intended for it to easily handle huge family gatherings. Sadie had left for her room right after eating or they'd have been six. The remains of funeral leftovers lay before them—a quiet supper. Until now.

"A lot changed for your father in the years you've been gone. He changed, too." Bella's words held the gentlest of reproaches.

"Apparently."

They sat like opposing countries at the United Nations. He and Harper took up one side of the table, Joely and Mia the other, and Bella served as the linchpin at the head.

"We always supported you girls and your decisions for college, careers, and building your lives away from Wyoming," she said. "But because of that, I think you owe your father the same respect and support. He always did what he felt was best for Paradise, and until the economy took a fall, he did a very good job of it. He kept the ranch going through a lot of adversity."

"Three generations have been through a lot of financial hardships, Mama," Harper said. "Somehow they managed to squeak through without selling out to any outside parties. You knew about his dealings with Mountain Pacific?"

"I only knew he thought about the possibility of selling some mineral rights. It has been the way out of financial crisis for many ranchers. I didn't know he'd actually set up a meeting."

"It's just exploration," Mia said. "If done properly, nothing will happen until we say so."

Cole squirmed. There were things he hadn't told Harper about his summer job, and this topic could easily blow up in his face. It didn't surprise him that she was upset by this. For years she'd led the stubborn, zealous fight of youth to keep everything on the ranch as natural as possible. Sam had sometimes voiced frustration with his second daughter because the things she'd wanted him to do—plant organic hay, raise free-range chickens, restore mountain prairie lands—were expensive and impractical.

"You tell them, Cole," she said. "You can't think it's a great idea?"

Damn.

"Harpo, I don't know. I don't have enough details."

"What? After how hard your family fought to keep your ranch intact and beautiful?"

"And how well did that work out for us?" He was no longer bitter about having had to sell the Double Diamond, but if he'd learned about a source of income before they'd done it, he would have snatched at it.

"Oh, come on. Would you have allowed all that machinery, all that oil rigging on your land? You didn't see where this was. Anything Mountain Pacific erected would be in the Wolf Paw Valley between us and the mountains. That magnificent view we're so proud of? Picture a lovely derrick or ten between us and Grand Teton. Picture black, oily landscape and habitat, not to mention loss of grazing land if one of them blows."

"You don't know they'd find oil at all," Amelia said. "It doesn't hurt to look."

"And if they do find a 'black gold mine,' as these people told me today? It's too late then, don't you think? We'd have sold our souls."

"Oh, that's not a little dramatic." Amelia rolled her eyes.

"So put your name in the 'for' column, then?" Harper's eyes shone with anger.

"I wasn't aware we were voting."

"We're not voting on anything," Bella said. "We're discussing. And in this issue, like the others, no decision needs to be reached tonight. Personally, I think it's a gift from the hand of God that Harper ran into these people. We are forewarned and forearmed."

"What's your vote, Mom?" Joely asked.

With a great sigh, Bella hugged herself and ran her hands quickly up and down her upper arms as if she were cold. For the first time since Cole had arrived home, she looked small, uncertain, and exhausted. "I don't want this beautiful piece of land marred by ugly man-made structures like oil wells. But I also know how bad things look on the books. I don't know yet what the right answer is."

"The real right answer is to sell and let someone else worry about it," Amelia said. "None of us has the time to deal with things like this. Honestly? I don't know what there is to discuss. This all makes it clearer than ever that we can't keep this place."

As it had ever since Mia had first made this declaration, a boulder settled more deeply and painfully into Cole's stomach. He couldn't bear the thought of selling Paradise Ranch now. Not when he was this close to getting the Double Diamond back. Once he had the money secured, he could pay off his debt to the Crocketts, and *then* they could sell.

"Doesn't heritage mean anything at all to you, Mia?" Harper asked.

"I don't see how you can ask that, Harper. You haven't exactly been gracing people here with your presence around here the last, oh, eight years or so. I'd say heritage means at least as much to me as it does to you."

To her credit, Harper's cheeks flamed with cherry-tomato spots of color. For one moment she looked like she wanted to counter, but her features relaxed in defeat. "Touché," she said.

Cole's heart twisted in sympathy. She'd never held her opinions lightly, but she usually knew when she'd overstepped her boundaries.

"I have an idea," he said. "Tomorrow, let's all take a ride out to where Harper met the oil company crew today. We'll have a good look at the land that's involved and then discuss it more."

"I think that's a wonderful idea," Joely said. "I'd like that."

"We don't have enough horses for all five of us right now," Harper said. "Dad's gelding and Rico and Neil's horses are the only ones here. Mom, why don't you have your horse anymore?"

"We had to put him down six months ago. Since I rarely rode anymore, I never looked hard for a replacement."

"We used to keep ten horses around here," Joely said. "What happened?"

"There are still tasks we need horses for." Bella gave a shrug. "Moving the cattle around close-in, the calving season, and a handful of jobs in the winter. But the trucks and four-wheelers were already indispensable when you were young. You know you can check a lot more fence in a day with a truck and a toolbox than with a few hand tools in a saddlebag."

"But there are so many places you can't get to by vehicle," Harper said.

"We can survey them by helicopter or plane. If we need to get someplace remote, we can determine from the air how to best do it."

"My dad still has his plane," Cole said. "He takes landowners up on a for-hire basis now."

"Still, no matter how convenient trucks and planes are, a ranch can't survive without good horses." Joely shared a troubled look with Harper.

"But more and more they can get by with fewer," Bella said.

A moment of uneasy silence fell after that. Cole found himself watching Harper from the corner of his eye. He could almost see her processing all the information she was taking in.

"So…" She frowned. "There used to be the one old-fashioned round-up every fall. The first herd would get brought in the last five or ten miles on horseback. Are you saying that's not done anymore?"

"There hasn't been time or manpower," Bella said. "All they do on horseback now is the last push into the main cattle yard and the sorting. Last year all it took was your father, Leif, Bjorn, Neil, and Rico."

"Not Bjorn's kids? Not Rico's? It used to be the best family time we had when it came to ranch tasks." Harper stared around the room. "Why aren't we all saddened by this? This is something we talked about all the time, around dinner tables and campfires and family outings.

How we'd never let the old way be forgotten. Now you're saying my own father allowed this to happen?"

"Sit down, Harper. What happened to my kind little artist?"

"That's what you think of me, isn't it? Still a little girl with her head in the clouds." She looked around. "What have we all let happen around here by leaving and staying away?"

"Don't be dramatic. As if we could have changed anything Dad decided to do anyway." Mia spoke quietly.

"We certainly could have tried." Harper's voice rose in agitation.

"Girls. Stop it." For the first time, Bella raised her voice. "Let me tell you what's happened since you've been gone. Ranching has continued to grow with the times. There are still many things we do the old way, but there are efficiencies and new techniques that have saved our skin many times by helping us get things done faster and for less money. We needed all the help we could get the past couple of years."

"The bottom line again. I see." Harper was not to be mollified.

"The line that gave you all food, shelter, college, and the lives you wanted, yes."

"Harper, you make my point. Isn't this just another nail in the Paradise coffin?" Mia sighed theatrically.

"Kind of a bad choice of words, don't you think?" Joely asked.

"Intentionally so." Mia leaned back in her chair. Cole stared at her. When had she turned into this cool, hard

Steve Jobs? "Our time here is dying—as surely as Dad died. I am sorry to say it, but there's no other logical way to solve this. Look, Harper. I know you don't think I understand, but that's not it. I hate all this as much as you do. But have you got time to go on a week-long round up so you can have your time to live in the past? Of course you don't. And neither do I. We *all* work. Does anyone have vacation time enough to come back here in between duties of your other job and run this place? Or fight off the *evil* oil executives for that matter? Don't answer, it was rhetorical. Bottom line is, who here honestly has time to fix all these problems?"

"I do."

Dead silence followed the quiet words. Cole stared across the table to Joely. Stunning, popular, Rodeo Queen Joely lifted a pale face to her siblings and mother. Her saucer-eyes looked like they belonged to a child who'd realized she'd taken a stupid dare—like maybe to walk across the Grand Canyon on a spaghetti noodle. But she lifted her chin.

"I have Mom, and Leif, and Bjorn and his family. I can do it."

"What about Tim? Your job in LA?" Harper asked.

Cole hadn't thought Joely could go any paler. She lowered her head and stared at her hands, which fidgeted on the table until she clasped them firmly together. When she'd stilled them, she spread them open and grasped the wedding ring on the fourth finger of her left hand. Slowly, with her mouth pinched as if the motion hurt like hell, she pulled the ring off and set it on the table.

"There is no Tim. There is no job."

Cole hadn't thought the silence could get any deeper either. Wrong again. He knew exactly what the others were thinking because the disbelief rocketed through him, too. This was Joely—perfect, tanned, admired, and always put-together Joellen Brigitta Crockett. Never a hair out of place, rarely anything but a smile on her face. Suddenly she looked like a ghost of that golden girl.

"Oh, Joely, what's going on?" Harper was the first to move, her anger evaporated and her natural empathy back in place.

She threw her arms around her sister, enveloping her face and shoulders. For a moment they clung and then Joely pushed her back.

"I couldn't bear to tell you," Joely said. "Tim left a month ago. Classic LA story—he got tired of me and found someone he says he loves more. Simple as that."

"Sweetheart, I'm sorry." Bella reached her, and this time Joely stayed enveloped in the embrace.

"I'm sorry, too." Her voice caught, diffused and muffled against Bella's slender arms. "I had no intention of telling anyone now. Even when Grandma noticed I was keeping something in. Like Harper said, this time isn't supposed to be about any of us. It's about Daddy. But I've known for months now I can't stay in LA. And I can't sit here and let anyone talk about selling Paradise when I was just starting to think I could come home."

"I wish you'd have told me," Bella said in a quiet voice.

"I couldn't. You would have had to tell Dad, and he..."

"He what?" Bella scoffed gently. "He loved you." Her eyes roamed the table, taking in everyone seated at its venerable sides. "Someday you'll believe he loved you all. Joely, family pulls together when something goes wrong. It doesn't matter that you didn't live here, this is home. Tell us what happened, we're here."

"We're all here, sis." Mia leaned forward and rubbed Joely's upper arm. "I'm sorry, too. Is it appropriate to call my brother-in-law a douche bag?"

Joely sat up and wiped tears from her cheeks. A small smile crept onto her lips. "You know what? Sure. He's a class-A douche. If there are rankings for such things."

Cole pushed from the table, stepped behind Joely, and planted a kiss on her crown. She'd been one of their Crockett-Wainwright band of kids, right along with him and her sisters.

"I'm sorry, too, Jo-Jo," he said. "I'll go beat him up for you if you want."

"Would you?" She tilted her head way back and looked up at him.

"I'm on a plane first thing."

"Thank you."

Cole patted her shoulder. He touched Harper's as well, although when she caught his eyes he wanted to do more than touch—he wanted to erase the mess of hard, sad emotions on her face.

Harper had always absorbed emotions like a sponge. Always taken on too many worries and championed too many causes. Now he could see her concern for every problem facing the family warring with her righteous indignation over her environmental beliefs. But what were her deep-down feelings? What was she burying inside to cause such confusion in her eyes?

He turned without explanation and made his way into the kitchen. Alcohol was rarely the right solution to desperate emotional times, but maybe this once Sam's medicinal cure would be a balm and a needed anesthetic—and Cole had something specific in mind.

In the wall between the kitchen and the dining room was an elaborate, built-in entertainment bar that opened from either side. Cole took his time looking through the variety of good alcohols Sam had stocked and searching out the item Sam had shown him once several years before. He found it still there, a golden, barrel-shaped bottle tucked into the farthest corner of the bottom shelf. Sam had said he was saving it, but for exactly what he didn't know.

"Well, Sam, you know now." Cole lifted the Scotch bottle and saluted the sky with it.

To connoisseurs, the odd-shaped bottle was apparently recognizable—a Glenrothes John Ramsay, one of only two hundred sent to the United States. Won in a poker game six years before, it went, Sam bragged, for a thousand dollars a bottle. Since nothing that rich had ever passed Cole's lips, he'd looked it up. Sure enough, Sam hadn't been ripped off—if a thousand-buck bottle of Scotch could be considered equal to money in a poker pot.

And since Sam wasn't here to protect his winnings, this seemed a perfect time to crack open the bottle. It certainly hadn't done him any good to keep it for posterity.

Cole found an etched-glass tray and pulled five low-ball tumblers from the shelves above the bar. Setting them artlessly on the tray, he hefted it and carried it along with the Scotch into the dining room.

"What's this?" Bella asked.

Harper sat beside Joely, holding one hand while Bella held the other. They were smiling now—anemically but genuinely.

"Your husband's secret stash." Cole smiled, too, fully prepared for Bella to protest. He assumed she knew about the Glenrothes. "I do remember one thing he taught every one of his daughters."

To his pleasant surprise, Bella nodded. "The John Ramsay. I'd forgotten all about that. Well done, Cole, sweetheart."

He nodded his acceptance of the compliment and distributed the glasses.

"Your father taught each one of you how to drink fine whisky," he said. "He definitely knew his Scotch. He had a warped sense of pride in the fact that every one of you learned to like it, too."

"His twenty-first birthday gift for each of us," Amelia said, "was a private tasting party. Our father was definitely one of a kind."

"Amen to that." Cole unwrapped the label from the bottle neck and pulled the stopper out with no more ceremony than he'd have used to unscrew the cap off of a bottle of Wild Turkey. "Like hiding this thousand-dollar bottle of Scotch in a corner."

"Oh my gosh! Are you serious?" Harper asked. "This is thousand-dollar Scotch? And you opened it?"

"Can't drink it without opening it."

Slowly he started around the table, pouring two fingers into each glass, finishing with his own. He set the bottle in the center of the table. Harper picked it up and peered at the label and at the white etched signature of John Ramsay across the swell of the barrel shape.

"Number two hundred fifty-seven of fourteen hundred bottles," she read. "Seriously?"

Cole shrugged. "That's what they say. Your dad told me there were only two hundred shipped to the United States."

"Heck," she replied. "We might be drinking our inheritance. I say bottoms up."

Cole lifted his glass and the others followed. "We haven't fixed anything," he said. "In fact, it feels like a lot is more broken than ever. But we're not going to discuss any more tonight. Agreed?"

A chorus of "hear-hears" made it so.

"And even though we each have our own memory of him and had a unique relationship with him while he was here, we can drink together to Samuel Crockett. We'll miss him. May he rest in peace."

"Rest in peace, Daddy," Amelia said quietly.

"Amen," Harper agreed.

Cole tipped his glass against his lips and let the cool, dark gold richness slide across his tongue and down his throat.

"Oh my," Harper said, her voice like a breathy prayer. "I haven't had anything that smooth and dry in a very, very long time."

"A little orangey," Joely said. "Maybe some vanilla."

"Oh, yes, your father would be very proud," said Bella, the sheen of unshed tears in her eyes. "Cole—I don't think there's any point in hoarding that Scotch. Pour again."

He almost laughed. He truly didn't believe in medicating problems—he'd had enough of that after high school—but the mood in the room was changing to one more appropriate for the night, and Bella needed that more than any of them. He poured again. Bella lifted her glass first.

"To my three oldest beautiful daughters. God grant you wisdom to go along with the brilliance you already possess."

More agreement and more glasses drained. Cole poured a third time.

"To Kelly, Grace, and Raquel," Joely said. "I wish they were here."

The Scotch disappeared a third time. Harper set her glass heavily on the table. "I think we need to drink to all the douche bags in our family." Everyone stared. She grinned slyly. "May one of them forever regret what he's done to my sister."

This time full-fledged cheering broke out, and when the whisky had been downed, actual laughter followed. There wasn't a lot of the John Ramsay left, enough for another couple of fingers each with a swallow remaining.

"To Mother." Harper lifted her hand for the final toast. "I hope you soar now on your own wings. Daddy can be your angel, and you will miss him, but you don't *need* him. You are the best part of each one of us."

For a group of people slowly getting drunk on very good Scotch, the response to that was subdued and heart-felt. Nobody chugged her last drink, and Cole swirled the amber liquid around the base of his glass. He knew another truth about the girls of Paradise Ranch—they all believed their mother had been downtrodden her whole life. After all, if Sam had pressed them to be what he wanted them to be, how much more opinionated would he have been with his wife?

Cole didn't know if their perception was right. Bella had never struck him as a weak woman. But he did know his father had said that nobody in Wolf Paw Pass knew why Isabella Holcomb had fallen and stayed fallen for Sam Crockett. They couldn't have been more opposite in temperament or interests. But stay with him she had, for thirty-five years. The girls' mother, at fifty-nine, only now showed the first fan of crows' feet at her eyes and the first miniscule droop beside her mouth to mark the approach of her next decade. Tonight the puffiness beneath Bella's lovely brown eyes were not the mark of a woman relieved to out from a man's thumb.

"This is very, very excellent Scotch." Harper stared into her glass, which still held half an inch of the Glenrothes. Her words weren't slurring, but they surfaced slowly, deliberately. Her thick, dark hair now fell unbraided in a beautiful, satiny drape along her cheek.

"It is." He drained his glass, pushed it away, and forced himself to stand so he wouldn't kiss her right in front of everyone. "I think it's almost time for everybody to go to bed."

Amelia smiled tipsily and winked at him. "Good idea. Bed."

He laughed at her loss of self-censorship. "Come on. Time for all good girls to go there. And nobody gets up early tomorrow, got it?"

Harper stood and braced both hands on the table. "Whoa. Did you see this stuff is, like, forty-six point seven percent alcohol by volume? It's the real deal, girls. Cole, if you get lost on your way to your room, you can come and get me." She grinned. "Or come and tuck me in to start with. I'll give you directions."

She was no more sober than Mia, and yet her words struck his blood like little hand grenades.

"You always were a fun drinker, Harpo. Go on and dream about me, but don't stay awake waiting."

She saluted him, hugged her mother and Joely, and stopped in front of Amelia. For a moment she hesitated, then Harper took her in a huge embrace. Cole sagged with relief. The Scotch had worked.

"You guys never let me finish," Joely said, still smiling over her glass of whisky. "I was serious. I'm flying back to LA day after tomorrow; I'm packing up my house, putting it on the market, and I'm driving back here in my truck and trailer. I still have my horse, and she and I are coming home. You all watch—I'll save the family ranch."

Cole didn't argue with her. Tomorrow, with a little hangover and the crashing weight of reality, Joely would probably fall out of love with this starry-eyed savior-of-the-ranch idea. Then again, he wasn't 100 percent sober either. He could be dead wrong.

Chapter Five

SHE DIDN'T EXACTLY have a hangover, just a thumping headache, but she sure had regrets. Harper remembered clearly every word that had been uttered the night before, including her ridiculous babblings to Cole.

Tuck me in? I'll give you directions?

Now there was a perfect example of why one drink should always be her limit. She was garrulous under the influence—and she'd never known how to run at the mouth with elegance.

Tuck me in. She groaned and concentrated on her feet. One step at a time. Don't think about her share of the thousand-dollar bottle of Scotch that, up until she'd gotten careless, had actually been a brilliant solution to the end of a truly awful day. The course of this day, even though it was already ten thirty in the morning, was still up in the air.

She trudged toward the barn, her old boots the most comfortable thing on her body. She'd kept them, along with a handful of sweaters and the ancient Carhartt jacket she used for ranch work, in a corner of her old closet where they awaited her infrequent visits. She suspected each of her sisters had a similar stash and wondered if they were always as surprised as she was to find their mother hadn't tossed the whole lot.

She crested the rise in the driveway that allowed her to overlook the impressive heart of the ranch. Her ancestors had known what they were doing when they'd laid out the basic work areas. Despite recent decisions, what her father had done to upgrade and make things run more efficiently only enhanced the beauty of the whole operation.

To the left stood the horse barn, the ranch's newest structure built ten years earlier. A horse owner's dream, it had solid oak stall doors, full plumbing, a huge tack room filling one end of the barn, and an extra room off the main rectangle, housing a repair shop for everything cowboy related, from tack to ropes to branding equipment to chaps. To the right was a cluster of buildings, a couple dating from the forties and fifties, and one, a small, meticulously maintained house that had been the main office from 1916 when Eli Crockett had founded Paradise Ranch.

Two cattle sheds and another huge, older barn, a machine shed, a blacksmith's cabin, and a modern log office not dissimilar to the main house completed the set of buildings. Beyond the ranch's micro city, however, the Paradise's majestic landscape spread out—the start of nearly ninety square miles of rolling hills and mountains, all smaller preludes to the Rockies. Two huge corrals that could be used for branding or sorting flanked the view, and beyond them, a glint from the small, tributary Kwinaa River flashed silver, and the mighty Rocky Mountains defined the horizon with jagged silhouettes.

Harper drew the sweet Western air into her lungs. It honestly smelled and even tasted different from the bustling, frantically moving, greasy air of Chicago. Slowly her headache faded and strength filled her limbs. She'd originally regretted her impulsive agreement to talk to Bjorn about using a couple of his private pleasure horses. But as her mind cleared, and the indignation from her meeting with Mountain Pacific caught fresh sparks, her mission suddenly seemed righteous. Not that she really wanted to run into Skylar Thorson again—she hadn't been particularly kind during their first meeting—but she wanted to get her family out to imagine the potential damage allowing the oil company onto their property could cause.

She was headed half a mile southwest of the ranch center. When he'd taken over Paradise, her father had set aside four ten-acre plots of land for his long-term employees. At the time nobody had known Leif would remain such a part of the family or that his son would bring back a Southern belle who'd stay as well. Sam had simply wanted his employees to have some ownership in their jobs. He rented the homes built on the acreages to full-time hands. After they worked for him two years, he offered the homes for sale to them. When they wanted to leave, the ranch bought the homes back, guaranteed. It had turned out to be a brilliant plan. Over the years, only Leif and Bjorn and their families had moved in permanently. The other two houses switched hands regularly, and most of the time served as rental properties.

Harper had chosen to walk rather than drive or ride to Bjorn's home. By the time she'd reached the front door of his stone-fronted ranch-style house, she didn't care who answered the door. She was ready with a smile on her face.

"Hi!"

She looked down through a screen door into the eager, round face of a boy child approximately five or six years old.

"Hi," she replied.

"You're Miss Harper. I saw you yesterday." He had a precocious tone of voice and precise enunciation. Impressive for such a short person.

"I am. I'm a friend of your grandpa's and your dad's."

"Howdy, Miss Harper."

Oh, they were going to have trouble with this one. That cowboy-slash-Southern charm combo was going to be lethal when he got to school.

"Howdy, sir. Will you forgive me if I tell you I don't remember your name?"

"Aiden Per Thorson."

"That is one of the most distinguished names I've ever heard. Is your dad or your mom home?"

"My mom's here. We're supposed to be in school, but she let us have the day off because of Mr. Crockett's funeral yesterday. She said we all need a day to play because life's too short."

Harper hadn't known Melanie Thorson possessed such practical wisdom. She'd always seemed overly structured and even a little unyielding.

"That sounds like a very nice thing to do."

"Did you know Mr. Crockett?"

For some reason his words didn't hurt or even sting. Harper found his serious question endearing and slightly comforting.

"I sure did. He was my dad."

Aiden took that in with a little bit of surprise. He studied her for a minute, as if he knew there was something special he should say but he wasn't quite sure what.

"Are you really sad today?"

Just like that he'd found precisely the right words. "I am. It's very nice of you to ask me."

"I would be awful sad if my daddy died."

"I know. I'm glad your daddy is fine. Is he working today?"

"He said he had to help Grandpa, because even though Mr. Crockett isn't here there's still work to do. The work didn't die."

Harper found herself wishing that adults—that everyone—could be this open and honest about death. No pussyfooting. No political correctness. Just pure emotion. Aiden Per Thorson was making her smile inside.

"That's something we all end up learning, Aiden. The work never dies. Your daddy and grandpa work really hard. I bet you work hard at school, too."

He shrugged.

"Aiden?" His mother appeared at the door and peered through the screen. "Harper?"

"Hi, Melanie. Sorry to bother you."

"Nonsense. I'm thrilled to see you, although I'm surprised it's so soon after the funeral. Are y'all doing okay up there?"

Every time she heard it, Melanie's lilting Carolina accent tickled Harper. It was so incongruous amid all the macho bombast of western Wyoming.

"We're fine, really. In a little bit of shock still, but we're muddling."

"I'm sure it's a comfort for your mama to have you girls all home."

"The triplets are gone already, but the rest of us have a few more days. And Joely will be staying on to start taking over some of Dad's work."

"Oh my, what a task that is," Melanie said. "Bless her heart; I'll be prayin' for her, you can believe that. Can you come in? I've got some fresh peanut butter cookies. Slipping in a little home-ec lesson even though I promised no school today."

"You must be the most organized person on the face of the earth. Mom, teacher, baker, friend. How do you do it?"

She stepped into the house. It did smell delicious.

"I don't always manage well. The older two are starting to fuss a bit about school and discipline. This time of year, when Leif and Bjorn are busy I sometimes do a lot of fudging with field trips. And now, since your father…Harper, I'm really sorry about your dad."

"Thank you."

"You'll let me know if there's anything at all I can do."

"I will. In fact, I'm kind of here to ask a huge favor right now."

"Name it."

"We need to go as a family to Wolf Paw Pass. Don't mention it yet, but yesterday I ran into a group from Mountain Pacific gas that claimed they were here on my dad's request. I'm not sure about that, but it's divided the family a little. I want everyone to see the area these people were talking about testing. I'm not a big fan of them coming onto the ranch."

"I don't blame you," Melanie said.

Melanie's agreement soothed Harper's inner turmoil a little. She didn't know what Leif or Bjorn's feelings about the situation would be, but if she had Melanie's support, it couldn't hurt.

"Not everyone will be adverse to the idea. It's a good way to supplement income if there is a reserve of oil or gas on ranch property. Still, there has to be a better way to make money than spoiling good land."

"So what can I help you with?"

"We only have three horses these days, but Mama said you and Bjorn have five. I'm wondering if we could borrow two mounts for a couple of hours this afternoon."

"Of course. I'm wondering, though, if there might be only two available today."

"Oh?"

"One is a pony—too small for any of you. Marcus took his horse, Scout, out this morning and isn't back. Bjorn's King threw a shoe yesterday and is a little sore until he gets it back on. That leaves Leif's Nellie and Skylar's Bungu. I shouldn't give permission to take him without asking Skylar first."

"Of course. The black-and-white Appy?"

"Her pride and joy. She bought half of him herself. The girl is horse crazy, but then, this *is* a ranch."

"We had six horse-crazy girls. I totally understand." Harper sat at the crisp, white lacquered kitchen table and took in Melanie's cheerful blue-and-red Norwegian color scheme. On one wall was a framed Norwegian blessing Harper had heard Leif recite a hundred times over the years. "*I Jesu navn gar vi til bords...*In Jesus's name we come to the table..." She smiled, hearing her father's voice mercilessly butchering the pronunciation whenever he teased Leif by trying it himself.

"Sure ain't a drop of Viking blood in your veins," Leif would say.

"Unless there were Vikings in Davy Crockett's genes," her father would reply haughtily.

"Probably were," Leif would say with a sniff.

Faintly Harper heard a question and pulled her eyes from the prayer, surprised that it of all things had dredged up the sorrow. She shook her head and turned to the plate of cookies Melanie set on the table.

"Sorry, what?" Harper asked.

"I asked when you have to go back to Chicago."

"Another four days. I have some preexisting commitments. Amelia has to get back to work in New York. I think, as of this morning, Joely's talking about taking Mom on a road trip to get her things from California."

"Your daddy raised some pretty smart girls." Melanie smiled. "You're all doing very well. He was proud of you."

So everyone kept saying. Harper smiled back—her rote acknowledgment of how great Sam Crockett had been. People said a lot of things after someone died. She bit into a cookie, and groaned.

"This is amazing. It's been ages since I've had a home-made peanut butter cookie. I forget that nothing compares—except maybe something with six pounds of chocolate."

"Well, that goes without saying."

"So, is Skylar here?" Harper changed the subject over a mouthful of thick, warm, chewy cookie. "I could ask her myself about her horse."

"I think she is." Melanie stood and walked to the kitchen door. She leaned through it and called her daughter's name. Instead, Aiden came running. "Have you seen Skylar?" Melanie asked.

"Uh-uh." He shook his head. "May I have a cookie?"

"After lunch. You've already had two."

"But pleeeeeeze?"

"Go. Find Skylar for me. Pleeeeeeze."

"She's not here."

"Oh?"

"She left."

"When did she leave?" Melanie's brow furrowed. "She should be telling me when she goes out."

"Like one second ago, about." He eyed the plate of cookies pitifully.

"Thank you for the information. Now you go and play."

"Howdy, Miss Harper." He grinned as if they shared a secret joke.

"Howdy, Mr. Aiden."

He beamed at her, his dimples deepening adorably, and turned to go—obedient yet impish. No doubt about it, the kid was already a lady killer.

"Six going on twice that." Melanie sighed.

Harper laughed and took another cookie. Aiden Thorson was the kind of kid who could make a person think about having her own. The idea had never seriously crossed her mind. Children didn't fit well into an artist's bizarre schedule, and with her history of drugs and dropping out of things, she didn't have anywhere near the credentials one needed for raising human beings.

"He's darling," she said, deciding she was just as glad Aiden was staying with a mom like Melanie.

AN HOUR LATER, Harper led Joely, Mia, and their mother over the trail Harper had followed the day before. Cole brought up the rear. She rode Skylar Thorson's black-and-white Appaloosa without the girl's approval, since nobody had seen her from the time Harper had appeared to ask for permission to use the horses. She'd only been on the horse twenty minutes, but Harper had decided she wouldn't give him back. He was a beauty, but he also had brains to spare. Bungu. All Melanie could tell her about his name was that it was an Indian word for horse, and that Skylar loved him more than life itself.

Joely rode the inexperienced Chevy, who belonged to Rico, the ranch hand. Cole had their other hand Neil's gelding, Paco. Bella rode Sam's gelding, Wheeler, and Mia rode Leif's mare, Nellie. As the sun filtered through the trees, highlighting the route toward the mountains and the open land beyond Wolf Paw Peak, Harper relaxed. Nobody seemed mired in anger or even dark grief any more. Maybe this whole idea would work. Or they were all nursing hangover headaches.

"Nice day for a ride."

Cole's voice startled her slightly and she laughed, embarrassed by the constant woolgathering that was making her so scatterbrained. A psychiatrist would excuse her, considering the events of the past week. Her family wouldn't consider it odd in any case. But she didn't like it.

"Hi," Harper said.

"Hi." He grinned, his face, shaded by the brim of his tan cowboy hat, was tough and angled and boyishly impish at the same time. "You doing okay?"

"Of course."

"Hey, it's not that obvious an answer to me. You didn't even say goodnight. And after all those promises…"

The wink he gave, underscored by a lecherous little grin, triggered a groan of dismay.

"Oh, don't even remind me. I'm totally humiliated, and I'm sorry. You plied me with way too much Scotch."

He chuckled. "It was good stuff."

"I guess it was, but honestly? A thousand bucks…" She blew a fart sound and swished her hand through the air. "Makes more sense to buy a Coach bag or Prada shoes. At least you get multiple uses out of them. And they don't make an ounce of sense to me either."

"I've always seen this lack of pretense in you. Fart noises and Birkenstocks, right? Real sexy, Harpo."

"Hey, you used to laugh plenty hard at the fart noises—at least I don't do them with my armpits like some people I know. And do you see Birkenstocks anywhere on my person? I know how to dress properly for this place."

"Awww, I'm just giving you a bad time. We were always good at that."

The reminder was mildly depressing. Next thing she knew he'd be stealing her boots and hiding them like he'd also done when they were kids. She didn't want to believe he still saw her as that short, stocky, fart-sound-making preteen from almost twenty years ago.

"Sorry," she grumbled. "Must be my thousand-dollar hangover."

"You don't get hangovers. I know that about you, too."

"So I don't drink much anymore. I've become a lightweight."

"What? Old Tris doesn't take you out to the finer establishments of Chicago?" He waggled his brow, and she leaned sideways in her saddle to sock him on the arm, finally laughing.

"Not to the seedy establishments either. Or to the movies. Or picnics. Or anywhere."

"Hey, then I'm one up on him. I'm taking you on a picnic."

"No. I'm taking *you* on a picnic." The new turn in the conversation rebooosted her mood.

"I've missed this kind of thing, Harpo. Glad you're still fun to tease."

At that her residual embarrassment from the night before along with her fears that she was only as good as a childhood memory to him, dissipated like magic. They rode in companionable silence, and the longer he stayed next to her, the more comfortable she grew, absorbing his quiet confidence, reveling in his easy manner and unwavering friendship. She gave up wondering why she was so hyperaware of him this trip and let herself simply enjoy.

He rode as one with his horse, left hand loose but sure on the reins, right hand relaxed on his thigh. Fascinated by the ridges of veins on the back of his hand, which defined the word masculine in visual form, she stared at the dusting of hair behind his knuckles and let her gaze meander up his arm to the roll of his plaid shirt sleeve below his elbow. Broad chest. Defined shoulders— obvious even beneath the loose cotton of his button-down shirt. Corded neck. Full lips—

She cut herself off as tension crept back up her neck and heat into her cheeks.

Leaning forward, she stroked Bungu's long, black mane as his head bobbed easily with his walk, and concentrated on his beauty rather than Cole's. She willed her friend to start talking again, suddenly craving the goofball she'd resented earlier. The goofball would be preferable—safer at least—to the strong, silent, movie star–looking cowboy.

They came around the base of the mountain, and this time no rumbling trucks marred the valley vista stretching before them. Her mother and sisters fanned out into a line, and everybody halted. For a moment only wind rustling in the hills and the snorting of the horses filled the warm air. A wispy bank of clouds trailed from the Tetons in the distance, like banners from Camelot.

"I haven't been here in ages," her mother said. "It is truly stunning."

"And now imagine a half-dozen oil wells," Joely said.

Harper could have kissed her for saying the words first and saving her from the obvious everyone had expected her to state.

"The first question would be whether there isn't somewhere else they could put them," her mother said. "Or explore. I suppose if this is where the oil is…"

"And what if it is?" Harper asked. "Can't we decide we don't want them here for no reason other than we don't want them? Maybe it doesn't have anything to do with politics or thinking one belief is good and another bad. Maybe it's our ranch, and we want it to look like this for the next generation."

Nobody countered her.

"As I recall, there's a great picnic spot around the next curve," Mia said.

"I'm all for that," Joely agreed. "I know there's chocolate in our saddle bags."

The entire mood lightened. Once they'd tethered the horses, their mother pulled a large, blue-and-white checked cloth from her saddle bag and shook it out on the grass beside a rocky outcropping. From the rest of the bags came a seemingly endless supply of sandwiches, fruit, carrots and celery sticks, two Thermoses of coffee and hot chocolate, and some magical plastic container filled with thick, gooey brownies.

Half an hour later, full and sated, they all sat back against boulders and sighed in contentment. "Bella, you are a true wizard—this was delicious," Cole said.

"It was a perfect thing for me to do today. Thank you," she replied.

"We could stay here," Harper said. "Ignore all the things there are to decide."

"I definitely like the sound of that," her mother said. "But I need to head back. I promised myself to work on some thank-you notes. I'd like to have them done before you girls leave—just because I'd rather be sad with you all around."

Joely wrapped her in a hug. "I'll help with that, Mom."

"I have a conference call at two," Mia said. "Then of course I'll help, too."

"We all should," Harper agreed.

"I'd like to take the long way back," Cole said. "Finish going around Wolf Peak and up across Kwinaa Ridge and see what the view is from there. Maybe it's a little more hidden and protected. How about if I meet you all back at the house?"

Harper's emotions swung wildly at his request. How much nicer would it be to continue riding than to go back and face funeral thank-yous? But her mother deserved her support.

"You shouldn't do that alone," her mother said. "We could take the extra time."

"Why don't you all go?" Mia said. "I don't have time before my call, unfortunately, but I can go back by myself—this is a perfectly easy, safe trail."

Harper studied her elder sister. Mia had been particularly subdued today—quiet and nonargumentative. She didn't know what that meant, but it did dispel her own defensiveness and made the afternoon and all the impending weighty discussions lurking in its shadows much less onerous.

"Harper, you go with Cole," Joely said. "I'll get us started on the notes. Mia can do the call, and you two will be back in a couple of hours."

"We could all go tomorrow," Mia replied, a hint of reservation stealing into her voice for the first time.

"No, no, we'd have to borrow horses again," their mother said, smiling at Harper. "You two go. We'll see you when you get home."

They packed up the picnic with no further discussion, and before she knew it, Harper was waving her sisters and mother down the trail. When she turned back to Cole, he was staring off across the valley again.

"You want to look for a place to hide oil wells, don't you?" she asked, trying hard to keep accusation from her voice.

She didn't relish bringing up the subject. It seemed like enough to be here, to absorb the beauty, the ripe scents of late summer. At that moment, she wanted Joely to succeed. Joely who *hadn't* changed her mind overnight. She wanted Mia to be wrong that selling Paradise Ranch was the smart thing to do.

"I want you to look at all the options, that's all."

"You think I haven't over the years?"

"I know you've looked at all the reasons you hate oil. I respect that, Harpo, I do." He nodded to the grass where they'd been sitting for lunch. "Come on, sit down. I want to ask you something."

"Fine."

He sounded so reasonable. She could be reasonable. She sat beside him, and he put one arm around her shoulders, pointing toward Grand Teton with the other. The little thrills of delight at his touch didn't shock her anymore. The shoulds and shouldn'ts of being this close to him, however, gave her no peace. The shouldn'ts were screaming at her.

She stayed beside him anyway.

"Look out there," he said. "What is it to you?"

"Stunning scenery," she said.

"No. It's stunning scenery to everybody. What is it to *you*? What do you want to keep it looking like that for?"

"Isn't that a self-evident answer?"

"Not at all. You want it pretty. You could travel ten miles down the road, see the same vista without oil wells, and what would this one little piece matter?"

"Because it's mine."

"Ah. Is it, though? Do you plan to be here? Plan to come back here with a family? Children? Grandchildren? That's what 'mine' means, you know."

"Good gosh, Cole." Anger rose quickly. "How am I supposed to know that? What is this, some kind of guilt trip?"

He took his arm from her shoulders and grasped her by both upper arms, turning her firmly to face him. "It's not. Of course it's not. There's no right or wrong answer for you. But I know what I want, and I will fight for it."

"Fight our family for it, you mean?"

"That's not at all what I mean. I'd like to work with you for it. With Mia, Joely, the triplets, and your mother. If there's a way to keep this place alive, I want to help find it. And it isn't just for the pretty view."

"What is this thing you want that you'll fight for? Kids? Grandkids?"

"Absolutely. The things my parents never got to have."

"And you'd like to give them a ruined landscape?"

"It doesn't have to ruin it. You saw one disaster out of thousands of oil wells."

"One disaster you can still see the effects of twelve years later if you go look."

"Oh, and you have?"

"As a matter of fact, I have. Last winter when I was home." He actually looked impressed. Harper glared at him. "I don't just talk through my ass, Cole. I do my research."

"Okay. I've never said you weren't smart. You're damn smart, Harper. And you care. I love that you care. But why hate this so much? Everyone uses oil. You flew here. You drove on asphalt made of petroleum. Finding oil here could help your family out."

"I wish I didn't have such a big footprint. I don't back in Chicago. I'm vain about that." She offered a tiny, sheepish smile. "But I don't have an alternative. Believe me, if I were smart enough to come up with an electric airplane, I'd be the first on that project."

"I believe you."

"Look," she said. "I know we can't go back to zero oil in this world. That's not my goal. But we'll never have other alternatives that are affordable if places like Paradise Ranch keep feeding into the big money oil pot. That's all."

"So it is purely philosophical for you?"

"No!" She wanted to throttle him for his dogged attack. So what if it *was* philosophical? Everyone had a philosophy. She was now seeing his, too. One wasn't right and the other wrong. "I do love this place. I do want it pristine. Why isn't that enough? You should want it pristine, too, for these illusory future grandchildren of yours."

"I want it to be, period."

"There are other ways to save it."

"I'll grant you that. Today we're exploring one way."

They fell silent, and he put his arm around her again. Maybe they'd drawn lines in the sand, but she appreciated that he wasn't angry. Surprisingly, her own irritation had gone, too.

"Do you want kids?" he asked.

What the heck? Her brain had brought the topic of children up just that morning. This had to be some weird kind of psychic disturbance in The Force, she thought.

"I haven't thought much about it," she said. "I don't think I do right now, the way my life is. You want a whole bunch, it sounds like."

"Two or three to carry on the legacy."

"Are you forgetting how well that didn't work for Sam Crockett?" She said it lightly, but a seed of melancholy sprouted deep within her.

"Sam Crockett has six amazing daughters. They'll figure out his legacy."

His questions stopped. He embraced her shoulders again. She stared a long, silent while into the distance, across a view she'd memorized years and years ago. She did love it. She loved it with every fiber of her innermost being. And despite Cole's points—valid ones, she had to admit—she would find a way to keep this untarnished for the future. Even if she came here alone when she was Grandma Sadie's age to view it.

Cole stretched his long legs straight out and smiled. He made no move on her, and she was glad, despite the continuing thrill of being so close. She relaxed into his strong, silent western hero side and followed his lazy gaze to the horses, still staked by the bushes they were contentedly decimating. He reached up to scratch his chest and closed his eyes.

His muscles contracted and froze into a giant, steel block.

"Oh shit! Shit! Shit! Shit! Harper!"

She shot to her feet at his sudden, frenzied cry, and he, too, rocketed to a stand. His hat hit the ground, his eyes rounded with genuine terror, and he flapped his arms and hunched his back like a drunken flamingo.

"What? What? Cole what's wrong?" She jumped to his side.

"It's in my shirt. It's flippin' *in* my shirt. Oh, freakin' God, it's big as my hand."

"What is? What are you talking about?" She didn't know whether to laugh at his ridiculous dance or panic along with him.

"I think it's one of those damn hobo spiders. What do I do? Those mother-effers are poisonous."

He clutched at his shirt, feeling for the thing he believed was going to dispatch his life on the spot. The strong, silent hero had turned into a babbling idiot. At least, she thought, now holding back a laugh, here was another thing that hadn't changed. His pathological arachnophobia.

She tried to catch one of his flailing arms.

"The first thing you have to do is stop jumping around like Pinocchio," she said, barely hanging on to her straight face. "Stand still so if there really is a spider, you don't scare it. Do you think it's bitten you?"

"Don't even say that." He whimpered.

"You big baby. Pull your shirt off." He stared as if he hadn't understood the command. "Stop backing up!"

"Give me a grizzly bear any time," he moaned.

"Where is this death-dealing creature?"

"You're not funny. God, it's still crawling."

She couldn't contain the laughter anymore. Even if it was a hobo spider, even if it did bite him, there was debate about how dangerous the bites were, and there were easily accessible antidotes. Her big, safe, strong friend was hilarious. With her palm, she pressed against his shirt and twisted it softly, feeling along his left pectoral. She jumped a little when she felt the inch-round bulge. Instinctively she gathered the fabric and captured the spider.

"Got him."

She literally felt the shiver shimmer through Cole's body. Tilting her head, she gazed up into his face, which was finally draining of panic. A woodsy, warm scent emanated from his flushed skin—even at his least macho, his power was substantial.

"Thank you." His breath floated onto her face. "You saved me."

"Unless you got bitten. Then I'm too late."

"I retract my thanks." He uttered a low growl as he worked his shirt buttons open. "You're evil."

"I'm enjoying this."

He shrugged out of his shirt only to wind up with Harper holding part of his snowy-white T-shirt along with the limp plaid fabric. "Great."

She couldn't say a word from a mouth suddenly as dry as mountain scree. The T-shirt stretched even more nicely than the sweater from yesterday over well-defined arms and pecs she absolutely didn't remember from the last time they'd gone river swimming. Where was that wiry, skinny kid when she needed him?

"Pull the undershirt off, too." She managed to choke the words out.

Cole shucked it, shivered, and brushed his hand roughly over his torso as if clearing away the last of his heebie-jeebies. Then he bent and brushed out his hair, leaving it with even more of its signature spiky messiness.

"Guess I've wrecked that mood," he said.

"Good thing you had a big, strong woman to take care of the problem."

"Yeah." He caught her eyes, and not a touch of embarrassment shone in his. "You know, I've always hated spiders. Don't know why, but clearly I haven't gotten any better. Thanks."

She stood less than a foot from his bare chest. For all the masculine scruff that showed up on his face by late afternoon every day, the skin before her was gloriously smooth and solid and pretty much the hottest thing she'd seen in longer than she could remember. She had to back away or risk reaching out to stroke the flat plane over his heart.

"I...you're welcome. Doofus."

He waggled his brow. "So, you gonna finish the job with the thing in my shirt or are you just going to stand there and hold it?"

"I think I'm going to make you ride back shirtless. If it happens again we don't have to go through this. You can brush it off."

"Oh no. Uh-uh."

She smiled at last and looked at the bunched shirts in her hand. Slowly she uncurled her fist. Cole backed away like a startled mustang. In the center of a web of wrinkles, stark against the white cotton of the undershirt, sat an inch-long brown-ish spider with classically freaky arched legs and two zig-zag brown stripes down its abdomen.

"Do you, like, sit and study spiders so much that you recognize them in split seconds?" she teased. "These guys aren't that easy to ID."

"Last summer Leif said he'd noticed a couple of spots infested with hobos. I leaped to the conclusion."

"You're a freak." She grinned and walked several feet away to shake the spider out behind a different rock outcropping.

"Wait, you aren't going to kill it?"

"Why? We invaded its home. It won't be back here before we leave."

"Now who's the freak?" He grabbed his T-shirt from her and held it up, inspecting every inch. "Bring on the well drillers—wipe out the spiders."

Harper shook her head and settled her gaze on his incredibly beautiful torso, flexing in preparation for donning the shirt. A snarky comment to cover her deep, *deep* enjoyment formed at her lips and hung there ready to fly, when a soft crash and sibilant spray of scree pebbles spun them both in place. Right above them on a slight path behind more large rocks, Skylar Thorson sprawled on her butt, scarlet creeping up her cheeks.

Chapter Six

COLE WATCHED THE disoriented teen scramble to her feet and back defensively toward the rock she'd apparently slid from. As she drew back, she gathered up a book of some kind and held it roughly against her stomach.

"Skylar?" Harper called. "Are you all right?"

Cole's first thought, since he could see the girl wasn't injured, was to wonder what she was doing there in the first place.

"Fine," Skylar called.

"Come on down here."

"I'll just go home."

"Oh no." Harper shook her head and crooked a finger. "Come."

The teen picked her way slowly down the short slope. She glanced at Cole but turned quickly away, a scowl on her face. Surprised, with no clue what he'd done to deserve the stink eye, he pulled his T-shirt over his head and smoothed it down.

"Well, well, hi there," Harper said when Skylar stood in front of them. "This is a surprise. Can I ask what you're doing here?"

For a moment she said nothing. "I heard you tell my mom where you were riding. They let you take my horse without asking me, so I came to keep an eye on him." Her pointed little chin rose in a small show of bravado.

"We looked for you so we could ask, but you weren't home."

"I wasn't that far away. They could have found me."

"Then I'm sorry. We would have left Bungu alone if you'd wanted us to. I get that you don't know me well enough to know if I'll ride him carefully. Still, that's not really a reason to come spying."

"It's not Bung-goo," she said, ignoring the apology and the mild chastisement. "It's Boong-goo. Everyone gets it wrong, even my mom. It's Shoshone for horse."

"Bungu." Harper pronounced it correctly. "I'll remember. Would it help if I told you he's every bit as brave and perfect as you said he was?"

Skylar's defensive posture eased—like any woman whose child got complimented. "He's a really awesome horse."

"He is. But this is a long way to come on foot. Seems a little extreme. You sure you aren't spying on us for some other reason, too?"

The teen shrugged. "I'm not spying. It wasn't hard to follow you. I do cross-country at our homeschool sports group. It's the only sport Mom lets me do because it doesn't cost much and the coach goes to our church. I could do chess, but I don't like chess."

"Bummer." Cole interrupted her. "Chess keeps your brain young."

"Don't mind him. He was captain of the chess team in high school. It was his only claim to glory." Harper fixed him with a teasing grin, but couldn't control her eyes as her gaze moved down his torso and back up. He grabbed his outer shirt.

Skylar, too, gave him a dazed up and down assessment. When he tried to smile at her, she whipped her gaze away again. The defensiveness returned.

"Like I said, I run a lot."

"Does your mom know where you are?" Harper asked.

"I come out exploring all the time. It's fine."

Cole exchanged a skeptical glance with Harper. "We had lunch earlier. Would you like a brownie or something to drink?" he asked.

Skylar shook her head and stuffed her hands into her jean pockets, her notebook, or whatever it was, wedged between one arm and her side. "Are you going to sell the ranch?"

Harper's jaw dropped.

"Who told you they might be selling?" Cole asked.

"I hear stuff. My grandpa talks to Dad, and Dad talks to Mom. And now you want to let there be oil wells here."

"Look," Cole said, hoping somebody who wasn't family wouldn't sound like he was sugarcoating the truth. "I promise, the talk you're hearing is just that, talk."

"We don't want to sell the ranch," Harper said firmly. "And we didn't invite the oil company people to come, our dad did. So we don't know anything about that yet."

Cole eased out a long sigh. In his opinion, a fourteen-year-old child didn't need to know anything about the business decisions being discussed on the ranch. All it would take was for her to blab to one friend, and some person in Wolf Paw Pass would start rumors—correct or incorrect. Paradise Ranch's problems could be spread across Wyoming.

"We should probably head out," he said, quietly ending the conversation.

Harper didn't argue and turned toward the girl. "I'm guessing you'd rather ride Bungu home. I'm telling you, if *I* ride him, I won't want to give him back. He's like driving a brand new sports car."

A smile darted across Skylar's mouth. "Okay."

"And how are you getting home, smart girl?" Cole turned to Harper.

"Maybe somebody will give me a lift?" She raised her brows and glanced from Cole to Skylar.

"Bungu doesn't carry double yet," the girl said. "He still kind of bucks."

Cole immediately felt the result of Skylar's announcement, as his pulse kicked into high gear. The idea of Harper sitting behind him on a horse for an hour and a half sent happy shivers coursing through his body. Right along with a little bit of dread. Cuddling with her next to a rock with the safe, unsexy topic of oil wells and the future between them was one thing. Having her sweet, very sexy body pressed up to his on the back of a swaying horse was quite another. Nonetheless, his lips and voice formed the words.

"Guess you'll have to ride with me."

Harper's wide eyes mirrored the tension in his body perfectly. "I guess you're right," she said.

Their mutual uncertainty intertwined and spread like an infection. He wondered if there was a vaccination against attraction.

Once the horses were ready to go, Skylar mounted Bungu, and Cole swung back up on Paco. Harper used a large rock as a mounting block and still had to encircle Cole's torso in order to hoist herself up behind him. She settled in behind the saddle, holding him around the waist as they jostled to get underway. He liked her touch. He reveled in the distraction of her body's pressure against him and marveled at the way she fit against the curve of his back like a soft, custom-made sweater. It took a solid fifteen minutes along the trail for him to get his mind, body, and voice to all behave together again.

"You ride as well as you always did." He finally teased her, when his words felt normal and his skin shivered only slightly from her touch.

"Hard to forget when a person rode before she could walk."

"The perks of being a ranch kid. We might not know the future, Harpo, but do you miss this sometimes anyway? Do you think about growing up here?"

"Sure I do. It was like growing up in Disneyland. And I never think I miss Paradise when I'm back home in

Chicago. Well, okay, I miss this—the horses—but it takes a trip back to remember how grand it all is. And after this visit, it'll be very hard to leave."

"I assume you really do think this art show is worth it?"

"What do you mean? Of course I do." Her half-wounded words pressed against his neck like a physical touch.

"All I mean is that you should be sure you're truly following your heart. Don't leave here for any other reason than it's exactly what you want. It's a first rate show, isn't that what you said?"

"It's exactly what I want. And I don't know how first rate my stuff will make it, but Crucible is a classy gallery—not a dive or a struggling, starving artist's place. My work will hang in the same hall as a lot of big name local artists. I'm excited and honored."

"All right then. That's what I'm talking about."

Cole let Skylar, ahead of them, take a solid lead. She rode like a ranch kid, too, easy in the saddle with a light touch on the reins and a long-legged confidence.

"You met our little spy before she showed up here," he said. "What's her story?"

Harper's answering sigh brushed the back of his neck. "I don't know for sure. I came across her sketching yesterday and found she's very talented for a fourteen-year-old. I only talked to her for five minutes. She and her brothers, Marcus and Aiden, are homeschooled. That's why they're able to roam around. Melanie gave them a vacation day today."

"I've heard that from Leif. He really thinks his grandkids should get into the public school in Wolf Paw Pass, but he says Melanie is a pretty devout woman. She thinks this is the way to protect the kids from bad influences."

"Skylar hinted yesterday at not loving school. But parents have to do what they think is best, I guess."

"You know, she's taken some sort of dislike to me," he said. "I got the hairy eyeball a couple of times. Never had that happen before. Is it because she's turned into a real teenager? What did I do?"

To his surprise, Harper chuckled. "Trust me, she doesn't hate you. That was no hairy eyeball; it was pure embarrassment she was trying to disguise. She thinks you're the only hot guy in Teton, Jackson, and Sublette counties combined. Which may be the entire geographical extent of her world."

"Very funny. I know full well I did not come up as a topic yesterday in your five-minute conversation with a fourteen-year-old."

"You're wrong. Don't sell yourself short, Cole. You're not all that ugly, you know. You're only eighteen years older than she is—there've been bigger age gaps in a marriage. That's what she's thinking."

"And that's not even a little bit funny."

"You just said it was. Make up your mind."

"You're itchin' to walk home. I can tell." He shook his head. The banter lifted his spirits and led him to familiar territory with Harper—where this new lust for her played a lesser role.

"Sorry. I don't know why I'm teasing you. In all seriousness, I don't know anyone who makes a better older crush for a teenager. You're the last guy who'd pay any attention to that—a good, safe, future-husband role model. She'd do worse than to pick someone like you. Much younger, of course."

"You are insane. Don't you dare ever counsel that girl." He laughed.

She rode silently for a bit, her hands on the saddle's cantle, her chest pressed to his back. "I shouldn't be having fun but I am," she said finally. "Thanks to you and your arachnophobia dance, and Skylar Thorson coming to steal her horse back."

"It's okay to have fun. Even when someone dies. Your dad wouldn't want anything different."

"Oh, I don't know. In his case nice asshole-ed-ness didn't include wasting time being goofy."

"Maybe he wasn't goofy, but he knew how to have fun."

"If you say so. I guess maybe he mellowed. One of the things I learned from Skylar was that he took an interest in her art and in her photography. He gave her an old camera of his."

"The old Minolta? I saw she was using it. Huh. Proves you never know about some people."

"Yeah." This time her voice carried the slightest note of hurt. "It would have been nice to find out before he was dead."

THE FAMILY RIDE did little to solve the issue of inviting or not inviting the oil company to explore Paradise land. Harper knew she, backed more or less by Joely, and Kelly down in Denver, was the stubborn hold-out for the nots. Mia, the other two triplets, and their mother insisted that learning what the land held in terms of oil would not constitute a decision to drill. Harper believed with her whole heart that if Mountain Pacific found deposits, the fate of Paradise would be decided.

A decision was easy to put off. The last two days before Mia and Harper had to leave turned into nothing but strings of disasters. One of the ranch's two, indispensable hay balers broke down, requiring a new, expensive part. Nobody could agree on what Sam would have done to replace it. That same day, their best breeding bull had to be put down. The day before Harper's plane was scheduled to carry her away from the mounting difficulties, another massive rainstorm overwhelmed the sump pump in the house.

After three hours helping rescue boxes, furniture, and rugs in Rosecroft's basement, Harper escaped from the house and searched out the only person who'd made her last two days tolerable. Even special.

Cole drew her like a new drug and scared her just as much. She'd been burned in college by her inability to say no to drugs and the wrong crowd. In his own way, Cole was both. She was going back to Chicago, and she couldn't deny the prospect had her adrenaline pumping. Falling for Cole was stupid on a practical level and equally foolish on an emotional one. They wanted such different things. She wasn't the one who could rescue the Wainwright legacy with him by making a passel of babies and raising them to take over the Double Diamond. For that he needed someone like practical, devout Melanie Thorson, not a crazy painter with dreams of national success for her art in her starry eyes.

And then there was Mia. She was no longer a factor in Cole's life. And yet she was. She'd curbed her animosity for Harper immeasurably over the past three days, but there was still an underlying current of irritation that sparked whenever Harper and Cole did something together.

There *was* a sister code. It had to be respected, even if it couldn't really be explained.

But despite everything that was wrong with building any kind of relationship other than friendship with Cole, she couldn't leave him alone. Whenever she was with him, his mere presence smoothed every wave of rough water in her life. Agree or disagree, he was a safe harbor, and Harper hadn't sheltered in one of those for so long. What harm could it do to enjoy it while she was here?

She headed for the barn, the place Leif told her he'd last seen Cole. She'd managed to ride every day of her visit, and since the rain had finally stopped, she planned to talk him into coming along on her ride for this last evening. He'd kissed her once—that day of the chicken wrangling. Since then he'd been far too gentlemanly. Despite all the reasons she wouldn't pursue him once she returned to Chicago, today she had a shivery, almost uncontrollable fantasy that she'd kiss him one more time: good-bye.

Late afternoon sunlight streamed along the barn aisle from front door to rear, mockingly cheerful after all the rain they'd had. Dust motes danced through the beams; the scents of hay, manure, wood shavings, and the uniquely sweet-musk odor of horse mingled and met her nose in the true perfume of a ranch.

She headed down the aisle, searching for Cole and Chevy and Paco's halters. She made it to just outside the tack room at the end of the barn before she heard the voices. It shocked her to recognize Cole and Mia. Knowing she should walk right in and announce her presence, Harper stopped anyway, not to eavesdrop but to decide if she should leave them alone.

"You keep forgetting I have a vested interest in this place," Cole said.

"But no moral authority to make decisions." Amelia's voice wasn't harsh, just firm.

"Of course not," he replied. "But I have the right to fight for my own family heritage."

Harper's intention not to eavesdrop failed. He was making the case he'd made with her, and she pressed herself around the corner into the last stall on the aisle and waited to see why.

"You do. I know how hard it was to lose your ranch. I know everyone thinks I don't feel anything for Paradise, but they're wrong. This is excruciating. The trouble is, it's all pure emotion around here right now. I'm only trying to be logical, but everyone thinks I'm the Wicked Bitch of the East."

"They do not. You need to give your sisters a chance."

"Joely? Believe me, I think she's smart and brave, but our *father* was struggling. He was a genius. What makes you think she can do what he couldn't? That's nothing against her. None of us has the answers or the time to support Joely, so why leave Paradise as a source of constant guilt and worry in our lives?"

"So you'd go back to New York and wash your hands of it all?"

"Yes. No. I don't mean that. Damn it, Cole, you're doing the same thing the others are doing."

"I'm only saying that Joely needs her chance before something irreversible is done with this place. And if she manages to hang on, Harper's point about needing to decide the ranch's overall philosophy on mineral rights is valid."

Harper's heart swelled with gratitude.

"Harper." Mia's derision came through clearly in one word. "Her take on this isn't any more realistic than it's ever been when it comes to running this place."

"Harper cares about a lot of things, and she's a smart woman."

Harper pushed herself away from the wall. She didn't need to hear her sister assassinate her character further. She wasn't quick enough.

"What's this little fascination you have going on with her anyway?"

"She's a fascinating person. And while you're wrong about what you're insinuating, you really don't have a say in my interests. Nor I in yours."

"But my sister? Really, Cole?"

"You're making up a relationship that isn't there," he said. "You have no cause to be jealous."

"Jealousy isn't the word. I have no regrets about you and me. I'll always love you and our friendship, that's all. It just tweaks a little to see you with Harper, I totally admit it."

"But only because she's your sister."

"Yes."

"That's ridiculous."

"Oh, probably, but it's real. But you don't even agree with her, and you don't even dare tell her you work for her enemy."

Harper froze again. *Her enemy?*

"She's emotional about the oil company. Why hurt her for nothing?"

He might as well have reached into her chest and squeezed her heart. Of all the people she loved, Cole was the one who'd never, ever made fun of her emotions. That aside—who was "the enemy"? She didn't want to know. She eased out of the stall and got four steps toward the main door.

"Harpo?"

At his voice, tears stung her eyes, but anger allowed her to dry them before they fell. She took two more steps, but he caught up and stopped in front of her.

"Don't talk to me," she said. "You might spill a secret I can't handle."

"Aw, damn. What did you hear?"

"Okay, fine. What's the big secret you've been keeping from fragile little me?" She punched the five fingers of her right hand into his chest. "I'm such a dumbass. I thought you were the one friend who kind of got me. Who kind of got everyone, actually. A cowboy with heart. Guess that's the fanciful little artist in me—making crap up, as usual."

"For cripe sakes, Harper. I didn't say you were fragile or even too emotional. Don't overreact."

"As usual?"

"All right, knock off the self-righteous anger. You're proving my point. You want the big secret? Fine. I do exactly what I've said I do, repair trucks and other mechanical machinery, but I work for UMI, Upper Midwest Industries, Oil Services—a subsidiary of Mountain Pacific. I don't have anything to do directly with drilling, but the oil company writes my check. And I get paid a boatload of money, which is why I'm close to having enough to buy back the Double Diamond. And I didn't tell you because I knew this would happen."

"What would? I'd get angry because you lied to me for five days? You play the sweet and understanding compromiser, but the entire time you've already chosen your side."

"I have no side."

"You've made it clear you're on the side of allowing Mountain Pacific in here to survey. Now I know exactly why."

"If you'd used half the brains I know you have, you'd have *heard* me when I told you why I want to explore all the options. I don't want Mia here to get her way and talk you all into selling either. I need this place to exist for another year."

"It's mercenary for you all the way. Get an in with the oil company and invite them to come save your old ranch at the expense of ours."

"I found the North Dakota job in the goddamn want ads, Harper. After months of looking. I did not conspire against Paradise. Your father was nothing but fair to me."

He raised his arms and let them fall helplessly to his sides with a loud slap. "You see why I didn't tell you?"

Guilt momentarily overtook her anger. "You're right. That all came out of my mouth because I'm angry at you, and I'm sorry. It's not the job. I have no right to tell you what you can or can't do. But you didn't trust me. I'm not fifteen. That's what hurts."

He stared her down for a silent second and then nodded. "I get that. Sorry."

"Thanks for that anyway. Look, I have packing to do. I'll leave you two to finish up your own argument. I'll see you before I leave tomorrow afternoon."

Amelia had been standing quietly in the doorway. Now she stepped into the aisle and touched Harper's arm. "Harper, don't be stupid. You can't go away angry."

"You know what, Mia? You're telling me not to be stupid, but here you are talking about selling the ranch with all the fervor I have for not selling. I don't know, I'd say we're equally unrealistic about the way we look at things." She spun away.

"Harper!" Cole called after her as she walked away.

"See you at dinner." Harper didn't turn around; instead, she pushed her anger firmly aside and forced herself to concentrate on how much she regretted the ride she wasn't going to get today.

Chapter Seven

SOMETIMES SKYLAR HATED her mother. She didn't know anyone else in the world who had as many rules that were all based around how important it was to be a Miss Goody Two-Shoes. Church on Wednesdays and Sundays, no sports where you might touch someone else or hurt them, no job in town until she was eighteen, no school in town because it was a bad influence, no friends because Paradise Ranch was too big and far away from town for anyone to come all the way out to hang with her.

And as of tonight? No art. No pictures. No camera.

Why, why, why had she told her mother the story about meeting Harper in the woods? When she'd said in passing she thought Harper might be mad at her, her mother had reached only one really stupid conclusion.

Skylar rapped on Rosecroft's heavy front door, her ancient Minolta in its padded case under her arm. She loved the Crocketts' huge log house. Its welcoming atmosphere always started on the sprawling front porch. Today there was the biggest wreath of sunflowers she'd ever seen on the front door. Four big wooden rocking chairs, with colorful yellow-and-blue cushions on their seats, stood in a semicircle like they were inviting someone to come sit in them. Five baskets of blooming flowers Skylar wished she knew the names of hung between the porch railing posts.

She fully expected Mrs. Crockett to answer the door. Or one of her daughters. What she didn't expect was for Cole to open it and smile as if she were the best surprise *he'd* ever seen on a front porch.

"Skylar! You keep showing up where I least expect you."

She embarrassed herself totally by losing her voice. He had on a dark blue T-shirt with the phrase "I have my reasons" in white letters across the chest. She couldn't help but picture no shirt at all. From her hiding place the day she'd followed Cole and the Crocketts into the hills, she'd watched him strip after he'd done that weird rag doll dance. He'd totally made up for that dorkiness by exposing the most amazing muscles—better than she'd ever imagined. She could still see them. She'd dreamed about them for three nights. He'd looked like all the pictures of hot guys she'd ever seen, but she definitely had never seen a bare chest like his in person. Gawking at him had sent her sliding down the side of the hill.

Now here he was in front of her. And she couldn't think of a single thing to say.

"Everything okay there?" He peered at her with eyes that were way more beautiful than even Liam's from One Direction.

"Uh. Yeah. I want to…came to see Harper. Miss Harper." Heat invaded her cheeks.

"She's here somewhere. Want to come in while I find her?"

She nodded and followed him into the living room, kicking herself, hoping he hadn't noticed she was a complete dork.

"I'll tell her you're here. I think she's still packing. She's leaving tomorrow."

Skylar thought a shadow flickered through his eyes. "Already?"

"Went by super-fast, didn't it?"

Skylar barely had time to nose around the gorgeous living room with its fieldstone fireplace and beautiful blue-and-white floral chairs and sofa before Cole returned.

"She said you should come up and talk in her room. Is that okay?"

"Yeah, sure."

His smile was so friendly. More than it had been when they'd met three days ago. She'd been afraid he hadn't liked her at all. The knots and butterflies inside started to loosen a little bit.

"You guys had to go back to school again?" he asked.

"Yeah, but our school is at home."

"That's kind of a cool deal, isn't it?"

"*You* can try it if you want."

She immediately regretted letting him hear the sarcasm. She didn't always keep her foot out of her mouth when it came to school. Who liked having their mom for a teacher anyway? She had a couple of friends in the homeschool co-op whose parents had let them go to the middle school in Wolf Paw Pass once they'd finished with sixth grade. But not her mom. She was paranoid about everything. What did she think was going to happen anyway? Drug dealers or gay people or witches were going to appear and wipe away all the stuff she already believed in like she had no brains of her own?

"Here you go." Cole cut through her thoughts.

She blinked and belatedly heard the echoes of words he'd said while she'd been whining in her head. "Sorry, what?"

"Here's Harper's room."

"No, before. I was thinking about something else."

Why was she blathering around him?

"I said it sounds like maybe you're a typical ranch kid. None of us liked school when it was still nice enough outside to do cooler things there."

She blinked again. He almost had it right. She wanted to tell him the ranch wasn't the only place that had cool stuff to do, although it was true she'd rather help with the calving than ever do math. She sighed, and kept her toes out of her mouth and herself out of trouble. "Yeah, I guess."

"You can go on in." He smiled. Her tummy tumbled in response. "I'll see you around."

He left her staring after him, wishing he'd at least told Harper she was there. Squaring her shoulders, she pushed on the unlatched door and entered a wonderland.

Harper stood beside a suitcase lying open on a double bed frame made of white-washed pine and covered in a quilt that had so many colors in it Skylar could have spent all day looking at the beautiful, intricate fabrics. She tore her eyes from it and took in the ceiling, sloped in two angles where the roof gables met. Each slope held its own huge quilt, unlike anything Skylar had ever seen. They were like pictures painted with fabric—one a profusion of flowers, the other a galloping horse with a mountain in the background. It looked so much like Wolf Paw that Skylar squinted and took a step forward to study it before she realized she'd moved.

"Hi," Harper said.

"Hi, Miss Harper, sorry to bother you." Her mother's drilled-in manners came out automatically as she continued to stare.

"You don't have to call me 'Miss,' honest." She smiled.

"Sorry."

"No, don't be sorry either. My mom made me learn to be polite, too, but you don't need to be formal. I heard you came especially to see me? I'm honored. And you're just in time."

That drew Skylar's focus from the rest of the bright paintings on the walls, the beautiful purply-blue-and-white curtains at the windows that matched a super full dust ruffle around the bed, and the amazing easel in the corner.

Honored? Nobody said that about a random visit from a neighbor kid. Skylar didn't have a lot of experience dropping in on people, but she knew that much. And in time for what?

"I…I have something to give back to you."

"Oh?"

Skylar remembered all at once why she really didn't want to be there. It was stupid to get upset over a camera that literally cost her money every time she used it, but a tiny lump formed in her throat when she tried to say what her mother had sent her to say.

She took the strap of the camera bag off her shoulder and held it out. "This," she managed.

True incomprehension filled Harper's face. "What is it?"

"Your dad's camera. It really should stay in the family."

Harper's reaction was 100 percent not what Skylar had expected. She covered her mouth with one hand and began to cry.

"Oh, Skylar, no. No, you can't give it away. I'm so sorry I made you feel like you had to give it to me."

She didn't bawl or anything. She just had tears running down her cheeks. Even so, it made Skylar want to cry, too. It made her miss Mr. Crockett even more. It made her not know at all what to do.

"It's okay," she said lamely. "My mom is right. He probably only meant for me to borrow it."

"No," Harper repeated, and wiped her nose with a snuffle. She turned and pulled a tissue from a box on the nightstand. After she wiped her eyes she turned back. "Come here and sit for a second."

She shoved the suitcase over and patted the quilt over the mattress. Skylar forced her legs to obey. When she sat uneasily on the bed, Harper joined her. "I need to tell you something."

"Okay."

"I was jealous that my dad gave you the camera."

"I know." Skylar surprised herself by saying so and rubbed her own nose self-consciously. Harper smiled even though her eyes were still shiny.

"But it's not because I want it. That's the truth. I was jealous because I never believed my dad cared about my art. He never told me he liked what I did and always seemed to think it was kind of silly. When you said he thought you had talent, I wanted him back for just long enough that he could tell me, too."

Skylar felt like she shouldn't be hearing this, and yet she was a little flattered, too, like Harper trusted her with something important.

"He talked about you." It was all she could think of to say.

"I'm glad to hear that." Harper's voice was calm but her eyes got a little wide. "I don't know why I told you this, because it sounds like you and my dad were friends, and I'm glad you were. I'm not trying to make you feel bad about him or me."

"Okay."

"I want you to believe me when I say I don't want you to give me the camera, and for you to believe me I needed to tell you the truth. I'm not a photographer anyway, I wouldn't ever use his camera, but you will. Right?"

"I love it. I take it everywhere."

"Then it has the perfect home."

"Do you mean it?" It was a stupid question. Harper wouldn't tell her she meant it and then be mean and say she didn't.

But Harper crying and the idea that Mr. Crockett hadn't even ever said he liked her work…it was rattling her brain. She couldn't believe someone else felt about their dad the way she felt about her mom.

"I do mean it, Skylar. I am sorry I was rude to you that day we met."

"It's all right."

"You know what? I never tell people about my dad making me sad. Do you think it could be our secret?"

For a second Harper didn't even seem like a grown-up. She seemed kind of sad but hopeful. Skylar had never had anyone ask her to keep secrets. Except Marcus who said he'd kick her butt if she told he had a Playboy magazine hidden in the barn. This was way different. This was a girlfriend secret.

"It's our secret," she said, and almost added that maybe Harper could keep her same secret, too. After all, she didn't think her mom liked her all the time either. But she didn't ask.

And then Harper stunned her again by leaning forward and giving her a hug. It was a nice, warm thank-you hug. Normally the only person who could hug her was Grandpa Leif, but Skylar didn't pull away until Harper did.

"It was a really nice thing, you coming to try and give me the camera. Thank you."

Skylar wanted to take the praise, but she knew she couldn't. "No. I wasn't the nice one. It was my mom who made me. She might not even believe me that you said I could keep it."

"I know your mom. I'll tell her. And you *were* nice. I'm sure it wasn't easy to come. But I'm glad. We're friends now, and I got to tell you I was sorry."

Friends! They were friends?

The she looked at the suitcase and sobered. It didn't matter. Harper was leaving tonight and she'd be gone. A stray thought came back to her.

"Why did you say before that I was just in time?"

"I was about to go to town. I have a couple of things I need before I leave for the airport. All I meant was that you had perfect timing."

"I was trying to get my dad to go to town today or tonight." Skylar stood and dug into the pocket of her jeans. She pulled out a yellow film cartridge. What she'd thought was her last roll of film from the Minolta.

"Is he going to take you?"

"Maybe tomorrow, he said. He's still working on the hay baler."

"Then come with me. We can go ask your mom, I'll tell her about the camera, and we can drop your film at…Where do you drop it?"

"At Kloster's Drug. They send it to the Walgreens in Jackson. Sometimes, if we go all the way to Jackson, Dad will take the film there himself."

"Well if Kloster's works for you, we can have it there in half an hour. Wanna go?"

Skylar smiled for the first time since knocking on Rosecroft's door.

"IS IT REALLY true that your family used to own half this town?"

Harper smiled across the booth in the ice cream shop at Skylar's unruly strawberry blonde hair and eager eyes.

The teen was a completely different person than the somber, nervous girl who'd come timidly into Harper's bedroom ninety minutes before. And what had started as an annoying interruption to her rotten day had turned into a blessing.

Skylar was nothing short of an enigma. Fourteen except for the moments when she acted twenty-one. Harper was piecing together a picture of a smart, lonely, scarily savvy girl who hinted that she hated being homeschooled but wouldn't say it outright. And Skylar was beyond a great distraction when it came to Cole Wainwright.

Harper swallowed the sadness that rose every time she thought about him.

"The Crocketts haven't owned much except the newspaper building and the feed mill since I've been around," she said. "But it's true my great-grandfather, Eli, helped build the town from the tiny little watering hole it was when he arrived from Kansas in 1916. Until my grandpa Sebastian sold most of the family's businesses and holdings, this was sort of Crockettville."

Skylar giggled. "What sounds weirder? Crockettville or Wolf Paw Pass for a town?"

"I don't know. I like Wolf Paw Pass. It's different. It sounds like the right name for a town between a big city like Jackson and a national park like Grand Teton."

"Yeah, I guess."

"You look like you're done. Was the Wolf Paw Chunk any good?" She winked knowing there wasn't anyone in the world who wouldn't think a flavor from Ina's Ice Cream Emporium was fabulous.

"Dark chocolate and milk chocolate ice cream with hunks of dark chocolate and milk chocolate candy? Uh, it was okay."

"Good to hear."

There was no Ina anymore, and she'd never run the store, but she'd taught her family to make darn good ice cream. Now the store was run by Harper's old schoolmate Bonnie McAllister, Ina's granddaughter. The staff—made up of Bonnie's husband and five siblings—had kept the tradition well alive. Quaint, homespun businesses like Ina's were a staple in Wolf Paw.

"Thanks for it," Skylar said.

"My French Mint Marshmallow was good, too, and you're very welcome. Anything else you need to do while we're here?"

"No. The film is turned in. Do you need to shop more?"

"I'm done. I don't have too much more time anyhow. It's one o'clock. I need to leave for Jackson by four."

"I wish you didn't have to go."

The statement took Harper aback. The girl barely knew her, and although Skylar clearly craved friendship, Harper wouldn't have expected a teenager to choose an adult.

"Thank you. It's hard to leave."

That was somewhat a lie. It hurt to leave things she felt so strongly about in the fate of other hands. Joely, however, was doing her best to seriously look at the books with her mother, research cattle with Leif, and research fairly the likelihood of Mountain Pacific finding oil on the ranch.

Maybe she'd find a way to pull off her ascension to the job of Paradise boss.

What Harper found less hard to leave was Cole and the confusion he caused in her emotions. In all honesty, his lie of omission was minor. People worked for oil companies. It wasn't a crime. The thought that he didn't see her any differently than anyone else did—as someone who was so single-minded of focus and so fragile of emotion that she couldn't be treated with the truth—however, hurt.

"Will you be back soon?"

"I don't know, sweetie. I don't have any specific plans right now." A prick of pain she didn't quite understand spread through her heart. "I'll come back if my mother needs anything. And I'll be back to visit. But I have a lot of exciting things going on in Chicago."

"Yeah. I get it." Her dull voice said she really didn't.

They left Ina's, Harper's mood slightly subdued and Skylar's slightly mopey. Mild temperatures had given western Wyoming a perfect summer this year, or so Harper had heard. Today the temp sat lazily in the low eighties, but a slight, fresh breeze kept the air from overheating. In hazy sunshine, they walked past stores Harper had known her entire life, as well as a smattering of brand new businesses. And they passed military families galore—the new heart of Wolf Paw Pass's demographic.

Thanks to the ten-year-old Veteran's Administration Medical Center between Wolf Paw and Jackson, along with the venerable military, fire, and police combined training facility west of Wolf Paw, the town's once-tiny population of several hundred had swelled to nearly two thousand.

Skylar barely paid attention to the businesses. The Have You Any Wool? yarn shop, next to A Piece-able World fabric shop got curious glances but no window shopping. They passed Wolf Paw Pass Office Supply, New Rags Clothing Boutique, Nelson Brothers Plumbing and Heating, and Wanda's Wolf Paw Gifts. They were almost past Wanda's elaborate Victorian door when Skylar stopped.

"Look." She pointed to a bright blue-and-green poster in the window.

They read it silently together.

The Wolf Paw Pass and Jackson Lions, along with Wolf Paw Pass Middle School and Jackson Southwest High School, present the third annual Warren A. Brenner VA Medical Center Art Exhibition and Competition. Participants from Jackson Hole Area Public Schools arts programs will be featured in a gallery-like showing combined with a fund-raising event for the arts in the public schools initiative. Winners will be chosen in five categories. Each winner will receive a $500.00 scholarship prize. One grand-prize winner will have the winning piece permanently displayed in the Brenner VA Medical Center. Tickets $5.00. Raffle tickets $3.00 to $25.00. Sunday, September 24th.

"Oh man!" Skylar rocked back and then peered again at the poster. "I've never heard about this before."

"It sounds really cool. I'm glad the schools are doing something like this."

"This is the problem with your mom being your teacher. We don't get to do anything cool like this. See, it says 'public schools.'"

"Maybe your mom could contact them and see if you could participate, too."

"She won't. She's on the homeschool co-op board, and they wouldn't do something where the money goes to the public schools."

She was definitely a quick analyst, Harper thought. She studied the teen's face and a sudden punch of recognition took her back. She'd once been right where Skylar was. Not maybe shut out of a contest, but shut out of acceptance. Thank God she'd had a great high school art teacher. She wasn't sure Skylar even had that.

"It can't hurt to mention it anyway," she said. "Maybe you guys could at least go to the exhibition and see what it's like. That might give your mom some ideas about things you'd like to do."

"Sure. Maybe."

Skylar shuffled on without another word. After a momentary flash of excitement while looking at the poster, she now let her shoulders hang with defensive apathy. A block farther along Main Street, they reached the car, her dad's old green Subaru Forester, parked in front of the Credit Union and a vacant lot that served as an access to Centennial Park and a network of hiking trails surrounding the town.

"Sorry the trip ended in a downer," Harper said.

"It's not a downer. It's the same stupid stuff."

"Yeah. There's a lot of stupid stuff, isn't there?"

She turned when a strange, high-pitched whine followed by a dull, uneven thumping, echoed from the lot. A random box bumped along the wall of the Credit Union.

"Oh my gosh, look at that!" Skylar took off toward what Harper could now see, three-fourths of the way along the building, was an animal.

"Be careful!" she called. "You've seen enough wild creatures on the ranch to know not to touch it."

Her words fell on deaf ears. Skylar knelt, hiding the thing from view, but clearly scooping it into her arms. Harper started across the grass. She met the girl along with the most pathetically eager black-and-white puppy that licked Skylar's face from the cradle of her arms.

"Goodness, what have we here?" Harper asked.

Skylar's angry face was back. "He was tied by a piece of clothesline around his neck to the punched-out handle on that cardboard box back there." She held out a piece of crumpled white paper. "This was on the box."

"Free to good home," Harper read. "He must have gotten loose from somewhere."

"There's nobody around." Her lip curled in scorn. "A puppy tied to a box wouldn't be that hard to catch him. He could have strangled if the rope got caught."

Once again, Harper caught a flash of herself at that age: the would-be champion of underdogs.

"I'm glad you got him free of it. We should probably take him to the police or maybe to Dr. Ackerman, the vet."

"Whatcha got there?"

Harper spun at the familiar, deep voice calling from the sidewalk. Cole leaned against the side of the bank like a poster boy for tight T-shirts and sexy jeans, with his hair mussed as usual, his arms crossed at his chest. Her ten seconds of arrhythmia gave way to annoyance at his cheerful insouciance.

"A puppy." Skylar recovered from her speechlessness first and started toward him, with a shy smile. "Someone left it here."

"Seriously?" Cole straightened. "How do you know?"

"We don't for sure," Harper said. "We're about to take it to the vet's I think."

"What will they do with it?" Skylar asked.

"If they can't find an owner, they'll bring it to the shelter in Jackson. Or find a foster place." Cole peered down at the dog in Skylar's arms. "Do you know if it's a male or female?"

"I didn't look."

"Can I?" He held out his hands.

"I think we can deal with this." Harper's temper lit. He didn't need to take charge of the moment as if she couldn't handle this either.

"I'm just takin' a peek," he said. "Or I'll hold him up so you can do the honors. I'm sure you know how to sex baby animals."

As if someone had tossed a red slushie in her face, Skylar turned bright pink. The lunatic, Harper thought, didn't he know what kind of trouble he could get into with a fourteen-year-old girl by blathering so carelessly. Besides, she'd warned him about the teen's crush.

"Knock it off, Cole," she said. "Give me the dog."

"What are you two so pissy about?" They both looked at hot-faced Skylar, whose fourteen-going-on-age-twenty persona took charge with sarcasm that she used to try and mask her embarrassment.

"Nobody's pissy," Cole said. "Harper is having a hard time leaving me behind."

"Cole is delusional because he's going to grieve when I'm gone."

"That's probably true enough." He forced his mouth into sad pout made ridiculous by the twinkle in his eye.

"Here." Skylar turned the puppy over to him.

"Traitor." Harper scowled but bumped her with an elbow, careful to show she wasn't annoyed with her.

It was pretty hard to stay annoyed with Cole either, watching his big hands with the little black-and-white pup. He roamed them across its back, feeling for any injuries or spots that might indicate it had been abused. She knew this because she'd seen him do it countless times on an injured calf or wild animal.

"This is quite a nice little border collie," he said. "I can't imagine someone abandoning a dog like this."

"My dad doesn't like border collies," said Skylar. "He says they're too intense. He likes Australian cattle dogs."

"You had collies growing up." Harper caught his eye, remembering, and understanding now why he'd taken such a quick interest in the dog.

"Jeff, Smitty, Lucy, and Turk," he agreed.

Carefully, once the pup had settled in his arms, Cole flipped it over and held it on its back.

"A little girl," he said. He stroked her tummy and handed her back to Skylar.

"Hi, girl." She cooed at the dog. Then she looked up, and for the first time in their short acquaintance, Harper didn't see the muddled light of a teenage crush in her eyes. "I don't want to take her to the vet. I'm taking her home."

"Whoa," Cole said.

"Oh, Skylar, I don't know—" Harper spoke at the same moment.

"We were supposed to find her." Skylar set her jaw and prepared to dig in her heels on the point.

"I can't let you come home from a field trip with me bringing a dog." Harper tried to make her denial light-hearted. "Your mom will ban me from playing with you."

Skylar was having none of it. "There are already three dogs around. What will anyone care if there's one more?"

"Border collies aren't like normal dogs," Cole said. "They take a lot of work and training. And puppies can mess up a lot of carpets and furniture before they're trained. That's a commitment a parent has to agree to."

"I'll get them to agree."

Harper exchanged a desperate look with Cole. She didn't have the authority to say no anymore than she had the authority to say yes, but he didn't look any more certain than she felt.

"Here's the thing," he said. "Even if you do keep her, she has to visit the vet and get shots and deworming and make sure she's healthy. That's expensive. And you really should check around town and make sure nobody still owns her or has claimed her.

"Well if they claimed her, they don't deserve her." Skylar held the dog more tightly, and it licked her face, whining and squirming to get closer.

"How about if we take her to the vet's, find out what she needs, and if your folks say you can keep her, I'll bring you back to pick her up tomorrow? Maybe Doc Ackerman will know where she came from."

"She can't stay alone in a cage. What if she had brothers and sisters and now she's missing them? She needs to be close to someone who'll keep her company. I'm taking her home, and my dad will bring us back tomorrow." Her features hardened into stubbornness.

"I don't know what to say." Harper sighed.

"I'd say you're bringing a dog home." Cole shrugged. "All we can do is look around the park a little bit and see if anyone's searching for a puppy before we go."

Harper checked her watch. "I'm sorry, but I don't have time to spend looking, even though I think you're right. I need to be at the airport in Jackson in three hours. Almost ninety minutes of that is travel time now.

"Nobody's looking for her." Skylar turned to Cole for support.

"I can help her look," Cole said. "If you thought it would be okay that I take her home."

"I don't know." That thought worried Harper considerably. Not because she didn't trust Cole, but because she wasn't sure she could trust Skylar to know how to act. One bit of fanciful reporting about time spent with "the only guy around here hot enough to date," and Cole could be in trouble. "I should probably be responsible for her."

Or maybe she'd lived in a big, dangerous city too long. She sighed.

"Yeah, probably," he said.

"What are you doing here anyway?" she asked.

"Your grandmother went looking for her favorite tea, and it turned out the crowd used it up the day of the funeral. Sadie looks tired today, I felt like she deserved her tea, and since you'd already gone, here I am."

He really was a nice guy. The jerk.

"I have a plan." Skylar interrupted.

She and Cole both turned. Harper was going to get whiplash trying to focus on the girl's sudden changes in emotion. She now looked like that thoughtful twenty-one-year-old.

"Okay," Cole said.

"We take her home. I'll get my mom's permission to keep her if we can't find any owners. I'll make up some flyers to put around."

Harper narrowed her eyes skeptically. "Promise?"

"Promise."

"I won't be here to check up on you."

"Oh, but I will." Cole shot Skylar a huge grin, which apparently was contagious, since she returned it without hesitation.

"Fine." Harper sighed. "It's on your head, chickie girl."

"Yup," Skylar agreed.

Cole touched Harper on the shoulder. "I'll see you when I get back."

She hadn't totally forgiven him, even though the hottest flame of her anger had died. "I'm sure you will."

"Harper?"

"What?"

"I should have told you."

"Yeah." She softened one notch more. "You should have."

Chapter Eight

TWO DAYS AFTER arriving home from Wyoming, Harper
thought she would have been over jetlag, over homesickness. Over Cole. Chicago had been home for four years
now, and if she lived there forty-four more, she doubted
she'd see all there was to see in the iconic city. The endlessly changing vibes always invigorated her, inspired
her, kept her sane.

Not this week.

This week the lights at night blinded like interroga-
tion spotlights from an old film noir. The 2.7 million
inhabitants all seemed to be crabby and obnoxious on
the same day. And the air reeked of gasoline fumes. The
best moment of that second day home came on her way
to a meeting with Tristan and the owners of the gallery,
when she passed a small manure pile left in the street by
a mounted police officer's horse. She actually slowed her
pace to pass it, and if she hadn't feared being picked up

for dangerously insane behavior, she'd have stood still beside it for a moment.

She couldn't deny it. She could barely hide it. She missed Wyoming. She missed the horses, her mother, even her sister. She missed Skylar and wondered about the stray puppy.

She missed Cole.

Her anger toward him had been infantile. They were grown-ups; they'd disagree. He'd apologized, but she'd blown it off. What had happened to her brain while she'd been there? She'd told herself a hundred times, she was better off here in the anonymous city.

Her mood improved when she reached Crucible and the warm, supportive enclave of her true peeps—as Tristan loved to say.

"Are you ready for this, darling?" Gil asked, when she'd joined them around the conference table in his office.

"I'm very excited," she agreed. "It's pretty surreal."

"Well, look what we got." Gil handed her a glossy brochure. "This'll make it real."

The informational brochure—about her! She held it almost reverently. Her portrait filled the front panel, and inside every one of her eighteen paintings that were to be displayed was reproduced and described.

"Oh, Gareth," she whispered. "You did this? It's…"

She had no words—she'd never been treated this professionally and respectfully in anything she'd ever done. Tristan patted her hand.

"Nice, isn't it, babe?"

"Thank you. This is so much time and expense. I don't know what to say. I feel like I won the lottery."

"You did," Tris said. "If you get these two on your side—you're golden."

"I'm beginning to see that." She hugged each of the owners in turn. "What can I do now?"

"Take a few of these. Pass them out to your friends, your enemies, your grocer, your cleaning lady, your—"

"Cleaning lady." Harper laughed. "Sure. She'll take a dozen and pass them out to the rest of my household staff. Sorry, I'm so excited I'm goofy. Of course I'll pass them out."

"Then, starting tomorrow you can come and begin supervising the hanging of the paintings."

"Me? You could hang them in the bathrooms and I'd be ecstatic."

All three men shared indulgent smiles.

"Don't make fun of me," she said. "I'm a total newb."

"You won't be by the time we're done with you," Gil said. "Now, let's talk about how you're going to circulate in the gallery."

She left Crucible an hour later, her head swimming with information and instructions. She could have been a queen being prepped for a coronation ceremony for all the protocols. How many people could this possibly involve for a brand-new artist? She'd be blown away if ten people showed up. But, whatever Gil and Gareth wanted she would do naked if they asked. Even for ten people.

She breathed a little easier with her stash of colorful brochures in her purse. Four more days to the showing and there was plenty to do. She'd start at the local library, move to a couple of her favorite window-shopping boutiques, and maybe make the rounds of her neighborhood businesses. Somebody would put up a brochure.

The spot in the street where she'd passed the horse manure had been cleaned. It was probably for the best, she thought. She didn't need horses, dogs, sisters, or old childhood friends on the brain. And it did no good whatsoever to wonder if she ever in a million years would have been able to talk her father into coming to see her now.

She'd never know. And that, too, was probably for the best.

COLE HAD GOTTEN his slender but muscular build from his father, Russ, and now at sixty-two, his dad kept in shape primarily by walking the halls of his condominium complex, helping with odd jobs whenever anyone needed him, and by flying his Cessna 172 whenever he possibly could. He made a tidy sum helping with cattle gatherings, wild mustang roundups for the Bureau of Land Management, and ferrying folks on occasion to meetings or gatherings if they were willing to pay for a pilot. In truth, he'd done well for himself since selling the Double Diamond.

Cole sat in his dad's sparsely furnished living room and lifted a beer, looking up when his father entered the room carrying two plates, each bearing a sandwich of thickly sliced roast beef. The man wasn't starving himself either.

"Thanks, Dad," he said. "Better than a feast."

"It's pretty unfancy for this being our reunion after an entire summer. Not counting the funeral, of course—but there was no time to catch up then. Damn it's still unbelievable. Sixty-eight and a heart attack out of the blue. How are the Crocketts doing?"

"Getting along. Finances aren't great for them either," he said vaguely. "Joely is going to try taking over the reins from Sam. I'll give her a hand along with Leif and Bjorn. But everyone else has had to go back to her home."

"Ironic, isn't it?" His father shrugged. "All those girls and not a rancher among them."

"Yeah, don't even get me going. But, this arrangement might work for Joely. She and Bella are taking a trip to California. They'll pack up Joely's stuff and move her out here."

"Hmmmm," his father said.

"Yeah. Sad. Sounds like she and her husband are separated."

"Shame. Hate to see that."

"Anyway, things will be quiet for a few weeks there. I'll help however I can."

"And the others?"

"Mia is the same. Fine, organized."

His dad laughed. "Gotcha. I love that girl, but she is one focused little filly."

Cole had to agree. He'd never been able to keep up with Mia. For every step he'd taken, she'd taken six. They'd never been in sync enough to make real sparks. "The triplets all went back to Denver," he said. "Their place is doing real well; they've opened a new location. It takes all three to run them both."

"Good for them. And Harper?"

"Uh…" His thoughts tangled up with each other as he sat there. What was she doing? Was she grateful to be back in the city? Would her little gallery opening be fun or a bomb?

"Cole?"

"Oh, Harper. She's doing great, too."

He told his father about the gallery show. About their ridiculous chicken adventure. About her new connection to Bjorn's daughter. When he finished, his dad was sitting deep in his armchair, wearing a definite grin.

He had a good relationship with his father now. For a while, after the ranch had been sold, he'd been angry. He'd never been given a say in his home's fate. But over time he'd grown to understand. Russ Wainwright was a proud man, and he'd done his absolute best by the Double Diamond. Selling had nearly killed him, Cole remembered. He almost admired his father more now for having weathered his personal tragedies with dignity and stoicism.

"What are you smilin' about over there?" He took another swig of beer.

"I'm your father—I watched you grow up with those girls. You've always had an eye for little Harper."

"Don't be ridiculous."

"All right, if you say so. But either way, you've got a thing for her now. Let's skip all the girlie denying and admit it. I know it's true. And for what it's worth, I approve."

"Aw, hell. Fine, Dad. She's beautiful. She's funny. She's grown up to be a kind, deep-thinking, nice woman, and

I was attracted the minute I saw her. But, and this is the truth, she's also complicated. She's got a thing about going out with me because of loyalty to Mia. Don't ask me to explain. I can't.

"She's also a progressive from the get-go, and while that's absolutely fine, she's pissed as all hell at me because we're talking about letting Mountain Pacific survey for oil and gas. So—there's not much hope for us."

He sighed. He missed her, damn it. He didn't want to—who needed the hassle? But even after being around her for one week, the world was black and white without her.

"Bah, ranch couples never agree on things," his dad said. "Politics, how to treat animals, where to burn the trash. All that doesn't matter if there's respect. You already sound like you have it for Harper."

Cole let out a choppy laugh and ran a hand through his hair. "I'm going to New York this weekend. Flying in and out to an oil producer's conference. I promised Bella and Joely that I would get all the information I could on modern drilling techniques. I actually thought about making an overnight stop in Chicago to catch Harpo's gallery show. Talk about ironic. She's already mad at me. What if I surprise her, and she finds out she's a stop on the way to an oil conference."

"Hell, son. You're afraid of a little argument with your girl?"

"Dad…"

His father laughed. "Okay. I'm giving you shit, sorry. But now I'm serious. I would give anything I own to have one more fight with your mama. Anything. I'm telling you. Go and pack your bags."

To his embarrassment, Cole found his palms sweating and his heart pumping adrenaline in sudden anticipation. The idea had been a random thought, which he'd pretty much dismissed. Now it seemed the only logical thing to do.

"You're serious."

"You bet I am. I can see you want to try this. Well, if you don't start with a spark, you'll never have a campfire."

"You're nothing but an old romantic." Cole chided his father, hoping to get a little masculine indignation from him.

"Why thank you," he said. "I do my best. Now finish your beer and sandwich and go start packing."

Cole snorted and picked up his beer. He had three days. There was probably time.

THREE DAYS LATER, Cole pulled open the seven-foot frosted glass doors to the gallery Crucible. He hated big cities, but he had to admit, the glitter-studded gallery party was danged impressive. And it was only a gallery showing for one unknown artist. He couldn't imagine how they'd treat a Picasso.

It hadn't dawned on him, however, that he'd need a tuxedo. He'd never needed one in his life, and he'd been picturing a little hole-in-the-wall shop that sold paintings, not the art gallery equivalent to a farm club for the Louvre. At least he'd left his work boots back at home and worn his dress hat. He scoffed at himself, catching his reflection in one of a dozen mirrored surfaces.

A trim man of about fifty approached, with thinning hair and a manner like a funeral director crossed with a high school English teacher. He assessed Cole's black dress jeans, white dress shirt, and gray woolen sport coat, with eager, curious eyes.

"Good evening, sir, and welcome. Is there anything special I can show you tonight? Would you like a brochure that introduces Miss Crockett's works?"

"I would, thanks." Cole took a glossy tri-fold pamphlet from the man's proffered hand.

"Are you familiar with her paintings?"

"Her very early ones," he replied solemnly. In truth, he hadn't seen much Harper had painted since high school. He was almost afraid to look around now for fear she was one of those weird-ass modern artists he didn't understand.

"We do have a few of her early pieces. We're honored to have her with us. Be sure to say hello. If you have any questions, I'm at your service; and should the situation arise, I can furnish you with a price list."

A price list? How frickin' much could a painting be that you couldn't put the price sticker on the side of the frame?

"Thank you." His eyes searched the small rectangular gallery without seeing anyone who looked like Harper. "Can you tell me where I can find, uh, Miss Crockett?"

"I believe she's on the second floor where her Paradise collection is located."

Paradise collection?

Cole looked straight up. Sure enough, he could see through white wrought iron railings into the next level.

"Spiral staircases are located on both ends of the room. There's an elevator around the corner if you'd prefer. I'm Gil Hargreaves, one of the owners of Crucible."

"Nice to meet you."

What did you actually say to the owner of a place like this? Nice paintings you have here? Do you have an ATM somewhere? Where's the sale room?

"I'm an old friend of Harper's. Thanks for showing her paintings." That seemed appropriate.

"We're very excited to have them." Gil Hargreaves gushed with enthusiasm. "We absolutely adore launching new artists. It's so satisfying to watch careers take off. Mark my words. Harper's is not in doubt."

Cole thanked him again and made for the wide spiral staircase to his left. After a quick climb he emerged onto the second floor to find it a starker space than the main gallery downstairs. Pale oak flooring and off-white walls reflected brightness from abundant recessed lighting. Floor-to-almost-ceiling walls served as separating screens to form three or four small rooms.

His heart thumped in anticipation. Harper had no idea he'd come, and he wasn't entirely sure how she'd react. He thought he'd managed to smooth a few of her ruffled feathers before she'd left Wyoming last week, but she'd still been plenty pissed off. The assignment bringing him off the ranch and through Chicago wouldn't necessarily help matters, but his father had been right. If he didn't pursue the spark now, he might as well give up on any kind of campfire. And giving up before he admitted to her how endlessly she stayed on his mind and how he hated the unhappiness he'd caused her, wasn't possible. He'd had to come. Besides, he'd never truly told her how proud he was of her blossoming success.

Judging by the scene around him, it was far more success than she'd led him to believe.

The moment he caught sight of her across the room, his heart slammed into his throat. He'd never seen Harper in anything other than jeans and ranch clothes or the long shapeless skirts and dresses she favored. Tonight she'd transformed herself into unique perfection, without a traditional ball gown *or* bohemian layers.

She smiled at a visitor, holding herself like a Wyoming princess. An ultra-dressy, multilayered skirt in some kind of snowy-white fancy fabric frothed around her hips and legs like a prom dress made of whipped cream. Her top, completely opposite, was a close-fitting denim shirt, with silver collar points and intricate white top-stitching. Cinched around her waist, setting off her curves, was a wide, tan belt with some kind of fancy edging. Sexy as that was, the whole beautiful picture was perfected by her cowboy boots—a classy, high-topped pair the same color as the belt.

His body's reaction was swift and shocking. He'd always thought of Harper as sexy. This...This was over the top.

He watched, mesmerized, for several long minutes, letting his reaction cool and his pride grow. To see her like this, animated and confident, was exactly what he'd always wanted for her. He understood in that moment why she said she didn't belong at Paradise.

After an embrace from the woman and a two-handed handshake from the man, the couple talking to Harper left. She stared at the painting they'd been looking at and ran a hair through her black hair, curled in long waves for the occasion. She smoothed her skirt and, with a squaring of her shoulders, straightened. Her eyes locked on Cole's.

Pleasure spiraled through him as her lips formed a sweet O.

Five seconds later she was in his arms, and he lifted her sweet, cotton-candy curves six inches off the floor.

"Are you kidding me?" she asked, her voice squeaking in excitement. "You're here? What are you doing in Chicago?"

"C'mon, Harpo. You couldn't go through your first art exhibition without any representation from the hometown."

Tears glistened in her eyes, with no hint of annoyance or residual anger. "I can't believe it. You just put the cherry topping on the night."

"I have to be honest. I imagined something a tenth this size. This is impressive."

She wiped a forefinger carefully beneath one eye and then the other. "I feel the same way. I figured five or six people might show up—pity visits, you know? Instead, Gil and his partner went above and beyond for me."

"Oh, yes. I met Gil." He laughed. "He's a big fan."

"He is. And I'm very lucky." She squeezed him again, hard. "I'm so glad you're here. I was feeling like that white feather in Forrest Gump—floating all over the place and not knowing where I was going to end up. There must be a hundred people here. And they act like I know what I'm doing."

Cole glanced around the room. "Have you *seen* the paintings?"

She smiled. "Thanks, but I don't mean the paintings. I mean people who collect art asking me the meanings of what I'm doing or how I chose my color palette. I'm sort of making this up as I go."

"You got a hug from the last lady. You must be saying something right."

He kissed the top of her head, wishing he didn't have to let her go, loving the feel of her in his arms.

"Show me around," he said, after reluctantly letting her loose. "My turn to learn about how you chose your color whatevers. And do you think you could tell me what your paintings mean?"

"You're cruel."

"Heard that before. But at least you didn't punch me when you saw me or run me off with a sharp brush."

"Or a palette knife?"

"Whatever that is."

"A dull blade. Very painful." She took him by the hand and led him to their left. "But no need to worry. You are officially forgiven. The fact that you're here makes up for whatever you might really think of me."

"I'm pretty sure this isn't the time or the place to tell you what I really think of you."

She stopped and peered at him, starting a slow, weird tremble in his stomach—partly because he hoped she'd ask him to tell her anyway, partly because she really was beautiful.

"You're probably right," she said.

His breath released slowly. "C'mon. Show me what you got."

She was good.

Very, very good.

Cole didn't know fine art from starving artist art, or a Monet from a Manet, but he knew that Harper had something special. That overused term he now understood: a gift.

Her subjects ranged from close ups of flowers to landscapes he actually recognized. She did especially well with skies and horses and mountains. But what stood out to him was the combination in each painting of reality and dreamlike fancy. A stalk of columbine bathed in reds and purples like it was framed by a sunset. A barn, very similar to the Paradise horse barn, haloed with bold, rather than soft and gentle, streaks of morning light. And his favorite—a grazing horse with hot patches of color bursting from the sky and mountain behind it.

"Lord, Harpo, when did you learn how to paint like this?"

"During my life when people were telling me I was wasting my time." She allowed a half-smile that told him she didn't mean the words with any kind of malice. "Which, I suppose, in a practical sense, I was."

"Not if you were doing this. Nobody saw this talent in you?"

"My mother always liked my paintings. Grandma Sadie, too. After a while, though, I didn't show very many people, until I moved away. I've read a lot artists' bios. I'm not alone in this. You're rarely accepted at first in your hometown. The Beatles, way back in Liverpool, might have been. Maybe Beethoven. A few authors. That's good company, I guess. And it's not like I'm famous. A lot of these people here tonight are bodies who like Gil and come to his openings for the champagne."

"They maybe came for the champagne, but they'll be won over."

They finished the upper gallery and the ten paintings that hung there. Then she accompanied him back to the first floor and showed him the eight pieces there—these with more urban settings and themes.

The biggest canvas was a cityscape about four feet wide by two feet high. The buildings in the background didn't give away any particular city, but they were detailed and interesting, even without identifying features. In the foreground was a playground with old-fashioned metal swings and a spinning merry-go-round. Rain poured through the scene, and what Cole now thought of as the signature swashes of Crockett colors in the sky hinted at a rainbow growing within the storm. Beside the swings, small, almost missed in the beautiful picture as a whole, a child, in rain boots and an open raincoat, leaped into the air, arms raised, feet clearly about to come down in a wide, shiny puddle. Harper had managed to make it all look like a misty, dreamy photo.

While Cole stared, two people joined them, another dapper man in a suit and bowtie, and a woman perhaps in her late fifties or early sixties; her chin-length black hair was frosted with gray.

"Ah, Harper, I'm glad to find you," the man said. "I have someone I think you'll very much enjoy meeting."

"Hi, Gareth," Harper replied, and turned expectantly toward the woman.

Cole studied the staid partner of the flirtatious Gil. He looked like a forty-year-old college professor right down to the bowtie and horn-rimmed glasses.

"This is Cecelia Markham," he said. "Cecelia, I present Harper Crockett."

Harper's body straightened, and her eyes lit as if Gareth had handed her six Christmas presents and a cookie. Cole shifted his attention to the woman, who smiled like a loving grandparent as she took both of Harper's hands in hers.

"I can't tell you how excited I am to meet you, Harper."

"Mrs. Markham. I'm honored. I hear so much about you. You've been a great friend to Gareth and Gil and a huge supporter of all our local art programs. I've wanted to meet you."

"Please, call me Cecelia. I've heard quite a lot about you, too. And I really think we'll all be hearing more after tonight."

"It's very kind of you to say so."

"I admit. I came tonight purely to see what all of Gareth's fuss was about. I expected to have a lovely time. What I didn't expect was to fall in love."

"Love?" Harper asked.

"With your paintings. I haven't seen anything that's touched me this much in years. It's fresh and different and yet classic."

Harper's eyes widened in astonishment. "I don't know what to say."

"Say thank you." Gareth's happiness was infectious. "Cecelia has purchased two of your paintings."

Cole couldn't help it. He knocked Harper in the upper arm with his elbow. "See? Told you so," he whispered.

"Oh, Mrs. Markham…Cecelia. I am flattered. Yes, thank you. Goodness that hardly seems adequate. Which paintings did you choose?"

"This one, for starters." Cecelia nodded at the cityscape. "It simply makes me happy. I love the rain, and this work captures perfectly why I do. The other is your Larkspur. The colors in that one are wildly perfect for my home."

"I'm completely flattered," Harper said again, and this time turned to Cole.

"I have someone to introduce as well," she said, smiling and taking his hand. "This is my best friend from Wyoming, Cole Wainwright. We grew up together, and he knows the inspiration for a lot of the paintings."

He shook hands all around, and from that point the night blossomed out of his control and into a whirlwind of greetings, congratulations, air-kisses, and Gil's frequent smiles and pats on the arm. Harper, despite what she'd said about feeling lost, flourished in the spotlight. Cole, despite hating the city and crowds and anything fake, found himself hard-pressed not to enjoy the weird

spectacle of well-to-do people discussing art and compli-
menting Harper.

By nine forty-five, Cole sat on a modern, black,
leather-and-chrome sofa in the corner of the gallery,
holding the third glass of champagne one of the circulat-
ing caterers had thrust into his hand. He hadn't taken a
sip of this one. One of the few things this shindig lacked
was a good craft beer. He pushed his hat back on his
head and rested his elbows behind him on the back of
the sofa. The crowd had thinned considerably, but people still chatted with Harper. The less formal crowd had
arrived as well, making Cole's jeans and sports jacket
less conspicuous.

"Hello, Cole Wainwright?"

He looked into the face of a man who made his
clothing choice not only inconspicuous but downright
elegant. The guy wore a long-sleeved, flowing peasant-
type shirt with a bolero tie, and he had a shoulder-blade
length brown ponytail was set off with a white bandana
à la Willie Nelson. He was the most anachronistic man
Cole had ever seen, stuck somewhere in a version of the
sixties.

For a moment Cole stared, but suddenly, with a rush
of insight, he knew exactly who the man was: Tristan
Carmichael.

Harper adored him, in her words. A flash of unadul-
terated jealousy made Cole want to toss him out the door
by his girlie shirt. Instead he smiled.

"We haven't met, but I think I know who you are," he
said, and rose to his feet. "Tristan?"

The man offered a boyish grin, as if pleased to be recognized, and held out a hand. "I am. Harper pointed you out. It's great you're here. She's pretty excited you are."

Cole's distaste for him eased a little.

"Mind if I sit? I was here at the beginning but had an emergency at home. I wasn't sure I'd make it back, but it looks like it's gone well."

Cole indicated another chair, and they both sat. "I think they've sold three of the paintings."

"That's what Gil said. I'm so happy for her. It took me a while to convince these guys to sponsor this, but I don't think they regret it now. Anyhow, I asked Harper to come out for a celebration dinner, and she said you're already going down the street to Pedro's?"

A thin, petty streak of satisfaction sliced through Cole. "Yup. I'm heading out in the morning so I grabbed her for tonight."

"I thought I'd ask if I could invite myself along. At least for a drink. I have some things I'd like to chat with her about."

Cole's satisfaction died, replaced by the full force of his jealousy. He had a few things to tell her himself. The last thing he wanted was a guy who didn't know hippies had gone the way of the dodo bird to monopolize the only chance he had at a conversation.

"I'd say that's up to Harper," he said, more sharply than he should have.

"Good! She said to ask you."

Well, shit, he thought. Showed how important a night out with him was to Harper.

"Guess it's settled then."

"Appreciate it, man." Tristan smiled at him.

"Don't mention it."

Tristan stood. "I've got a few people to chat with before we're done at ten. See you in a few. Looking forward to it."

"Sure thing. Who isn't?"

The man had to be an idiot not to hear the insincerity in his voice, but he smiled anyway.

He stood once Tristan had melted into the small crowd, walked around a corner to the men's room, sneaked in, and poured his champagne down the nearest sink. Somehow, the shine of Harper's triumphant night had taken on some unwelcome tarnish.

Chapter Nine

HARPER KNEW COLE didn't like Tristan. In a way his jealousy was flattering, even though it was completely unnecessary. The two men couldn't have been more different than a stallion was from a loyal puppy. Tristan had been a very-short-term love affair four years ago, but he'd turned rapidly into nothing but an amazing mentor and friend. Cole was…Well, she didn't have a clue what Cole was. She did know he definitely didn't have to be jealous of anyone.

But tonight she didn't worry for one second about smoothing things over. Cole would be fine. All that mattered was he and Tris were two of the most important people in her life, and they were both here after the most important event of her life. She felt the significance of this like a celestial sign. Life was about to change.

All the memories that had held her down—the childhood teasing about having her head in the clouds, her bad choices and weak-minded mistakes and missteps, her father's lack of belief in her talent, even the way he'd pulled the plug on her official studies—had taken a back seat to the thrill of Cecelia Markham telling her she'd bought the paintings.

Suddenly Chicago seemed shiny, and her dreams seemed possible again. Even having Cole here, which should have reminded her of her earlier doubts and her homesickness for Wyoming, only told her that it was possible to hang onto both worlds. He'd come, after all. She could go back there, too.

She took in Cole's boredom with Tristan's lengthy description of his latest trip to South America with amusement. Even grumpy and with his blunt cowboy sarcasm at the ready, he was the sexiest man in Pedro's by far. Maybe the sexiest man in all of Chicago. In fact, the way her blood zipped through her body just looking at him, she believed he might be the sexiest man anywhere.

For tonight only, she didn't feel an ounce of guilt. Mia didn't have to know he'd come. Or maybe she already did know. He'd come as a friend, that was all. Her zooming pulse was her own problem. None of the reasons it was a bad idea to be with Cole had disappeared. But tonight, she couldn't make herself follow those bad ideas to their ending places.

Tristan held up a glass of gin and tonic. "And the guy says, 'that burro won't take you to the corner, much less the border.' Proof, I guess, that you shouldn't go car shopping in Brazil after four *caipirinhas* and a tequila shot." He took a swig of his drink.

"I'm writin' that down, buddy." Cole lifted his tall stout to his lips and downed three inches, rolling his eyes at Harper over the rim of his mug.

She laughed. "I'm glad you didn't buy either a car or a burro," she said. "And I'm glad you're home. Sounds like an amazing trip. You brought back some nice art pieces and learned a new fiber dying process. We all win."

"So, Cole my man," Tris asked. "Where are you off to so early tomorrow? Too bad you can't hang around a while and absorb some of the Windy City's culture. Go to an art class taught by our girl here. She's got some talented kids in the shelter program."

Cole looked uncomfortable. Harper set her hand over his and squeezed, loving the hard prominence of his knuckles and the soft patch of masculine hair beneath her fingers.

"Don't listen. I know how busy you are at the ranch this time of year. It's nearly time to gather the cattle and start the shipping. I'm sure there's no time to goof off in Chicago."

"Not that I wouldn't love to see what you do," he said.

"I teach a bunch of inner-city kids and adults to use paints and brushes. It's fun for them, but not all that exciting to watch."

"I'm sure it's fun to watch you." He winked, and her cheeks heated in pleasure. "But I promised not to hide things from you anymore, so I have to admit that I'm not headed straight back to Paradise."

"Oh?"

"I'm headed for a conference trade show in New York City. Something called the Atlantic International Oil and Gas Expo. For no other reason than I can gather information from neutral parties without pressure from Mountain Pacific."

Her stomach lurched in dismay. She struggled to keep her hand on his, but slowly it slid away. She felt bereft. "I see. So Joely's made a decision?"

With swift deftness he caught her fingers again, flipped her hand into his and held it tightly. "You don't see. And Joely doesn't seem prone to making any more quick decisions, so no, nothing's been decided."

"What's Mountain Pacific?" asked Tristan.

"A gas and oil company that wants to drill on the family ranch," she said.

"Ooh." He wrinkled his nose as if warding off a foul stench. "Bad karma if you go that route, man."

"I agree." Harper left her hand in Cole's this time. It turned out, even if she disagreed with him, as long as he held her hand, there was safety in her world.

"Before Joely and your mother make any decisions they want all the facts," Cole said lightly. "That's all I'm going after. What exactly is involved in the search for oil or gas? What happens to the land?"

She knew this was a reasonable business practice. Sound and smart, in fact. It didn't make her feel any less betrayed by her family. Was she truly the only one who didn't look at this as a dollars and cents issue?

But she wouldn't lose her cool with him tonight. Not when everything had been so perfect, and not with Tristan sitting feet away.

"Fair enough," she said. "I wish you good luck getting straight answers from people who want what you have to give."

"Harpo." Cole placed a finger beneath her chin and forced her to look up. "This *is* fair enough. It's common sense, that's all."

"You're right." The words weren't as difficult as they'd seemed in her head. "I wish someone besides me would say no just because."

"Why don't you put up some windmills?" Tristan sipped from his glass without looking up, as if he'd spoken absently to the liquid and not the others present.

Harper sat back into the booth with a thump. *Windmills. Solar power. Isn't that a brilliant idea?*

"Now, hang on." Cole, peering at her, seemed to read her mind. "One of the big reasons you don't want oil extraction at the ranch is because it will uglify the landscape. You tell me a whole regiment of those giant, alien-looking windmills isn't going to spoil the view of Grand Teton."

That was true enough. Windmill farms stretched for acres and weren't exactly natural-looking either.

"Thing is, man, you can put windmills anywhere, relatively speaking. You aren't beholden to pockets of dwindling resources in the ground." Tristan spoke again.

"Exactly," she said. "And the bottom line is, it's more than the ugliness. Windmills won't spill oil and ruin groundwater. If the view across Paradise land has to be spoiled, I'd choose a hundred acres of windmills over five acres of oil wells."

"Well." Cole sat back in the booth and grabbed his beer. "I gotta admire the way you stick to your guns."

She closed her eyes. She didn't want to discuss this anymore—it had taken the glitter off the evening way too abruptly.

"I'm sorry," she said. "I shouldn't be spouting off at all. I left. I live here. I don't have a say."

"Sure you do. Until Paradise isn't yours any longer, if that even happens, you get an opinion."

"Harper Crockett have an opinion?" Tristan grinned from across the table.

"You aren't funny. I'm a mild-mannered little farm girl in the big city," she said.

For the first time, the two men exchanged actual looks of camaraderie. "Whatever you say, Mama." Tris held up his glass again. "Then how 'bout we forget the windmills and toast three sales?"

"Hear, hear." Cole hoisted his beer.

"Toasted." She raised her half-gone Long Island ice tea.

With one last shock for her system, Cole leaned forward and kissed her, slowly, chastely, but hard enough to send her insides tumbling like Jack and Jill down their nursery-rhyme hill, and leave her shaken and confused at the bottom. He raised his head and smoothed the skin beneath her lip.

"I'm proud of you, Harpo. Really proud. May you end up in the Louvre."

"To the Louvre," Harper agreed, while his hands trailed fire across her cheeks and then fell away.

HE WOULDN'T STAY overnight with her. After the Champagne, more drinks, the heady sensation of being Queen for a Night, and the sale of her work to people who loved it, Cole's self-control was probably smart. She'd have thrown all her caution to the wind in the wake of the unfamiliar giddiness of success. It was better one of them remembered they were just friends.

He came from his hotel at eight o'clock the next morning to say good-bye. The world still felt shiny, and her newly discovered belief in herself hadn't disappeared. She greeted him at the door of the house she shared with four other people, her emotions a mixture of gratitude and sadness.

"I still can't believe you came," she said. "It means so much."

"I'm glad I was here. You are an amazing woman."

"I wish you could stay a while."

"You know what?" He took her into an embrace. "I do, too. But maybe it's better this way. We might do something we'll regret if I stay this time."

"Would you regret it?" The innuendo didn't need to be explained.

"Honestly?" He pulled back and asked the question with his eyes as well. "No. But you would. I'm not what's good for you right now. I saw that last night. You're on the brink of getting exactly what you've dreamed of, and what I want is for you to go for it."

She didn't want to admit it was true. "Will you come and visit again?"

"Will *you*?" He winked.

"I'll come home at Thanksgiving."

"Let's see where we are then. Besides, there's this sister thing you and Mia have to work out."

The reminder of that stung more than waiting until November to see him again. "Does she know you came to see me?" she asked.

"No."

"You should tell her."

"It has nothing to do with her, Harpo, can't you see that? And I don't talk to her. Why would I call her out of the blue and tell her I came to your show?"

"She might care."

He sighed. "I don't get it. If she cares, she shouldn't. If you care, you shouldn't."

It was so reasonable. He had to be right. But two sisters and the same man...and one of those sisters was *the* Amelia Crockett?

"I know."

It was all she could say.

HE HUGGED HER again, this time lifting her off the ground with the strength of the embrace.

"I'll be there when you come in November," he said. "I'll be in Wyoming until they bury me there, remember?"

"With the children and grandchildren." She forced a smile, truly sad for the first time.

"Yes. But there'll be none of them by this Thanksgiving."

He didn't kiss her. And when he'd gone, she wept, because he was wrong. She did need him now. And she wanted him. But she couldn't have him—not if she wanted to build on the amazing foundation that had been laid the night before. And she did.

But a brand-new vision of children with Cole's stunning eyes, lying in the arms of some other woman who Cole would choose to share his dream, lodged in her mind— ghosts from a future she didn't want to think about.

She'd pulled herself together by the time her phone rang an hour later. Her spirits lifted when she heard the cheerful voice of Cecelia Markham on the other end.

"Harper, love, when do you have a free day for lunch with me next week?"

"Me?" she asked, her brain sluggish. "Gosh, almost any day. Tuesday I have the most free time, since I'm off until evening."

"Tuesday it is. Would you like to meet at the Chicago Cut Steakhouse on LaSalle? Unless you're a vegetarian, dear, in which case, I have a second suggestion."

She laughed. "No, my family raises beef. I'm far from a vegetarian. I'd be happy to meet you there."

"It's nothing too fancy, but it's very nice. Tuesday then, at eleven thirty?"

"This is awfully nice of you," Harper said. "Is our meeting about anything in particular? Can I do anything for you before then?"

"No, but I definitely hope you'll do something for me after we've met. I'll explain it all next week. Congratulations on a lovely show last night."

Once they'd hung up, Harper looked around at the large, old living room in the house she shared with her roommates. Her sisters would call it a commune, but it wasn't—even though all of the five who lived there contributed to the finances, the food, and the household needs. Her sales from the gallery opening would net her five thousand dollars—a fortune. Harper couldn't remember the last time she'd had an extra five *hundred* dollars. Heck *one* hundred dollars. The deep secret she kept from her family, from Cole, from everyone but the people in this house, was that in every sense of the word, she was a starving artist.

She made barely enough at her community education teaching jobs to pay her share. The newly gained money would allow her to pay Tristan back for the plane ticket to Wyoming, for the funeral, and her housemate Sally back for the loan to buy last night's outfit.

She danced with glee at the idea of taking her full turn filling the fridge and the pantry rather than offering her usual occasional pizza and paltry handful of groceries. What a blessing it would be to have relatively unlimited travel money for work. And maybe she'd splurge on a new easel—not that her ten-year-old faithful friend with the splints made from wooden spoon handles didn't do the job serviceably enough.

If there was money left, she'd actually put it in her bank account. She still had one although anything she put in would have to compete with moths and cobwebs.

WITH A NEW skirt and vest, a pretty scarf, and her bills paid, Harper rode to the restaurant on Tuesday with no mass-transit hiccups, no unruly passengers, and no delays. She arrived with fifteen minutes to spare and was waiting for Cecelia when she arrived. The woman greeted her as if she were royalty, showered her with more praise for the paintings she'd purchased, and described where they were already hanging. She went on to extract every detail she could about Harper's jobs at the three community centers where she worked and the kinds of students who took her classes.

By the time they'd each consumed every bite of their exquisite steaks, Harper had shared more with Cecelia than she had with anyone besides Tristan. She set her fork down for the last time, set her napkin on the plate and groaned as politely as she could. She truly didn't need anything more from this lunch.

"*That* was delicious. And I'm kind of a steak snob after growing up with prime Wyoming beef cattle."

"You've had a fascinating life, my dear. It's no wonder you have such a variety of inspiration for your work."

"Thank you, but it's simply the way I've chosen to express my experiences. Everyone has a life full of inspiration. Not everyone likes to paint."

"Not everyone *can* paint, Harper. You must know that."

"I do. I feel very fortunate. I thank God every day that I can express my visions this way."

Cecelia leaned back slightly as if to take in more of Harper's frame and demeanor. Cecelia's long jacket of ecru silk flowed richly over a striking brown-and-black African print blouse. Black slacks fitted her slender frame like custom couture—which, Harper figured, they probably were. Her brown, black, and off-white, bone-and-stone jewelry was chunky but tasteful, her shoulder-length bob classic and elegant. She oozed wealth but dripped charm.

"Have you ever thought of treating your art as a vocation?" she asked.

"Do you mean paint full time?"

"Exactly."

Harper held back a sigh of longing. Her entire life she'd wished for more time to paint.

"I wish I could even fantasize about such a thing." She smiled. "I paint whenever I can, but it's never enough."

"Have you ever heard of an arts patron?"

"Sure." She narrowed her eyes warily.

"Most commonly, in this day and age, people who support the arts do so by giving to museums, art collections, and the like. I have done that in the past. But there are also a few old throwbacks to the days of private patronage. Harper, there's a reason you've heard my name and knew who I was. I have made myself the biggest pest at art shows and galleries in and around Chicago. I love art. I love new artists."

"And I'm so grateful."

She smiled. "I've been trolling."

"Trolling?"

"For an artist I could, to be crass, buy." She laughed, a fun, musical sound.

"Buy an artist?"

"Of course not literally. But I would like to sponsor you. I'd like to commission several paintings, perhaps a dozen or eighteen. Then I'd like to pay you a small stipend so you can concentrate exclusively on painting."

The world spun, even though Harper sat securely in a thick, comfortable banquette. Never in her wildest imagination had she pictured this being Cecelia's reason for lunch today. Or any day. Or anybody's reason ever to invite her anywhere. A patron?

"I'm not sure I completely understand."

"It's all right. This is a highly unusual request, I know, but I've thought about it a great deal, and I have lots of time to explain it. You have plenty of time to think about it."

Harper forced herself to hold back the questions bubbling in fast-rising, disbelieving effervescence. Think about what? A stipend? Twelve paintings? What kind of—?

"What?" She focused again when she realized Cecelia had spoken again. "I'm sorry, my brain is trying to take this all in."

Cecelia smiled.

"I'm sure it is. But it shouldn't be. You completely deserve this. I want to see you go places, my dear. All I said was I'm talking about a rather substantial time commitment from you. I want to make sure you know exactly what that entails."

"All right." Her stomach rocked and danced. This was real. An honest-to-goodness about-to-be offer of something she'd never imagined. "I'm all ears."

"First of all I have two homes, one here in Chicago, the other quite a large place I recently purchased on the ocean in South Carolina and hope to use for winter entertaining. That home is in the process of being renovated, and I have always dreamed of having it decorated thematically by one very special artist. That artist is you."

"I don't even know what to say."

"Nothing yet." She laughed. "There's more. I also have a bed and breakfast I inherited from a cousin who passed away several years ago. It's a Northwoods lodge along the Canadian border in Minnesota. It's dated and needs fresh décor. I don't need to spend much time there, but it is a thriving business, and I do send a lot of my friends to visit.

"So, you see, I think I can start out by giving you exposure as a very up-and-coming new talent through people who spend time at my properties. And, while all this is going on, I'd like the world to meet you."

"If this doesn't sound too rude," Harper said, "what are you getting out of this?"

"Not rude at all. I'm getting a lot of very valuable artwork, for starters. Second, I'm getting the pleasure of calling myself the person who discovered you. In two years, that will be worth a lot."

Heat from excitement as well as embarrassment rose in Harper's face. She longed for a cool breeze, yet dreaded the thought of this all being a dream she might blow away with the slightest stray breath.

"That's a lot of faith in someone completely untested and unknown," she said.

"But I have that faith." She patted Harper's hand. "That's why I'd like you to think about a commission of thirty-five thousand dollars, which I'd pay over the course of the first year. For that you'd agree to the first twelve paintings. The only other thing I would require from you would be a promise to be available on occasion to attend social gatherings where I could introduce you as my artist."

Harper's ears buzzed with the white noise of utter disbelief. Her brain had clicked off after the words "thirty-five thousand." She couldn't comprehend such a stratospheric amount of money for her crazy paintings. Paintings that didn't yet exist. She'd heard of such things, in fairy tales and circles far removed from the ones in which she traveled.

"Oh, Cecelia." It took a moment for her to form a coherent thought. "That can't be right. Nobody does this—it's far too generous."

"Harper, in my world now and my late husband's world before he died, of course people did this. They did this kind of thing all the time. And it is a very good thing to do with one's money. It's not a real estate takeover or a high-stakes gamble. It would cost me three times as much to buy a top-of-the-line car or boat or horse or any of the million things wealthy people buy for pleasure. Your talent is my pleasure. It's that simple."

"My heart is pounding; I have no idea what to say. Again. This is the most incredible thing anyone has ever done for me."

"Well, I want you to think about it. Think about it very hard. It's going to put us in each other's pockets for the next year. You may come to hate me." Her smile said she didn't really see that happening.

"Never."

"I don't think so either. And, that, my dear Harper, is what this lunch was all about."

"Thank you. Whatever happens. Thank you."

"My joy and my pleasure. Now. I have to ask about your name, Harper Lee Crockett. I could make all kinds of suppositions about it, but I'd love to hear from you how you came by it."

"Your suppositions would probably all be right. My father had very eclectic heroes and heroines. I'm named after the author Harper Lee, and I am Davy Crockett's ninth cousin twice removed. Somebody worked it out."

"That's the most marvelous thing! Can you imagine the hook your beautiful name will be for getting people interested? This gets better and better, my dear! I'm thrilled."

Harper could hardly breathe for excitement, although the first taste of commodity pricing, as it were, over her name gave her a twinge. But it was nothing. There didn't seem to be a downside to this. She wanted to dive into the deal like an Olympic champion into a pool. Still, she knew she had to think about it for appearances sake. Probably for her own sake as well.

"I do hope you'll consider this—I know it's a lot to ask. But I have great hopes and plans for you. And once you've considered it and come up with what you need and want to add to the deal, I hope you'll say yes."

She thought two things simultaneously: Cole would be so excited, she couldn't wait to tell him, and she already knew there wasn't any question of her answer.

Chapter Ten

SKYLAR STARED AT Cole sitting comfortably on his horse. He leaned forward with his forearm resting on the saddle horn and laughed at something Grandpa Leif told him. She loved looking at him, even though he never looked back except to tease her about her new dog or the way she complained about school. She knew she should think of him as an old man, but she couldn't. Every time he flashed his smile, her heart melted—like in the romance novels her mom didn't know she read. The ones Grandma Sadie let her borrow and promised not to tell about. For a really, truly old person, Grandma Sadie sometimes acted younger than Skylar's own parents.

She sat up straighter on Bungu and scanned the hills for cattle. They were in this five thousand acre pasture somewhere. Her dad, Cole, and Grandpa Leif were waiting for a radio call from Cole's dad, Russ, who was surveying the area in his plane. The two ranch hands that still worked for Paradise Ranch, Rico and Neil, had their families with them and were spread out on horseback waiting for word. Rico's black lab, Shaggy, and Neil's husky-lab cross, Lolly, criss-crossed the field between owners.

This was one part of ranch life Skylar loved—gathering the cattle. There were three herds, each in a separate place. This first gathering of the early fall was of the closest-in herd and was always the most fun—everybody helped, from youngest to oldest; nobody was sick of the work yet; and this fall, for the first time in as long as she could remember, they weren't going to use a helicopter to drive cattle—just some four-wheelers.

They usually brought the cattle in the last half mile and sorted them on horseback. Today they were starting farther away—about five miles from the ranch—and would have an old-fashioned mini cattle drive—a one-day exercise so they could appreciate the old ways. Those were Joely's wishes, handed down before she'd left for California with Mrs. Crockett three weeks ago. Skylar's dad had told her this once-a-year drive had been a tradition for years, but Mr. Crockett had stopped it a while back. Joely and Mrs. C were due home today or tomorrow, and Cole wanted to be able to tell them the tradition had been revived.

Skylar couldn't have been happier. She thought Joely was making some good rules.

A faint familiar whirr caught her attention, and she shielded her eyes to stare into the blue September sky. She saw the helicopter approaching straight toward them, and she frowned. The whirr morphed to a tell-tale whoop and she pointed to show her brother Marcus.

"What's that? I thought we weren't using a chopper this year."

"We aren't." Sixteen-year-old Marcus met her frown and copied it.

Moments later everyone could see the big, white-and-silver helicopter.

"It's a medi-vac chopper," Cole said. "Must be coming from the VA."

"Seems a might low," Leif said. "Don't like seeing them. Means someone's life is probably changing, and not for the better."

"Oh, don't think like that." Skylar's mom chided them. "Somebody's life is being saved."

The chopper passed overhead and continued on. Skylar watched it with an odd premonition in her stomach, but everyone else went back to work before it was out of sight. She didn't like thinking about the kinds of injuries that required an air lift. Although, she reminded herself, because roads were far apart in this part of Wyoming, an injury didn't have to be that serious. One Interstate highway did cut through a corner of Paradise, but that section of road was a long way from anywhere an ambulance could get to quickly. Medical helicopters weren't uncommon.

She shook her head. Her mother was always warning her about the gloomy thoughts she often let grow. Normally the admonition to cheer up irritated Skylar to death. Now, however, her mother was probably right. She didn't want to dwell on accidents on a day like this.

She turned Bungu toward her brother, ready to follow him as she'd been doing all morning. His horse Scout knew everything there was to know about working cattle and made a great partner horse for Bungu who was still learning. The walkie-talkie on her father's belt squawked. At the same moment, Cole's did the same. Then her grandpa's followed. Cell phones didn't work out here in the middle of the ranch, but the radios had ranges of around eighteen miles, sometimes more if there weren't any hills or other things in the way. To have them all go off meant someone was hailing them.

Her dad pulled his unit free and pushed the talk button. "Bjorn here. That you, Sadie?"

"Bjorn?" Miss Sadie's voice crackled with age and distance. "You all need to come back. Right away. There's been an accident."

Skylar's blood froze.

"Sadie? Tell me what's going on." Her father's voice soothed, even as he exchanged worried glances with the other adults.

"Chet Reynolds is here."

Chet Reynolds was a Teton County sheriff.

"Bella and Joely. Chet says it isn't good."

"What?" Cole grabbed his radio. "Sadie? It's Cole. Darlin' let me talk to Chet."

The rest of the conversations and crackles and moans of disbelief blurred after that. With sickening clarity, Skylar realized the chopper they'd all seen, flying low, had been heading for the accident scene on Highway 191, twenty-five miles from the ranch. The knowledge made her want to throw up. She'd known something was wrong.

The cattle were allowed to disburse into the pasture without a second thought. Her grandpa, her dad, and Cole launched themselves, with Rico's and Neil's youngest kids, into the pickup truck that served as a chuck wagon, and disappeared toward the ranch at breakneck speed. Skylar, left behind with her mother, Neil and Rico, Marcus, and Rico's wife, Sarah, to make the ten-mile ride back home leading three horses, paid only enough attention to know Joely and her mother weren't dead, and that Joely, the most seriously injured, was unconscious and badly hurt. Something about a logging truck and broken chains and logs smashing through the car windshield. After gleaning that much, Skylar let herself go numb.

The ride home seemed to take forever. All Skylar could think about was that there'd been a funeral only a month before. That one was still fresh in her mind. She didn't think she could stand another one. And definitely she couldn't handle two.

She expected to find chaos when she got back, but the ranch yard was quiet. She wanted to run and find Cole, but her mother made her help with the horses first, and by the time they all reached the main house, there wasn't any chaos there either. Even so, Skylar recognized the pall that permeated all the rooms. It was as crushing as when Mr. Crockett had died.

They found Grandma Sadie cradled in the oversized arms of the living room armchair. She was wrapped in blankets, and Cole squatted beside her. At first she thought Grandma Sadie might have finally succumbed to grief, but she was the one speaking. As Skylar approached the words became clear—and immediately comforting. Grandma was praying.

The Crocketts had always been known as good church-going folk—at least according to her mother. "The girls slipped a mite after they moved away." She could hear her mom's voice, telling her the story as a warning, so she wouldn't become one of the ones who strayed. "We all hope they come back to the fold in time. You'll have to remember to keep them all in your prayers."

The funny thing was her mother cared about God and religion more than anyone Skylar knew, even the pastor at their church in Wolf Paw Pass. But when she said the Crockett girls had slipped, she didn't say it like she thought less of them. It was sometimes impossible to figure out what things her mom would take a dislike to, like going to school in town, and what things she'd be tolerant of, like the Crockett girls who'd "slipped."

"So please cover Joely and Isabella with your precious spirit and lead them through the valley back to us," Grandma said, her eyes closed. "And pour your love and mercy over the rest of the girls. Comfort them. Let them know you are with them as you are with their sister and mother."

The words were kind of old-fashioned and churchy. Skylar mostly didn't know what she believed. Her dad didn't say much about religion. Sometimes religion was all her mom talked about. When Skylar was out riding and drawing, she thought there must be God somewhere. When he was being stuffed down her throat, she was sure people were making him up to scare her.

Grandma Sadie's prayer didn't scare her. It was sure and strong, like she was just reminding God to do those things instead of asking him. When she finished, Cole kissed her cheek and stood.

"You okay?" he asked when he saw Skylar.

She nearly cried. Not a single other person had asked her how she felt.

"I'm scared," she admitted and the admission caused a miracle. He put his arms around her and held her in a huge hug.

"I'm sure you are. We all are," he said. "It's pretty hard to be brave when we don't know what's going on. Your dad and your grandpa went to the hospital. They'll let us know."

"Are they going to die?" It was a question she normally never would have voiced, but she was braver than usual with Cole there. She held onto his waist, and he felt more solid and strong than her own dad.

"Aw, honey, I sure hope not," he said. "I don't believe they are, but that's because I'm hoping so hard. I wish I could lie and tell you I knew they were going to be fine. But you're big enough to know that I can't make a promise like that yet."

"I know."

He pulled away and patted her on both arms. "Hey, where's that pup?"

She'd forgotten about Asta. "She's in her kennel in the barn."

"Why don't you run and get her. Bring her here. I'll help watch her. And, hey, even if she pees on the floor, it's more important for you to have a friend right now."

Wasn't he her friend? She'd rather stay here with him. She also knew he was right.

"Okay," she said. On her way to the back door she stopped and looked back. "Did anyone ask you if you're okay?"

He smiled, his eyes a little surprised. "You're a nice girl, Skylar Thorson, anyone tell you that? I'm okay."

She felt a little better, like she did after she'd been helpful around the house or the barns. The satisfaction didn't make the cloud hanging over the whole house go away, but she wasn't as reluctant to leave by herself. She'd taken good care of Asta as she'd sworn to her parents she would when they'd very reluctantly allowed her to keep the pup. She didn't want to mess that up now. Cole was right about her needing a friend, but more than that she needed someone to take care of the way Cole had taken care of her.

"Hey, Skylar?"

She turned back to his call, her heart thumping at his smile. "Yeah?"

"Could you ask Rico if he'd call Dr. Ackerman? Tell her we need to postpone the pregnancy testing on the cows tomorrow. We'll call and reschedule."

Her heart floated. He was trusting her with ranch business. Easy stuff that anyone could do—but he'd asked her. "Sure, I'll tell him. Anything else?"

"Come back quickly. I don't want you wandering around by yourself—we all need to be together. 'Kay?"

At that her heart officially soared. She could be here for him—she definitely could. Maybe people were wrong. Maybe a crush wasn't ridiculous after all.

Chapter Eleven

HARPER MADE BJORN take her straight to the hospital from the airport without stopping at home. The terror eating like acid inside her had only slowed its burn as they neared the VA medical complex, and then it had only quieted because she knew she'd finally be able to talk to the experts herself. There wasn't much of her family there to give her details. She trusted Leif, Bjorn, and Cole to tell her everything they knew, but after imagining the worst for twelve awful hours, firsthand information would be a gift.

She'd been disappointed that Cole hadn't picked her up, as he'd said he would, even though she had no right to expect it from him. Bjorn explained he was basically running the ranch at the moment, and in the past eighteen hours he'd spent most of his time trying to figure out how to be two places at once.

She absolutely couldn't hold that against him.

Bjorn parked in the massive lot at the front of the hospital. Panic hit Harper anew as they entered the cheerful but imposing medical center lobby. Beautiful paintings depicting each branch of the military hung in solemn watch near the doors. Two American flags and a Wyoming state flag flanked the pictures. Warm colors and natural-wood furniture softened the military presence.

"Mom was in the National Guard," Harper said in a whisper as they headed for the elevator bank. "After fifteen years of service, I get why she's eligible to be here. But the only tie Joely has to military service, as far as I know, is her husband, and she said he isn't in the picture anymore. Doesn't she have to be in a civilian hospital?"

"Yes," Bjorn replied. "But this is a far better equipped trauma center and was closer to the accident. They flew both your mom and Joely together."

"Will they move Joely?"

Bjorn grimaced. "They can't yet, Harper, honey. They don't dare."

The words twisted the knife of fear deeper into Harper's heart. Oh, God, she prayed. How could this be happening again?

They reached the ICU on third floor, a huge, open space with a futuristically designed nurses' station in the center and glass-walled rooms around the perimeter. Soft lights bathed everything except the rounded counters and overhead light fixtures in the middle. Harper marveled at the mix of sterility and warmth some designer had managed to achieve.

After they registered at the desk, the male RN who took them toward her mother's room treated them with such careful respect, Harper wanted to shake him. His demeanor hovered too close to sympathy, and that was scarier than the thought of what she'd see inside the room.

The first person she saw was Leif. He sat in a recliner at the foot of the bed, feet on the floor instead of elevated, elbow propped on one chair arm, his chin cradled in his hand. He looked naked without his cowboy hat, his bushy gray hair starting to need a trim. His head popped up when the nurse knocked softly on the open door.

"Harper. Darling." He practically bolted from the chair and had her in his arms seconds later. For the first time, she wept. She hadn't even looked at the bed yet. "I'm sorry you have to come home again for this. But I'm awful glad you're here."

"I'm afraid to ask how she is."

She knew the list of injuries her mother and Joely had each sustained. Her mother's were the least serious on the surface: a hairline fracture above the left eyebrow, a severe concussion, a broken leg, a bruised spleen. It all sounded horrific, but she'd heal if the swelling in her brain got no worse. Right now, they were trying to prevent hematomas from forming and hoping the swelling would go down without surgery.

Leif released her and placed a firm-but-wrinkled hand on her cheek. "She's sleeping. They have her pretty well sedated due to some swelling around the brain. But she's been awake, honey. She's a tough bird, your mama."

"Have you been here the whole time?"

"No, we all take turns. But she hasn't been alone. Joely either. Go on, take her hand. She looks bad, but don't let that worry you."

She didn't want to see her beautiful mama any way but as she always was, glossy-haired, much younger looking than her fifty-nine years, perpetually positive, and agreeable. What she saw when she faced the bed pulled a gasp from the pit of her stomach.

"Oh, Mom! Oh no."

Her mother's beautiful chestnut hair tufted out from a swath of gauze around her forehead. Almost no unmarked skin was left on her face—every inch seemed covered by a scrape, a small cut, or a brown pockmark. It took a long moment and a deep breath, but finally Harper bent and kissed one damaged cheek.

"I love you," she said. "I'm so sorry this happened. I'm sorry I wasn't here."

She sat with her mother, talking and murmuring words of encouragement without regard to time. The longer she stayed the easier it got to be there, even though her heart still hurt. The regular rise and fall of her mom's chest was comforting, and the color behind her bruises and cuts at least made her look alive, if painfully so. She didn't notice the others had left her alone until she looked up to find the room, with its muted light, quiet and empty.

"She's gonna be all right."

Harper spun her gaze to the door as Cole stepped through it. No thoughts, no analysis preceded her leap from the bed. He met her in the middle of the room and caught her into the folds of his soft shearling-lined denim jacket, letting her burrow into it as she prayed to escape the reality in the room.

"I thought you were out with the cattle," she said.

"I was. But Rico, Neil, and Bjorn sent me packing. I'm sorry I missed your plane."

It didn't matter. Only this mattered—the combination of his wind-scented coat; the cradling warmth of its lining, the warm, musky scent of his skin; and the hard heat of his chest beneath her cheek. She wanted nothing more than to be part of him, to never leave this sanctuary, and maybe to weld his arms to her body so he'd never be able to let her go. For the first time this trip, she let herself forget about Mia and indulge in fantasy.

"That's nothing to be sorry for."

Warm lips rested on the top of her head. Slowly her body molded to his, tension drained from her shoulders and spine, and reason returned. Her brain kicked back into gear. With huge effort, she relaxed her python-squeeze on his torso. He lowered his kiss to her forehead.

"Hi," he said. "You okay?"

"I'm okay."

"Have you seen Joely yet?"

Oh, God, Joely. She hadn't forgotten, she'd just pushed her sister far to the back of her mind until she'd come to grips with her mom.

"No."

"Melanie is sitting with her now. I sent Leif down to get something to eat. I can wait here when you're ready to go visit her."

"No!" She latched back onto him again. "Please come with me. Everyone says she's much worse than this."

"It's not good, sweetheart."

All she let herself hear was the *sweetheart*.

After a moment more of indulging her childlike help-lessness, Harper pulled away again, hating her fear, hat-ing her need for someone else to show the strength.

"I'll go. I need to see her. But does it make me awful that I don't want to?"

"Of course not. None of us wanted to come yesterday either—not to see this."

The walk to Joely's room across the ICU floor took thirty seconds that dragged like a broken clock. Every-thing felt broken in this place—a place that existed only because of damaged and shattered people.

Melanie stood when they reached Joely's door. Her smile was wide and sincere as she embraced Harper as Leif had. "She'll be glad you're here."

Such a silly, clichéd thing to say, Harper thought absently, avoiding looking at the bed. Joely couldn't be glad about anything at the moment.

"It's wonderful of you to be here, Mel. This is above and beyond when you have a family."

"Above and beyond Christian charity and duty? Non-sense. And it's only a duty because it shouldn't have hap-pened. We love you all—Joely and your mom are family to us, too. Now, you two go in. Be warned. Don't get freaked out if buzzers go off and people come running. She's fighting hard right now."

Those words nearly sank what remained of Harper's bravado. She only nodded and took Cole's hand. Melanie edged out of the room and, finally, there was no choice but to face the truth.

It wasn't Joely lying in the bed. The person there had purple-and-yellow skin, eyes swollen shut, a head swathed in bandaging, a disfigured jaw, and tubes snaking everywhere as if attaching the body to the Matrix. Nothing of her sister, save the relatively unscathed hand lying atop the covers, looked like the stunning beauty that was Joely Crockett.

Harper's stomach roiled in unacceptance. "No!" She began to cry. "Oh, God, how can she survive this?"

"She will." Cole drew her close and murmured into her ear.

He let her creep forward to take Joely's uninjured hand but held her from behind, his arms securely around her waist, his body a brace at her back.

"Joely," she whispered. "It's me, Harpo. I'm here now, and I'll stay as long as you need me. The other girls are coming, too. We'll take care of you."

"That's exactly what you needed to tell her," Cole said. "She'll know. I believe that."

He was pulling out all the cowboy poet stops. Had he always been this way? She didn't remember. Maybe her brain was muddled when it came to him, too. Whatever the case, childhood now seemed a million years ago—shattered by the all-too adult truth surrounding them.

"I'm so shallow," she said, loud enough for both Cole and Joely to hear. "All I can think about is how broken her beautiful face is. I don't want her to be disfigured."

"You know what? That means you're thinking positively. It's better than despair. The universe is telling you something."

For the first time, she smiled. "You sure are in touch with your feminine side today, Mr. Wainwright. You don't have to make stuff like that up for me."

"Who says I'm making it up?"

She leaned back for a few seconds against his solid, safe chest, still not thinking in any depth about what she was doing.

Melanie headed home, and Cole insisted Leif do the same, insisting they could keep an eye on both Joely and Bella until after dinner. For two hours they alternated between the ICU rooms. Twice, a response team rushed to Joely's side, pushing drugs, stopping terrifying seizures. Each time, Harper lost a slice of faith. Each time, Cole shored it back up.

They played cribbage in her mother's room. They played Go Fish at Joely's bedside. They talked about pregnancy testing the cows, about the aborted old-fashioned roundup, and about hospital coffee.

They avoided the topics of oil wells or selling the ranch.

Even more assiduously, they refrained from talking about the saddest part of the accident so far—the mare Joely had been bringing to Wyoming that hadn't survived the terrible accident.

Harper found the hospital and all it held a terrible world—more surreal than the experimental drug times that had gotten her kicked out of college. She never talked about them, and yet she'd go back to her wasted years and shout her weaknesses to the universe if it meant guaranteeing Joely's and Mom's recovery.

"Are you sure you don't want to go back to the ranch?" she asked Cole as the dinner hour neared. "This has to be excruciatingly boring for you."

"It's not boring at all. You're here."

At that one line, she panicked.

"Cole. Don't. Don't say that, I feel guilty enough. I need a rock and you're it—the safest place I know right now. But the emotions are so raw—like at Dad's funeral. The feelings don't mean—"

"Harpo. Stop. You're overthinking again. I said I'm with you, so it isn't boring. I like being here with you and for you. That's all. I didn't propose."

His smile, amused and tolerant, sent her sinking, embarrassed, into the recliner in her mother's room.

"Man," she said. "I'm sorry. I'm such a wreck."

"You have every right to be. But trust me, then, to have your back. There's time much later to sweep you off your feet."

Oh, if only you could. Or maybe you already have. "Good luck with that."

"How little you really know, Miss Crockett."

"How little any of us knows about the Crockett sisters." The surprised voice from the doorway made them both turn.

Amelia stood there, dressed as haphazardly as Harper had ever seen her in a pair of dark-blue sweat pants, a pink turtleneck beneath a multicolored ski sweater, and a pair of red cowboy boots. She hadn't been due in until the next day, and for an instant Harper stared at her, waiting for the know-it-all, take-charge sister to appear. Instead a tear traced down her cheek.

It took no more effort to run to her than it had to run to Cole. They grabbed each other, and to Harper's astonishment, Amelia squeezed tightly.

"Is she okay?"

"Mom seems stable." Harper straightened. "How did you get here so quickly? I thought you had surgery scheduled."

Amelia shook her head. "It wasn't life-threatening. I rescheduled and rearranged everything for the next two weeks, pulled what clothes I had in my hospital locker out, and got on the first flight I could."

"Who picked you up here?"

"I took a cab. I didn't want to make anyone take time to come get me when I wasn't expected."

She didn't add anything about needing to be here to check on the medical staff's decisions, not trusting anyone to organize things, or being indispensable. Harper chalked it up to shock and the weird mind tricks the ICU played on them all.

Once she and Cole walked Mia through the shock of seeing both patients, some of Mia's medical calm surfaced, but it turned out to be a welcome comfort. Giving a rare glimpse of her true bedside manner, Mia engaged the staff with intelligent questions Harper never would have thought to ask, even managing—with sweet talk and dogged logic—to peek at the charts; something she definitely shouldn't have been able to do without another doctor's approval. By the time she'd been at the hospital for an hour, everybody had in-depth knowledge about the true nature of Joely's and their mother's injuries and prognoses. Not that the knowledge was encouraging.

Finally, Mia gave the staff a rest from her inquiries and settled in for her watch shift. She turned her doctorly intensity on Cole and Harper.

"It's nearly six o'clock, you two. You should go home and take a break. I'll be fine for now. I'm used to long nights."

"What about dinner for you?" Harper asked. "We can stay a while longer."

"You think hospital food scares me?" Mia snorted. "Believe me, I'm good. We're all in for some long days, I'm afraid. Go. Rest. You'll be needed later."

"Someone will come and spell you in a few hours," Cole promised.

Mia waved a hand in dismissal. "Don't worry about that. I got the original admitting doc to agree to come in and talk to me before he leaves for the night. He's here until midnight. I'll stay until I see him. If we need to leave them for a few hours overnight it's not necessarily a bad thing."

"I'll come back first thing," Harper said.

"Perfect."

Hugs flew abundantly. Harper wished with all her heart that this ease with her sister would remain. Maybe it would.

"Don't harass the docs too much," Cole said, grinning slightly.

"What, and be untrue to my nature? Dream on," Mia replied.

Harper turned away and sighed. It would be good to leave, she decided. Getting away from the beeping monitors, the walls steeped in worry, and her two family members wrapped in pain could only help.

"Call if you need something or if there's news," Cole added.

"Of course," Mia replied. "I'm going to Skype with the triplets a little later. We'll talk about whether they need to rotate coming up."

"I'm sure we'll all have to deal with our schedules as we learn more," Harper said. "I can stay a while."

"That's good." She smiled.

"Tell the movie stars I love them." Harper offered one last hug and followed Cole gratefully from their mother's room.

Exhaustion struck as they waited for an elevator.

"You all right?" Cole asked.

"I'm glad to be leaving. I feel awful because you and the others have been here for two days with this."

"We've all had time to acclimate. You need your chance to absorb it all." They entered the elevator. "What would you say to not going right home? I've been hoping you'd let me take you to dinner so we can talk away from the family."

"I think that sounds wonderful."

"There's a new place in town called Basecamp Grill. They have great food and even greater cheesecake."

She sighed with pleasure and slumped against the wall of the elevator as it finished descending. "What's that they say in the military? You have the conn, Mr. Wainwright."

The elevator doors parted on the main floor.

"Okay, soldier. Basecamp and cheesecake it is."

Chapter Twelve

NOTHING SHOULD HAVE seemed right in the midst of all the worry and uncertainty, but everything *was* right in Cole's world with Harper at his side. They passed the closed shops on Main Street, heading for the newest eatery in Wolf Paw Pass—a converted grain mill that featured not only a firewood stove but an attached craft brewery started by a guy Cole had known back in high school.

Since the town had grown with the building of the medical center and the presence of more military, Mickey Franz's little home-brewing hobby had become a local hit. Wolfheart, he called the stuff. To beer aficionados it was apparently top notch. And the food was excellent, too. Once inside, they were led to a corner table near a fireplace. The room smelled like a fragrant campfire, and amber light filled the restaurant, glinting off the full wall wine rack along one end. Harper collapsed into her chair and wiped her fingers across her cheeks and eyes. A sigh rolled from her lips.

"You must be exhausted."

"Yes, but so's everyone. I'm all right."

"This is hard. No sense trying to pretty it up. You were great with your mom and sister, though. You talked like they were right with you, listening."

She shrugged. "Nervous blathering."

The emotions she'd cycled through this afternoon and evening had let him see every nuance of Harper Crockett—fear, shock, determination, despair, forgiveness, desperate need. It had been an insight into his evolving history with her. She'd been cute in high school. She'd been lovely and feisty as a college co-ed. She'd been ethereal and unreadable as a twenty-something. He'd been blown away by her passion at her father's funeral and then by her paintings in Chicago. Now he was simply love-struck. Like a kid, like a moony-eyed calf, like a big dork. Whatever legend said about cowboys being tough and hard wasn't true. Tonight he was living proof.

"I've missed you," he said.

"I've missed you. Thanks again for staying all day at the hospital. It would have been hard alone."

"Happy to."

Silence fell, the first real quiet between them since she'd flown into his arms earlier that day. He could only hope that had meant something more than a reaction to grief, but he wasn't sure. She still held her distance. Even he didn't know exactly when it had started for him, but since their time in Chicago, he didn't doubt what he wanted in the least.

"Can I start you with something to drink?" A waitress in a khaki skirt, white blouse, and hiking boots stood beside the table, cheery and encouraging.

"I'll have a Wolfheart Stout," he said.

"Do you have a Riesling?"

"Yes. A glass?"

"I'm tempted to order the whole bottle." She smiled faintly. "But, no. Just a glass."

He chuckled. "You can drink a bottle, as far as I'm concerned."

"Nope. I'm a sloppy drunk. Puts every brain cell that isn't killed to sleep. I've seen enough coma-action today."

"It's good to hear you joke about it."

"Yeah? Well it makes me feel guilty."

"Stop. Nobody will ever doubt how awful this is for you. You need to be okay, and laughing helps. However lame the joke."

"It's surreal, Cole. The whole thing. First Dad, now Mom and Joely. Is this some sort of end-of-the-line curse? Is Amelia right? Should the rest of us get out before Paradise kills us all?"

The words dug into his heart with surprising force. "No, honey, no. There's no curse. Things happen, bad things. You know that. We ride it out, that's all." He studied the play of emotions that crossed her face. Fear, exhaustion, a touch of anger. He nearly lost it himself when the sheen of tears coated her eyes but didn't fall. "Do *you* want to sell Paradise Ranch?"

"I…don't. But if anything happens to Joely, it's all over. There's nobody. You said you don't want it. We went through all this."

"I know. I know. But this is no better a time to be talking about that than the day of your father's funeral was. We have to let Joely and your mom heal, and then there can be decisions."

"I know you don't want to sell yet. But how close are you to being able to buy back the Double Diamond acres? Maybe that's what you should do."

His heart hurt even more. She'd hit the center of his personal dilemma and didn't even know it. Six weeks earlier his only motivation had been getting the Double Di back. But since Sam's death, he'd been more intimate with Paradise's inner workings than he'd ever had a reason to be. Joely had given him the ranch's books to look over, and she'd asked his advice on everything from cattle, to employee management, to Mountain Pacific Oil and Gas. He had some opinions about where Sam had gone a little wrong, but he'd also seen the incredibly well-oiled machine Sam had run. He still wanted his land, but in four short weeks, he'd also become invested in Paradise.

"A full year minimum. They've laughed me out of the bank twice already. Mostly I need to show a steady income for that much longer. Plus get together the rest of the down payment to make the loan feasible."

"So we need to try and keep the ranch another year at least."

"Look. Joely made a decision to try and make that work. Let's honor her wishes and take one day at a time. What dredged all this deep interest up anyhow?"

"Death. Dying. Losing the ranch person by person. I'm scared, that's all."

For the second time that day, she let a tear slip from the corner of her eye. It traced half way down her cheek before she wiped it away, but another formed to take its place. Cole stood, dragged his chair around the corner of the table until it was right next to hers, and pulled her into his arms. All he wanted was to protect her. Harper looked at everything from such an emotional perspective. Her artist's eye and her artist's soul tried to make beauty from everything, and there was no beauty to be had in any of this.

Her body felt fencepost stiff in his embrace. He rubbed her upper arms. "Breathe, Harpo," he said.

But once she did, a sob surfed out on a long, quivering wave of air. The sound cracked the dam she'd held in place all day.

"Okay," he said as her body slumped. "This is good."

She covered her mouth with one slender hand and buried her face, leaning from her armless chair to his, half-sharing his seat. Her tears fell silently with only the occasion hiccup. He nodded and mouthed it was okay to the waitress when she brought their drinks. A few people sent them empathetic glances, but he ignored them. At last, Harper sniffed a final time and straightened, covering her face with a cloth napkin.

"I'm sorry."

"I'm not even going to bother stating the obvious."

She set the napkin down, and even though her eyes were puffy, she looked clearer, more at peace, and all the more vulnerable for having showed him the tears. Normal Harper would have averted her gaze, apologetic for being too sensitive. This time she didn't. Instead she searched his eyes, looking for something. He didn't know how to ask her what it was, but his gut tightened, his pulse notched upward, and his instincts led him into leaning forward.

Every fraction of a second that brought him closer, he expected her to jerk away, but at the very last of those seconds she closed her eyes. He took her delicate chin in his fingers and tilted her lips to his, slipping a kiss onto her mouth with all the certainty he could fake.

She yielded. Her lips molded to his, soft and salted from her tears. He maneuvered the angle of her head with his touch, and she allowed it, following the kiss, playing along with the changes of pressure and stoking sparks. Fire flickered to life in his stomach. Unlike the potent lightning of their first kiss, this one wasn't over in a flash. She didn't pull away. She opened her mouth before he did.

The lightning struck then.

Deep, surprising, and hot, it left behind more smoldering and more flame, steady, bright, intense. Their tongues danced, and hers was every bit as talented, as enticing as he'd imagined. She suckled his, she gave him hers; he slid his fingers from her chin to her ear and pulled her head closer. She groaned—a tiny, satisfied sound to which his body responded with age-old life.

He pulled away slowly and then pressed back for one more tango before he relinquished the kiss.

"What is this?" she whispered. "I don't even know if this is appropriate."

"We're figuring out feelings. Everything's appropriate."

She smiled half an inch from his mouth. "Don't use hyperbole on me, cowboy. I can think of a lot of things that wouldn't be appropriate here."

"I'll find us a place where they *would* be."

"Whoa. What happened to my sensitive, take-it-slow cowboy?"

"He's my alter ego. I sent him to the corner."

"Can I talk to him again?"

"Aw, hell." He grinned, loving this side of her. "What do you need him for?"

"To tell him it's time to order cheesecake. Maybe real food, too, but I definitely like cheesecake after a cowboy kisses me. With lots of chocolate."

"Hmpf. So much for the seductive power of the bad boy. Where's a dumb romance novel when I need one?"

She only giggled at him.

They ordered and ate their meals, keeping the light, teasing tone they'd adopted after the kiss and limiting their conversation topic to Harper's new relationship with Cecelia Markham, the woman Cole had met at the gallery showing.

They finished dinner and the waitress took their cheesecake orders, clearly relieved that everything remained all right after the earlier crying spell. Once she was gone, Harper excused herself to the ladies' room, and Cole finally took his moment to cover his eyes and blow out the confusion of the day. For all his bravado, he didn't feel that confident about what to do with his growing feelings for Harper. He could see the looming problems. She wasn't staying. He wasn't leaving. Was it really fair to start anything when it was doomed to fail? A relationship that had never been truly real with Amelia had been strange enough. Trying to make a real relationship with Harper couldn't help but be a cosmic mistake.

But how could he stop?

"Cole—look what I found."

She slid into her seat, handing him a large blue-and-green poster advertising the Lion's Club high school art competition.

"Where'd you steal that from?"

"The front desk." She gave a guilty smile. "I'll bring it back, but this is in less than two weeks. Do you know if Skylar ever talked to her mom about getting in?"

"Not a clue. Nothin' she's mentioned to me."

She thought a moment. "How is she? Skylar?"

He almost didn't understand the question. How was Skylar Thorson? She was a fourteen-year-old nice kid. "She's...fine? She still has that stray pup—"

"She does! Her folks let her keep it?"

"Yeah. She named her Asta. I guess it's the name of Bjorn's childhood dog, and he couldn't say no."

"See! You do know how she is."

"I know she has a dog." He truly was bewildered at the conversation.

"But she wanted so much to be in that art show."

His head spun at the topic change. "Okay. How do you know that?"

"From the look in her eye when she saw this poster the day she found her dog. And from the disappointment when she saw the contest was for public school students."

Well that explained it. She'd deduced something from nothing. He didn't know any more about the way women worked than most men did, but he understood that women had some sort of belief in the gods of voice tone and eye rolls.

"Sure. Of course."

"You're such a guy. Don't you pay attention?"

"I'm real glad you noticed I'm a guy. And I believe the right answer here is, 'no, I admit I never pay attention.'"

Her smiles, after all the tension and worry that had kept them at bay since she'd arrived home, were a relief. She aimed one at him now filled with mock pity.

"You've been trained up well by someone, cowboy. Lucky for me."

"Long as you're happy, sweetheart."

Their cheesecake arrived, hers topped with extra chocolate and his with butterscotch and walnuts. She dug in without hesitation, and when she closed her eyes and groaned, he only wished he could make her react that way again for him. He forced the thoughts away.

"Seriously," he said, returning to the unsexiest topic he could. "Why are you thinking about Skylar?"

A wisp of embarrassment crossed her features but then she looked him in the eye. Her lips closed over her fork a second time and slicked it clean. He swallowed.

"I know it sounds dumb," she said, mumbling over the mouthful of cheesecake. "I feel a connection with her. She's a lot like I was when I was kid—a little lost and kind of misunderstood."

"I shall call her Mini-Me." Cole used his best Dr. Evil voice.

"Don't you dare make fun of me."

"I'm not. I couldn't resist, sorry. I'll be good, but you didn't honestly feel lost and misunderstood, did you?"

She said nothing for a long moment. She didn't even take another bite of cheesecake.

"You wouldn't know because you were the only one who ever *seemed* to understand. You stuck up for me when people made fun of my daydreaming and my drawing."

"I did?"

Harper had been famous for having her head in the clouds and her nose in a sketchbook, but he'd thought everyone found her cool and insightful and nice. That was simply how he'd looked at her and why he'd liked being around her. And what he found so steady about her now. She hadn't changed. He teased her, but her concern about Skylar and everyone and everything else was what made her special.

"Until you started dating Amelia." She averted her eyes with a self-conscious smile. He caught her chin again.

"Really?"

"This is stupid. It was more than a dozen years ago."

"But I want to hear. Was I a jerk after I dated her?"

"No! No. You were…busy. That's about the time we stopped riding around the two ranches like wild cowboys and grew up, that's all. I missed my friend. But here he is, so it's all good."

He glanced around their table. Nobody was looking. He shoved his chair back, grabbed her hand, and removed the fork from her fingers. With a firm tug he pulled her to a stand and backed her into the hidden corner behind their table.

"We were good friends. I think we still are. But what if your friend wants more of this?"

He didn't kiss her slowly this time. He pressed his way into her mouth without waiting for an invitation, bracing for her to shove him away but prepared to stand his ground. She gave a squeak of surprise but then met his insistence with her own demanding tongue. Sparks flew across his scalp and down his spine.

Her mouth was hot and sweet with chocolate, cream, and wine. Her tongue slid against his expertly, playful and stunning. The flying sparks gathered in his stomach. His body hardened so quickly, his lack of control shocked him more than Harper did. He'd meant to act the macho cad for a few teasing seconds to divest her of any memories of them as kids. Instead, she banished their childhood ghosts all by her little lonesome.

When she did push him away, he was no longer braced for it. She held him at a literal arm's length, her tongue on her upper lip, her breath loud enough for him to hear it, and unsteady as a newborn filly.

"Stop. This is so not smart."

"Felt pretty smart to me. Would it help to go someplace less public?"

"After I finish my cheesecake."

"I'm glad to know where I stand in the hierarchy."

"Pretty far below chocolate. But above almost everything else." She touched his lip with a soft fingertip.

"And tell me again," he said. "Where's your good old friend now?"

"Still right here, I hope," she whispered. "Although he's shocking me. No matter how much I keep fearing he's going to kiss like a...well, a brother, he—"

"Doesn't. You'd better be about to say 'doesn't.'"

"He absolutely, unequivocally, *so* doesn't."

BY THE TIME she and Cole got back to Rosecroft, Harper's brain was in a state of agitated confusion and guilt. Her sister's ex-boyfriend could kiss like an angel, and then turn her on like nobody she'd ever been with—and she'd been with more guys than she wanted anyone to know about. She felt like she'd sold out to the devil himself. The bottom line was, a person simply didn't go after her sister's old boyfriend.

Still, she didn't pull her hand away when Cole held it on the way home. And she managed to live with the cocktail of bliss, guilt, and worry that made up her roiling emotions even though they consumed every thought all the way home. She wasn't expecting Skylar to nearly bowl her over as she stepped through the door.

"You're back! How's Miss Joely?" Skylar all but ran into her in the foyer, stopping short and scooping up the black-and-white pup that was three times bigger than when Harper had first seen it.

"Hey, Skylar." Cole answered for them both. "If nobody's called here with other news, things are pretty much the same."

"Nobody called."

"Skylar! Hi." Harper gave the girl a one-armed hug and set her suitcase on the slate tile so she could pet the dog. "This little girl has sure grown. Congratulations on getting to keep her."

She scratched the puppy behind its perked-up ears, and each of her fingers got thoroughly doggy kissed. Skylar flushed with pleasure and pride.

"My mom made me make signs to put around town, and I had to report her missing to the sheriff. But after ten days, nobody called or anything. I named her Asta."

"It's a beautiful name. Cole told me you named her after one of your dad's old dogs."

"Yeah. She's really smart. She's pretty much house trained, and she can already herd the chickens, but she doesn't know why she's doing it."

"They're incredible dogs. So, how are you?"

"Okay. It's nice you're back again." As soon as the words were out, she looked as if she wished she hadn't said them. "I mean. I wish you didn't have to come back. You know?"

"I know, sweetie. I know. I hate this."

"Are they going to be okay?" Skylar bit her lip.

"Amelia says she's very hopeful about our mom. Joely's not doing as well. All we can do is pray she stabilizes, and then the doctors can figure out more."

"They won't let me go see them."

"Do you want to?"

She shrugged. "I don't know. Yeah, kind of. Like I should tell them to get better myself. Mrs. Crockett—your mom, I mean, she's always been cool to me. But my mom says it's best if no kids are there."

"Skylar, honey, if you want to go, you tell me. I'll take you. You're not a kid. But you don't have to, either. It's not very much fun to see them. They got pretty badly hurt."

"My dad said they…" She stopped and shook her head.

"They what?"

"Miss Joely especially doesn't look like herself."

Tears pricked Harper's eyes, but she held them at bay. All the excitement over Asta had faded from Skylar's features, replaced by sadness and worry that she'd say something to get herself in trouble. Harper wasn't about to let Skylar think she'd made anyone cry.

"She doesn't. She looks very beaten up. And she needs all the good thoughts and prayers she can get. You tell me anytime what you want to do."

"Okay."

"Come on. I want to see my grandma. Is she still up?"

"She's waiting for you. And I'm supposed to go home now that you're here."

"Oh." Harper looked at her watch. "It's only eight thirty. What if I call your mom and ask if you can stay? I want to ask you something."

The girl's eyes brightened. She glanced from Harper to Cole, flushed a little—so the crush hadn't diminished—and nodded. "Okay. What do you want to ask?

"Let me get my stuff put away and give Grandma Sadie a kiss hello, then we'll talk."

Chapter Thirteen

SOMEONE HAD BEEN working overtime in the kitchen. The room gleamed like one of Amelia's ORs. And the cookie jar, which had never been empty when they'd all been kids, was filled to rim with some kind of amazing chocolate shortbread something. Chili simmered in a Crock-Pot, and bowls of creamy cheddar cheese and thick sour cream were covered and waiting in the refrigerator.

"I wish we'd known about this," Harper groaned, as she lifted the lid on the aromatic chili. "Who's the wonderful elf that did all this?"

"Grandma Sadie and my mom," Skylar said.

"You want some?" Harper asked as she got out mugs for coffee.

"No. I ate some earlier." She sat at an empty spot at the kitchen table. "Oh, but, thank you."

The manners she'd been drilled in again. Cole set a glass of milk and the cookie jar in front of her.

"Eat up," he said. "Get your strength for Harpo's grilling."

The teen frowned. "About what?"

"Stop teasing her." Harper admonished Cole. "There's no grilling. I want to talk to you about your art. I've been thinking about it ever since I was here last month."

"Really?" Skylar picked up a thick, rectangular cookie as if this were no big deal, but her hands shook. "I've been drawing as much as I can. Cole showed me pictures of your paintings. They're amazing."

"Thank you, sweetie, that means a lot. What I really want to know is if you ever asked your mom about that art show and competition that's coming up in two weeks."

She looked genuinely surprised. "You remember that?"

"I do."

Her features closed up. "I told her about it. She barely paid attention. She said she'd heard about it, and it was only a fund-raiser for the public school district. It's not something she wants to support—didn't I tell you that's how she'd be? I'm pretty sure she thinks public schools are where the devil teaches or something."

"I doubt she thinks that." Harper reined in a smile. "She wants to make sure about the quality of what you and your brothers are learning that's all."

"Well she's not a good art teacher, I'll tell you that. She lets me get art books and books on photography from the library, but she thinks that's all I need. I have a friend, Christy, who goes to our church, but she's in the regular middle school. They have painting class, and drawing class, and even a pottery class for art. Our co-op for homeschooling has an art class or art activity once a month. It's completely lame."

From the way Skylar's voice ramped up in volume and frustration, Harper knew she'd pulled a cork out of a dam. Her heart went out to the teen again.

"It sounds frustrating. But I don't see why the people running this competition wouldn't let some students from outside the public school join. It's more money for them."

"My mom says the co-op needs her money, and she'd rather spend it there. She already pays taxes to the school district."

A tidal wave of sympathetic frustration rushed over Harper. How many times had she heard her father complain about the cost of materials for her extra-curricular art classes because he'd "already paid taxes, so why don't the schools use their money with more discretion if they were going to offer these kinds of courses?"

She'd hated that argument. She still hated it.

At least someone was trying to raise money to help fund the arts. School districts all over the country—certainly in Chicago—were struggling to hang on to any art and music programs.

"Do you have anything you would want to put into the exhibit if you could enter?" she asked.

Skylar sat back in her chair and bit her lip in sudden uncertainty. "I don't know. I didn't let myself think about it."

"If I talk to your mom, *will* you think about it?"

"Uh, yeah. But I don't have anything framed or with a mat on it even."

"That's pretty easy to fix. I'll bet the rules will say what kind of finishing you have to do."

"It would be cool to have my picture hanging in the VA center."

That confident wish told Harper all she needed to know. Deep inside, Skylar thought maybe she was good, and that was all any artist needed. The feeling wouldn't always be there—in fact, most of the time it would be replaced by towering doubt. But like with faith, all a person needed was a mustard seed's worth of belief in herself.

"Give me a couple of days, okay? Things are crazy here—I'll talk to your mom as soon as I can."

"She won't say yes." Skylar's dejected face proved she believed the verdict had already come down. "But I can't believe you're willing to ask her. It's…thanks."

"Don't be so pessimistic." Harper smiled. "This is a good little battle for us to take on. It'll keep our minds off of the bad things."

She didn't let herself think that if the worst happened, this whole conversation would be moot.

THAT THOUGHT HIT at two o'clock in the morning when Harper's eyes flew open in the wake of a nightmare that left her gasping and certain her sister had died in the horrible crash. She thrashed in her covers for a few seconds before coming fully awake with a pounding heart.

"Keep her safe. Keep her safe. Please, please keep her safe." She repeated the prayer like a mantra until her pulse calmed and she could make herself remember that a nightmare wasn't a prophecy. She buried her head in her pillow, letting the ghostly remnants of the dream fade.

She might have succeeded in forcing herself back to sleep but for the faint sounds of movement in the house below. Curious, she flipped to her back and listened. The slight squeaking of hinges, a drawer rolling out, and definitely footsteps, sent her swinging out of bed.

She slipped on her favorite pair of woolen Haflinger shoes and threw a sweatshirt over her pajama top. The weather had been unseasonably cool in Chicago, and now she knew it was because they'd been getting blasts of Wyoming's early chilled September air. She shivered and grabbed the extra quilt off her bed to wrap around herself. The person downstairs maybe didn't want company, but she worried it might be her grandmother, unable to sleep. Not that their super-matriarch couldn't fend for herself, but she was ninety-four.

The comfort of tiptoeing through her house, following the dim light from the kitchen, drove the last of her dream away. She'd lived in more apartments, with more different roommates, in more different states than she could count. But none of her houses, apartments, or shared living spaces in the past ten years had replaced the home Paradise and Rosecroft still were. The insight surprised her.

The sight of Cole in the kitchen surprised her more.

He stood at the stove, stirring something in a pan, his plaid sleep pants not so baggy she couldn't get an appreciation for his strong butt muscles and bare feet. A box of hot chocolate mix sat on the counter beside him. She smiled.

"Want a little peppermint schnapps to go with that stuff?"

He started slightly and turned, his slow grin turning her sleep-deprived joints to something soft and weak like Play-Doh. She swore his hair didn't look a whole lot more disheveled in the middle of the night than it did during the day. It gave him even more of the rakish appeal that had been affecting her cool so strongly in the past weeks.

"Is that your remedy, alcohol?"

"Remedy for what?"

He looked a little sheepish. "Kinda had a nightmare. Poor Coping Skills R Us."

"Oh, hardly. I'm sorry, Cole. My dream wasn't so hot either."

"Then maybe schnapps is the answer."

"Nah. Virgin hot chocolate is good enough for me."

"There are so many, many places I want to go with that line."

Her use of the line had been half purposeful. She wrapped her quilt more tightly around her shoulders and shot him an evil smirk. "Typical. Stupid boy humor again. But in the interest of full disclosure—since we've kissed and all—if I'd meant a drink *for* virgins, I'd have to pass."

"Not me. This boy is pure as little lamb's wool."

"Oh, kill me now." She laughed.

"Never. I've chosen you to teach me the ways between a man and a woman."

Her heart pounded up into her throat. "You really don't want that," she said. "The things I know might scare you."

The words didn't feel quite as funny as she'd intended. Suddenly she'd reminded herself of the all the bad things he didn't know about her past.

"I don't think a little bitty thing like you scares me much."

The unexpected touch of his hands on her shoulders sent ripples of pleasure cascading for her fingertips and toes and the tips of her ears. She shrugged into his hands.

He pushed back the quilt and drew her into his arms. "This isn't a very romantic way to say the words 'I want to start something with you,' but they and hot chocolate are all I have." He kissed her slowly and then turned back to the stove, dumped two packages of the mix into each of two mugs and added the water he'd boiled. He handed her a mug and added a spoon. "Here, a virgin drink for a new start." She stirred the cocoa numbly. "Harper, you have to notice, too, that whatever this new thing is between us feels like way more than just something."

Warmth flowed through her stomach and her heart before she'd taken a single drink of the chocolate.

"Yeah," she said quietly. "Doesn't mean I know what it is, or if it's okay."

He grinned but didn't touch her. She tingled inside anyway and sipped the chocolate.

"Potent stuff here, cowboy. I saw how much mix you put in here."

"Don't question expertise. I've been drinking this stuff since before you were born."

"I didn't say it was bad. I learned this was the way to go in a lot of cold, basement apartments over the years."

"I think I'd like to hear about Harper Lee Crockett: The Lost Years."

"No. Really. They aren't anything to write home about. Which is probably why I rarely did."

She led the way into the living room, carrying the quilt and her mug. She set the blanket on the back of the overstuffed sofa, and then put coasters on the glass-topped coffee table. Cole settled into one end of the sofa and held out an arm. Gratefully, she snuggled beside him and hugged her mug between her palms.

"Harper Lee," he said. "Why did your parents name you after her? And why don't I know this?"

"Because my mother would not let Dad name me Scout from the book, so he named me after the author. He said it was his favorite book of all time. And I never talked about my name at all when I was a kid. I hated people asking me if I'd read the book, if I liked the book, if I'd ever met Harper Lee, if I'd ever written to her. Would you believe, I didn't read *To Kill a Mockingbird* until I was twenty-five?"

"Seriously? You didn't have to read it in school?"

She shook her head. "No. I'm glad, though. I wouldn't have appreciated it then. On any level. I was too pie in the sky for such a weighty subject."

"And what did you think once you read it?"

"I was blown away. I think I cried for two days after finishing it. But now I never, ever tell people it's my favorite book because they all say, 'oh, isn't that sweet?' I'm a walking cliché. But it is my favorite book."

"Another thing you have in common with your dad."

"Another? Maybe the only."

"Are you kidding? You're so much like him it's eerie sometimes."

She pulled away, slightly wounded, and looked at him critically. "That's not funny."

"Come on. Why do you think you used to butt heads so often? You're opinionated, but you know exactly why you hold those opinions. He was very much that way. You love beauty. Your appreciation of it comes out in your painting. His came out in weirder ways—his chicken coop and his exacting office décor. The way he directed the orientation of this whole house so he could see the view. He had to find acceptably macho ways to express it, but he liked beautiful things."

"Then he must have thought my art was anything but beautiful."

"He was always afraid he'd lose you if he encouraged things that would take you from the ranch."

"Yeah, how'd that work out for him?"

"Not well. He was an idiot about that. But don't think he didn't love you. He talked about all his daughters the last three years—probably before that, too, I didn't work for him then."

She settled back into the crook of Cole's arm and sipped the chocolate.

"You said you needed a year to buy back the Double Diamond. If we keep Paradise, is it really an option?"

"Getting the ranch back into the Wainwright name is what's driven me since we sold it, I guess, but sometimes it seems a little hopeless. Big loans for little guys like me are pretty much impossible. My only strategy is to be debt-free, build a strong four-year work history, and have a decent down payment. That part is up to the famous Crockett sisters now. I know what your father set as the selling price—it may be more reasonable than what you six will need."

"What makes you think we'll *need* any particular amount? The biggest thing for you is the same thing it is for us—can you make the ranch viable even if you can afford to buy it back? We're all in the same leaky lifeboat here."

"Which is why it sometimes feels hopeless."

Harper reached around him to set her mug down and rested her cheek against the soft, white V-neck T-shirt that constituted his pajama top. "I don't like to think of you feeling hopeless. You've always been unflappable. How can I be freaked out about things if you already are?"

His chuckle vibrated sexily beneath her head. "There's a difference between feeling down and being freaked out. It's not like we're talking spiders here. I won't die if I can't buy a ranch."

Laughter, welcome and healing, spilled from her, and she clung to him even harder. "You have to be the only person on the face of the planet who would compare running into spiders to losing a family ranch and have the spider end up as the worse outcome. Who tortured you with spiders when you were in your formative years?"

"I don't know. I was born with a fear so deathly I can't look at a realistic picture. You know that kid's song about the spider in the water spout?"

Harper giggled again, twisted in his arms and made the eensy-weensy spider with her fingers. He forced her fingers apart.

"Terrifying," he said. "You can't even kill a spider with a flood. It doesn't get any worse."

"*The Lord of the Rings* must have given you nightmares for a year. Oooh and Harry Potter..."

"Do you know people show those movies to children?" He wrapped her tightly again. "You'd better do something to atone for dredging up all these horror images."

"Hey, buddy, if *you're* not afraid of little old me, I doubt a seven-foot spider would pay me any attention at all. I'll throw shoes at it, but you might have to run and get Grandma Sadie to help, too."

"And Kelly, and Leif, and probably Skylar." He yawned and pulled her closer yet, dragging the quilt off the back of the couch and wrapping it around them both. "My little burrito. No more talk of spiders. I'm trying to maintain the illusion of the unruffleable super hero."

"Not Spiderman, I'm guessing."

"He wouldn't even be my friend."

Silence enveloped them along with the warmth from the quilt, and Harper tried not to let herself lapse back into guilt. Cole was fine with this. He claimed Mia should be, too. Harper wanted the same freedom.

"Doesn't this feel even a little bit weird to you?" she asked, feeling for emotional footing.

"No. This feels right for the first time in a very long while. It's kind of chick flick romantic, I'd think. The start of a love affair. Aren't you going to get all mushy about it?"

"No." She pushed herself away again. "I can't do this if I look at it as a love affair. I'm not stealing you from anyone. I won't—"

"Harpo!" He grasped her upper arms. "Since when does a love affair have to be something illicit? My father had a love affair with my mother until the day she died. And your mother and father were the same. Give us a break here."

"But...love? It's a scary word."

"That's enough." He threw off the quilt and turned on her. With a serious light in his eyes that startled her, he pushed her backward onto the couch cushions and covered her with himself. Once he'd stretched fully atop her, he pulled the quilt up as well. "I have loved you as a friend for as long as I can remember. Is it weird that my body and my head can no longer see the tomboy I used to think of as my coolest buddy? No, it's a miracle. Stop throwing up roadblocks and reasons we shouldn't try this. Love isn't scary, Harper. It's an adventure—we've had a lot of them. Let's take another one and see where we end up."

As always, he freed her by tearing through the constraints she put on herself as if they were no more than paper.

"Okay. You're right."

She kissed him—her idea, her initiation, her excitement—and dragged the quilt over their heads to make a hot cocoon where all she could do was feel in the dark. He tasted of chocolate and smelled like soap and sheets and heat. He let her play against his mouth with her lips, biting the soft skin lightly, dotting kisses around his face, seeking out his tongue. But he only allowed her to maintain control for those first few moments of exploration before he pulled away and started his own assault. Trills and shivers of excitement radiated from her mouth to her stomach as he delved with his tongue, turning the kiss from exploration into warm, wet plunder.

He found her neck, the skin behind her ear, and the hollow of her throat. Trills turned to full-fledged waves of desire, twining down her body and building, layering her in heat. Awareness of their thin night clothing, the lack of any barriers but two layers of cloth between her suddenly aching body and his hardening one, hit her like a sledgehammer. It would take nothing to turn this into much more than the start of an adventure. The equivalent to hitting Class Five white water was two sets of sleep pants away.

"Cole," she whispered, the words thick.

"Shhh. Trust me."

"Fine, but I don't trust me."

"Good." He laughed softly against the hollow where her neck met her shoulder. "It'll make me look like a hero when I don't take advantage of that."

She couldn't help but giggle.

"Doesn't mean I'm a Boy Scout kind of hero, though," he continued. "I lied about that virgin hot chocolate."

"Oh dear, really?" She held his head and groaned as he tickled the spot behind her ear with tiny nips of his teeth and nibbles from his lips. A million mini electric shocks burst through her body. "So I don't need to teach you how it is between a man and a woman?"

"I think we're both pretty capable."

He pushed himself down her body and lifted the hem of her pajama tank top to expose her navel. With soft kisses, more tiny scrapes of his teeth, and moist strokes of his tongue, he drove her senseless by working his way up the skin of her stomach to her breastbone and to the sensitive flesh of her left breast. He spanned her waist with his hands, slipped them beneath her and slid up her spine to cradle her back. Gently, he lifted her upper body to his kiss.

The tip of his tongue flicked against her nipple. Arching in pleasure, she bit her lip over a groan, conscious, barely, of her grandmother's bedroom on the far end of this main floor.

"I've been imagining this for far too long," he said.

Every inch of skin flushed with erotic pleasure at the idea of him picturing her body. "You thought about this?"

"Imagination is a guy's best friend. Girls have the advantage. Unless we're on a beach, you can see a lot more of us than we can of you."

"Like during spider attacks." She wriggled beneath him, loosening his hold and scooting downward until she could grasp his hips and yank them to her. There might as well have been nothing between his long, hard erection and her body. With a sharp sigh she nestled him against her and wrapped her legs around him. "I've relived that half-striptease you did for me too many times to count."

"What? Girls are shallow, too?"

"Oh yeah."

She rocked beneath him, knowing it was putting a match to tinder but unable to stop herself. He slid along the perfect sweet spot and groaned right over her whimper of delight.

"I told you I couldn't trust myself," she said.

"You don't have to. I've got this."

She closed her eyes and gave up the fight with herself. "Trust me," he'd said. She was beyond being able to do anything else.

Two glorious minutes later she knew she'd been wrong to trust anything. Her body poised at the moment of no return and there was no way to back away from the cliff.

He coaxed her with a whisper. "Sweetheart, let go."

She crashed into her orgasm at the mere vibration of his words in her ears. Wave after wave buffeted her, but she was safe in his embrace and the wildness couldn't break their contact. She rode the slowly undulating crests time after time until finally, slowly Cole brought her to the end of the ride's crazy heat.

"See, I told you I couldn't trust you."

"I'm sorry," he replied.

He kissed her on the eyebrows and on the nose. Languid heaviness spread through her limbs, and all she felt were his arm beneath her neck, his hand on her cheek, and her knee between his thighs.

"What about you?" she asked dopily. "Your turn?"

"In a minute. I'm not going anywhere."

"I don't think you're a real cowboy. A real cowboy wouldn't be this patient."

"It's the nice guy alter ego, remember?"

"I do. But now I want the bad cowboy."

"I'll see if I can find him for you."

"Git along little doggie." She mumbled the words, and her eyes felt incredibly heavy. "Although that doggie's not really very little."

"Anyone ever tell you, you're very strange?"

The world softened, and the dark deepened and she murmured something in return but she knew Cole was too far away to hear her.

Chapter Fourteen

"WELL, THIS IS COZY."

That was Mia. How strange. Cole heard her voice as if it came through a wall. No, a quilt. He ignored it. And was jolted from sleep by a screech.

Okay, that was Harper. He opened his eyes as she scrambled out of his sleepy hold.

"Mia! I'm so sorry. We couldn't sleep and got talking and we must have—"

"Good Lord, Harper, quit babbling." Mia snapped. "You're a grown woman. You can do whatever you want."

"But this has to look like—"

"Like you two slept together? Yeah."

"But we didn't…" Harper glared first at him and then at her sister.

"Um, well, we kind of did."

He supposed his first words were less than politically correct under the circumstances, but he grinned anyway, wanting to soften Harper's discomfort. The pain in her face, however, proved her distress was real. And he did have to admit, Mia didn't exactly look happy either.

Which confused him, too.

"Mia, I should have talked to you first," Harper said.

"Look." Mia sank into the armchair across from the sofa. "I'm telling you right now, I don't care what you did or didn't do. I'm too tired to care. I'm too annoyed to care. I'm too frustrated to care. I want to go take a shower and crawl into bed for a few hours before I go back to the hospital. But I need to update you first."

Cole handed Harper the quilt they'd both been wrapped in, and she bundled herself in it then started to stand. He pulled her back down. She wasn't going to run away from him because of a little awkwardness. He wasn't convinced Mia's mood had anything to do with them anyway. Acting guilty would only make everything worse. Harper sat back down but kept her hands clutched inside the quilt.

"How are they?" she asked.

"It was a long night for Joely. She suffered three seizures, and about all I can say is the last one was less severe. She'd been quiet for three hours when I left. It's impossible to tell yet whether this is part of the healing process or if there's permanent injury. She has no reflexes in the crushed left leg, but there are normal reactions in all her other limbs. The contusions in her brain are located behind the ocular orbit—her eye socket—and behind the frontal lobe. It doesn't look like there's severe damage to the frontal lobe itself, which is good. But there is a lot of swelling in the brain and she's getting a lot of steroidal meds to counteract it."

Cole's heart went out to both sisters. Mia recited the facts like a computer, barely remembering to translate the medical terms. Harper held her blanket-covered fists against her mouth, eyes dull and wide.

"Do they think she'll be okay in the long run, though?" he asked.

"The next twenty-four hours will tell," she said. "If the swelling starts to recede and the seizures stop, then they can start to be very cautiously optimistic, but for now it's just waiting."

"Not a lot of good news," Cole said, and rubbed Harper's back through the quilt.

"Well, there is where Mom is concerned. She woke up about five this morning.

"Oh, thank God." Harper covered her eyes briefly with her hands, and her shoulders heaved with one grateful sob. Cole rubbed harder.

"In her case, the swelling in her brain has gone down, and her vitals have stabilized. She's in quite a bit of pain, so they're dosing her up pretty heavily right now, but I was able to talk to her for about half an hour. She doesn't remember the accident, but she remembers everything up to it, as far as I can tell—the trip and that they had Joely's horse in the trailer. She's devastated about the horse, and about Joely, of course, so we're not going into too much detail. All Mom really knows is that Joely isn't awake yet."

"I'm glad you were there," Harper said. "Truly. I wouldn't have understood anything going on. You could help Mom understand."

Mia rubbed her eyes and didn't say anything at first. "I don't know," she said. "I probably didn't make any friends. I demanded a lot of information and got a few people out of bed that won't soon forget. There's one patient advocate who put me on his shit list almost right away."

"Patient advocate?" Harper asked.

"He's an ex-military liaison whose job it is to coordinate between the doctors and the patient and the family. Well, I'm both a doctor and family, but he didn't for one minute care to treat me like a medical person. I'm not a hospitalist doc at the VA, so I have no standing to request specific treatments. And as a family member who isn't her husband, I'm entitled to medical updates, but not to personal information such as insurance status or her medical history. Of course, I wouldn't for a minute overstep my bounds medically; that would be unethical because I'm not on staff and not Mother's physician. But I do understand what's going on, and I demanded to be in on the consultations. This dude pretty much escorted me out of two meetings. So I went over his head."

"Did it help?" Harper asked.

A weird, satisfied smile flitted across Mia's lips. "I got private meetings with the doctors at six o'clock this morning. Let's say, I wouldn't want to be crossing the street when Lieutenant Liaison drove by."

"See?" Harper actually giggled. "I told you I was glad it was you."

"If they let me back in later this afternoon, I'll know I didn't cause us any permanent damage." At that she rose.

"That's the story as much as I know it. I really do need to sleep, though. I'll be less adversarial after a nap."

"I'll go up this morning, and I'll take the overnight shift," Harper said.

"There'll be plenty of us here."

Amelia turned for the stairs. Harper met Cole's eyes, and the misery in her face broke his heart. He stroked her hair and kissed her temple. "It's okay," he said. "She's tired."

"Mia!" She called after her sister. "Thank you."

"It's what I do," she said as she kept walking. "Make waves."

"I'm sorry you found us like this. We really couldn't sleep."

Amelia turned back then, a frozen smile on her face. "I told you. Don't worry. For crying out loud, you two are adorable together."

When she'd disappeared up the stairs to the bedrooms, Cole gathered Harper into his arms. He tried to get her to look at him, but she held herself stiff.

"You lied," she said.

"About?"

"She's mad at me. This isn't okay. It's against the sister code; I told you that."

"You can't help you who love and don't love," he said. "I don't love Amelia. She doesn't love me. How is anything you or I decide to do against any sister code?"

"You're a man. You wouldn't begin to understand."

"Well, I sure do admit that outright."

Her hands flew, soft and desperate, to his cheeks. Her eyes beseeched him to understand. "I slept with you last night, and it was wonderful."

He grinned, but his relief ebbed when she pressed her palms against his chest and pushed him firmly away.

"Come on, Harper."

"But it can't happen again. Not until I talk to Mia."

"About what?" Frustration rose like heat.

"It's mixed up in our heads, too, believe me. But we aren't like guys. We don't want you comparing us, even if you never mean to do it. There's a sort of eeew factor between sisters."

That did it. He stood and stared down at her. "An 'eeew factor'? Excuse me? That's about as insulted as I've ever felt."

"No, no. It has nothing to do with you. It's between us—Mia and me."

He blew his breath out in a hard sigh. "Fine. I've told you I don't understand this, but it's apparently real. You're right, she was pissed. So you two work this out however you have to."

With no apology he left the room. He truly did not understand this "code," at least not the way she'd described it. Compare sisters? He growled in annoyance, stopped, and stomped back into the living room.

"For your information, there is no comparison between you and your sister. Even if there were anything *to* compare, it wouldn't happen. I've never felt this way about any other woman—and if you think that's an easy thing for a man to say outside some romance novel, you're wrong. So take your…your 'eeew factor' and sleep with that next time."

Harper's mouth dropped open. He turned again and this time made it all the way out of the room.

"YOU LOOK LIKE you could use a friend. Or a dog. Or a good nap."

Harper lifted her head and met Melanie's smiling hazel eyes.

"Or all three," she replied, and stood from the recliner in her mother's hospital room.

Arching her back, she yawned, gave her eyes a hard rub, and looked at her mother sleeping peacefully. It had been so good to reach for a hug earlier and have her return it. She'd been awake a few times in the three hours Harper had been with her. Each time she stayed awake longer and sounded a little stronger.

"There's no change in Joely's room," Melanie said, her soft Southern accent somehow making the unwelcome words easier to take. "But she hasn't had a seizure in the past hour since I got here. It's been about eight hours now, they said."

"Little miracles, one at a time," Harper said.

"Let's go get some coffee, or maybe even some lunch. They'll sleep."

Harper checked her watch—one thirty. Coffee sounded good. Lunch was probably necessary but sounded awful. "Sure," she said. "I could use a walk."

"I already got us a pager from the nurse's station. If anything happens, they'll let us know."

The hospital cafeteria had a surprisingly excellent reputation. The scents from behind the long counter offering multiple dishes cooked and created on the spot, nearly awakened Harper's appetite. She ended up with a bowl of Italian wedding soup and a half a grilled cheese sandwich. Melanie ordered a BLT and chips.

"What are the kids doing for school today?" Harper asked when they'd found a table by the large picture window. "You're taking a lot of time to help us out, Mel. We don't know how to thank you."

"There's nothing to thank me for. Over the years your family has come to our aid plenty of times. I told you, you all are family. I set out lessons, and Skylar will help Aiden."

"She's a bright girl. Very talented," Harper said. "I feel a little bond with Skylar."

"She talks a lot about you, too."

"Could I ask you a few questions about her? You can tell me to mind my own business any time."

Melanie laughed. "Ask anything you like. Skylar is an open book written in a foreign language. You'll be lucky if I can answer any questions about her."

Harper laughed. Melanie's words proved she knew her daughter better than anyone.

"Do you know what a good artist she is?"

"I know she loves to draw. I have no artistic ability, so I figure I'm prejudiced when she shows me her drawings and I like them. It seems an awfully big compliment for you to say she's got talent."

"Her talent is raw, but it's there. I know she takes a lot of photos, too. I haven't seen her photography work, but I'll bet she has a good eye."

"Now there's a hobby that's been a little too expensive for my tastes. She manages to earn the money to have her film developed, but I wish she'd save for a digital camera that would cost less in the long run."

Harper nodded sympathetically. "I hear you. But in all honesty, it's true there are things you can do with film that you can't with digital. Once you get hooked on it…"

"So I hear all the time." Melanie sighed. "She lobbies on a regular basis for a darkroom. That's definitely not in the budget."

"That's okay. She's doing fine with the process she has. She's still figuring out what she wants to do anyway. A darkroom might be premature."

"Thanks. Will you tell her that?"

"I will." Harper agreed. "Meanwhile, I know a couple easier things she wants. She'd love to have access to some art classes. Did you know that she'd love to go to a public school? Has she ever talked about it?"

"Only once a day. Sometimes once an hour when she's really angry with me. But, that's why we take part in the homeschooling co-op. It gives her a few other influences besides me."

"So, going to a public school isn't an option in your mind?"

She expected defensiveness—especially after hearing Skylar's assessment of her mother's view on the evils of public school. And she'd seen firsthand how strict Melanie could be. Instead, Melanie shrugged.

"I've told all the kids that once they get to high school, they can choose depending on how they're doing and how much trust they've built. There comes a point at which they have to learn to deal with the world. Skylar isn't there yet." She laughed. "I can't let her go to town without her coming home with a stray dog. What will she come home with if I let her into the world of middle school? Anything from a boy to a copy of *Playgirl*."

"Given those two options, a boy her own age might not be such a bad choice."

"Bite your tongue. I hope she stays moony-eyed over Cole Wainwright."

Harper's heart skipped a beat. She'd wanted to be furious with Cole Wainwright for being so dense and unsympathetic that morning. But with the hot memory of what they'd shared, she couldn't possibly stay angry. In fact, she felt a little bereft on his behalf for leaving him unsated and robbing her of watching his pleasure. And then he'd gone and thrown his last dang zinger at her. "I've never felt this way about a woman before."

Who could resist a line like that?

And yet, she had to.

"She's not super subtle about Cole, is she?" Harper asked.

"Thank goodness he's the man he is. I trust him completely."

Harper's heart warmed further. What sorts of amazing things must he have done to inspire such confidence in an overprotective mother like Melanie?

"He's a good guy. A younger version would keep your daughter safe, that's for sure."

"Let me know if you find one of those." Melanie laughed.

"Boys and crushes aside, did Skylar tell you about the art festival and competition in two weeks?"

"She mentioned it. It looks like it's mostly for public school kids, and all the fund-raising goes *to* the school district. That would fly in the face of the reason I keep my kids homeschooled. I pay taxes already to a district I don't use."

Harper wanted to groan in frustration. There was nothing but Melanie's own choice dictating that she not use the school district.

"So, it's not the event itself you object to?"

"No. But it is expensive. It's only five dollars to attend the show, but it's fifty to enter it. The district is subsidizing part of the entry fees, but they wouldn't for Skylar or the two other kids she's got riled up about going."

"So they *would* let the kids enter?"

"I don't know for sure, but I expect so—more money for them."

"Okay, Mel, I'm about to overstep my bounds, but if they would allow her to enter, and if you'd consider allowing her to enter, I'd like to pay Skylar's entry fee."

"No, I couldn't let you do that."

"Look, here's the thing. I would have gone crazy without my high school art teacher, Mrs. Hodges, encouraging me. And now I have a wonderful woman back in Chicago who's commissioned quite a few pieces of my work and is mentoring my career because she believes in the value of art in the world. I'm not suggesting Skylar is going to make art her living, but I can pay the luck I've had forward. It's one little opportunity for her. And who are these other two students?"

Melanie lost herself in thought for several long moments. Her face gave nothing of her feelings away. When she looked back at Harper, it was with stern resolution.

"I don't know how I feel about supporting the schools. We do art projects in the co-op, and Skylar is always involved in those. I'm not sure why that isn't enough." Harper started to protest, but Melanie held up her hand. "I know it isn't, and I can't preach to my kids that they should explore all their options if I don't let them do it."

"I like that." Harper smiled.

"No disrespect intended, Harper, but I don't want Skylar to get the idea she can forgo other subjects because she has a passion for art. You're getting a break with your paintings, but that doesn't happen very often. I hope you won't encourage her to follow her heart at this young age. She still needs guidance."

"Of course she does." Harper swallowed the small bubble of resentment that rose at Melanie's insinuation, but she tried to understand. The world was a scary place, and truly, Harper didn't want Skylar to go through some of the fires she'd endured on her way to the start of success. "She also needs to explore what she loves best, so she doesn't resent the rest. I think that's what happened to me. Let's make this art show a reward for her doing well in school. I'd be honored if you'd let me help."

Melanie shook her head, trying to look stern. "You and your dad. You could argue successfully before the Supreme Court."

She and her dad again. It was beginning to feel like the gods were trying to torture her with these comparisons. "Maybe so."

"All right, here's the deal. If you promise to keep this low-key, I'll okay the activity if the school district allows it."

"You're the greatest, Mel." Harper covered Melanie's hands. "Skylar will be really happy."

"Skylar." Melanie shook her head again. "Maybe I'm hoping this will serve to cure some of her apathy and a little of her anger. She's not a bad kid, but some days I feel like I'm losing her."

"She's growing up. I hear it's hard on parents."

"Just wait. You'll have one soon enough, and you'll see how painfully right you are."

Have a child of her own? Harper held in a snort. Now there was a scary thought for the world. "You know what, Super Mom? I'll take your word for it."

Chapter Fifteen

COLE PULLED HIS old, indestructible Range Rover into a diagonal parking spot in front of Dottie's Bistro—the oldest and most beloved of Wolf Paw Pass's cafés—and rubbed his eyes. This meeting had originally been set up for Joely and her mother, but in light of the accident, Leif and Bjorn had agreed he was the most knowledgeable person to talk with Baumgartner and Pearce from Mountain Pacific about their preliminary surveys of Paradise land.

Cole didn't want anything to do with it.

They hadn't told Harper about the meeting, a decision Cole thought wrong-headed. Mia had made that decision. It was better, she'd said, to go to Harper with all the facts rather than risk getting her philosophical dander up before the facts were known.

Cole disagreed. She shouldn't be kept out of any planning, even if to avert a battle, and he didn't like being in the middle of the sisters' duel. Nonetheless, here he was, the designated lackey. Harper would undoubtedly see this as him not keeping his promise again, no matter how reluctantly he was performing the task.

Once he'd located the oil company reps in the homey, cabin-like restaurant, Cole watched Magdalen Pearce rise from her chair at an oil-cloth covered table and approach him like an exuberant realtor greeting a potential buyer. He nearly walked away. Instead he gritted his teeth and took her handshake. It rivaled that of a strong marine.

"Mr. Wainwright. Cole," she said. "I'm glad you're here despite all the tragedy of the last two days. How are Mrs. Crockett and her daughter doing?"

"Nice of you to ask," he said, warming slightly. "Mrs. Crockett is improving. Joely is in very critical condition and hasn't regained consciousness since the accident."

"I'm so very sorry."

"My condolences and good thoughts, too." Brian Baumgartner stood behind his boss and offered his hand as well. "We hope for full recoveries for both of them."

"Thank you."

"Sit, please," Magdalen said. "We have some exciting news to share with you."

Cole took a seat between the two and removed the Stetson he'd worn in hopes of looking the part of Paradise Ranch's representative. "You do remember this is strictly an informational meeting," he said. "I'm not authorized to make any decisions today. The family members will do that."

"Of course," Brian said. "We completely understand. This is a huge undertaking and nothing to be taken lightly."

He began the show and tell without further extraneous chit-chat by pulling two paper rolls from a briefcase beside his chair. He handed one to Magdalen and rolled the other out on the table. Cole was startled to see a detailed aerial photograph of Paradise Ranch, a little like an unnerving spy photo, covered with contour lines and symbols he couldn't decipher.

"This is a map of the land area we chose our survey sites from. The shaded areas indicate the areas we felt were worth exploring based on geological features and below surface radar. As you can see, coming up from the south, we believed there was a lot of potential."

"Impressive," Cole said.

The next map Brian laid out was actually a sheaf of perhaps ten maps that were far more colorful than the aerial photo. Large blocks of red, green, and yellow covered the map topography.

"These maps are the results of what's known as a Play Fairway Analysis. They're common risk segment maps or what we sometimes nickname traffic light maps because of the colors. In this case, what you need to know is that the green sections indicate a high potential for geological structures that mark oil pockets and a low risk of failure if we explore further. Red indicates a higher risk that exploration will be unfruitful. Yellow is a medium risk. As you can see, we have a lot of green on these maps."

What followed for the next hour was a presentation on the areas of Paradise where Mountain Pacific wanted to focus further exploration. The next step involved minor drilling and the building of a temporary service road at the south end of the ranch. It also meant that, from the time exploration began, Paradise would receive lease payments for the right to use the land it explored. The ballpark figures they quoted were enough to make Cole catch his breath. And that, they told him, was the tip of the iceberg.

What made his heart sink was that, other than a section in the southernmost part of the ranch, most of the potential lay directly in the valley between the house and the Teton Range—the most beautiful scenery on the ranch, and the area Harper, Kelly, and Joely—his heart sank further—were going to fight for with the most vehemence.

"So, Cole." Magdalen sat back in her chair when they were finished, as satisfied as if she'd served the best Thanksgiving meal ever documented. "What do you think?"

"I'm very impressed with the thoroughness of your report," he said. "But I don't think anything until I talk to the Crockett family."

"Do you feel confident in recommending they move forward?"

"You know, I'm honestly not going to say much more today. What I will promise is that I'll tell them that if they move forward with you, I know you'll be straightforward and honest with them, and that you'd be sincere in your desire to make this an easy experience for them."

He half quoted their own sales pitch, but he had been impressed with their honesty as far as he could assess it. He picked up his hat from the chair next to him and held it on his lap.

"I also promise to talk with them about this as soon as I can, given what's going on. I hope you'll be patient waiting to hear from them. As I told you, some of the family members have concerns, so there'll be a lot to address with them."

"We understand completely. And anytime they want to meet with us themselves, you have them let us know." Magdalen stood with Cole and shook his hand again.

"I will," he said. "Thanks for the good information. It's very helpful."

They all walked out together and parted after more well wishes for Bella and Joely. Cole's head spun with numbers and statistics as he climbed into the Rover and set the large folder filled with copies of all pertinent documents, estimates, and facts on the passenger seat. Suddenly, he dreaded going back to the house. In the first place, he had no idea what configuration of Crockett women he'd find. Kelly was due back from Denver for a few days. Harper could be there. Harper and Amelia could be clawing at each other in the mud for all he knew—and the thought was not remotely enticing.

In the second place, he didn't want to have this discussion about Mountain Pacific. The income potential was phenomenal when viewed in light of Paradise's current financial situation, but emotions about the issue ran high and hot.

He nearly took the road west out of town and headed for the old Double Diamond. He'd only been back to check things a few times in the four and a half weeks since Sam's funeral. The house he'd grown up in wasn't as grand or imposing as Rosecroft, and it didn't have a name, but it brought him some comfort to know it still stood and would be there when he got the title to the land back. It pulled at him now. He could go there, throw a sleeping bag on his old bed, since most of the furniture, minus what his father had taken to furnish his condo in Jackson, still remained. He could pretend he didn't have any obligations to the Crocketts.

He sighed and turned east on the road that led straight to Paradise.

A misnomer today if ever there was one.

HE'D IMAGINED EVERY scenario possible except the one he actually found in the Crockett kitchen. Honest-to-goodness laughter greeted him, and once in the cozy room, he found Harper, Kelly, Melanie, and Skylar hunkered around the table, heads together over a paper in the center, smiling and laughing. The pup, Asta, skittered under and around the table, chair, and human legs, adding a yipping contribution to the sounds her people were making.

"Cole!" Kelly saw him first and jumped from her chair, crossing the room at a trot to give him a welcoming bear hug. "I'm so glad to see you. How are you, handsome?"

"Handsome as ever, glad you noticed. How are you, Kel? I'm at your service, by the way. A greeting like this is worth a lot."

He hugged her tightly and let her go.

"Don't promise service if you aren't going to deliver, Mr. Wainwright." Her serious eyes twinkled.

"Oh, I'll deliver."

"Excellent. I'll let you know when I need you. I like having handsome men in my debt."

"Hmmm," he said. If any one of the sisters could gather a flock of men to do her bidding it was Kelly—probably because she'd never truly play the part of a seductress, and that was a darn attractive quality. "So, ladies, what's going on here?"

Asta discovered him then and jumped at his legs, resting her baby front paws on his shin and wiggling with pathetically hopeful eyes. He took a small step back so she stood on the floor, and when she tried to follow him he knelt and took her head gently in one hand. With the other he pushed lightly in front of her tail.

"Sit, Asta," he said once.

The pup had no idea what he meant and let her butt plop for half a second before she was up wriggling again. Nonetheless, he scooped her into his arms. "Good girl," he crooned while the dog licked his chin and cheeks as if he were the sweetest treat she'd ever found.

He approached the table, finally finding Harper's eyes. His pulse raced ahead of his speech and tongue-tied him for several seconds. The last words they'd shared early that morning hadn't been the kindest, and that had been primarily his fault. How she felt now was anything but obvious.

"Hullo," he said at last.

"Hi," she replied.

Cole put the pup in Skylar's lap. "She's a smart girl. Did you see how she didn't fuss when I made her sit? You can start training her already to behave the way you want her to. She won't remember yet that she should sit before someone pets her, but do it every time and she'll figure it out super quick."

"You know about training dogs?" Skylar asked.

"My dad's hobby was training border collies. I learned from him."

"Can you show me?"

"Sure."

Harper's eyes warmed from impassive brown to hot cocoa rich. "A man of many talents," she said.

"You have no idea."

She granted a smile and sent his insides into a hopeful freefall.

"So, guess what?" Skylar pulled his attention back to her.

"What?"

"Harper talked Mom into letting me enter the art contest. And she went to the high school and got the okay even though I don't go to public school, and then she got me the entry form."

"That's pretty big."

"Look!"

She grabbed the two-sheet form from the table and handed it to him. Asta squirmed to be released and hit the floor running.

The forms were straightforward and 90 percent filled out. "Hey, there's no name and no category, the two most important things. You forget who you are and what you're doing?"

She laughed. "We were talking about what name I should use. I kind of don't want to be Skylar."

"Nice, right?" Melanie said with an exaggerated sigh. "A good Southern family name, and she wants to ditch it."

"Who do you want to be?" Cole asked.

"Sky," she replied.

"That's pretty." He wasn't sure if he was supposed to praise it or not. He was vastly outnumbered here.

"Sky Bluewaters," Kelly said, eliciting a few giggles.

"Sky Pie. Sky Limit," Harper said. "I think we're all a little over tired. These aren't that funny."

"I might have to agree."

"Sky Thorson." Cole set the application back down in front of her. "I'd go with that. Sounds artistic. But, it's up to you. Your whole name is pretty classy, too."

There, that should get him off the diplomatic hook. Skylar looked up at him with some sort of mist or foggy veil in her eyes. She picked up a pen and wrote carefully then handed the application back to Cole.

SKY THORSON

"All right then," he said. "One decision down."

"I don't know what I'm going to enter, though," she said. "I don't have anything I did especially for this that's good enough. I kind of want to paint something new."

"I told her she has notebooks full of beautiful work." Melanie shrugged.

"Or I can enter a photograph," Skylar said. "But I can't decide."

"Can you enter one of each?" he asked.

"You can, but it's expensive."

"That part doesn't matter," Harper said. "Like I said before, if you feel like you have a new idea, work on it. Otherwise, enter something that came from your heart. If you try to plan something you think will win, you'll lose yourself. Art isn't for competitions. Competitions are to highlight art."

Skylar sighed. "Why am I doing this again?"

"Oh no, you don't." Melanie sat back and crossed her arms. "Miss Harper went to bat for you. Don't back out now."

"I'm not backing out." Skylar frowned at her. "I'm just nervous."

"That's completely normal," Cole said.

"I guess. But I wish I could be like those French artists or whatever, who take their paints and sit on the top of a hill somewhere they've never been and paint for hours."

"Haven't you ever done that?" Harper asked.

"My gosh, Harper used to disappear for whole days," Kelly said. "I remember that even from when I was a really little kid. Dad used to get so mad because she missed chores and a few times came home after dark."

"Hah, don't you even think about it." Melanie laughed, but shook her finger at Skylar.

"I bring my sketchbook out," Skylar said. "But I've never brought the paints. You always say they're too expensive to take outside." She looked accusingly at her mother.

"They are. I can see them getting smashed in your saddle bags or dropped and lost. Call me over-frugal."

"I wouldn't lose my *paints* for crying out loud."

"You need a writer's retreat." Kelly nodded emphatically. "Remember, Harper, how you used to make them up for yourself?"

"I did." Harper's eyes took on a faraway look. "When I figured out my Dad got less upset if I planned ahead, I would have my own overnight in one of the range cabins out in the far summer pastures."

"Cool!" Skylar grinned.

"No." Melanie repeated.

"All right," Harper said, straightening as if coming out of a trance. "Leave the entry categories blank for now. It's Wednesday. You have until Friday to decide. And this is one instance where you should decide with your heart, not your head."

"Okay, Skylar." Melanie stood. "We need to go home. I haven't been there since this morning, and it's nearly dinner time. Aiden's been with your dad for the past two hours—we'd better get them out of the barn."

For the first time Skylar scowled. "I had him all day. Can't I go ride before dinner?"

"I suppose. But you have an hour, that's it. Afterward you can entertain your brother or you can make dinner, your choice."

The teen shot a helpless look around the table. When she settled on Cole, she stuck out her lower lip. "Probably a choice between fried liver and boiled tongue. Oh boy."

He sputtered. "You're funny, kid. Go with the liver. I hate food that can taste me back."

"That's so old the last time I heard it I fell off my dinosaur," she said and grinned.

"And the Dead Sea was only sick." Cole wrinkled his nose, indicating he knew the joke stank.

"And God was just a kid."

"Skylar," her mother warned. "Don't cross the line."

The teen rolled her eyes, and Cole bit his lip to keep from saying something irreverent to Melanie. Skylar stood, gave a quiet wave good-bye and followed Melanie toward the door.

"Let me know if you need me at the hospital," Melanie said. "I'm happy to take a shift, anytime."

"Thank you," Harper replied. "You've been a Godsend. I'll call."

Once the Thorsons were gone, Cole sat in Skylar's vacated chair and couldn't resist any longer. "I didn't realize God doesn't have a sense of humor in Melanie's world."

"You don't know that by now?" Harper smiled. "Mel's wonderful. And if you approach her the right way, she's pretty open to things. This contest is proof. But, nope, if you use the name of God, it had better be in a reverent manner."

"Oh, man, I'm in big trouble then—with him, not Melanie."

"He's beyond laughing at me." Harper propped her elbow on the table top and plopped her chin into her palm. "He just pats me on the head and says, 'Oh well.'"

"You, the sweet and thoughtful Crockett sister?" Kelly stood and patted Harper's head. "I thought God used you as a model for his angels. Anyone need more coffee?"

"I'll have some," Cole said over Harper's laughter.

Harper sputtered. "Angels? Yeah. The fallen ones."

"My turn to laugh," Kelly said.

"You clearly missed my formative years."

"Sure. Sex, drugs, rock and roll, and a little crazy artist thrown in. Okay, whatever." Kelly brought Cole a steaming mug of coffee.

Harper smiled, but the uptick in her lips was a hair sluggish. "Enough about me. I want to talk about Skylar."

"What about her?" Kelly asked. "She's excited about this. You did a great thing talking Melanie into letting her enter."

"That was easy," she said. "And that should be the end of it, I know. But all that talk about my old retreats gave me an idea. Assuming everything stays the same or improves with Mom and Joely, what if I took her and maybe her two friends from the homeschool co-op on a retreat? Maybe they can all talk about what they want to enter and what it means to enter, and maybe I can turn it into part art history lesson and part practical lab—let them find secluded places to work."

"Where would you take them?" Cole asked.

She looked straight at him.

"I hoped maybe you'd let us use your house. None of them has been there—maybe Skylar, I don't know. There are so many beautiful views to paint. We could ride over on Friday morning and come back Sunday."

"There's not much in the house," Cole said. "But there are places to bunk if they bring their sleeping bags. You'd have to consider food."

"Yeah, lots of logistical issues," she agreed.

"Doesn't mean it wouldn't work. I certainly don't care if you want to use it. I was thinking this afternoon I ought to check on the place one of these days."

"Speaking of this afternoon," she finally gave him a genuine smile. "Where were you?"

He stood and lifted his coffee mug, wimping out on the whole conversation for now. "I'll tell you after supper."

"Why?"

"Because you're in a good mood now. Why spoil it? Think about it, and let me know if you need me to do anything over at the house to get it ready. I'll bring the mug back after I check in with Leif."

He escaped with a little guilt but everyone's mood intact. Plus, he did want Sadie and Mia there when he told everyone what Pearce and Baumgartner had reported. He definitely only wanted to go through that conversation once.

Chapter Sixteen

A DULL ROAR. That's what their mother had always said life was "down to" if there were no disasters in the hour before dinner. Harper took on cooking duties around four o'clock; Mia took Grandma Sadie to visit Joely and their mother; Kelly prepared for her stint at the night watch and popped in and out of the kitchen to play sous chef. Cole disappeared completely.

A dull roar. Outside and inside Harper's head. Now that the adrenaline rush from getting Skylar involved in the art show had ebbed, Harper rethought the wisdom of her rash suggestion to organize a retreat. She'd have dropped the whole insane idea except that, while still under the influence of impulsiveness, she'd contacted the other two students' parents, who'd already filled out their application forms, and sounded them out on the idea. Both kids and their parents loved the idea. She was stuck hoping Melanie would be equally excited.

She was an impetuous idiot. Three teenagers: Skylar at fourteen, Lily Brandeis who was fifteen, and Nate Swanson, the oldest at sixteen. The worst possible combination of hormones.

Teenager worries, however, only shared space with anxiety over her sister. It looked, thank God, like her mother was going to be all right, but the only positive for Joely was that her seizures seemed to have stopped.

Then there was Cole.

She wanted him to wait for her brain to catch up with her heart—and her body. But he flirted shamelessly. It helped nothing that her own brain was insubordinate.

Deep down, she didn't want Cole to stop pursuing her. The sight of him sent her thoughts into a tailspin and her body into mutinous shivers, and the more she told herself he was forbidden, the more she couldn't keep her eyes off of him. The more she admonished herself to talk to Mia, the more she wanted to ignore the whole sisterhood code.

On the other hand, he wouldn't tell her where he'd been that morning, and the only thing he wouldn't talk to her about was the subject of gas and oil. As much as she wanted to feel his arms around her, she wanted to slug him to the moon for hiding information from her—again. So what if she got upset over the idea of oil wells? Couldn't he simply get mad, too, and duke it out without treating her like the crazy girl-bomb nobody wanted to set off?

And why was she obsessed with stopping the oil company anyway? She didn't live here. The majority should rule and she should let it go.

"How's the spaghetti coming?"

Kelly bounced into the kitchen, lifting Harper's spirits in half a step. She truly loved having Kelly home again. She was a perpetual sunny spot in a dark week.

"Tell me." Harper offered her a spoon.

Kelly smacked her lips after tasting the tomato sauce. "It's pretty good. I'd maybe throw in a couple pinches more salt and then add some basil. Fresh if we have it."

"We do. I knew you'd know how to fix it."

They laughed and talked their way through the meal preparation. By the time the family began filtering in for dinner, the spaghetti was cooked al dente, the sauce perfected, broccoli steamed, and a salad and breadsticks were ready to share.

Everyone showed up. Mia, Grandma Sadie—and Cole, who staked out his spot, right next to Harper. Close enough for her to catch the delicious scent of his after-shave, splashed on, she surmised, to cover the effects of an afternoon in the barn. It had worked.

"Mom did great this afternoon," Mia said. "They had her sitting up in bed. Tomorrow it's on to the chair."

"What about Joely?" Harper turned directly to Mia. "Do you know anything more?"

"I wish I had the magic answer," Mia replied. "Brain injuries are difficult because no two are really alike. She could still come through fine. You'd like to see some improvement within twenty-four hours of the accident, but for serious brain contusions like Joely has, this isn't unusual."

"When are they going to move her? Doesn't she have to go to Jackson?"

"Funny thing." Amelia half scowled at the spaghetti twirled on her fork. "I had a chat with the irritating and mostly unhelpful former lieutenant, otherwise known as the pain in the ass Gabriel P. Harrison."

Harper laughed. "I don't know why you hate him so much."

"Yes," Kelly agreed. "I met him this morning. He's super good-looking. Why would you not want to be nice to him just in case he, oh, looked at you?"

"Because in his case, beauty is only skin deep."

"He's been perfectly pleasant to me. But I haven't talked to him much," Harper said.

"Yeah, well, I'll spare you the details. The bottom line is, I went over Lt. Harrison's head, again, spoke to the director of the advocates program about Harrison's obstructionist attitude, and lo and behold if I didn't get some answers about Joely and Tim."

"What's to know about Tim?"

"Joely glossed over the particulars of their separation, although it turns out Mom knows since she was just in California with her. The divorce isn't final. Tim is fighting her on separation of assets. I don't know the financial details—we can't unless something happens to..." She looked at her plate and composed herself for a moment. "Anyway, the good news is that, since Tim was in Iraq, got a purple heart, and is eligible for full benefits, Joely is covered. She doesn't have any other insurance of her own yet, so were she to go to a civilian hospital, she'd be in deep financial trouble. Looks like Tim's selfishness is going to bite him in the ass—he gets to pay his wife's medical bills."

"Well, praise the Lord and pass the parmesan." Grandma Sadie lifted the last of a glass of Shiraz. "One should never wish evil on another human being, but exacting a pound of flesh from one who hurt my grand-daughter? I'm not too old to find that satisfying."

That broke the tension around the table.

"We definitely all want to be like you when we grow up, Grandma," Harper said.

"What?" she asked. "Old?"

"And irreverent," Harper added.

"Speaking of irreverent." Cole caught everyone's attention. "I have something to confess to you, Harpo. And to report to the rest of you. Since we're talking about Joely, you should know I followed up on her decision from a few weeks ago to get more information about let-ting Mountain Pacific drill on Paradise land. Today I met with the technology analyst and her assistant. I'm sorry we didn't tell you first, Harper. We wanted to know if they said anything remotely worthwhile before making a big deal out of it."

So, she'd been right about where he'd gone. Harper's resentment started to rise, but she tamped it down and faced the knowledge with an unexpected calm. He'd told her what he'd done without prompting, he was info-gathering only, and he was cute in his apologetic tizzy it was impossible to stay angry with him. Plus, she'd downed two glasses of wine. Who could hold a grudge?

"Okay," she said, as pleasantly as she could. "*Was* there anything worthwhile?"

Cole looked like he might fall off his chair.

"Uh…there was plenty that was interesting, definitely. Who are you and what have you done with Harper Crockett?"

She was a little pleased at his reaction. She had him off-guard. "Don't push your luck, Cole. Just tell us what they said."

"Okay." He grinned at her, and the wine went to work even harder on her humor, and maybe her libido. "They told me you all could make a whole lot of money in land leases and mineral rights should the wells pan out."

"Did they actually find oil?" Grandma Sadie asked.

"They found geological markers that strongly suggest the presence of oil. They would need to drill three test wells in order to be certain."

"And that means construction of access roads and heavy equipment," said Harper.

"Temporarily, yes."

"How much money?" Mia asked.

"There's no set amount yet, of course," Cole said, his voice rising slightly in the first stages of excitement. Harper took a deep breath and made herself listen. "There'd be a land lease to negotiate, and that could be up to five thousand dollars an acre or more. If the well produced, you'd get royalties based on a percentage of how much was extracted. That's just the start—it's complicated. But you could be looking at several hundred thousand dollars over time."

"Holy crap!" said Kelly.

"That's a lot of money," Mia agreed.

"It's not all at once, remember," Cole warned. "It will take time. But, yes, in the long run, it could certainly solve a lot of financial problems."

"I don't suppose they talked much about the down sides to this." Harper asked as mildly as she could.

"They didn't, but I can give you a list. Each well would require the clearing of up to two acres of land; there'd need to be areas for high-volume liquid storage for hydraulic fracturing; there's no way of knowing what any long-term surface damage might be; the month-long drilling process is dirty and noisy; and it does disrupt the view and any grazing or other land use around the wells. And you'd have to make sure any drilling didn't affect your fresh water wells."

"Not to mention the chances of a disaster," Harper said. "Spills, wells breaking, or malfunctioning."

"There are a lot of safeguards nowadays, but yeah."

"Well," she said, looking around the table. "It is very interesting. And the money sounds like it would be significant. I still vote no."

"You don't even know where they're talking about drilling," Amelia said.

"It doesn't matter to me, Mia. But here's the thing. I don't live here. Joely is the one who'll ultimately make the decision."

"We don't know that," Mia replied softly.

"I'm choosing to know it." For the first time, anger took hold of her words, but more on behalf of Joely than about the oil, although the thought of sucking ancient finite resources out of the earth beneath Paradise wounded her soul.

"Most people with land pray to find oil on it," Mia said. "And here we are with the company courting us. It seems like it would be a rare person who'd turn down such money."

"I know. This is why we have no choice but to drive gas-engine cars, for the most part, still wear shoes and clothing made from petroleum products, still heat with coal and gas, and emit crap into the air. People don't want to change. It's about the money. I get it. I get that I'm a weirdo."

"You're not a weirdo," Kelly said. "You care."

"But what's the smart thing for the family?" asked Mia.

"What's best is however we end up voting." Harper released a long sigh, straightened, and stood. "Let's see what happens with Joely in the next few days. If nothing changes, we'll come back to this in a week, and we'll vote on the next step. Fair enough? Meanwhile, who wants ice cream for dessert?"

"Hey." An hour after dinner, Cole found Harper in the barn, saddling Chevy. "Where are you heading at seven o'clock in the dark?"

She glared at him, and he laughed. "I'm going to talk to Melanie. I've gotten a thumbs-up from the other two kids' parents for a retreat. I'm not sure how Mel will react."

"Would you let me ride with you? There are still dangers in the dark. Two of us will make more noise."

She assessed him, as if searching for an ulterior motive. "I'll be perfectly safe, you know. It's only a mile, and the road hasn't changed in twenty-five years. But if you behave yourself, I'm fine with good company."

"Let me grab Paco out of the pasture. It'll only take a minute."

"No hurry. She's expecting me before eight. Lots of time."

It only took him ten minutes to grab the big quarter horse out of the paddock, give him a quick brushing, and throw his own big stock saddle on the broad back.

"I forget how much fun it is to watch a cowboy work with his horse," Harper said as they headed out of the yard and toward the dark road leading to the ranch houses.

A half-moon shone down, bright enough to give a few shadows some definition. A cool, fall-like breeze made him glad for his hat and lined denim jacket. He was well aware that he wasn't supposed to flirt with her right now, so he tried to obey. Although it was hard to resist teasing her.

"I've been thinking I'd like to find me another good horse," he said. "Remember Barney?"

"Gorgeous and brilliant."

"Owned that horse almost fifteen years, all told," he said. "Nearly half my life. Had some serious cow sense and loved bad weather."

She laughed—a genuine, happy sound, not one filled with the standoffishness of that morning or the tight control of their dinner conversation. The civility of which still astounded him. "He was one of a kind," she said. "He and my mare, Sheba—best buds, too."

"I haven't thought about Sheba for a long time. You did have a thing for mares."

"I like mares," she said. "Joely likes mares. The other girls hated them. Mia claims she can't get along with them to save herself. Kelly and Grace liked the steadiness of geldings for showing." She hesitated. "Oddly enough, my dad liked mares, too."

"He did."

A shadow crossed Harper's face. "When Joely wakes up, we'll have to deal with the death of her horse."

"We'll all be there for her," he said simply, and she nodded.

In the somber silence, he watched her sway in the saddle like he had the day after Sam's funeral. She'd complimented him on his cowboy skills with a horse, but she'd been born and bred a cowgirl. She might think of herself as a city girl now, but she hadn't forgotten a single thing, and she was a far sexier rider than he'd ever be. He loved the way her curves eased into the dips and swells of the saddle. Harper had never been fat, but she'd been gifted with her grandmother's feminine curves, whereas all the other girls had received their father's long, slim build. Those curves had fit so well into his arms last night…He tore his eyes from her as his thoughts moved into dangerous territory.

"You were pretty understanding tonight about my meeting with the oil people."

She shrugged. "I figured out that's where you'd gone. There isn't any other topic you'd hide from me. But in the end you told me, and I've known all along you were going to gather the information. I can't be mad about that. But I don't want to talk about it now. It's too nice out to argue about anything."

"So no talking about us either?"

"What do you want me to say about us? That I like how you kiss? That would be an understatement. That I was embarrassed when Mia walked in on us this morning? That would be an understatement, too. How do I reconcile the two?"

"Get over your embarrassment."

"Didn't I say it was too nice to argue about anything?"

He sighed. He'd harbored the silly, secret idea that getting her alone like this would soften her. Instead, she buried everything and frustrated him in far more ways than one.

Melanie welcomed them and let them into the warm blue-and-red kitchen. They were immediately accosted by Aiden showing off his latest schoolwork.

Small children delighted and befuddled Cole. They were like puppies with the ability to talk, and while that and the fact that they ruled their parents' world a bit too easily scared him a little, he liked imagining what it would be like to have his own. He had no idea if he'd be any kind of a good dad, but he had his father as a role model. Russ had done all right given the hardships he'd endured.

Harper, on the other hand, claimed to have no ability with children yet took to them like she'd been born a parent. She was patient with Skylar, speaking to her with respect while understanding she was a teenager. She would make a terrific mom.

She explained her mission to Melanie with such enthusiasm, Cole didn't see how the woman could refuse. And yet, somehow, she came awfully close.

"I know the kids would love it," Melanie said, "but I'm not sure it's appropriate. You'd have two young teenaged girls with an older boy. I know Nate, he's friends with Marcus and a nice kid, but the girls really go for him. I would rather you do something at your house. Or maybe at the barn."

"It's honestly not the same, Mel," Harper said. "The ability for them to find new scenery to paint—things they haven't seen—is so valuable. And because they're exploring and seeking out these places by themselves, it's freeing."

"But you just made my point exactly. I don't like the idea of them wandering in the woods where they can possibly be alone and face temptation. Not to mention sleeping arrangements. It's a regular house. You can't exactly separate them by floors. You can't be responsible for a sixteen-year-old boy and two young girls."

A tinge of pink crept into Harper's cheeks. She opened her mouth and closed it again. Cole didn't think, he spoke.

"Oh, didn't we say? I'll be there, too. It'll be my job to keep an eye on young Nate. There won't be a problem."

"Really?" Melanie asked.

"Uh…" Harper stared at him but deftly covered her shock. "Yeah, really."

"And you two? No bad role modeling for the kids?"

Cole couldn't believe the words had actually come from Melanie's mouth—was there anything the woman wouldn't say? He bit his cheeks hard to keep from teasing her with some snide remark and looked to Harper for support.

"Oh, you don't have to worry about that even a little."

Well, that wasn't even close to the kind of support he'd had in mind. She'd sounded entirely too okay with the good role model part.

"I guess if that's the case, I might be willing to ask Skylar if she's interested. Is it okay if I bring her in here now? Go over a few rules if she wants to go?"

"Sure." Harper chirped like a happy canary.

To nobody's surprise, Skylar was over the moon. Even her mother's warnings and instructions couldn't dampen her excitement. It was nice to see—she'd been so down lately.

"All right!" Harper said when Skylar had agreed to all the conditions. "It's settled. We'll leave here Friday early afternoon. I'll e-mail you, Lily, and Nick with a list of things to bring, okay?"

"Thank you!" Skylar threw her arms around Harper's neck and then shocked the heck out of Cole by doing the same to him. "This is going to be the best weekend of my life!"

"THIS IS AWESOME! Oh my gosh, thanks for bringing us here. I think I could sit right in the house and draw all weekend."

Lily was the talker of the group, and Harper laughed as the fifteen-year-old entered the half-empty ranch-style house Cole had grown up in and stared around bug-eyed as if it were a fully decorated and functioning mansion. Before she'd passed away, Charlotte Wainwright had shared many a decorating session with her friend Bella Crockett, and they'd both turned out beautiful rooms and décor. Even though the Wainwright house had been unlived in for three years, some of the stylish earth-toned furniture and art remained. Russ had taken only what he wanted and lived frugally in Jackson. Cole kept the house up when he was home, and Sam had used it as a guest house on occasion. There were two empty bedrooms and two still fully furnished, a sofa bed in the den, and one oversized, overstuffed, comfortable couch in the living room. Plenty of space for five people.

"There's a TV room past the kitchen that way." Harper pointed. "There's a pool table in the basement. I have no rules about when you can or can't use them, but I hope you'll take this weekend seriously and spend some time creating. I've got a couple of art activities for you, so this will meet the criteria of a school field trip. Cole and I will make the meals, but you all have to help clean up. You can stay up all night if you want to, but no wandering around outdoors other than to the edge of the first field to the lookout spot after dark—it can be dangerous at night, as you all know. The rest is up to you guys, okay?"

As Harper expected, there wasn't much painting that evening. Nate and Skylar played pool while Lily cheered them on. Then she and Skylar watched a romantic comedy while Nate and Cole built a fire in the fireplace and teased the girls about their sappy movie.

Cole moved about the house like a wolf in his home den, confident, alpha, and protective. He took to the kids naturally, doing exactly what he'd advertised to Melanie—making sure there was nothing untoward or dangerous going on. Yet Harper knew he didn't do any of it consciously. Nate gravitated to him. Skylar mooned over him. Lily talked his ear off. For all Harper had been shocked at his announcement he was coming, it was blissful to have him there.

The smiles he sent her from across a room, the way he role-modeled chivalry by helping with dinner and dishes, the way his movements—hands, back, torso muscles, legs, butt—made for a better movie than anything they could put in the DVD player, gave her a sense of contentment she'd rarely known.

She wanted to hold onto it forever. But there was Chicago. Now there was Cecelia. And Mia.

Mia. She closed her eyes and made herself analyze the whole sister code intellectually for the first time. She'd always felt it was real—you didn't date someone your sister had loved.

But, why not? Really, honestly, why not?

The usual list was easy to make: It was wrong to hurt your sister by taking a man she'd left behind and cruelly remind her of a love gone bad; it was wrong to make your sister feel like you'd won someone she couldn't keep; it was wrong to make your sister wonder if the sex was better with you.

Sister. Sister. Sister.

Harper stopped herself. Why was this only about Mia?

Because where Cole was concerned, she'd always been in Mia's shadow. Mia was the captured princess. Mia was the homecoming date. The prom date. The girlfriend.

Mia had let him go.

What did she, Harper Lee Crockett, want?

She sat in an armchair in the basement and ogled Cole, who bent over the pool table helping Nate line up a shot. She wanted to stare at him like this without guilt. Kiss him without feeling like she'd stepped out of line with her sister.

She wanted to deserve him.

She'd never deserve him. But couldn't she enjoy him?

She'd wounded him when she'd said she didn't want him comparing her to Mia, but whether he did or not wasn't something she could control. She either trusted him to love her for herself or she didn't. For her part, she'd never dwelled on his physical relationship with Mia. If she did that, he'd have the right to think about all the men she'd been with.

The truth hit her over the head like a rap with a pool cool. She didn't care about Mia and Cole's past. She was worrying about things from her childhood—things she'd conditioned herself to believe were obstacles.

Could it be that simple? Let the past go? Her eyes misted with tears of disbelief. It couldn't be.

Nonetheless, she balanced her sketch book against raised knees and moved her pencil carelessly and quickly over the paper. A dozen rapid studies of Cole's body quickly filled four pages, several sketches a page...his hands on the cue, his shoulders hunched to take aim, the long line of his back. This one was of his seat and the back of his leg, a firm, muscular, denim-covered curve leading into taut, broad hamstrings. She captured the shapes and then filled in the detail of belt loops, tucked-in shirt, and pocket stitching after he'd moved from his position.

She caressed the drawing with her pencil strokes, adding the folds of denim around his backside from memory, staring at the paper, remembering how safe that body had made her feel a mere three nights before, sleeping on the sofa. She shaded the pocket carefully. She'd snuggle up to this backside in a heartbeat were there no children around…

"What are you working on so intently?"

His unexpected voice elicited a full-fledged gasp from her, and her gaze flew to his. With flaming hot cheeks she could only stare a moment, her mouth too dry to form words. And for the first time, she didn't feel guilt.

"You okay?" Amusement filled his eyes.

"Uh, lost in the moment." Her voice was raspy. "It happens."

"Can I see?"

She managed to flip the sketchbook pages slowly, closing it without revealing the embarrassment that would accompany letting him see his rear end in her drawings. "Nope," she said blithely. "Nobody sees the pre-sketches until I know what I'm doing.

For a second his smile seemed too knowing, as if he actually had seen what she'd done and was only teasing her. Then he nodded. "Fair enough. Want to play?"

She looked across the room to where Nate was hanging up his pool cue. The very last thing she wanted to do was play. The heat creeping through her body needed to dissipate. That wouldn't happen sharing the pool table with Cole.

"Thanks," she said, and uncurled herself from the chair. "But I think I'd like to walk out to the lookout and see if the moonlight is casting any fun shadows. I haven't worked on a night painting for a long time."

"Okay," he replied.

"Maybe I'll ask the girls, too. You boys have any desire to join us?"

"Nah," Nate said. "I thought I'd try sketching some things I saw along the trail today from memory."

"Sounds like an awesome idea." Harper turned to Cole, raising her brow in question.

"Ask the girls. Maybe I'll build a fire out back."

Her heart battled between relief and disappointment. "Okay. That'll be a good way to end the night later."

The girls agreed to go with her and gathered their sketchbooks and cameras. Harper grabbed a carrying case holding her portable easel and a set of paints. With promises to be back soon, the three of them set out on the quarter mile walk across the Wainwright's old backyard, through a shallow stand of trees and out into a clearing on the top of a small bluff. It wasn't high enough to pose a falling danger but stood elevated enough to provide a stunning view of every kind of landscape feature this part of Wyoming offered.

Even in nine o'clock darkness, and although she'd seen this view hundreds of times, the scenery left Harper breathless. The waxing moon hung high enough to turn the valley before them into purple-and-periwinkle shadows. The Kwinaa River, which wound through the entire ranch, was at its widest here, circling the base of a bluff taller than the one they stood on. Beautiful pastureland stretched beyond the river, rising slowly into undulating hills that rolled on toward the same part of the Teton Range visible from the main part of Paradise Ranch.

"Tell me what colors you see," Harper said. "What paints would you pull out?"

Their answers flew. Purple, black, blue, azure, white.

"Do you see the forest green? How about yellow ochre?" Harper asked.

"Red." Skylar pointed to a near shadow.

"Yes," Harper agreed. "My point is, you all see this differently. Everyone could paint this scene and not one finished piece would look like another. That's the magic of art."

The girls wandered the bluff, ooh-ing over new perspectives, each finally settling in a different nook. Harper set up her easel and a thin piece of canvas board. In the light from a low-watt flashlight, she squeezed six colors onto a paper palette, used an elasticized hairband to affix her flashlight to the easel so it shone on the canvas, and took out a pencil.

For a long time she sketched in basic perspective lines and the rough outlines of a few key features. She glanced at the girls periodically and smiled at Skylar's attempts to use a rock as a camera tripod. For the most part, however, she lost herself. They'd left things in status quo at the hospital, and Joely's care was in the doctors' and God's hands; the cattle gathering had been rescheduled for next week. For one perfect moment, there was nothing she could worry about. Her first brushstrokes flowed onto the canvas.

The colors began to pop, and the scene emerged—a study in darks from blacks, blues, purples, and greens layered with diamond splashes of brights: gray, yellow, and pink moonlight. She squeezed a final color onto her palette, now smeared with her mixed hues, a bright turquoise she mixed with purple to get the halo around the fat, gibbous moon.

"I don't know which takes my breath away more, the real scene or what you captured of it."

She spun in place and stared at Cole, her brain as fuzzy as if she'd been sleeping, not working. Immediate panic shot her pulse rate through the roof, and she stared around wildly for the girls. Understanding dawned horribly. She'd gone into the crazy trance that overtook her when she loved a painting. She'd failed to keep Skylar and Lily safe.

"Oh no, where are they? What happened?"

Cole laughed, its resonance cutting through her panic. "Harpo, it's fine. Everyone's fine. Except maybe you. Do you have any idea what time it is?"

"No, no." She held her wristwatch up to the flashlight and gasped. "Oh my gosh."

"Yeah. Nearly one in the morning."

"This is not possible. Oh, Cole, I'm so sorry. What happened to the kids?"

"They're total lightweights. Sound asleep all of them by midnight. Definitely not natural party animals. I don't think any of their parents tolerate much hanky-panky."

She gazed at her surroundings, still stunned that she'd disappeared so completely into her own private world. "I'm really sorry I abandoned you with them. Thank God you're here. You're so good with them. They adore you."

"Because you adore me, too?"

"Dream on." Relief that all was well started slowing her heart at last. "Thank you, Cole. What kind of chaperone am I? I'd have been in big trouble had I zoned out like this and been here alone. Heaven knows where they would have ended up."

"Are you telling me you need a keeper, Harper Crockett?"

He took a step toward her, and she brandished her brush at him. "I do. Desperately. But one with a clear head and some self-control."

"Oh, my head is clear. One hundred percent. Give me a test that measures clear-headedness and I'll pass with extra credit."

She didn't get another word out before he grasped her wrist, removed the brush from her fingers, and took her paint-smeared palette from the other hand. He set both on the ground and straightened.

"Are you going to tell me you don't want this?" he asked.

Her head spun with all the thoughts from her evening's introspection. She knew she'd still have to talk to Mia sometime, but it was going to be a very different talk than she'd once thought. She closed her eyes and leaned into him.

"I wouldn't dream of it."

Chapter Seventeen

HE STOLE HER breath with the kiss—a claim-staking lock of his mouth onto hers. How he could be powerful and gentle at the same moment baffled her, but she lost the ability to analyze the question as soon as her brain had asked it. The muscle-weakening, bone-liquefying invasion of his tongue, and the resulting hot dance against hers sent fireworks surging through every nerve in her body. She pressed back with her own tongue and set off another wave of sparklers and cherry bombs.

With a groan she thrust into his mouth and tasted him, warm and savory and familiar now, like her new favorite wine. She withdrew and let her head fall back when he nipped lightly at her bottom lip. Shivers ricocheted through her stomach. He kissed down her chin and beneath it, traveled down her neck and flicked his tongue into the hollow of her throat.

So softly she barely felt anything but the electricity, he ran a thumb over her breast, kissing her ear when she gasped.

"Like that?" he whispered.

"Stupid question," she whispered back. "But this isn't safe. I might not be able to control myself. I have a history with you now."

"Trust *me* then."

"Oh no. You said that before, and I ended up sleeping with you." She smiled in spite of herself.

"Probably shouldn't happen tonight."

He pushed her backward three steps until her back met the face of an upright boulder marking the edge of the bluff. She relaxed against it gratefully and arched her back until she curved into his body, meeting the hard outline of his obvious arousal with her pelvis.

"Is that a pool cue in your pocket—?"

"No. I'm just very glad to see you."

" 'Trust me' he says."

With a little moan of desire, she grasped his seat through the denim of his jeans, squeezing and caressing the solid curves she'd drawn and dreamed of touching just hours before. The pressure brought him fully against her, and he rocked slowly upward. Heat exploded through her core.

"Oh, Cole. We really, really have to stop soon."

"Yes. I know."

He captured her mouth again, and she tugged harder on his hips. Once more he traveled down her body with his lips, and this time he unzipped her sweatshirt and delved beneath the hem of the turtleneck underneath it, pushing the soft fabric up and over her bra. A moment later, the satin was out of his way as well, and he closed his lips over the tip of her breast.

"Oh, I really don't trust you now." Her breath came in a rush, and she released his seat and lifted her fingers to his hair, diving into the soft spikes.

He lifted his head, pressed a kiss on her nipple and then moved his lips to the valley between both breasts. "Think how silly you'll look when you find out you still can." He nibbled on the second soft swell of skin. "Trust me, that is."

He assaulted her already rubbery bones with equal treatment of her second breast, and when he stopped he ran his hands up her sides and placed a thumb on the tip of each, circling the damp skin with butterfly-light rotations.

"You really are beautiful," he whispered.

"You make me feel that way," she admitted, reveling in the cool air on her skin while his hands, with their reverent touch, drove hard shivers through her body. "I don't very often."

"Why not?"

"Age-old insecurities. Comparisons to my sisters who all got the long, tall, model bodies. I got the five-foot-four body."

"You got the sexy body with the curves in all the right places. Don't you dare be one of those gorgeous women who says she's fat."

"I'm not fat; I know that. I'm the cute one, not the elegant one. That's a direct quote from my father, by the way."

"Your father didn't have the tact God gave a bull in a crystal shop. Don't listen to his voice in your head anymore. You're different from your sisters—you're the most beautiful."

He pulled her bra back down, adjusted her shirt, and closed up her sweatshirt, hugging it together in front of her. Softly he kissed her, and she had no idea what to do with the feelings he'd evoked. The concept of anyone thinking her more beautiful than her stunning sisters was foreign to her. The fact that it was rugged, beautiful Cole, only made tears threaten to fall.

"Don't cry," he said lightly. "I told you I'd stop."

"I think I'm crying because you did."

"Aw, hell, I can fix that."

He pulled her into another kiss, this one softer—sensual, deep, and slow.

They both heard the high-pitched gasp at the same moment and pulled apart, eyes meeting in a question.

"Hello?" Cole called.

Nobody answered. A second later, footsteps pattered away through the leaves in the woods.

"What was that?" he asked.

Her heart sank. There was only one thing it could have been. Nate wouldn't have gasped like a girl. Lily would have burst in on them like an excited little squirrel.

"Skylar," she said. "She must have seen us."

There was no sign of Skylar in the main living areas when Harper and Cole stole back into the house. They found her bedroom door closed.

"The light is off," he said. "Maybe we didn't hear her after all."

"Maybe not, but we should peek in to make sure she's here. It would be awful to find she'd slipped out and we didn't know it."

Harper cracked the door open enough to let light from the hallway illuminate the bed. The tips of Skylar's strawberry blonde hair stuck out from beneath the blanket.

"It couldn't have been her we heard," Cole said once they'd closed the door again. "She couldn't be this sound asleep already if she was out in the woods five minutes ago."

"Don't put anything past a fourteen-year-old girl with a crush."

"You still believe she has a thing for me? She's been perfectly normal ever since you first mentioned it. Personally I think you're seeing things that aren't there. She's just a nice kid."

"And you're just a nice guy who's such a guy. I hope you're right. We'll know tomorrow morning."

SKYLAR HELD HER breath until the door closed and blackness filled the room again. She'd known they'd heard her in the woods, and she'd known they'd come right back and check on her. This had been the best defense she could think of. She rolled onto her back, unclutched her fingers from the blanket, and stared at the ceiling with tears burning in the corners of her eyes.

Cole and *Harper*?

She should have known. She should never have told Harper how handsome she thought Cole was. Now Harper had noticed him and moved in.

Deep inside, Skylar knew her thoughts were foolish and silly, but her chest literally ached since seeing Cole with his lips against Harper's. She hadn't meant to make a sound, but the kiss had totally shocked her. It hadn't been any weenie, friendly little kiss either. It had been one that made Skylar's stomach flip in wonder and excitement. It should have been forbidden. If her mother ever heard that the two chaperones had been out in the woods kissing and Skylar had seen them, she'd be furious.

At first, a small, mean-spirited corner of Skylar's heart wanted to tell her mother exactly what she'd seen. But she'd never do that to Cole. And she liked Harper. Harper was the first person in the world to take Skylar's side on anything—and to make this whole dream happen had been amazing.

She buried her head in her pillow and let a few confused tears wet the pillowcase. She had to get through the weekend without letting Harper know she'd seen anything or that she cared. She'd already scoped out a few spots where she wanted to paint. She wasn't sure if she'd come up with ideas that would work for the contest, but looking for one would keep her away from Harper. And from Cole.

Finally, after plotting her strategy, as much as it felt completely lame and she hated it, she made one last adjustment to her pillow and snuggled into its softness. Now that she knew Cole was at least in the house, she felt safer if not better. Closing her eyes, she let herself drift to sleep at last.

What happened the next morning threw her whole plan off track. Lily and Nate greeted her from their seats around the dining room table. Cole stood at the stove with a huge, handsome smile on his face.

"Hey, Sky, can I make you some pancakes?"

"Yeah, okay."

But then Harper handed her a mug filled with hot chocolate and pointed toward the living room.

"Come with me?" she asked, and Skylar had no choice but to nod, sure for a second she was in trouble.

But when Harper sat on the sofa and patted the seat next to her, she was the one who looked guilty. "I think I need to apologize to you," she began. "You came back outside to the lookout late last night, didn't you? I don't care a bit if you were there. I only want to make sure it was you."

Skylar had not prepared for direct confrontation. She wanted to lie and put her plan to ignore the whole situation into practice, but she couldn't. She'd been told often enough in her life to cheer up and stop being so gloomy but never that she was a person who couldn't be trusted.

"Yeah." Her voice felt half its strength.

"And you saw me kissing Cole."

Skylar's face flamed with embarrassment. She didn't want to talk about this. "So? It's not my business."

"You're right."

That surprised her. Skylar shrugged.

"On the other hand," Harper continued, "I promised your mother everything would be appropriate this weekend. I'm sorry we got personal when you guys were around."

"So basically you don't want me to tell my mom."

"I would never say that. You tell your mom anything you need to. This is about you and me." She hesitated as if she wasn't sure she should say the next thing. "And, I think I might have made you angry because I know you like Cole, too."

If her face had been hot before, it was burning now. "No. No, I…don't."

"It's okay. Cole is…kind of awesome. Right?"

She could only shrug again.

"Anyway, I want you to know I'm sorry. There won't be any more embarrassing kissing during the weekend."

That should have made Skylar feel 100 percent better. Instead, her stomach fell, like she was disappointed or something. She scowled. "Why would you even tell me that?"

"I like you. I've started thinking of you as my friend, and friends should be honest with each other."

She had to think about that. How many times had she been told to be honest, be honest, be honest? No adults had ever said they had to be honest back.

"Do you love him? Cole?"

The question tumbled out. She couldn't believe she'd asked. Harper looked a little surprised.

"I…don't know," she said. "I like him very much. But I don't even live here, so I don't think it matters."

"What if you did live here?"

Harper laughed. "Then you and I would have to duke it out over him."

Somehow, no matter how Skylar felt when she started talking to Harper, she felt better when she was done. Harper wasn't like the other adults in her life. She didn't take everything so dang seriously and make Skylar feel like she had to do the same.

"Yeah," she said. "That would suck."

Her mother would have lectured her for an hour about her language. Harper only laughed.

The rest of the day turned into one of the coolest of her life, and nothing could have surprised her more. Harper knew so much about painting and drawing it was like a paintbrush turned into a magic wand in her hand. She gave them lessons on shading and on perspective and on famous painters. She had books for them to look at and new paints for them to try. But she wasn't strict about the lessons or anything. Everything was simply more fun when she talked about it. And when they were done for the morning, she let them wander anywhere they wanted. They could work or think or search for things to draw or paint. For hours. The only rule was, if they took horses and went farther than a mile away, they had to bring a walkie-talkie with them. And they could stay out until sunset, but they needed to be back to the outlook by dark.

Skylar felt like a grown-up. Like a real artist.

And she created the picture she knew she would enter in the exhibition. She got the idea from one of Harper's art books containing a picture of one famous artist's draft sketch and then his finished painting. Skylar started by sketching a mountain path and a sweetly kissing couple in the bottom left corner of the canvas. Beyond the couple, the entire Kwinaa Valley and the Teton Range spread across the canvas. The beginning of the path in the corner and the leg of the girl remained a pencil sketch. As the picture evolved, the shading grew more detailed until it burst into the whole rainbow palette of colors Skylar always saw in the mountains. By the time she had the canvas nearly filled and finished, she loved it.

She wanted to call it Hopeful World.

"That's amazing."

She turned around in her small copse of trees to find Nate. At first a small fist of resentment that he'd invaded her private painting spot squeezed in her chest, but then he smiled. He had a dimple in each cheek and bangs that fell across his forehead in a super-cute, pop singer kind of way. She couldn't help but smile back.

"Thanks," she said. "Are you looking for a place to paint?"

"No. I stayed around the house to paint. Now I'm hiking to clear my brain. I found this and thought maybe you were here somewhere."

He held up a small, pink-and-white striped knit glove, the kind that were only a couple of dollars at Kloster's Drug.

"It is mine. I didn't even know I dropped it. Thanks, Nate."

He stepped closer and peered at her painting. "You got those shadows perfectly. I've kind of been wondering, do you think you could help me with one of my drawings?"

He pulled off his backpack and unzipped the main pocket. From it he took his sketchbook. Flattered and nervous, Skylar waited while he flipped pages. He handed it to her. "Here," he said. "I tried to get the shading on those flowers right but it isn't quite. Can you see what the problem is?"

She did. The solution was simple. He had the light source twisted around a little bit. Her nerves vanished, and she sat cross-legged on a patch of grass with him beside her.

"See how you have the light coming from over here?" She pointed. "And then the shadow in front of the plants? You have to move it to the side."

That was all it took to get Nate playing with his pencil, asking questions and reworking parts of the drawing. Skylar pulled out her own sketchbook and doodled while they talked. The time flew past, and before they realized how late it had gotten, the shadows had fallen over the stand of trees where they worked.

"We need to go," Nate said. "It'll take us a good half hour to get to the house. We'll be back well after dark."

"Do you have a walkie-talkie?" she asked.

"No, I didn't think I was coming this far."

"I'll pack up my stuff. I need to be careful with the painting 'cause it's still wet."

He carried the eleven-by-seventeen canvas for her, finding his way on certain feet through the growing darkness. By the time they reached the house at last, it was fully dark and Skylar braced for the lecture sure to come. Even Harper wouldn't forgive breaches of the after-dark rules. She knew all too well the animals and dangers that lurked after sundown for people who weren't prepared to be outdoors. A wet canvas and a few paintbrushes wouldn't do any good against a cougar or stepping off the edge of the bluff.

What they found once inside was as far from a lecture as they could get.

Harper and Cole sat in the living room with two other adults who seemed vaguely familiar, although Skylar couldn't place them. Lily stood in the kitchen stirring a pot of spaghetti noodles.

"What's up?" Nate asked her.

"These two showed up about ten minutes ago," Lily replied. "Cole and Harper seemed really shocked to see them, and they needed to talk, so I said I'd finish cooking the spaghetti. Where have you guys been?"

"I was painting by another overlook and Nate was out hiking. We found each other and were working on our drawings together. All of a sudden it was getting dark."

"You know how good Skylar is with shading and dimension, right?" Nate replied. "She helped me with that flower picture."

"Cool. You'll have to show me."

Skylar couldn't believe how amazing Nate and Lily were being. They didn't seem like they thought they were better than she was or like they were there to compete with her. They seemed like real friends. She knew them from the homeschool co-op, and Nate and Marcus had hung out a few times, but she'd paid only passing attention to them. Suddenly she felt like she'd found kids from the same planet her dad always told her she lived on.

"What did you work on today?" Skylar asked, still fighting a little shyness. Lily was such a good artist.

"I practiced painting pictures of different parts of the house." She shrugged. "It sounds boring, but I wanted to see if I could make wood look realistic. And I painted an old truck I found in a shed. Cole said it was his grandfather's. It was fun."

"Look at this one Sky is working on."

Nate held up the canvas, and Lily stared at it for several long seconds.

"That is awesome," she said. "You should enter that in the contest."

"I was thinking I might," Skylar admitted. "Do you really think it's good enough?"

Lily smiled. "You could win with a painting like that."

Skylar could have died right then and gone to heaven happy—which is what Grandpa Leif always said when something went right. To get praise from her friends felt better than anything had in a long time.

COLE HEARD THE kids come in and nudged Harper with an elbow. "We should take this meeting to the porch," he said under his breath.

She nodded. "Little ears could mean big gossip."

The visit from Magdalen and Brian might have been a complete surprise, but what they'd come to report was even more stunning. Once they'd all found seats on the three-season porch off the side of the house, Cole leaned toward them, still amazed.

"So you got some further results from the explorations. Large deposits, you said?"

"Deeper analysis on two sections of land that piqued our technicians' interest," Brian said. "The findings were so exciting they rushed their results."

"What sections of land?" Harper asked.

"Part of easternmost two thousand acres. Not far from where we are right here," Magdalen said.

"The Double Diamond." Cole steepled his fingers, elbows resting on his thighs. "What are these results?"

"Potentially the largest deposit of oil on the entire ranch. Of course, this is still no more absolute than the other results, but the indicators are extremely exciting. Should you go ahead with the project, we would recommend starting with exploration in these areas. We could be talking a great deal of money."

"Wow," Cole sat back. "That's…who knew?" He turned to Harper. "Pretty enticing wouldn't you say?"

They hadn't spoken about oil since dinner earlier in the week.

"Why would it be any more enticing to me than oil elsewhere on the ranch?" Despite the slow burn in her eyes, her reply was still calm. "As with the other information, this has to be discussed with the others."

"Of course it does," he replied. "In fairness, the week you asked for is almost up, and now we're talking about enough income to save the ranch."

"Don't you mean save two ranches?" she asked. "That *is* still your priority, right?"

Her accusation slammed him, not with guilt but with indignation. His first thought had not been for his own financial well-being, but for hers. Still, she was right. Finding oil on the Double Diamond would not hurt his situation one bit.

"I think you're talking about events that affect the future much more than the present," he said. "Any benefit I personally got out of this would depend on what kind of an arrangement the *current* owners were willing to make."

He hadn't meant to get peevish, but her calm was disintegrating slowly into stubbornness. That was the Harper who dug in and fought the hardest.

"Good to know that has to factor into the discussions," she said.

He looked away, frustrated. Why couldn't she let go of her stubborn idealism long enough to see what she was rejecting out of hand?

"You still don't need to make any decisions about this now." Brian broke the building tension. "We only wanted to stop by and let you know about this so it could factor into your decision making."

"We appreciate the information," Cole said.

"We'll be on our way." Magdalen stood. "You two obviously have much to discuss. We'll wait to hear from you once you've spoken with the whole family."

Once the two were gone, Cole sighed with relief. At least he could talk freely to Harper if outsiders weren't involved. But instead of finding Harper ready for a discussion, Cole met her halfway across the porch back to the living room.

"Aren't you even going to stay and duke it out?" he asked, trying to lighten the mood.

"With you?" She spun. "No. The bottom line is this isn't any of your business. This is up to my sisters and me."

Her words stung. She was absolutely right, but since Sam's death Cole had grown accustomed to status as an honorary family member. He didn't expect to make final decisions, but he'd taken for granted that he'd be given a voice along with the others. She'd just cut him out.

"I see. Well, you're right. I'm sorry I misunderstood and thought we were closer than that."

"You and I disagree philosophically. People disagree all the time. That doesn't have anything to do with us personally."

He couldn't argue with her, yet tension followed them into the kitchen where the kids had finished making the pasta and were setting the table.

Harper stopped in front of a new painting leaning against the end of one counter. Even Cole could see it was beautiful.

"Who did this one?" Harper asked.

"I did." Nervousness shimmered in Skylar's uncertain eyes, and the hands she shoved into her back jeans pockets trembled.

The painting showed colorful, sunset-painted mountains and, silhouetted in the foreground, a couple embracing and sharing a kiss. For a moment it took him aback, filling him with fear that he and Harper had put something inappropriate in the girl's imagination. But the picture was a perfect study of beauty and innocence.

The unique way it grew out of a simple black-and-white drawing gave it a sense of something being discovered.

Harper turned. "It's gorgeous, Sky. I'm really proud of you."

"It's okay?"

"Far more than okay. It's—"

The "Imperial March" from Star Wars rang through the kitchen, followed immediately by a sharp intake of breath from Harper.

Cole stiffened. "What?"

"Mia."

"Wait. She's Darth Vader on your phone?" He grinned.

"It's not funny." Color leached from her cheeks as her anxiety rose. "She wouldn't call if something wasn't up."

"It's okay, honey," he said, sobering dutifully. "Do you want me to answer?"

"No. No, I need to."

She picked up the phone, hesitated one last second and then slid her finger across the screen.

"Hello? Mia?" They all listened. "What? When?"

It was impossible at first to tell what kind of news she'd gotten. Only her eyes gave anything away—they shone like deep dark pools of shiny brown paint. So slowly they barely noticed it happening, she broke into a grin. "Okay. Okay. I'll come as soon as I can."

She ended the call and stared at them all for a few seconds. Then, as if she hadn't had an angry word with him in her life, she threw herself into Cole's arms. He held her as if they were alone in the woods again.

"Joely's awake."

Chapter Eighteen

"I WISH WE could stay for a few more days."

Harper accepted Lily's giant hug and squeezed her back. The kids' supplies and overnight bags now filled the back of Cole's car, and the three were ready to climb in. Harper wished they could stay longer, too. It had been a weekend successful beyond her wildest dreams.

"Would you do it again sometime?" she asked.

"Anytime," Lily replied.

"I wish this was a class. Or a camp," Skylar said. As far as Harper could tell, she'd been the most affected by the weekend. "Everyone who wants to draw should come and have you teach them."

She followed Lily's example and threw her arms around Harper's shoulders.

"That's sweet of you," Harper said. "But you guys did all the work."

"I got a lot out of what you told us about perspective." Nate smiled at Harper. "You gave us good things to work on."

"I'm so glad." Harper couldn't stop a swelling of pride. "And you all told me you know what you're turning in tomorrow for the exhibition. I'd say you accomplished what you came to do."

She'd almost considered calling all their parents and requesting another day or two to work, but it was time to go.

There was Cole and the conflicted emotions he evoked. There was a fear of pushing Melanie a little too far. And, most importantly, there was Joely.

Beautiful, broken Joely, who'd awoken and, according to all reports today, was pleasing the doctors with her improvement. She hadn't been fully coherent the night before, when Harper had left the kids with Cole to go visit her, but seeing her moving and responding had been as good as seeing her fully recovered. And the weight now gone from Harper's shoulders had turned today into a brilliant gift. Even her anger at Cole had dulled to annoyance.

Now he circled the front of his car and surveyed the kids and Harper.

"Everyone got what you brought?" he asked. "I don't get back here too often, so it might take a while to retrieve anything you forgot."

"We went through the house pretty well, didn't we?" Harper asked.

The kids all nodded.

"Hop in then," Cole said.

Harper climbed into the front passenger seat, buckled the seatbelt and settled back for the ten minute drive. When they were underway, she started at a nudge from Cole's hand against hers. When she relaxed her fingers, he grasped them and squeezed. For a moment she resented how easily he ignored and glossed over their problems. Then the shivers of excitement from his touch trumped her grouchiness, and she clasped his hand in return.

"Successful weekend?" he asked.

"A miraculous weekend."

"It was fun. Right guys?" he called, and received another chorus of yeses, filled with a lot more enthusiasm than teens usually showed.

"You going to see your sister when we get back?" he asked.

"I'm planning to."

"Would it annoy you if I tagged along?"

"No." The question surprised her. "Of course not."

"You forgot in the wake of the good news how ticked off at me you are."

So he did remember.

The idea of resuming the oil conversation sent weariness flooding through her. She was sick of the subject, sick at the thought of Mountain Pacific getting its hands on her property, and sick of fearing she and Cole would forever be on opposite sides of the issue. She tried telling herself the whole argument was not important. That in light of Joely's recovery, and in return for her family being safe again, she could find any business decision acceptable.

But in order to believe all that, she had to ignore a constantly growing ache in her stomach.

"I'd never forget. I'm totally angry with you."

"Oh, good, I was beginning to worry."

As they dropped the teens off one by one, Harper wished her words were true. She was annoyed that Cole refused to take her side, but she wanted to be *incensed*. True fury would make her life much easier. She could chalk the fling with Cole up to out-of-whack emotions, spend her last weeks here, and go back to Chicago with no encumbrances. Her sisters could work out whatever they liked with Paradise and the oil company.

But there was no fury, and a piece of her heart railed at giving up her share of Paradise. An even tinier piece of her heart understood that Cole was only protecting his interests the way she was protecting hers. At least he was actively trying to solve his problems. She was only throwing up roadblocks.

THAT NIGHT JUBILATION shouldn't have been such a huge part of the gathering in Joely's room. On the surface, things still looked too serious for celebration. Mother had experienced a setback and developed a fever from a mild infection. Joely still slept 90 percent of the time, and spoke mostly incoherently when she did awaken. Her sleep, however, was natural rather than coma-induced. Mia promised their mother's condition was almost to be expected. The prognosis for both Crockett patients was better than it had been since they'd been admitted. How could there not be celebration?

Kelly, now at the end of her visit and jubilant that she'd been here for a miracle, broke more than one hospital rule by sneaking Champagne into the rooms. Not even Mia complained when Kelly rubbed a drop of the sparkling wine onto Joely's lips, and everyone watched her tongue emerge slowly to make a careful circuit around her mouth. They cheered at her thin smile.

"You children are disruptive and undisciplined," her mother said when Harper surreptitiously offered her a quarter inch of Champagne in a tiny paper cup. "The staff will kick us all out."

Harper bent to hug her tightly. "Oh, Mama, if only they would."

By the time they'd emptied the bottle of sparkling wine, nobody had drunk enough to be inebriated, yet they all giggled like curbside winos. Harper doubted the staff was blind to their breach in the rules, but she figured everyone was equally relieved at the good news.

For the first time since the accident, they were all asked to leave overnight. Joely and Bella would sleep better if they weren't worried about someone trying to be comfortable in a bedside chair. Nobody objected.

"We'll continue the party at home!" Mia waved to Harper and Cole as she ducked into their mother's car with Kelly.

The green Forester rolled out of the parking lot before Harper and Cole had reached his Rover. She climbed in beside him filled with relief and exhaustion.

"Party on, huh?" Cole asked. "It's been a while since the Crockett girls have thrown a wild bash. Mom's away, so her kittens can play. And on a Sunday night." He clucked with mock disapproval.

"Ugh." She laughed as she leaned her head back against the headrest and closed her eyes. "Partying sounds like a lot of work. Besides, I was never part of those illegal bashes."

He nearly choked on his own snort. "Good one, Harpo."

"I was the quiet, artistic one. Remember?"

"Your quiet was deceptive. When you weren't talking or drawing you were figuring people out. You're still that way."

"No." She shook her head. "I used to think I was such a great judge of people, but I don't anymore. My wild ways after I left home killed that ability."

"I know I teased you about partying, but I can't imagine you were *that* wild."

Maybe she'd had just enough Champagne to loosen her tongue too far. She didn't want to go near this subject, and yet her mouth opened and the truth spilled out.

"You're wrong. I did every single thing short of getting pregnant that we good Crockett girls had been taught never to do."

"Sex and degradation from the best-behaved sister of the six. Got it." He chuckled again.

She didn't reply. If that was the Harper Crockett he remembered and still compared her to, he was sadly mistaken. Her cheeks stung. She'd never wanted Cole to know how much she'd rebelled after leaving home. Or that her conduct during that rebellion was the real reason she'd made such infrequent visits home over the years.

"Believe me, I'd rather you live in your fantasy world," she said.

He reached for her hand. "You're telling me you went a little crazy and experimented with things?"

"That's one way of putting it."

"So? Do you think the rest of us didn't do the same?" He squeezed her hand. "I had my share of passed-out nights."

"In a jail cell?"

Oh, Lord, what was making her do this now, after such a great day?

He turned his head in the dim car interior and stared. "Okay, this is interesting."

"More than once, in fact. And it's not interesting—it's mortifying. The first time, it was one of the many men I let try to prove to me I was desirable and worth loving who'd talked me into supplementing my pot—bad enough where I came from—with some old-fashioned uppers. To this day I don't know what I took over the course of the time I was with him. It was only by the grace of God that he was a small-time dope dealer—no heroine, no meth. Twice he had to bail me out when I was at parties without him and passed out with other friends.

"Thank God, too, I was old enough that my parents didn't need to get the phone call from jail. The last time I got picked up, it was for, quote, returning a wallet, end quote to one of this guy's friends. It was filled with cocaine. I absolutely did not know it, but it took some fancy tap-dancing with a court-appointed lawyer to get out of that with thirty days and a year of parole. At least I never saw that guy again."

She loosened her hand, fully expecting him to drop it. He clamped it tighter.

"You went through a rough patch. You did some dumb things. You got out of it."

"I wish it had been that straightforward." She rubbed her eyes with her free hand. "Damn, Cole, don't make me tell you the rest."

"Oh, you bet I'm going to. In for a penny…"

She laid her head back against the seat and fought with herself. Cole waited silently and she loved him for that. Finally she straightened. What choice did she have? She'd started this herself. And even though she'd only ever told her story to counselors, this telling made her ugly past seem slightly less horrifying than it was in her head.

"Well, I guess you haven't kicked me out of the car yet," she said.

"I'm not going to."

"Fine. I didn't know how to make good choices anymore. I went through several more boyfriends, and while none of them was a drug dealer, the crowds we hung with definitely knew how to party. And knew how to pull the wool over a parole officer's eyes. I was a quick study. Mind you, I was in school, too. Art school—something I supposedly loved. And I totally screwed it up. No quick study there. I failed class after class. Only passed the actual hands-on labs. It was after two years of this that I got kicked out. Not flunked out—literally expelled."

"That explains why I heard you'd dropped out of college," he said, perfectly calmly.

"That's about the only kind thing my dad did for me in the whole mess. Not spread the truth."

"He found out?"

"He was paying for school. He had to find out. And believe me, it did not go down prettily with Sam Crockett. I never could count all the times he said 'I told you so.' And, of course, Dad paying for college was a thing of the past. No second chances. I could never afford to go back. But, he and Mom did keep their promise to not tell what really happened. So, aren't you lucky? You're one of maybe five people who know how close I came to permanent loser-hood."

She pulled her hand from his this time. No she hadn't killed anyone, but it was humiliating all the same to be the only imperfect Crockett girl.

Cole retrieved her hand again. "Tell me the good part now," he said. "How you didn't give up. How you got back to being stunning, wonderful Harper—the one who's sitting here with me."

"Stunning and wonderful? Wow." She laughed a little ruefully. "Six weeks of rehab, a bunch of counseling, and Tristan Carmichael."

"You met Tristan in rehab?"

"No. He taught an art class I took once I was out. Tris was the first to tell me I was talented enough to make it big. We had a six-week-long, I guess you'd call it affair. By that time, though, I was done with meaningless relationships, and there was no sexual attraction between us. There was an artistic one, though. We've been friends for four years. He's the big brother and in some ways

306 LIZBETH SELVIG

the loving father figure I never had. He turned my life around."

That was it.

She felt fifty pounds lighter even though the story hadn't come out as tragic as it had been while inside. And here Cole sat, still driving, still squeezing her hand.

"I have officially stopped detesting Tristan Carmichael."

"About time. He's never been a threat to you."

He remained so quiet she panicked briefly. They neared Paradise's driveway, and he kneaded her fingers together thoughtfully.

"Cole?"

"I'm trying to decide if I heard what you said correctly. Tristan's not a threat to me. Does that mean I'm in a position where someone *could* be a threat? Are you telling me I have a chance to be your fella?"

He grinned at the road ahead of him. Harper's heart soared. "You got a chance to be my fella when you didn't sing 'Beauty School Dropout' from *Grease* after you heard my story."

His laughter floated through the car, rich and reassuring. "You're kidding."

"Not. Two truly mean girls in rehab. They got disciplined. But to this day I can't stand that movie."

He said nothing, just turned into the driveway, but to her surprise, he drove straight past the house and continued to the barn. No lights shone from any of the buildings. Cole turned off the engine and opened his door. Seconds later he opened hers, too. She unclipped her seatbelt.

"Wheeler lost a shoe, I guess," he said. "Bjorn will put it on in the morning, but he's in because they don't want him lame tomorrow. I said I'd check on him."

He flicked on the light in the barn. Most of the horses were still in the pasture. They wouldn't start coming in at night until the snow flew. Wheeler nickered as the light caught his bright white blaze.

"He looks fine." Harper reached the horse and stroked his neck.

"Yeah, she does."

Cole wasn't looking at the gelding. He grasped Harper's shoulders from behind, spun her in her tracks and pushed her gently to the stall door next to Wheeler.

"You don't need to relive all that stuff you told me anymore, Harpo." The words touched her one at a time, hot, sweet-scented breaths, earnest and adamant. "You have me. And I think you're brave and smart. You fell and you got up. It made you kind and empathetic and too ready to deny yourself. Stop worrying about everybody and believe you deserve your life."

It was exactly what she'd tried to tell herself the first night at his house by the pool table.

He claimed her mouth, and familiar pangs of desire erased any thoughts of speech or resistance. She wrapped his neck with her arms and pressed into his body, taking his tongue hungrily into her mouth and twisting her head to get closer.

They kissed. They kissed longer. They parted and then pushed back together. Teeth scraped lips, lips sought cheeks, chins, and earlobes.

Heat blazed into the deepest feminine part of her and pulsed, begging for the touch of his body against hers. She pulled away.

"I want this. I decided that during our retreat. I know I have to get past all my hang-ups."

"You know none of them matter to me, don't you?" he said.

"It matters to me a lot what you think. What everybody thinks."

"What about what you think?"

"I'm still figuring that out. I still can't believe I told you everything."

"Harper, people have done much worse."

"I know. But to me it was huge. A blot I can't erase on my life. I need to think about this. About us. About where I belong."

"I'd like to see if we could belong together."

Chicago glittered in her mind, but it loomed a little like a diamond-studded jail cell.

Cole let her go, but he didn't step away. He pressed another kiss to her lips, and even with no hold, no bodies inciting excitement with friction, the touch of his mouth was pure, hot, and meaningful all by itself.

"Tell me one thing," he added. "This isn't because of the oil disagreements? That's decision making is all. You know that, right?"

She smiled wistfully. They'd come full circle, and the circle encompassed all the parts of her life that still tripped her up and messed with her head.

"It's everything, Cole. It's the future. It's our different dreams. It's the oil. It's maybe less about Mia, now, but I still want to talk to her. And with Joely sick, how do we know where oil fits into her plans? This is too complicated."

"Okay. Take it slowly. I get that. Just know that I'm getting used to having you around. If I'm not jealous of Tristan, then I'm pretty jealous of Chicago."

She stepped back and turned again to the horse. Wheeler nudged her hand, looking for a treat. "And then there's that. How smart is it to start something when I don't live here?"

Once again the odd hollow in her stomach burned. It had never hurt before to say she didn't live here; in fact, she'd relished it.

One more time the barn circled around her as Cole spun her in place and shocked her with a thrust of his hips that pressed her back against the wall. She stared at him with the coarse, solid wood bracing her back until his kiss, hard and desperate and matching the strength in his body, forced her eyes closed. He rocked his pelvis into hers and cupped her ears as if clinging to his very life force. Yet his weight neither frightened nor threatened. Instead, flames engulfed her core as he stroked against her once and then twice and then cruelly released her. When he stepped back, she couldn't breathe.

"We could overcome the distance."

His quiet words were in juxtaposition to the thunder pounding through her veins. They sent a thrill low into her stomach and yet another rush of heat between her legs. She grabbed a handful of his shirt in each hand, bent on figuring out how to push him away and pull him closer at the same time. Pushing won out.

"We haven't even been together under normal circumstances since this whole insane thing between us started. Every time we're together it's a crisis—something that's forcing me to need you, to want protection and safety, and for you give it. But that's not normal living."

"Aw, Harpo, you're a hot old mess aren't you?" He drew her back for one last kiss on the forehead. "Tomorrow. We're finishing the roundup. Come along. Forget all the crises and the questions. Get a little ranch normal back in your blood and see if that doesn't make you feel better."

For the first time in ages she grasped hold of a suggestion and embraced it with 100 percent enthusiasm.

"A normal day." Her grin came easily. Her sharp-edged fear and even some of the pain of physical longing dissipated into excitement. "You're on, cowboy."

Chapter Nineteen

COLE RESTED A forearm on his saddle horn and smiled across a sea of cow butts to the two girls on horseback trotting toward the herd. Ahead of them gamboled a white-faced calf maybe four or five months old. Harper drove from the left, Skylar from the right, each of them held her hat in a hand and waved it gently, keeping the calf trotting toward its mother. The cow—evident because it faced the oncoming baby from the edges of the herd—scolded in low, exasperated-mother moos, and Cole laughed. Some things were universal.

Skylar let out a whoop when the bovine pair was reunited. Harper, relaxed and easy and sexy as always in the saddle, slowed her horse to a walk and fell in beside the girl. They lifted their arms and slapped a high five above their heads. Cole sat up and pressed Paco forward.

"Good job," Harper said. "You and Bungu make a great cow pair. This was a naughty little calf and you kept right up with him."

As if to agree, the cow butted her babe with a sharp flick of her head, and he scooted up to join the herd. Skylar giggled.

"He was exploring. The creek bed was way more interesting than the walk home."

"Welcome back," Cole said, meeting up with them. "He must have wandered a ways."

"A good half mile down the creek bottoms. Little dickens," Harper said.

Her smile warmed him like a sunbeam. She'd looked damn gorgeous in her Chicago finery, but nothing could beat her curvy hips clad comfortably in soft denim, her legs draped around her horse's sides, and her black bangs peeking out as she settled her hat back on her head. The addition of her Lady Stetson made her big, shining eyes pop even more. She looked like a sexy sprite.

She looked happy.

In fact, she'd worn this happy smile and lost the worried, uptight tension she'd been carrying from the moment he'd made her promise to come on the roundup today, and he had every intention of keeping her in this mood as long as he could. She needed the break.

"You should go tell your grandpa you've got the calf back," Harper said.

"Okay. Where are you going to be?" Skylar looked at Harper almost as adoringly as she looked at him.

"I'll keep her behind to help push," Cole said. "Come on back when you've updated them at the front and found out if there's anything we need to know."

"Sure!" Her face shone with relief that they hadn't banished her. "I'll be right back."

She turned Bungu and loped off along the edge of the herd. Twelve hundred head made a long line when stretched lazily along the last few miles of the valley toward home. This fake roundup was a wonderful tradition, Cole had decided. He could see Mia and Rico ahead on the left and Kelly and Neil on the right. Up ahead would be Bjorn and Marcus. In between were Rico's two kids and Leif, and two dogs. Asta was still too young for such a long day, but Skylar had studied the behavior of these two so she'd know when her own pup was ready. Keeping the little border collie had been good for her. Everyone smiled. Everyone remembered how good it was to be outside moving. Yes. This was a good thing.

"That was sweet of you," Harper said.

"What was?"

"Telling Sky she could come back. You're good with her. You let her enjoy this teenage phase without encouraging anything."

"Aw, heck, I like the kid. And her parents are the best—salt of the earth like my dad says. But she needs a little freedom to learn about the world. Then again, I dunno, I really have no idea about kids, especially girl kids. I open my mouth and crap comes out. You're the one who's great with her. You were a natural with all of them this last weekend. Skylar worships you."

"I'm a novelty. Life on a ranch is never dull, but it can be lonely. I at least had sisters. And you. There aren't a lot of kids her age around here."

Silence fell, and they rode through it comfortably, easily, as if they'd done it all their lives. They had, in some ways, of course, but not like this. Not like partners with all the thoughts, worries, joys—and sparks—of adulthood between them. The knowledge that Harper had to leave soon pricked the back of Cole's mind, edging toward pain like a constant tapping in the same sore spot. It didn't matter that they disagreed on things—he liked discussing those things with her. It didn't matter that she believed she'd had a bad past—he'd lived and worked with oil and construction crews; he was no saint. He didn't want her to leave.

Unfortunately, he didn't know how to convince her to stay.

Skylar rode back long moments later and settled into a walk beside them, sandwiching Cole in the middle. She reported that they were only about two miles from the main holding corrals and should be there in an hour or so—well before dinner, which Melanie and Sadie were preparing back at home. After that, the teen seemed to pick up on the silent contemplation and fell with them into the easy quiet.

Cole could have ridden in the peacefulness all the way to Canada.

They reached the outermost of six huge pens, each the size of a football field, while still half a mile from the main barns and the house. That's when the easy peace ended and the fun of sorting began. It wasn't so much detailed or difficult work as it was slightly chaotic, as steers were separated from cows and calves. The weaning would take place tomorrow and the rest of the week, when cows were tested for new pregnancies and the babies sent off in mopey collections to cry with each other away from their mothers for the first time. Today, none of that mattered. As the herd pooled into the ranch yards, the moos and squeals along with the dust and pungent cow reek mingled with shouted directions from Leif and Bjorn.

Skylar and Marcus were as helpful as any of the adults. They had no fear, directing their horses after scuffling steers, cutting off calves, and working together to funnel groups into the right gates. The teamwork had never ceased to amaze Cole. No matter what went on everywhere else, working the cows brought out the best in everyone. Good-natured ribbing and shouted praises flew abundantly. Satisfaction was everyone's top emotion. A little over an hour after they'd arrived, the herd had been sorted into six pens containing roughly a hundred and fifty head each. The cattle dug into abundant hay and vied for automatic waterers, settling quickly.

The riders gathered at the last pen, grins on every face.

"All right!" Marcus practically swaggered in the saddle. "That was awesome."

"You two are becoming indispensable," Leif said. "Good job, grandkids of mine."

"Amen to that," Kelly said. "I haven't been on a gathering for years. You guys reminded me how much fun it was when I was a kid."

"Joely would be proud," Bjorn said. "I admit, this always was a fun tradition."

"Joely always was the beasts' champion," Harper said.

They laughed because they could, now that Joely was likely going to be all right. Relief curled like warm hearth smoke in Cole's chest. He'd worked closely with Joely for several weeks before the accident. She was a little naïve and idealistic, but she was darn smart and a fast study. Over time she'd make a good landlord for Paradise Ranch. Any of the sisters would, come to that. They all knew their ways around horses, cows, and hard work.

He shared a quick smile with Harper. A pang of regret took him over. If he had Harper by his side, he'd consider running a big place like this. Raising their kids to continue both ranch legacies, teaching them to ride the way Skylar and Marcus…He chopped off his thoughts with an abrupt turn of his head. Such musing daydreams were far out of line.

"One down, two groups to go," he said. "Busy week coming up."

"We moved the two smaller groups into nearer pastures last week," Bjorn added. "We'll get through this bunch in the next three days and then go after the next."

"I wish it would take a month," Marcus said. "No school is the best."

Skylar smiled and nodded. She'd turned in her art piece to the contest that morning, and from the way she spoke about it only when forced to, Cole figured she was plenty nervous. Harper had talked to her about ignoring rejection, and she'd done a good job easing Skylar's fears.

Her smart, sensitive words had probably impressed him more than they had Skylar—it was another example of the thousand things he was growing to love about Harper Crockett.

They all rubbed their horses down and took plenty of time making sure they were treated like the vital partners they were. Even if they didn't participate in weeklong roundups anymore, they were still indispensable. Paradise was definitely going to need a couple more good cow horses.

He sighed, his mood sobering slightly. He did love the idea of more horses, more time in the saddle, sticking around where, even in the barn, he could feel the cool breeze tugging at his hat through the open door and leaving its rough kiss on his skin. He'd give anything to get his dad back on a horse, too. To erase the stigma and hurt from losing the Double Di and give it all back. But more horses were another expenditure—the tip of a very large iceberg of costs. There was barely enough to cover salaries and feed for the winter at the moment. He had to pray the price of beef had risen as much as his research showed him it had.

For now, they'd all simply have to take top notch care of the horses they had. New ones might be an expenditure for next season.

When they trooped into the house, everyone was more than ready for a feast. And the women who'd chosen to stay domestic for the day didn't disappoint. Platters of short ribs appeared on the big dining room table along with mounds of garlic mashed potatoes, tender beans fresh frozen from Bella's garden, fruit salad, and Melanie's delicious cornbread. Through the boisterous meal, everyone laughed. Cole delighted in Harper's high mood, relieved that she even shared it with Mia. Maybe one more day of ranching would turn the tide on her outlook.

The landline phone rang as Sadie was about to produce her signature chocolate cake for dessert. Mia jumped to answer it and everyone's conversation froze, knowing it could be news, good or bad, from the hospital.

"Hello?" Mia said, her features twisting as she listened intently. "Oh! Certainly. She's here. Can you hold for a moment?" She covered the speaker and pointed at Harper. "It's for you. Cecelia Markham."

Pure surprise crossed Harper's features. The rest of their tablemates breathed a collective sigh, and the chatter started up again. Harper took the phone from her sister and headed to another room, casting an uncertain look at Cole. He shot her a thumbs-up. Cecelia Markham had only brought good things to Harper's life. This couldn't be a bad call.

He was wrong.

She returned a solid ten minutes later, her face as crestfallen and pale as if there'd been yet another disaster.

"I have to go back to Chicago," she said. "First thing tomorrow morning."

"THERE YOU ARE."

Harper stopped the soothing rock of the front porch swing with her toe and smiled without looking at Cole. He'd gone to help check the cattle, and she'd gone to say good-bye to her mother and Joely. She'd known this conversation was coming, too, but she'd put it off as long as she could.

"Hi," she said, as he eased his handsome frame onto the wooden seat and put his arm around her.

"It's all going to be okay, you know," he said. "You'll be back soon."

Would she? While Cecelia had been her usual kind self, she'd all but ordered Harper back for a special party organized to celebrate her recent sponsorship of Harper's work. It was important, she'd said, for these movers and shakers to meet her. And it sounded as though Cecelia might have scheduled holiday appearances for her from now until Christmas. Cole could not possibly know if it was "all going to be okay." But she loved that he tried so hard to make her think so.

"I don't know," she said. "It's a little like I have a job now. It's a job I love, but I owe Cecelia a lot, and I want to do my best for her. She's creating so many opportunities for me to meet people and make a real career out of painting. How can I promise anything to Paradise? To you?"

"All you have to promise is not to give up on this new thing we've got. Don't throw up roadblocks. Don't be such a pessimist. See what happens."

"You're a cock-eyed optimist."

"Promise."

"I promise to see what happens."

The growl that emanated from his throat made her laugh even before he clasped his hands around her neck and shook them. "You're impossible."

"Gosh, I've pretty much heard *that* my whole life."

"Yeah, and I sure don't have any trouble knowing why," he teased. "But for some damn reason, I like you anyway."

"It would be a lot easier if you didn't like me quite so much. And vice versa."

"But not nearly as much fun."

"Yeah, fun."

"You promised not to be a pessimist."

"No. I promised to see what happens."

"Let me show you."

He kissed like he'd taken lessons from Casanova, Rhett Butler, *and* Upside-Down Spiderman and now surpassed them all. The soft touch of his lips set her body trembling, and shivers blazed across every inch of skin when his fingertips stroked her cheeks the moment he delved into her mouth. He tasted her reverently, as if she were the most exotic and precious of wines. He pulled her into the kiss inexorably and stoked the fire inside of her like a master, until she wanted him no matter what the consequences.

Until she scared herself out of the fog.

She jerked away, her movement the opposite of his skillful tenderness.

"Harper, what?"

"I'm leaving in the morning. What good does it do us to keep starting this and then having to screech to a halt?"

"We wouldn't have to screech or halt." He brushed his knuckles along her jawline. "Morning is a ways away."

"And what? Complicate this by going to bed? What if I liked it?"

She tried to joke, but deep inside it wasn't funny. The idea of loving Cole frightened her. She didn't want to live on planes. She didn't want to fall any more deeply in love with him than she already had.

"You would like it."

"Arrogant." She attempted a smile.

"Believe me. I don't think for one second it would be one sided."

"Nice save."

He tried to gather her to him again, and this time it wasn't fear of him but fear for herself that forced her to push him away and stand.

He sighed and pinched the bridge of his nose, tired and disappointed. "Fine," he said.

It *almost* changed her mind. "I won't make love to you just to leave afterward," she said. "That's how it would always be after that, stolen lovemaking. Like you and Mia used to have. I do remember that."

He stood then, his features more than disappointed.

"Run away, Harper, if that's what you have to do. But at least be kind enough to stop comparing us to Amelia and me. This is nothing like we ever were. Ever. I resent that you keep making this out to be a sister swap."

She hung her head. He was right. It wasn't fair. It was one of her countless reasons for not wanting to hurt him or get hurt herself.

"I'm sorry." She raised up to kiss his cheek. "You're right. You aren't that kind of person; I know it. But I can't do long distance. Not when a relationship needs more care than that. Not to mention what Paradise needs. We have to leave it in the hands of the people who will be here every day to care for it and make decisions."

He didn't reply. She'd finally made her point. When she turned he didn't stop her, nor did he see the tears beading in her eyes.

She closed the front screen door quietly behind her, gulping a deep, calming breath. Closing her eyes, she leaned back against the door.

"He's right, you know." Mia's voice beside her drew a sharp gasp from Harper's throat.

"Who's right about what?" she asked.

"Cole. We've never had, in all the years we were together, what's grown between you in two months."

"But…" Harper tried to find the right words. "You were perfect together."

"For about two years. In high school. After that we were on again and off again more than anyone ever knew. And you are right about one thing—long distance is hard. But mostly it wasn't even that. We were pretty much trying to live up to our own hype and everyone else's hopes."

"Wait. You stayed together for us?"

"I think we wanted it to work at first. It sounded good on paper." She laughed. "Two ranching families united. Could it get any better? But then I got my dream job, and his dad lost the Double Diamond. We were finally able to step back and admit what we'd known for a long time. We liked each other. We didn't love each other. I doubt we ever really did."

Harper's mind whirled. This was not the picture she'd ever had of Mia and Cole. How many secrets had they all kept from each other over the past twelve years?

"But wait. You haven't liked it when Cole and I are together. The other morning when you found us on the couch, you were angry."

"Do you want to know the truth? I was annoyed at first. I was never jealous—but I kept thinking that if I didn't want him, I didn't want any of you to want him either. It was reflex. But then I started to watch you both. You two are perfect opposites and yet exactly alike. He's calm and level-headed. You're passionate and emotional. He's all about the facts. You're all about the feelings. And yet, you're both so nice it hurts."

"I am *not* nice." Harper laughed. "Not if thoughts count."

"You know they don't. Besides—you get to be the emotional tree hugger. I get to be the bitch. Don't even try and take that from me."

"You aren't—" Harper covered her mouth to hold in laughter at Mia's candor. She couldn't remember the last time they'd had a conversation like this.

Mia waved her hand. "I am. Sometimes. But the other morning? I wasn't mad, I was shocked. Because I'd actually been thinking maybe you two were perfect for each other and that I should even tell you. Then you went and beat me to the punch. Plus—I *was* tired and mad at that frickin' stupid Lieutenant Busybody Harrison."

"Aww," Harper changed the subject briefly. "He's adorable."

"He's an arrogant, ex-army megalomaniac." For a moment there was silence and then Mia laughed. "Oddly enough, I've heard that about myself."

"Not from me. Maybe I called you a know-it-all. When we were kids."

"I know there are more problems between us than Cole. But I told him when we split up three years ago that I wanted him to have someone perfect. Whatever our issues have been, Harper, you're that perfect one, and I don't want to see you lose each other. Despite what you think, I'm not cold or heartless."

"I don't think—"

"Sometimes you do. You all do. Ever since we were kids. And…" she held up her hand to ward off Harper's protests. "I thought—sometimes still think—you're an idealistic ostrich with your head in the sand."

"I see. So is this something we should talk about now, all these years later?"

"No. Maybe. Harper, I'm sorry. I guess I perceive your life as one big hippie love fest, and I've never known how to deal with that."

"I don't even know what that is." She thought her heart should be breaking over these revelations, but the truth made her feel like she could say anything. "What is it you think I do?"

"Truthfully? I have no idea. Isn't that sad? I imagine you bringing people together with tambourines and singing Kumbaya. You do have an uncanny knack for uniting. Maybe not this family so far, but you're wonderful with people."

"You must be good with them, too. You're a doctor after all."

"I can be. And I can be tough—as everyone loves to point out. I'm a surgeon. I spend limited time with my patients. It's easy to have a great bedside manner for consultations and talking to relatives after an operation."

"Why are you suddenly bringing all this up?" Harper crossed her arms. "Because I'm leaving?"

"I don't blame you for being suspicious. We don't have a good track record, do we?" Mia studied her nails, rubbing one with a thumb. Hesitating. "Tonight it's about Cole. Later, maybe I'll tell you how envious I was of you as a kid."

"Ex*cuse* me?"

"I was jealous of how you managed to be yourself in this place where conforming was always the expectation."

"That's the craziest thing I've ever hear—me being myself. I hid it all the time. It is true. We were expected to be nothing but good little cowgirls."

"Yeah. And after I told Dad I didn't want to run this place, ever, I was very far from being a good Crockett cowgirl."

"You thought Dad was mad at *you*?" Harper snorted derisively. "He was so disappointed in me—wasting my life on frivolous pursuits."

"Are you kidding? He thought you were amazing."

"I'm not even going to dignify that with a denial. You're the one who had his heart in your palm."

Mia didn't say anything for several long moments. She finally looked up with shining eyes. "Maybe we're both a little right. I don't think I can work all that out right now. But I'm not bringing this up because you're leaving. It's because I wish you weren't."

"Good grief." Now she'd heard everything.

"I've been watching all of us since Mom and Joely were injured. Every one of us is fragile. I feel like I should be able to fix them, and I can't. You're torn between here and Chicago. The triplets want to come and help. I think we owe it to them to work harder on figuring out what to do with this place. For some reason, I think you and Cole might be a big part of that."

"That's where you're wrong."

"I don't know…"

"Do you still want to sell?"

"I don't know that either. Maybe selling is the right thing. Maybe not. All I have learned is that it's not something to be angry about. I've been really angry. I'm sorry."

"Mia, I…I don't know what to say. I have to go back. I've got a big new opportunity in Chicago. I can't stay here."

"I know that, too. It's just, it feels like it's you and me right now. The triplets are fantastic and smart, but they're so young. Joely's still critical. Mom's in no shape to figure this out. Grandma is living out her time."

She was right. The weight had been there for days now, unnamed but heavy on Harper's mind.

"Could you ever come to Chicago?" she asked, surprising herself with the question. "We could…talk. Some more?"

Mia nodded. "I'd like that. I still wish you could stay."

"You haven't met Cecelia Markham."

"No. But I've met Noble Westin, our chief of staff. I'll pit him against your Cecelia any day."

Harper had to laugh. "I'd like to see that. Except I like Cecelia."

"It's good you like your boss."

"She's not a boss…"

"She's telling you when to come back to work, Harper. If it looks like a duck…"

Harper bristled slightly, but her sister was right. "Whatever you label it, I'm obligated to fulfill my part of our agreement."

"It's true. You are. You're a professional now." She sighed, but for once it wasn't in exasperation. "Look," she said. "I started this whole thing because I really believe you shouldn't give up on Cole. You two have something special, as new and unexpected as it is. Don't run away from it."

"Yeah," Harper said, scowling. "About that eavesdropping."

"Wish I could say I was sorry." Amelia stood. "Think about it. He's a pretty special guy."

"Yeah. He is."

They stared at each other for a moment, and then Harper reached in first for a hug. Mia's embrace eased another load of bricks from Harper's shoulders.

"I will think about what you said," Harper told her. "You've given me a big gift. I didn't want to hurt you with Cole."

"I know."

"I'm more worried about leaving Mom and Joely. I'm leaving you alone with them. That's a lot. You'll call me if you need help? Despite what I said, I'll tell Cecelia Markham off and come running."

"Do not worry about that. I'll check in with you every day. I promise."

"Thanks."

"Oh, Skylar was here looking for you earlier. Be sure to talk to her tomorrow before she heads back out to help with the cows. You'll be missing her show."

If Harper's world hadn't already been tilted completely off its axis, the bottom would have dropped out then. How could she have forgotten that?

Chapter Twenty

For the first time since moving to the city on Lake Michigan, Harper found Chicago all but intolerable. The party Cecelia had thrown to introduce Harper to some of her friends and clients had been successful, but it felt excruciatingly stuffy after the few days spent in the company of horses, cows, and Cole.

She missed Cole. It would have been so much easier if she didn't.

Cecelia was nothing but sweet and solicitous, and yet there was a new air of propriety in her pride. Harper couldn't put her finger on it. It wasn't smugness, or vanity, just an overprotective, over-helpful, over-mothering sense that managing Harper's career was the new most important thing in her life. It was impossible to be ungrateful. But Harper was slowly seeing exactly the number of strings that had come with the generous grant.

She spoke to her mother every day. Joely wasn't up to talking yet, still sleeping most of the time. But they were getting her up when they could. Raquel replaced Kelly as the triplet at home and kept her up-to-date on everything. She didn't hear any more from Mia. Or Cole.

The Sunday of the art exhibition, Harper consoled herself by painting and waiting for news from Raquel, who'd promised to attend. The regret at not being able to see her kids' pictures on display stung. She'd tried to empower them to do something brave, and here she was, unable to follow through.

Not that she didn't appreciate the time she did have to work on her own pieces. The decadence to have all day for painting blew her away. Still, she missed the interaction with other artists—even budding ones at a Chicago community ed center, or baby ones on a makeshift retreat in Wyoming.

Her phone didn't ring until well after ten. She saw Raquel's number and answered breathlessly. It wasn't her sister.

"Hi, Harper?" A quiet, half-timid voice came through the phone.

"Skylar?" Her heart pounded with happiness, which was silly, but the surprise delighted her. "How are you, sweetie? How was the show?"

"Well…" The long pause had Harper on the edge of her stool, and when Skylar spoke again the words were no longer uncertain. "I won!"

Won?

"Won?" She jumped from her seat.

"I won the whole thing. The best entry. They want to hang it at the hospital. Oh my God, Harper, can you believe it? Raquel let me call and tell you myself."

"That is fan*tastic*, Sky. I'm jumping up and down for you!"

She skipped across the room, hugging herself, wishing desperately she was in Wyoming to hug her young friend instead.

"Yeah. I was pretty shocked. They said it was one of the most sophisticated paintings from a middle school artist they'd ever seen."

"Baby, that's cool. Oh, I'm so proud. And proud of myself for seeing your talent." She laughed.

"Harper?"

"Yeah, sweetie?"

"Thank you. You made this happen."

"Bah. I read a sign. The talent is all yours. I'm so glad you called."

"Sure. Hold on."

The rumbling, happy voice that followed Skylar's still didn't belong to Raquel either. "Well, Madam Art Teacher. What do you think?"

Her regrets hit full force. She wanted to hug him. To celebrate. To be there. "I'm totally blown away," she said. "How was it? The coolest?"

"Absolutely the coolest. She deserved it, Harpo. Her painting really is phenomenal."

"I'm sorry I wasn't there. I really am." She hesitated. "How...how are you?"

"I'm fine. I've been so busy I haven't had time to check on you, though. We've got the second herd sorted and preg tested. Third group gets sorted tomorrow. Almost done. We should have a decent crop of calves. The cows are looking good. We might have caught a break—prices have gone up."

"Oh! That's wonderful!"

It was all so normal, much more boring and mundane than the parties she had scheduled through the holidays. And yet, all she could think about was the sound of cattle mooing and snorting their way into pens after the long walk from their summer pastures.

"Sorry," Cole added. "Totally boring. It's my life at the moment. Everyone's life."

"No, it's not boring at all. I want to hear."

"But the girl of the hour is about to get taken out for a late treat by her mom and dad. Nate and Lily are coming as well, and Raquel and I will represent you."

Tears welled in her eyes. "I wish I could fly back and join you."

"Aww. Harpo, we'd wait for you."

"Tell her I'm proud of her. And the others, too."

"Lily got an honorable mention in her photography category."

"That's fantastic."

"Nate's being as nice to Skylar as if he'd won. Mia thinks there's a little something there. I don't know. Skylar barely looks at him as far as I can tell."

Harper laughed. "Be glad, Cole. Your days on the pedestal might be coming to an end."

"I should be jealous?"

"Yup. I think so."

"Girls. You're all fickle. Okay, gotta go. But we wanted you to know."

"Thanks. Will you...call again? Sometime? Keep me updated?"

"Sure. If you want me to."

She hesitated, about to break her own edict about not fostering something they couldn't continue. "I do."

She waited for a snarky comment, but he chuckled. "Talk to you soon. Go paint pretty pictures."

She hung up and stood over her canvas, liking what she saw but hating the thought of finishing it now. Two of Cecelia's paintings were already complete. This one would have to wait. She turned on her phone again and scrolled through her address book to Tristan's name.

"Hey!" she said when he answered. "Do you know any decent bars open late? I'm looking for someone to drink a toast with."

Tristan's laugh held none of the warm, sexy comfort that Cole's did, but he was a friend, he'd never turn down a good glass of wine, and he appreciated good art. As a stand-in for celebrating in Wyoming, he'd have to do.

SKYLAR STARED UP at the cold, dark heavens and tried to let the crowding stars comfort her as they always did. She loved the night sky, which was why she had chosen two in the morning to leave. This early Wednesday morning, however, anger consumed her and left no room for comfort. The stars were no more than hot white pinpricks in the black sky. She'd never been so furious with her parents. Ever. In two days she'd gone from celebrating the most wonderful thing that had ever happened to her, to hating almost everything about her life.

She tightened Bungu's cinch and heard Asta crying in the barn. Skylar almost relented. The puppy had grown to double her original size in the past six weeks, and she was smart as could be, but she wasn't quite big enough to trek into the mountains. She'd be fine for two days until Skylar got back. And if Skylar didn't go now, she'd say something really stupid to her parents and be grounded for life. She might be anyway after this, but if she'd learned anything growing up on a ranch it was that you had to get your anger under control or you couldn't do your job.

She was going to climb her anger out on Wolf Paw Peak, but she highly doubted she'd ever forgive her mother this time.

Not display her winning picture?

Her eyes still burned from the hours of tears she'd shed after the edict had come down.

So there was a couple kissing on the painting. There wasn't anything weird about it—you could hardly see any detail at all because they were silhouetted. But her mother was such a freak. She acted like a nun or something.

"This is not an appropriate way to show off your first artwork," she said. "People will expect you to do more of the same. You're only fourteen, Skylar. You can't be painting love scenes already. There'll be another art show. Why don't you go paint something equally beautiful but without the sex?"

There was no sex. It was a stupid kiss. Her mother was…well, she was what Grandpa Leif said about bats and shit and crazy—but if anyone heard her repeat that, she'd get a toothbrush full of soap.

So she was running away. Well, not really; she wasn't that stupid. But she'd tried to find someone who'd sympathize with her, and nobody was around except Grandma Sadie. Everyone else was at the hospital or had gone home or was out doing fence repair. And Cole had flown off to Chicago. Which kind of made her mad, but only because she knew he'd be on her side and now he was gone. So she had to go and figure out what to do next by herself.

She checked the cinch after tightening it and made sure her thick bedroll behind the cantle was secure. October had arrived, but she knew how to pack for camping in the cold. There wasn't any real snow yet, just a dusting on the peak. She'd take her time and follow the trail she knew until dawn. Then she'd take a nap in her pup tent and make it to the top by evening. She'd camp overnight one more time and come home. Maybe she'd have a plan by then for convincing her parents to change their minds. She'd camped plenty of times on trail rides, and her dad and brother were experts. At least she'd show them she wasn't some baby who shouldn't have her picture hung in public.

She zipped her jacket up to her chin and pulled on her fleece mittens. The air was cold, but she'd dressed for frigid temperatures. Even though the slight breeze would be at her back, she knew cold could settle in unexpectedly when you were sitting on a horse. She had plenty of food, like energy bars and peanut butter crackers, along with water in her saddle bags. She knew where the safe streams were anyway. And she had long underwear and a mummy-style sleeping bag in her roll. The idea of her adventure sent adrenaline surging through her veins. She'd wanted to do this forever. Everything felt perfect. And exciting. And only a teeny bit scary.

"Come on Bungu," she said, and she lifted her foot into the stirrup.

COLE DIDN'T REMEMBER the West Chicago neighborhood looking so shabby the one time he'd been here before. Now, in the growing twilight, he could see the unkempt lawns and the overgrown gardens that signaled lack of care on the residents' parts. Not that he cared that much about appearances, but this was where Harper lived. He didn't want to think of her in an unsafe place.

The house she shared with four roommates was better maintained than some of the others, but the stone steps up to the front door were cracked, and the foundation plantings were late fall dry and wildly overgrown. The privacy fencing looked new, however, and although the blue shutters badly needed painting, the white house color wasn't too old.

Cole hesitated before ringing the bell and hoped Harper had gotten his text. He hadn't warned her he was coming until he'd landed at O'Hare. Faith and audacity—that's all he had on his side after imagining he'd heard genuine longing in her voice the night of Skylar's big win. He hoped she'd let him in. After that he couldn't guess what would happen.

Still, he laughed at the thought of Harpo turning anyone away. She would never have to worry about not properly entertaining angels unaware. Yet another thing he loved about her.

He pushed the bell.

The door flew open in fewer than five seconds, and her greeting surpassed his wildest hopes. She was in his arms like an ecstatic puppy, hugging him, peppering him with kisses, burying her head in the crook of his neck, and laughing.

"What are you *doing* here? I couldn't believe when you texted you were on your way from the airport."

"You said I could check on you." He unwrapped her arms and pushed her far enough away to smooth the sleek, flowing dark hair from her face and kiss her forehead and then the tip of her nose. "Otherwise, no excuse except that I missed you, whether you missed us or not. And I came to show you that twelve hundred miles is not insurmountable."

She mirrored him, cupping her hands around his jaw and smoothing his cheeks with her thumbs. With a happy smile, she placed a sweet kiss on his lips. "Of course I missed you. I miss everyone, right down to the cows."

"Would you like to prove it?" He kissed her back, his heart flying with hope.

"How?"

"Let me in?"

Her laugh added pure joy to his hope. She grasped his hand. "Oh, all right. C'mon, there are only two of us home at the moment. It's not even chaotic."

He entered the warm, eclectic living room, filled with mismatched furniture and bright, bold colors, and waved to one of the roommates, Natalie, watching television in a corner.

"Welcome back to Chi-town," she said with a wave of her hand.

"How long are you staying?" Harper asked.

"Three days. We finished with the cattle. There were two days of downtime before we start fencing. Leif was going to work on some tack mending, and I asked for some vacation. Gotta leave Friday."

"Will you...stay here?"

"I have a hotel room. Wasn't sure where we stood, so I didn't presume. We'll talk about it."

"Well, I took over the third floor and spread out to paint. Molly moved into my old room on the second floor. It's a little more private up there."

"Whoa, are you inviting me to see your, um, etchings?"

She smiled. "No etchings, sorry to say. The space isn't even very presentable—smells like paint and linseed oil. But you can come up and see what I've been working on the past week. Has it really only been a week since I left?"

"Eight days," he agreed. *Eight long days.* "I'll come up, but please tell me I can take you out tonight. Isn't this supposed to be the best place in the world for pizza? I'm starving."

"Poor thing."

"Yeah, they don't feed you much on planes anymore."

"I wouldn't want that fantastic body to waste away."

The light in her eyes flared hot and strong. He wanted to pinch himself to make sure he wasn't fantasizing. This wasn't the Harper who'd pushed him away and run practically screaming from his arms in Wyoming.

"What do you know about this body?" he teased.

"I refer you back to that spider incident again. And I've seen the bottom half in a whole lotta pairs of nice, worn jeans."

"I'll be danged. Who knew you were paying attention?"

She only grinned and led him up two flights of stairs to the open, full-floor room on the third level. "Not presentable" took on humorous clarity when he entered her space. A single bed, thick with blankets and rumpled sheets, stood unmade against one wall. Clothing spilled over the sides of a wicker basket, whether dirty or unfolded he couldn't tell. In a far corner he took in a dorm-sized refrigerator covered with boxes of granola bars and a basket of bananas and a few other random pieces of fruit. Next to it was a trash can in the same state as the laundry basket.

Laughter rose helplessly, and he moved to a chair covered in clothing. For some reason the disorder thrilled him. His eyes lit on a scrap of black lace and he bent over. With one finger he lifted the bra off its pile and dangled it like a prize.

"Now this is the kind of messy room I like. Am I learning something about the real Harper Crockett?"

He fully expected her to snatch the bra from him and stuff it away; he almost looked forward to her discomfiture. The surprises, however, kept coming.

"I'm afraid so. I'm a pathetic slob." She pulled the blankets and comforter carelessly up to cover the bed, which didn't make it look that much neater. "And that's one of my favorites. Don't be stretching it out."

His mouth went slightly dry. "Do tell." He could definitely do a fantastic job of stretching it out given the right circumstances. "I'm not sure this is a safe location for a boy like me."

She approached him slowly and ran one finger up the front of his sweater. "Oh, I think you're old enough to learn about the world, Cole. It's a girl's room. It's just a bra. Most of us wear one."

He wrapped his arms around her, and lowered his mouth. The bra dropped to the floor behind her back. "Okay, then it's you who aren't safe with me in the room."

"That I believe."

"Harper, are you all right?" He grinned. "Or is this what Chicago does to you?"

She rested against his lips for a moment. He shivered when her hands threaded under his arms and clasped behind his back.

"I am totally confused and happy that you're here. I know I'm acting crazy, but that's how I've felt since I left the ranch."

"That might be the most awesome thing anyone has ever said to me."

"That's pretty sad."

"It's not. It means you miss us."

"Not 'us.' I miss you."

"Nope, I'm incidental. You miss Wyoming."

"Say you'll move here, and I'll prove it has nothing to do with Wyoming."

"Okay."

Her eyes filled with the light of disbelief, and she disengaged from their embrace. "Really?"

"Harpo, I've decided I'll follow you anywhere. That's really why I'm here."

"You aren't on your way somewhere? You aren't here to give me news?"

"I'm here to take you for pizza and then to bed."

He'd done it, rendered her speechless, and he grinned like a fool. He certainly wasn't here to force her. He hadn't even meant to say those words. But the spark of desire behind her surprise almost chased away his desire for food.

When she found her voice she used it coyly for the first time. "Well then. With that much to fit in, we'd better get a move on to that pizza place."

SHE COULDN'T STOP staring at him.

Their conversation covered the most mundane subjects, but the way his lips moved around the words, interspersed with sexy bites of Gino's East deep dish pizza, made cows, dogs, beef prices, and pasture rotation the most scintillating topics ever to be discussed in public.

He'd asked her if she was all right, and now she knew the answer—she wasn't. His unexpected appearance had shattered every resolve she'd made about being with him, long distance or otherwise. The sense of perfect peace that settled more deeply into her cells the longer they sat astonished her, and the longing for every ordinary ranch activity he mentioned took her totally aback. Here she was, in the heart of one of the biggest cultural centers in the world, and all she could think about was missing out on watching Skylar's little border collie learn how to herd cows.

"Are you even listening?" Cole's amusement only sent his lips into an even sexier upward curve.

"I'm watching you," she replied honestly, propping her chin in one palm.

"All well and good, but I asked if you want another glass of wine."

She laughed. "Oh. Sorry."

"So do you?"

"No. Thanks, but you might take advantage of me if I get any loopier."

"I might anyway."

Heat in her cheeks had become a familiar sensation over the course of the evening. In fact, he could raise the temperature in her entire body with the most unexpected lines. She'd given up trying to anticipate when those lines might come and why they could be the most ordinary of subjects. She loved the easy conversation. They discussed things the way they might have rehashed an ordinary day as a long-married couple—

Her thoughts ground to a halt.

Married?

The word had never once come into her thoughts, and suddenly she found herself wondering if she *could* ever marry this man. The notion was insane. And yet part of her believed if he asked her right this minute she'd say yes.

Ridiculous. She'd already enumerated the problems with simply being a couple. Marriage would be like diving purposely into a pool of quicksand. His hands slipped up over the backs of hers and pulled her again into the present.

"Can you come back home for Christmas?" he asked.

Memories from childhood Christmases flooded her and she smiled. The one time when every sister had been equal in the eyes of Santa, and by extension their parents, had always been the heart of the year. It had been the only time her father took multiple days off from all but basic barn chores. Three days—and the hands and their families had all gotten the same time off. Times of actual fun.

"I'd like to," she said.

"Your mom will be home in a week. Joely might be able to come for a visit by then."

"How is she really?"

"No sugarcoating, honey. She's in rough shape," he said, serious for one of the first times. "Physically, she'll be okay in the long run, although nobody knows if she'll get back the use of her left leg. Her biggest problem right now, though, is severe depression. Nobody can really get her to talk about anything since she learned about the loss of her horse in the accident."

"I hurt so badly for her. I try to call her most days, but she can't talk for long."

"Well, keep it up no matter how hard it is. She needs those calls. And if you can tell her you'll be home in six weeks or so and you want to see her up and about, maybe she'll have some incentive."

A twinge of guilt settled on her. She shouldn't be discussing the seriousness of Joely's condition yet thinking only how she wanted to crawl right over the table and the pizza to wrap herself around Cole's body. How crass was that? But his mix of hard sexiness and soft caring was suddenly irresistible. To make it worse, his hands on hers shot tingles up her arms.

"She'll be okay," he said. "It's just going to take time."

"How'd you get to be so nice?"

"Am I?" He grinned.

"Sometimes."

"What am I the rest of the time?"

"Irritatingly attractive."

His brows lifted and waggled like Groucho Marx. "Here's to irritating the hell out of you, Harper Lee."

Chapter Twenty-One

"YOU HARDLY EVER see this." Harper leaned against Cole on a bench in a cold, clear park located on three dark blocks outside the city center. She laid her head on his shoulder and pointed between tree tops to the patch of night sky and the pinpricks of starlight so difficult to spot beneath Chicago's overpowering glow.

"Rare as the northern lights in Texas." He stroked her cheek with one finger, reaching across their bodies to do so and enveloping her in warmth and shivers at the same time.

"You're bothering me," she murmured.

"I was bound to since you wanted to walk to the hotel."

"Buses are much slower going. It's only six blocks."

"And you wanted to stop here."

"Because you noticed the stars." She smiled into the dark.

Without warning he pushed her upright and then pulled her around on the bench until he could tug her leg over his lap. She crawled onto him.

"Now I'm really going to bother you," he said and stopped any reply with a hard, deep kiss.

Her body awoke fully. Liquid heat rushed to the spot where she pressed against him, and a hard shaft of desire drove straight up between her legs and into her stomach. He pressed upward and doubled the shots of pleasure.

"I admit it," she said against his lips. "I'm afraid."

"Don't be. C'mon, Harpo. Let go of the silly sister code and believe—"

She pressed her finger to his lips. "Amelia told me to get over myself."

"She did?"

"She told me to grab you and run."

His dopey grin almost made her laugh. "I always knew she was intelligent," he said.

"I don't want to talk about Amelia."

"Okay. Why are you afraid?"

"Because even if this isn't the old Harper resurfacing, the one who's only looking for acceptance, it's a new Harper who'll like this too much. I still don't know what I'll do when you're gone again."

He kissed her in answer, thoroughly, a little punishingly, as if to brand her with something she couldn't lose no matter where he went. When he stopped he held her cheeks firmly between warm, firm hands.

"One step at a time. Step one was proving I can get to you, like this, anytime I want to."

"What's step two?"

"Proving we work together."

She rocked against him and moaned as pleasure radiated from her center, enveloping her senses, intensifying, and heating her blood until there was no such thing as a cold park bench or the chance of being discovered. No such thing as fear. Cole was right: one step at a time. He moved beneath her, hard and perfectly matched to her body. Her breath hitched and released as every nerve fiber vibrated, and she knew two more strokes, maybe one, would push her over the edge.

"Like this." His breath, hot and literally steamy, melted into her ear. "And, baby, if you're ready to start right here, I'm with you."

"I'm not. Ready." She forced herself to rise from his lap and take his hand. The October night air, crisp and invigorating, temporarily cooled the heat in her body.

"Harper." He groaned and stood with her.

"No. No, I'm not running this time. I just see step two as something completely different. You almost proved three seconds ago how well you and I are going to work together." Step two is execution. And I'm not wasting my first time in a spot, however beautiful, where I can't have you all to myself. I'm not sharing you with the cold."

"Or that guy over there." Cole pointed at a man in a flap-eared cap shuffling down the path.

She sputtered and covered her mouth with a gloved hand. Cole's chuckle rolled into a belly laugh, and he pulled her to his side, wrapping her with both arms and making her hurry the rest of the way to the hotel.

FIFTEEN MINUTES LATER Harper drew open the drapes in Cole's room on the twenty-seventh floor and stared at the neon city, now spread at their feet. The pewter sheen of Lake Michigan glistened straight ahead of them. The whole scene glittered like the stars in the park.

"This is a beautiful room."

"Not anywhere near as expensive as it looks," he said. "Midweek, one of those hotel-finder sites."

"That's my economical cowboy."

He appeared behind her, reflected in the dark window like a dream lover.

"Am I? Yours?" His arms encircled her from behind, and his fingers laced over her stomach—not dreamlike at all but solid and thrilling.

"Pretty sure. Do you see anyone else in the room who'd take you?"

She watched his reflection again, as he bent his head and placed his lips at the side of her reflection's neck. The hot, throaty chuckle that filled her real ear and, the soft, exploring lips that touched her skin against her throat sent chills lancing through her body. The ethereal picture of them in the glass juxtaposed with the physical sensations on her body tantalized like a sensual optical illusion. The magic set her aflame. She watched herself sink on wobbly knees deeper into his hold before she closed her eyes and spun from the vision into the reality of his embrace.

"For a minute I thought you were my imagination," she said, opening her eyes again. "Thank the good Lord you're not."

"Believe me, I'm not. Let me get rid of that ghost for you."

He strode quickly across the room, flicked off the light, and the room went dark, until the city outside the window sent its glittering play of lights upward and turned the darkness to soft shadows. He returned and their reflections in the window were gone. All they could see were the diamond-bright lights of Chicago.

The time of languorous build-up had passed. Every fiber of Harper's body begged for him, and the heat from the park flared anew. She pushed his fleece-lined jacket off his shoulders and down his arms. Her boring gray wool car coat followed his to the floor.

Feverishly she worked the buttons on his dress shirt through their holes. As soon as the shirt hung open, he followed her lead, making short work of her sweater by slipping it over her head with a flourish.

His shirt and T-shirt hit the carpeting. Her bra took the ride as well.

"Gorgeous," he whispered when they stood skin to skin clad only in jeans and shoes. "Harper, you're so—" He cut himself off by leaning sideways and dipping his head to her breast. She gasped in delight at the scrape of his teeth and the wet heat of his tongue circling first one tip and then the other. He didn't hurry nor did he linger, as if his mission was to carefully but quickly lay the fuse that would bring a final implosion to all the perfect places.

He sank to his knees and reached her navel with his kisses. She giggled and then shivered violently as he worked the button and zipper of the jeans she'd worn in honor of his visit. He turned her in place, and she could see out the window again while he worked the jeans half-way down her hips and reached around her to slip a long, hard-fingered hand down the soft part of her belly and beneath the waistband of her panties. Farther and deeper he sought heat, and found it. She moaned at the first explosive shudder from his intimate touch.

"No, please, I want to do this together!" She wasn't above begging.

"Hush," he replied softly. He pressed up against her from the back, pushing her into his oh-so-talented fingers. "We are together, I promise. This might be more for me than it is for you."

"Not possible."

"Yes. Oh, yes it is. Are you ready?"

Colors burst as the full explosion hit first in one special spot and then spread like seismic waves along every nerve and into every bone and muscle. His hand moved and the aftershocks slammed her—brilliant, strength sapping, and exquisite.

"No," she whispered when she could form the sound. "That was all for me. Sorry."

She opened her eyes and for a moment the world in front of her was nothing but neon fairy lights. Then she was in Cole's arms and the lights faded away, replaced by the beautiful shadowed planes of his face. She rubbed his cheek. "Thanks for that, cowboy."

He snorted a laugh and nuzzled the palm of her hand. "Never thank me for that, honey. Then I'd have to thank you. We'd be thanking each other all night and there's too much left to do to waste time jabbering.'"

"Such a practical cowboy," she murmured, her pulse finally coming back down from the stratosphere.

COLE SCOOPED HARPER into his arms and let her feet touch the floor only long enough so he could throw back the bedspread on the California King and drag down the neatly tucked sheets. He dug into his pocket and tossed two foil packets on the table beside the bed. His body ached and begged him to hurry, but he forced himself to show the last vestiges of restraint and dregs of chivalry by cradling Harper once more in his arms and setting her gently in the middle of the bed.

She weighed nothing in his arms, and she still vibrated like a guitar string, with a note that belonged only to him. "Together," she'd said. Leave it to her to want that rather than pleasure for herself. He'd almost felt guilty because all he'd wanted was to feel her fall apart in his arms. Like some macho caveman who could force the girl to tremble.

He'd gotten his fantasy and then some.

But his body wasn't impressed. It wanted more.

"Okay, mister, now it's my turn." Her voice startled him, and her soft smile sent a bolt of anticipation through his stomach and deep into the base of his spine. "I know you like denim, but there's far too much of it between us."

He nearly lost it then and there when she set to work on his fly button, resting her hands on the aching length of his hard-on, tracing the zipper before she found the tab. The rasping of the metal teeth was nearly the sound of his undoing.

She literally stood up on the mattress then and balanced on first on leg then the other while she removed her soft, chic, city boots and then wriggled out of her jeans. His eyes went wide, and his throat went dry when she stood there with nothing on but the scrap of silk that he'd already invaded once.

It took her no time to sit back down, pull off his boots and socks, and then direct him to rid himself of his jeans. If he'd thought for a minute she was going to be a timid or reticent lover, she dispelled that notion the moment he lay open to her admiring eyes.

"That is nothing less than impressive, cowboy," she said, and took the foil packet from the bedside table herself. When she'd taken care of it and him, she slid her body up the length of his. She locked their kiss and drove her tongue deep into his mouth, searching and stroking, mimicking intimately what his body so badly needed.

He pulled her against him and groaned in surrender.

"I'm sorry," he said. "But this isn't going to be all soft and slow and romance-y."

"I'm counting on that."

He flipped them effortlessly and bracketed her head with his hands, arching above her. "Tell me if you're not ready."

She adjusted beneath him and wrapped his hips with her legs. "I'm more than ready."

Her eyes closed and her head tilted back as he slipped into her, and she moaned through a smile of pleasure. He sank deeper and groaned at the perfect fit of her around him and the pure fulfillment simply being one with her brought.

The satisfaction lasted three seconds. Then she moved and quiet pleasure disintegrated.

For several giddy, uncoordinated strokes they looked for a rhythm—new lovers unfamiliar with each other's likes. But what could have been awkward became a sensual game of discovery under Harper's patient humor and skillful movements. One moment they struggled, the next they soared into a synchronization that took them far past exploration.

Three strokes, four, and Cole was thrown over the brink, his breath lost, his awareness gone, his body quaking with release. From far below, a gentle, feminine cry followed him into space, or wherever he'd come to ride out the waves of pleasure. Harper. With utter satisfaction he knew this had been her moment, too.

SHE LAY CURLED in his arms, the last of her emotional tears dried, the power that had blasted her into another orgasm dissipated, and the sense of safety and warmth wrapping her like a cocoon.

"I was right," she said. "I'll never survive you leaving."

"Aww, you will." He laughed. "You got me roped and hog-tied, too, and you don't hear me whining." He squeezed her tightly.

"Oh, that's real romantic."

"Purebred lady killer. That's me."

"And we call you a cowboy poet. Brother. Give him a little lovin' and the romance flies out the window. So, now what?"

"Now you give me fifteen minutes, and I'll show you romance."

"Only fifteen? After what you just did to me? I won't be ready that fast."

"Sweetheart." He pulled from their embrace with a snort. "Know what? I'm going to start right now proving you don't know yourself."

His lips found the hollow beneath her ear and used it as the quivering starting point for an inexorable journey back down her body. He started on the way back up when a wailing version of "Folsom Prison Blues" made them both nearly jump from each other's arms. Cole's eyes flew open and every ounce of languor drained from their shadowed blue depths.

"That's Leif," he said, worry immediately replacing sleepy sex in his voice. "It's nearly eleven here. He wouldn't call at any time much less now unless something was wrong."

Harper's pulse danced with fear, and she let him sit, biting her lip at the sight of his muscled seat as he rolled from the bed to find the phone in his jeans pocket.

"Leif?" he answered. When he spoke a minute later his voice sent cold chills through Harper's heart. "Oh shit, Leif, are you sure? Where have you looked?"

"What?" she asked drawing up behind him and pressing her cheek to his back.

He took one of the hands she had snaked beneath his arms and patted it. "Look, I'm with Harper now. Let me talk to her and see if she has any ideas. I'll call you back in five minutes, okay? . . . Yes I will. Don't worry, we'll find her. Talk to you in a few."

He punched the soft keys on his phone and spun in Harper's arms.

"What's wrong?"

"Skylar disappeared. She seems to have taken her horse and run off. The pup is missing, too."

"What?" Fresh panic struck. "Why would she do that? She should be on top of the world."

"Long story." His voice turned grim "Turns out, the first time Melanie ever saw Sky's painting was at the art show. Skylar wanted to surprise them. But, now, Melanie won't give permission for the painting to be hung at the VA. She says it's too explicit for a fourteen-year-old. She wouldn't even have let her enter it had she known."

"Are you *kidding* me?" Panic was replaced by complete disbelief.

What in the world was wrong with Melanie?

"Skylar left sometime in the middle of last night and hasn't been back. It's been almost twenty hours, it's dark now, and they're starting to panic. They've called everyone she knows and searched all her regular hangouts around the ranch. Leif thought maybe she'd said something to one of us that might give them a clue."

Harper's brain spun trying to think of anything the teen might have said. "Did they try your house?"

"Good thought."

They moved around the room gathering their strewn clothing and brainstorming ideas about places on Paradise land that could conceal a teen, a puppy, and a horse from diligently searching adults. The longer they talked, the crazier the ideas forming in Harper's brain became. When they were dressed and Cole grabbed the phone to call Leif back, Harper stopped him.

"We need to go back."

He didn't say anything, and she could tell he was calculating the practicality of that plan.

"They could find her any second, honey. It might be a done deal by the time we could get back."

"Then I'll believe with all my heart it was buying tickets home that proved lucky. I'll pray that's exactly what happens."

"I thought you had some social obligations two days from now."

"I don't care."

"Harper..." His voice trailed off, leaving his concern unspoken.

But she knew why she had to go back. Skylar had done exactly what it had taken Harper nineteen years to do—leave home because nobody understood her. In her own teenage years, Harper hadn't had anyone to take her part. That couldn't happen to Sky. This had to be settled now, even if Harper had to shake her friend Melanie into understanding what she'd done to cause this. It wasn't her business to tell Melanie and Bjorn how to raise their daughter, but they had to understand what Skylar needed from them.

Aside from stupid, archaic, pious rules.

"Tell Leif we'll be home as soon as we can get there. I'll find the next available flight. I'll pay for your ticket switch."

"For crying out loud, that's not the issue."

She stopped ranting and took a deep breath, floating her fingers down his cheek. "I know."

IT WAS BETTER to ask for forgiveness rather than permission.

Harper intoned that to herself over and over during the hour flight to Minneapolis, the first leg of their flight home. Timing made it impossible to tell Cecelia the new plans before they left. This flight would land in Salt Lake City at five in the morning, and they'd booked a small commuter flight that would get them to Jackson by six thirty. They'd be to Paradise before seven. She'd call Cecelia then and face the consequences, but with the grace of God the trip would prove to have been unnecessary, and she could fly right back.

If this was insanity, so be it. Harper knew she'd make this decision a hundred more impractical times if it meant Skylar was safe and Harper could hug the reckless girl to her heart. Cole never once questioned the rash decision. Men were supposedly the logical, practical sex, but if this made no sense to him, he didn't say so. His forbearance only heightened the love still spilling over from their quick first night together and made her crave more.

Cole's Range Rover awaited them at Jackson Hole Airport mere hours after leaving Chicago. Harper called Leif, Bjorn, and Mia, but nobody answered. Frustrated, she texted everyone and finally got a short answer from Raquel: "Out checking the trail, little coverage, be back home in an hour. No sign of Skylar."

She read the message with a groan. "Oh, Cole, this is not good."

Her heart had sunk to what felt like her stomach and sat there like a boulder. Cole took her hand. She appreciated, a little perversely, that he didn't make false promises.

"Call Cecelia," he said gently. "Get it over with. Once we're home, we'll be too busy to think about Chicago."

Home.

She took in the scenery flying past them. The Teton massifs—Grand and Middle Teton, Mount Owen, Mount Moran—names and silhouettes Harper had learned in the crib. She drank in the unusual geology that made mountains look as if they'd been set mid-prairie like the blocks of giants' children, with no foothills, just the stunning valley landscape leading her…home.

Skylar was missing, but at least here Harper could think and breathe and believe they would find her. She grimaced at her phone, found Cecelia's number, and dialed.

"Harper, darling!" Cecelia didn't bother with the standard hello. "This is a lovely way to start the morning."

"It's good to hear your voice, too," Harper replied. She took a fortifying breath. "But I'm afraid this call is going to disappoint you, and I'm sorry."

"Oh? How could you possibly disappoint me?"

"I left Chicago last night, and I'm back in Wyoming."

"Oh dear! Has something happened to your sister or your mother?"

"No. Not this time. It's little Skylar. I told you about her—the budding artist. She's run off from home and has been missing for almost thirty-six hours."

Cecelia let silence hang for several seconds. "You flew back for someone who isn't your family? When are you coming back?"

It was the first remotely uncharitable thing Cecelia had ever said.

"I came back to help look for her, yes. I'm sorry, Cecelia, it's something I had to do. I feel very connected to this girl. She's as close as family, and I want to be here for her the way you've been there for me. I'm not sure when I'll be back. If she's found today I'll try and get back for the party tomorrow. But I hope you understand that I have to stay until we know she's all right."

Once again silence met her explanation. When Cecelia spoke, her tone was cooler. "Of course I understand you wanting to help a young girl. I'd be more sympathetic if she were a relative. I've made a lot of preparations for this gathering, and many people are expecting to meet you."

"I am sorry." She truly was. "I'll try my very best to get back on time. I promise. I'll send Tristan in my place if I can't. He's wonderful with people, and I'll make sure he has a greeting and heartfelt apology to pass on to the guests."

"I hope the child is found safely, you know that. I am disappointed, however, just as you suspected. I hope this won't be a habit, Harper, dear. I do have a lot invested in you."

This was a side of Cecelia she hadn't seen, and even though she understood her benefactor's unhappiness, Harper fought down a quick flash of resentment. She'd braced herself to apologize yet again when Cole's fingers closed over hers. His encouraging smile boosted her certainty in what they were doing.

"I know you do, Cecelia," she said into the phone. "And please don't think I'm taking this lightly. I'm so sorry. But forgive me; I was hoping you'd be sympathetic. I didn't understand your amazing generosity would cost all my personal freedom. You see, I'd like to be a tiny bit like you. Support Skylar the way you have me. I'm worried about her."

"Really, Harper, I do understand—"

"I'm sorry, Cecelia, we're arriving home. I need to check in with my family. I promise to call you tonight and let you know what's happening."

"All right." A heavy sigh came over the phone. "I'll wait to hear all is well."

When Harper ended the call, she dropped the phone like a hot branding iron into her lap, and her hands began to shake. To stop them, she covered her face.

"She was pissed. What have I done?"

"Hey." Cole's voice commanded that she look at him. "You stood up for what's right. You stood up for yourself. Well done."

"She's right, though. She's invested a lot in me."

"And she'll get a lot from you in return. But she isn't your keeper, and you aren't on a monitoring anklet. I'm proud of you."

"You are?"

"Always. It was nice hearing you take no guff about this. Cecelia Markham is a grown woman, and she'll survive. If she's helping you for the art, then this will blow over. If she's in this for herself, then you're right to tell her you have to rethink things."

"You don't think I was rude?"

He touched the corner of his mouth with one finger. "Kiss me."

She huffed out a laughed and leaned over. He turned his head to meet her lips and kissed them with a quick, loud smack. He looked back to the road.

"You apologized multiple times. You promised to fulfill your duties the best you can. I do not think you were rude. Forget about Cecelia for now. Let's go help find a little girl."

Chapter Twenty-Two

"I DON'T HAVE the heart to yell at her now." Harper whispered to Cole, and he nodded his agreement as Melanie moved robotically around her big kitchen, putting on hot water for tea, wiping away tears at measured intervals.

"Not that you should yell at her anyway." He kissed her forehead.

"I know. I feel awful for her. Where could Skylar have gone?"

It was a useless question, but Cole didn't point that out. Obviously if anybody knew...He sighed helplessly. An hour after their arrival, he and Harper, along with Melanie, Aiden, and Grandma Sadie, were the only ones not actively searching. Bjorn, Leif, Mia, and Raquel, along with Neil and Rico and their families, were scouring the ranch on horseback and by truck as they'd been doing for two days now.

"Are you sure we shouldn't go get changed and help?" Harper asked.

"Leif will be back soon," Melanie replied. "He's going up in the plane with your dad, Cole."

His stomach sank further. If they were resorting to air searches...

"How do we know she's on the ranch?" Harper asked. "Couldn't she have ridden off to somebody's house? One of the other kids?"

"We aren't sure," Melanie said. "We've called everyone Skylar knows. Nate and Lily have been trying her cell phone since last night.

"The pond in the south pasture? The drivers' shacks out along the trails? The river bottoms?" Harper reeled off one Paradise landmark after another. Melanie nodded at each suggestion. They'd looked everywhere.

Mel stifled a quiet sob. Harper rose, the peasant-style flowered skirt she'd worn for traveling flowing to the tops of her worn cowboy boots. Over it she wore an extra-long cardigan sweater. Everything was fluffy pink and dark maroon, and Cole wanted to gather her to him like an armful of baby goose down or sweet cotton candy. She took Melanie's defeated form into her arms.

"They'll find her," she promised.

"I can't believe you came all the way back for this." Melanie sniffed and wiped her nose on a sleeve. "You're so good to us. To Sky. This is my fault. She was furious with me."

Cole braced for Harper's rebuke, but it didn't come.

"There'll be plenty of time to talk to her about why she did this."

"Oh, I pray so."

Bjorn returned to the house first, looking like a man who hadn't slept in thirty hours. He accepted Harper's warm hug and shook hands firmly with Cole.

"Anything? At all?" Melanie asked.

Bjorn shook his head and scrubbed a hand over his mouth. "Dad's meeting with Russ now."

"My dad has flown a lot of search missions," Cole said. "If someone can be found, he'll do it."

"Either of you want to go up with them?" Bjorn raised his brows, and Cole looked at Harper.

"I don't," she said. "I had a thought. I'd like to go talk to Betty Hodges, the high school art teacher. She probably talked to Skylar a fair amount during the competition, since she coordinated the exhibit and the judges. Maybe there's the smallest chance she overheard Sky say something that would give us a clue." She looked at Cole with smoky eyes and touched his cheek. "But you feel free to go. I'll be fine."

"I hate to leave you."

"No. Don't worry a bit. I'll check on Grandma and then take a run to the school. It's what, Friday? I have no problem interrupting Betty even if she's in a class. After that I'll canvas all the businesses in town in case she stopped in somewhere before heading out to wherever she went."

"Dad *could* use another set of eyes…"

"Absolutely. Go. I'll be back before you're done. Promise."

He kissed her. The effortlessness of their decision making together warmed him. She'd known exactly what he wanted and needed to do to help and exactly what to say. They would work easily together. If only…

He wrapped his arms around her for a last hug. It reminded him of the night that had been cut short, but he placed his lips against her ear. "Thank you," he said. "It's good to be here."

"It is. Thanks for not saying out loud that I'm insane."

"Well, you're not…"

They were interrupted by a rapping at the back door. Melanie's head jerked toward the sound, her eyes hopeful. Cole strode to the door, pulled it open, and found a somber-faced Nate Swanson on the stoop.

"Hi," the boy said. "I'm…I'm here to do more than try to call Sky's phone."

Harper rushed past Cole and threw an enormous hug around Nate, looking small against his gangly frame. "It's wonderful of you to come," she said. "I'm sure the group will take all the help they can get."

"I had a cool time with her at the retreat," he said. "We got to talk, and I—" His cheeks deepened in color and he shrugged. "I hate thinking something happened to her."

Cole hid a sad smile. Harper was right. There was something budding between Nate and Skylar. Well, damn, that was good.

"You haven't heard or seen anything about where she might have gone, Nate?" Melanie stepped forward.

"No. I figured if she hasn't been found, then she wasn't up the mountain, right?"

"The mountain?" Cole asked.

"Wolf Paw."

"They've looked up as far as she could take a horse," Melanie said. "She wouldn't go farther and leave Bungu. Besides, she's not allowed to climb higher alone."

Nate caught Cole's eye, skepticism in his face. Even Cole heard the breakdown of logic in Melanie's words.

"She really loves that mountain," Nate said. "All she told me was that one of her goals was to summit by herself."

Melanie's jaw went slack. Harper clamped onto Cole's upper arm. "Do you think...?"

"What exactly did she say?" Cole's heart rate had doubled, but he forced his voice to stay calm.

"That's all," Nate replied. "Except, that's why she had so many sketches of the peak. It's her favorite."

"It has to be the answer!" Harper squeezed his arm tighter. "She has to be up there."

"Nate, how'd you like to take a flight around Wolf Paw Peak?" Cole asked. "We're about to head up—sounds like that's a good place to focus."

"Sure!"

"We have to get permission from your folks," Harper said. "I'll call your mom if you like."

"Yeah, okay." Nate nodded. "Thanks."

"And I might wait here, then," Harper added. "Let's see what you find before I go running into town."

"WE'LL GO ANOTHER half hour, then set down to regroup." Cole's father banked the Cessna 172 left and headed for another pass across the face of Wolf Paw Peak.

Two hours into their search, the three men and the teen in the plane hadn't given up hope, but they fought off frustration without saying so out loud. Weather luck was with them. Colder temperatures had ushered in a cloudless blue sky with clear visibility. Unfortunately, the scrub juniper and cottonwoods of the lower mountainside turned into thick stands of Douglas fir that obscured most of the ground until the tree line gave way to scree and bare rock near the summit. They'd scoured the landscape but had seen nothing.

Cole glanced at his dad, taking in the beloved tanned face with its burgeoning crow's feet and neatly trimmed salt and pepper beard. Far more, even, than on the back of a horse, Russ Wainwright was truly in his glory while at the controls of his plane. He could forget what he'd lost and escape into the freedom of flight. His hazel eyes switched between scanning the surrounding terrain and his engine instruments, eyes sharp and focused as a hawk's. Behind them, Leif and Nate pressed their foreheads to the small back windows, old and young, quiet and subdued.

"You all got what you need back there?" Cole asked. "Water, another energy bar?"

"Look." Nate's one word broke the cheerless atmosphere in the cabin.

"What?" Leif turned to him.

"A flash of something kind of bright blue."

"Marcus told us his pup tent is blue and that it was gone from the shed," Leif said.

"I'll turn her tight and let's see if we can spot it again," Cole's dad replied.

"In a little bit of a clearing," Nate said.

It took two more passes to spot it again, but when they did, there was no mistaking that the blue wasn't a natural part of the surrounding geology.

"Okay I have the GPS coordinates," Cole's dad said, reading them off the flight display attached to the center of the yoke. "Let me climb up to ten-thousand feet to radio this in, then we'll head back. Good eyes, there, Nate."

The teen grinned self-consciously, and Cole laughed with relief as Leif ruffled the boy's hair and the Cessna ascended to a good radio reception height. His dad keyed the mic.

"Casper radio this is Cessna November Six One Eight Papa Juliett. We've spotted a possible tent on the west rise trail, about a half mile from the tree line. I have GPS coordinates when you're ready to copy. Over."

"Cessna One Eight Papa Juliett, ready to copy those coordinates."

"Can we get back in time to go with them?" Nate asked when the transmission was complete.

"Probably," Russ replied. "Depending on how long it takes us to get back."

"And if we're on the ground when they get some news?" Cole asked.

"I'll call them and give my cell number. Don't you worry. Everybody strapped in and ready to land?"

"Let's go," Leif replied.

MELANIE BURST INTO tears when Bjorn raced into the kitchen bearing the news that something blue had been spotted in the trees along one of the main hiking trails up the mountain. Harper hugged her, too, and then did the same to Aiden. She'd changed from her skirt into her standard ranch uniform of jeans and sweater and was ready to go.

"What can I do?" she asked. "Do you want to ride with them, Mel? I'll stay with the kids."

"No. Of course I want to, but it would be best if I stayed by the radio. I'm not the strongest rider anyway. But would you go, Harper? You know the mountain almost as well as Marcus does."

"Of course." Harper didn't tell Melanie how excruciating staying back would have been.

"Marcus has been to the summit most recently of anyone," Bjorn said. "He'll come. I'll go and so will Rico. Sounds like Cole and Nate are on their way back as well."

Harper's pulse bounced in relief.

"We'll take anyone who wants to come," Bjorn added. "Once we're close to the area we'll need to spread out to actually find her. The coordinates aren't exact."

"We'll find her." Harper nodded with certainty and hugged Aiden again until he squeaked.

"SHE'S GOT A good memory if she came this way," Marcus said, riding ahead of Cole at the line of ten searchers now three-fourths of the way up the mountain. "I took her with me here once, probably a year ago. It's one of the only ways you can get this far on a horse, but it's not that easy to find."

"Skylar is nothing if not intrepid," Bjorn said. "Stubborn and smart. But why would she not come home? It's been almost three days."

The afternoon sun hung low in the sky as it approached three o'clock. It was slow slogging up the trail, which had wound through multiple switchbacks for the past two hours.

"We won't get a lot farther," Marcus said. "Maybe a mile. If she's camping past there, I don't know how she got the horse up with her. If she did."

"Doin' okay?" Cole looked over his shoulder, and Harper smiled. He'd kept an eye on everyone the entire trip, as she'd known he would, but she savored the times he asked her especially. It was overprotective and unnecessary, but the chivalry gave her chills of pleasure.

"Doin' great," she replied. "You?"

"Yup."

Harper rode Wheeler and looked behind her at the line of riders. Bjorn, Nate, Rico and his son, Neil, Raquel, and Amelia. Mia had been the nicest surprise, showing up ready to ride with an enhanced emergency first aid kit in her saddle bags. "I pray you don't need a doctor," she'd said. "If I come maybe I'll be unnecessary."

Exactly what Harper had said to Cole about coming back to Paradise in the first place.

Another half hour passed, and the trail grew steeper and rockier. Conversation ceased as the group concentrated. At last Cole held up a hand to halt their progress. Marcus had stopped twenty feet ahead and twisted left and right in his saddle, searching for landmarks.

Or a tent.

"We can't ride any higher," Cole said. "It's going to have to be on foot."

"There was that tiny little spur back about a mile that headed to the north," Bjorn said. "It's at the wrong altitude, but maybe a couple of us should go back and follow that."

"I'll go," said Raquel.

In the brief silence that followed, as everyone gathered his and her own thoughts, a shuffle of leaves and a tiny sound, like the yip of a fox or the whine of a coyote pup drew Harper's attention to the left of their trail. She stared into the undergrowth but saw nothing. Giving Wheeler a touch with one heel, she squeezed next to Cole who sat on Paco studying an old Wyoming geological survey map he'd pulled from his pocket.

"Hey," he said.

"Over there." She pointed. "I swear I heard something."

"What?"

"An animal? Leaves rustling. Probably a squirrel or a rabbit."

They watched, and then Harper heard it again. Definitely a whine. She swung her right leg over her saddle and threw her reins over Wheeler's head and toward Cole.

"You be damn careful," he said, grabbing the reins.

She ducked beneath the lower branches a tall fir tree, stepping as quietly as the needle-and-fern-covered ground would allow. Six steps in, a shrill bark made her jump. Her heart pounded in hope.

"Asta?" she called softly. "Puppy?"

Another bark followed, and Harper delved three more steps into the woods. She found the border collie tangled by one foot in a patch of vines and roots.

"Oh, baby!" She cooed at the dog. "Look at you. What happened? Where's your owner, girl?"

She pulled her pocket knife from her jeans, silently thanking her father for teaching her never to ride out without it, and cut through the winding tendrils of fern and weeds that had wound around Asta's paw. Once free, the dog crawled into Harper's arms, licking and whining and covered with burrs, but otherwise apparently unhurt. She carried the pup out of the woods.

"Look who I found," she said.

Bjorn was off his horse in three seconds. He grabbed the dog and held it fiercely. "Oh Lord," he said. "She *is* here. Skylar!" he shouted. "Sky, it's Dad. Can you hear me?"

For a few minutes they all took turns calling her name with no luck."

"Put Asta down," Harper said quietly. "Maybe she knows which way to go from here."

Almost reluctantly Bjorn set the dog on the ground. "Where's Skylar, girl?" he asked. "Smart dog, you can find her."

At first Asta did nothing but wiggle and sit. But Bjorn pointed away from their group. "Find Skylar. Where were you going when you got stuck?"

All at once, as if she understood, Asta stood and trotted past the line of horses, continuing up the trail without looking back.

Cole took charge. "Bjorn, Nate, Mia, Harpo, come on, we'll follow on foot. The rest of you, search this area. See if you can find anything more around where the dog was found. Rico, Neil, you have walkie-talkies?"

They both nodded.

Harper knotted Penny's reins and looped them over the saddle horn. She took the rope attached to the halter beneath Penny's bridle and tied a quick release knot to the sturdiest tree branch she could find. The others did the same, then they headed up the trail after Asta, who'd already disappeared around a bend.

"I saw her duck into the woods to the left up about thirty feet." Cole pointed.

"I saw!" Harper stepped up her climbing pace until they reached the spot. "Asta!" She called for the dog.

The dog barked.

A second later they came across Bungu in a small opening between trees. He was staked and grazing contentedly on the sparse grasses and weeds. From the eaten-down state of the circle, it was clear he'd been there a while. The gorgeous Appaloosa whinnied when the humans appeared. Bjorn approached him, gave him a thorough check by running his hands over every inch of his body and legs, and patted him hard.

"He's okay. Clearly Skylar did this intentionally. I wouldn't think she'd be far from her horse."

They left Bungu and chose a direction based on a few broken twigs and some stomped-on brush. It took five minutes to find the blue tent.

"Skylar!" Harper raised her voice another notch. "Sky? Are you here?"

Bjorn charged up behind them to the door of the tiny, two-man tent. Asta came from behind it and scratched on the nylon. Harper scooped the dog into her arms.

"Skylar did everything right," Cole said, his gaze roaming the makeshift campsite. "The door is away from the prevailing wind. The fire pit is cold, but she dug it deep into the wet ground. There's no food in the open…"

Bjorn unzipped the door and they all heard a muffled groan.

"Skylar?" Bjorn said. "It's Dad. Are you okay? Sky? Honey?"

His tall frame disappeared slowly into the tent, but a moment later he backed out, his face ashen. "Amelia?" he called. "She's burning up with a fever, and I can't get her to talk."

Mia, along with her saddle bags, disappeared into the tent. Harper heard her talking, coaxing gently. Five minutes later she reemerged.

"She's got a fever of a hundred and four and she's pretty out of it. I'm guessing it's flu, but it could be something she ate, or a bite, or any number of things. We need to get her out of the tent so I can look her over more thoroughly. She's dehydrated, too, so we need water."

A few moments later, Skylar lay on her sleeping bag outside the tent, her head rolling side to side, her lips dry and pale. She opened her eyes a few times while Mia examined her, pulling up sleeves and pushing up her pant legs to look for injuries or bite marks. Bjorn stroked his daughter's hair. Nate took her hand, apparently no longer caring whether anyone knew of his feelings. Harper stood beside Cole, one arm snaked tightly around his waist, one holding Asta like a football. She bombarded heaven with prayers.

"I'm pretty sure she brought a flu bug up here and got progressively sicker." Mia tucked a blanket up to Skylar's chin. "She needs a trip to the ER to have her bloodwork and electrolytes checked and determine whether this is bacterial or viral."

"We can't get a helicopter up here," Cole said. "Can we take her off the mountain on horseback and have one meet her there?"

Mia brushed the teen's pale, dry forehead. "She feels pretty awful I'm sure, so she won't like it. But, yes, if someone can support her, she'll make it."

"She'll ride in front of me," Bjorn said firmly. "We'll get you home, honey."

Skylar's eyes opened into little slits. "Daddy?" she whispered.

"Yup, I'm here. We all are. We were worried about you."

Skylar grimaced and closed her eyes. They flew open again and rested on Nate. "You're here, too?"

"I had to help find you."

"I made it to the top," she murmured. "Told you I would."

Chapter Twenty-Three

"I'M SICK OF hospitals."

Harper leaned her head on Cole's shoulder and sighed. The couches in the waiting area at St. John's Medical Center in Jackson were comfortable enough, but that didn't make the waiting pleasant. He drew her close.

"Yeah, honey, I am, too."

"Shouldn't be too much longer, but I'll see what I can find out." Mia stood, patting Melanie's shoulder and holding a hand out to Aiden, who wasn't sleeping. "C'mon, little mini Norwegian. Let's go ask about your sister."

"Sissy will be all right." He took her offered hand.

"Yes, she will be."

Harper caught Mia's quick smile. Cole squeezed her shoulders.

"Glad to see you two have put down the verbal bazookas," he teased.

"Yeah. I am, too." She smiled and laid her arm across his stomach, caressing his side as she wrapped him in a hug.

A moment later Mia returned, Aiden skipping beside her and a lab-coated male doctor trailing behind them. Bjorn and Melanie stood, faces twisted with anxiety.

"Mr. and Mrs. Thorson, I'm Dr. Wagner, and I've been taking care of your daughter. She's going to be fine."

Melanie wilted against her husband. Bjorn's shoulders heaved with relief. Even though Mia had been fully reassuring, this was the official word.

"She indeed has the flu," Dr. Wagner continued, "and she got pretty sick. I'd like to keep her a day or two so we can give her some fluids and make sure no pneumonia develops. She'll be able to go home the day after tomorrow, maybe even tomorrow afternoon barring any complications, but she won't be feeling very well for several days."

"We'll do whatever we need to for her." Melanie raised her head, wiping her eyes. "Can we see her?"

"We're moving her to a room now, and you can meet her there. Just a couple people at a time, she doesn't have much energy. And you might want to keep the little one away. She's contagious for the next few days."

"We'll be careful," Melanie said.

"She's a strong young lady." Dr. Wagner shook hands all around. "She'll do fine. If you hang tight, I'll have the nurse come and tell you what room she's in."

Harper's relief and happiness was tempered by creeping exhaustion now that the adrenaline of worry had disappeared. She would have gladly left with Cole and let Skylar's parents take care of her this first night, but Melanie insisted they stay and at least say hello, along with Nate.

"You are three of her favorite people," she said. "Seeing you will make her feel better, I know it."

They settled into their lounge seats again. Melanie and Bjorn discussed their daughter quietly, speculating on why she'd run off and what they should do once she was well. For the second time Harper bit her lip to keep from overstepping her bounds. And yet the reason she'd come wouldn't leave her mind.

She'd come to take Skylar's side.

With fists clenched and her pulse drumming with a sense of injustice, she told herself she had to wait and see what Skylar had to say. Maybe Melanie would ease up on her decision about the painting once she and her daughter talked, and Harper's own anger would prove unnecessary.

They all looked up when a trim older woman, closer to Leif's age than Bjorn's or Melanie's, entered the waiting room and scanned the area, settling on their group and marching toward them with heartfelt sympathy on her face. Betty Hodges, the high school art teacher and the recent exhibition coordinator, carried a large, flat rectangle wrapped in brown paper and tied in bright yellow raffia cord. Harper rushed to meet her.

"Mrs. Hodges!"

"Oh, nonsense, Harper, I thought we agreed it was Betty. You're not my student any longer." She accepted a hug.

"Betty."

The old teacher let her go and approached Bjorn and Melanie. She offered them her free hand. "I heard Skylar had been found safely, and I had to come and tell you how relieved I am. You must have been very frightened."

"It was a scary few days," Bjorn agreed. "It's nice of you to come. She's being moved to a room now. They'll keep her for observation a day or two."

"I'm so glad."

"Won't you sit and wait with us?" Harper asked. "They'll let us see her in a few minutes."

"Oh no, dear, no," Betty said. "I won't stress her; she needs her rest. I only thought that since her family would all be here at once, I'd bring this for you to show her. Part of her prize was getting her painting professionally framed and ready for display. The hospital donates that part of the award. It turned out so beautifully that, under the circumstances, I thought Skylar would like to see it before we hang it. Might make her feel better."

Harper stared at Melanie. She hadn't told the judges she wasn't allowing the picture to be hung? Bjorn took a step away from his wife, a grim set to his mouth.

"Mrs. Hodges," Melanie began. "I'm afraid I have some news about Skylar's painting…"

Anger simmered dangerously in Harper's chest, rising before Melanie even finished her first sentence. She wouldn't really be this heartless would she?

"Her father and I have decided the painting is much too sophisticated and explicit to be displayed as the first work of a—"

"Wait!" Harper shot from her chair, pulling away from Cole's warning touch. Like a phoenix rising from the ashes of her own memories, she looked at Melanie the way she'd always wanted to look at her father—in the face, with no apologies. "You can't do this, Mel. Not to the daughter you love."

"Excuse me?" Melanie, confused and frustrated, turned dark eyes on her.

"Please. Come with me for a minute. Let me talk to you privately. I need to say something."

"Say it right here, Harper."

"No. This isn't an ambush. I'm not trying to undermine you, but I want to give you my insight before you make this decision."

Bjorn, Mia, Leif, and especially, Betty Hodges stared at her in puzzlement. Cole held up his hand. "It's okay," he said. "Melanie, you know she'll hound you like a beagle after a ground squirrel if you don't go."

Mel closed her eyes briefly and released a pent-up sigh. "Fine. Because you've been such an incredible friend. But I don't even let friends mess with my parenting decisions."

Shades of her father.

"I understand."

When they'd moved around a corner past a bank of elevators, Melanie stopped her. "What's this about, Harper?"

"Why did you let Skylar enter if you weren't going to let her hang the picture?"

She didn't hesitate. "She wanted us to be surprised by her painting at the show, and she didn't show it to us beforehand. She was right. We were more than surprised. But I didn't want to make a scene at the competition, and I didn't think for a moment she was going to win."

"You wanted to know why she ran off. I can tell you exactly why. Telling her the picture can't be hung was only a peripheral reason. Do you know what a damaging thing you said to you daughter?"

"I really don't think this is any of your business."

"Oh, I know it's not. But I'm sticking my nose in anyway, because you are as good as a member of the family, and you need to hear this."

"I don't think I do."

Harper ignored her. "For one thing, you told Skylar you don't think she's talented. For another, you told her you have no faith in her. And, finally, you told her that even though the thing she loves is definitely something she's good at, it isn't important."

"I never said any of those things."

"You did. Loudly and clearly."

"Fine, you said what you needed to say. Thank you."

"It's a kiss, Mel. A sweet, schoolgirl kiss. Are you telling me you don't believe teenage girls think kisses are romantic? It doesn't have anything to do with sex, but that's beside the point. I don't care if you keep the painting from being hung. That's the part that's none of my business. But you'd better make it up to Skylar by telling her she's the most talented, beloved girl in the world. Because if you don't, you'll lose her and she'll lose you—the way I lost my father." She held back the tears that threatened to turn her emotional argument into a blubbery joke.

"That's a little over the top, don't you think?" Melanie crossed her arms, her anger mitigated by a hesitant uncertainty in the depths of her glare.

"Melanie, it's far from over the top. This is what my father did to me my entire life—dismissed my feelings about my art. I not only ran away, I never wanted to come back. It's taken me years to get past it. Don't do that to Skylar."

For long, strained seconds Melanie only stared at her. Her eyes hardened again and without a word she walked away. Harper slumped against a wall and covered her mouth with her hands.

"Hey, there."

She looked into the sea of intense blue that made up the color of Cole's eyes. He lifted her chin and kissed her softly. When he stepped back, she caught Betty's quiet smile from behind him.

"I'm very sorry," she said to them both. "I only tried to tell her—"

"It's all right," Cole said. "Whatever you said to her at least made her stop and think."

"She took the painting and promised to give it to Skylar," Betty added. "And she didn't say another word about not letting it be hung. Cole explained to me about Mrs. Thorson's decision."

"So she changed her mind?"

"She didn't say that." Cole shrugged. "She said she would be getting back to the committee soon."

"All right." Harper wiped at her eyes and nose. "If there's a chance she'll tell Skylar how proud of her she is, then it's worth losing a friend."

"You could never lose a friend." Cole kissed her forehead.

"If that's what you told her to do, she'd be foolish to be angry with you." Betty nodded sagely. "Art brings out the passion in everybody, Harper. You know that better than most. What great artist hasn't suffered for her work?"

Harper choked. "That's too cliché for words, dear Mrs. Hodges."

"Yes." She laughed. "I suppose it is. But even though art is a very individual pursuit, there are some universal truths—suffering is one. Not all suffering is tragic. But whether you're a painter, a writer, an architect, a musician, or a mentor, there's some pain involved in creation. Everyone goes through pain. We're lucky to have an outlet."

"I'm not an artist and I understood that." Cole grinned. "There's even pain—the very best kind, mind you—when you fall in love with an artist."

"Mr. Wainwright. How come I never had you in my classes?"

"Because everything I draw looks like a cow face."

"Maybe I could have changed that."

"Well I'm sorry now I never had you for a teacher. You're a wise lady."

"I bestow an honorary A-plus on you." Betty winked. "And this is the sad part of this entire episode. This could be the last of these competitions we see here and my last year of teaching art at Southwest. I had visions of enticing Skylar's parents into letting her attend public high school when she's done with middle school. Many homeschool parents make that switch. But, with the severe budget cuts we're facing, art and music are on the chopping block."

"What?" Disbelief gripped Harper's chest. "You can't be serious."

"I'm afraid I am. It's going on everywhere across the country. You've taught art, Harper, you know as well as anyone. When money falls short, school boards see the arts as extraneous. Fun but unnecessary."

"It's not true! What happens to students like Skylar—like I was? Art made school bearable."

"They wait until college or they find their own ways."

"Is this decision already made?" Cole asked.

"The preliminary budgets are just coming out, and the programs are slated for cutting. But the decisions aren't final until the school board discusses the numbers and votes."

"There must be something we can do." Harper twisted her hands together in anxious energy.

"Get the word out. Try to convince the public how necessary the arts are. But, sadly, even though this community has a contingent of folks big on arts, it's very small. We aren't powerful enough, I'm afraid. We'll try. But…" Betty patted Harper on the arm. "For now it's miracle enough that Skylar is safe and that she has a huge talent and a few people who'll encourage her. With luck, her mother and father will be among them. It's a good day's work. Tomorrow will fight its own battles."

Harper wanted to say more, to find some assurances in the wake of what felt like a looming disaster, but Betty turned and headed for the elevators, a wise lady perhaps, but a small figure in the midst of a storm.

"I feel like she whacked me with a sledge hammer," Harper said when Betty was gone. "Of course I know arts programs are in trouble, but not here. Not where things have always been the same."

"It's sad," Cole agreed.

"I wish I had five grants like the one from Cecelia. I wish I had her money. Dang it, I'd fund the program myself."

"Three kids at a time, Harpo." Cole pulled her close and rested his chin on her head. "You made a world of difference for three kids a couple of weeks ago. That's all you can do."

"A drop in the bucket."

"A drop at a time is how that bucket gets filled."

She craned her head back and stared. "You really are a sappy doggone cowboy poet, aren't you?"

"When I'm not flying around the country trying to convince stubborn artists we belong together."

"Artists? There's more than one."

"Sometimes it feels like it. For example, this one here in my arms. She's about as sexy as they come. I got a girl in Chicago who wears these purty long skirts and feels like a bunch of soft, sweet hotness in my arms. I love that. But you—you belong in denim and boots. Unless, of course, you're wearing nothing."

"Denim or nothing?"

"Sounds like a poem in the making to me. Wanna come back to my place after we visit Skylar?"

"Nope."

His eyes widened in honest surprise. She raised up and kissed him. "I want to come now. Let's leave Skylar with her mom and dad for tonight. If you'll go grab my purse and jacket and tell Mel I love her, I'll follow you anywhere. I'll fix things with her tomorrow."

"You sure you don't want to tell her yourself?"

Harper shook her head. "She needs to process how she feels. I don't want her to think she has to be nice to me tonight."

"I'll get your things. I'll tell her you love her."

She grabbed the back of his sleeve as he turned, yanked on it, and spun him back to her. She wrapped her arms around his neck and pulled him into a long, deep kiss. Liquid rushed to her core and mush infiltrated her joints. She pushed him away again with succulent sweetness.

The words sat on her tongue like scared divers afraid to leap from the springboard. She tried. She almost made it: "I…love you, too." But the words wouldn't form.

"Hurry back," she said out loud.

"Your mind is racing."

Propped on one elbow beside Harper in the bed in his old room, Cole traced a finger languidly beneath her closed left eye, down her cheek, and around to her earlobe. She smiled when he drew an imaginary line down her collarbone and circled her breast. He could see the peak of her nipple pop against the soft, pale green fabric of her sweater.

"It is racing," she admitted. "Hard to turn off a day like this. Skylar being so sick. Melanie's anger. Betty's news. Now I think after I see Skylar tomorrow, I should fly back to Chicago. I could make Cecelia very happy."

"Would you make Harper very happy?"

"Sure. Nobody would be mad at her anymore. Except Melanie."

"I don't think you should be contemplating things that don't make Harper happy."

"It's not all about Harper."

He ran his thumb over the tip of her breast. She shivered. He kissed her through the sweater, and she squeaked in pleasure. "I respectfully disagree. It should be all about Harper. How can she be happy living her life if it's all for other people?"

"Those other people are helping her get what does make her happy."

"Doing what?" He kissed her other breast. She grasped his head and held it to her.

"Letting me paint. Sending goose bumps and shivers through my entire body..."

"Okay. That last one *I'll* allow."

He pushed himself down the bed and rolled on top of her jean-clad legs so his mouth was even with the hem of her sweater. Pushing it slowly upward, he rested his kiss above the waistband of her Levi's.

"You could come back to Chicago *with* me again." Her breath caught along each word as he kissed his way up her stomach to the space between her breasts.

"I would, but I was only staying through Friday, which is nearly past. You and your sisters do actually pay me to work around here. I suppose you could fire me."

"You're fired," she murmured. "And now rehired. To do this all day long."

He pushed her sweater past her breasts and rose to his hands and knees. With only a little fumbling he helped her pull the sweater over her head and tossed it to the floor. Before she could lie back down, he flicked the hooks on the back of her bra, pulled it off, and sent it after the sweater.

"Oh yeah." He grinned as she nestled into the mattress and he stretched out on top of her. "I accept the position."

"Do you really think you'd make a good missionary?"

Laughter burst from him like water from a newly discovered spring. She never failed to surprise him with something wonderful or caring or silly or slightly naughty. Suddenly all he wanted from her was tumbling, sheet-twisting, laughing naughtiness. She obliged, and their peals of laughter mixed as their mouths met and parted, their noses bumped, and their hands flew to buttons, shirts, zippers, and socks.

Before he knew it, she was atop him, her long, dark hair disheveled and flowing across her creamy skin, heavy over his knuckles as he reached for her perfect, round breasts.

"You misrepresented yourself, Mr. Wainwright. Missionaries are not giddy. I expected much more serious dedication from you."

"You will find nobody more dedicated than I am," he promised. "But if you want somebody more serious, you'll have to search elsewhere."

"You stay right where you are. I'm done searching."

"Good to hear."

He rolled to a sitting position and pulled her into his lap, tugging on her hips, and settling the sweet cleft of her against the heat and hardness only she could allevi-ate. She held him around the neck, moving against him, arching and stroking until he couldn't breathe.

The last straw dropped when she slipped one hand between them and slid back enough to add finger strokes to the erection he didn't think could get any stronger. He dropped his head back and groaned.

"Baby, that's about gonna do it if you aren't careful."

"I never said be careful." She kissed him.

"Then turnabout is only fair."

He closed his eyes and slid his hand beside hers, swirl-ing a finger through the soft tangle of curls. Her cry and the clench of muscle around his hand nearly made him lose it.

"See," he said. "Torture isn't nice."

"No. But try and stop."

"We have to." He removed his hand.

"Have to?" She whimpered.

He laughed and took her hand from him, groaning his regret. "Patience, love."

He stretched enough to reach the foil packet on the night stand beside the bed. She closed her eyes.

"Oh bother," she said. "Give me that. You'll be too slow."

She was not slow. Once she'd made him even crazier by rolling the soft latex expertly over him, he cupped his hands beneath her seat and lifted her. In one smooth motion he lowered her again and slid slowly into her, whimpering as her velvet skin encased him in heat. He made her move slowly, guiding her hips, extending the torture, closing his eyes as she moved up and down with athletic grace. He moved closer and closer to the brink as he listened to her breathing grow ragged.

She arched her back with a cry that penetrated to his core, and then she collapsed against him, pushing as if she couldn't get close enough. Spasms wracked her muscles, and she clung to him, shivering and gulping for air.

"All right?" he asked. She nodded, allowing a tiny choked laugh to escape, followed by a clear sob. "Hey." He tried to pry her from him, to check on her, but she held his neck more tightly.

"No! You," she said. "You now."

"Oh, baby," he said in her ear.

With a swift, masterful motion he pushed them together onto one side and flipped her to her back. He never left her soft, deep warmth and moved without a lost moment into a timeless rhythm as perfectly tuned to her motion and her body as if they'd been designed to for each other. Three strokes. Four. Hard and smooth. Five and she grasped his butt, pulled him tight to her and let him fall from the cliff right into her soul.

His release took long torturously phenomenal moments during which he lost all frame of reference and sense of time. Only her voice, soft, filled with humor, brought him back to Earth.

"I think you passed the job interview."

He wanted to laugh, rouse himself, and go again, but he had no power to do anything but collapse and worry that he was going to crush her before motion returned to his body.

"I don't care if I didn't. Don't you dare let anyone else try out for this position. Ever."

"Okay. You've got the job anyway."

"I made you cry."

"You mean man."

"Awww. I've heard it's a talent to make a woman weep."

"I've never met anyone with that talent, so I wouldn't know."

"Proof I'm the perfect man for this job. And, I'll make you a bet. I can do it again."

"I like a cowboy with confidence," she said, and pulled him back down on top of her for deep, rejuvenating kisses in the tangled sheets.

Chapter Twenty-Four

SHE'D ALWAYS SCOFFED that the term "soul mate" had been invented by some ancient romance writer, but after the night with Cole she had to change her mind. There wasn't any way Harper could write off the night as meaningless fun, even though three beautiful, star-reaching "times" had definitely fit the very definition of fun. It was what happened when they weren't making love, when everything they said and did flowed between them as effortlessly as breathing, without awkwardness, embarrassment, or effort that altered her view. As if Harper-and-Cole had always been.

She was a believer.

She was also confused and torn. How could she pick between a soul mate and life dream?

The next morning she entered her mother's hospital room, a new one on the general medical-surgical floor. Bella was still under careful watch, but she'd graduated. With luck, she'd be ready to go home in a week.

She looked beautiful. Now that she could shower and dress in her own pajamas, she was back to being elegant Bella Crockett—put together and lovely even in a hospital bed. Harper found her knitting a stunning filigreed shawl with the enviable skill she'd only ever been able to pass on to Grace.

"Hi, Mama," she called softly.

The soft click of needles stopped. Her mother looked up and smiled. "Darling. I'm so happy to see you."

Harper kissed her cheek and lingered for a long, tight hug. When she straightened, her mother patted the mattress. "Sit. Tell me why you look so sad about being happy. What's going on?"

How in the world did her mother do it?

"What makes you say that?"

"I know my girls," she said. "Don't try to get out of it."

She hadn't officially told her mother about her feelings for Cole. They hadn't officially told anyone, although they didn't need to announce the obvious, she supposed. Like everything else about her life at the moment, words to describe it seemed weak and insufficient.

"It's Cole. Cole is messing up everything."

"However is our sweet boy doing such a thing?" She smiled in the all-knowing way that had been confounding, and sometimes terrifying, children since the creation of mothers.

"He…" She stopped the elaborate explanation she'd planned and shook her head. "He's making me fall in love with him."

"And? Is it working?"

Her raised brows and calm hope drew a sputter from Harper. She took her mother's hand. "It's working maybe a little too well. I've lost all ability to think straight."

"Sounds like love to me."

"But he and Mia…for so long."

"Cole was never feisty enough for Mia. He has too much of a poet's soul, too much of kindness. Mia needs someone to stand toe-to-toe with her and love her for the mover and shaker she is. Cole needs someone to ground him—to prove there's more to life than trying to regain the past. That, my sweet daughter, is you."

"Oh, Mom, I don't know. He deserves someone less needy."

"Didn't I tell you I know my girls?" She smoothed a strand of Harper's hair. "What is it you think you need?"

"I don't know if I've ever been able to answer that question. Just someone who accepts me for who I really am and what I really love to do."

"You've always had that, Harper."

"Right. Sure I have. From the time Dad told me he had no idea what planet I lived on half the time to the day I devastated him by getting kicked out of school."

"You don't think he told all his daughters he thought they were from other planets?" She chuckled. "You girls had your father bamboozled and lost from the days you were born. He was a rancher's rancher drowning in estrogen."

"He never once told me he was proud of my talent. Never once encouraged me to pursue what I loved. I had to leave home for that."

"He kept every drawing, every painting, every picture you ever made him, did you know that? I can show you his "Harper Box" when I get home. Of course he was proud of you."

Harper's mouth dropped open. "He had a very strange way of showing it."

"I never said he did everything right. He was stubborn, and he was focused. I look back now and realize I should have forced him to do some things differently. But that wasn't easy to do with him. He loved the way he loved—quietly but deeply."

"I wish he could have troubled himself to tell a person."

"I know, honey. You're right. You don't say it easily either, though. Do you?"

She sat there, convicted on the spot. Her mother's words drilled into her heart, and her breath caught in a mixture of embarrassment, mortification, and denial. Cole. Patient, kind, loving Cole. She'd had the words on the tip of her tongue so many times. And yet…

"I wish people would stop trying to compare me to Dad. I'm nothing like him."

"Oh ho, darling Harper. You are the most like him of all."

"Pierce my heart why don't you?"

"I'm not trying to pierce anything. But one of these days you have to embrace the truth. You and your dad both did things far differently than anyone else in the family. You both ran away and holed up when you were wounded. You were both opinionated and extremely brilliant about those opinions. You both make decisions as

much from the heart as from the brain—a way of feeling
what's right. Highly evolved intuition, I used to call it."

"Or the ever-popular 'flighty' according to Mia."

"For the record, Mia was far flightier than you ever
were. She jumped from one interest to another until she
settled on medicine. As much to be rebellious as anything. But you? You never wavered. You knew who you
were from the time you could hold a big fat crayon."

"If this is all true, then why did Dad always act like I
was the black sheep? Why did he take away my sketchbooks as punishment or belittle the degree I wanted?"

"Because what he didn't have that you do is true
empathy. He never saw, either, how much alike you were
to him. He was wrong to see your talent as impractical.
But don't mistake that for not loving you."

She didn't know what to say. It wasn't that her mother
had shaken the world or foundations of Harper's life, but
her view of everything she'd ever believed about herself
now stood on its head.

"I loved him. And I disappointed him."

"He knew you loved him. And no parent likes to see
his child go through what you did. He hurt for you. He
also had his own brand of tough love. But he understood
making mistakes."

"It's hard to hear this. I never thought he forgave me,
so it was hard to forgive him."

"And yet you're such a loving, caring, amazingly
warm person. I loved your father deeply, but I wouldn't
say he was warm."

"I got that from you."

She smiled and patted Harper's knee. "We are champions of the underdog. So we're back to what you want."

"To have it all. Cole. Cecelia Markham's patronage. No oil on Paradise Ranch. Cole?" She added the second "Cole" with a tiny smile.

"Then go be the true love of his life. Give him a dream."

"Oh, Mom. I want that. But his dream is to stay here with someone who will help him get his ranch back. I don't live here. He can't live in Chicago."

"Your heart is the only thing that can find you an answer, my sweet. I wish I had something better."

Harper's heart despaired. "But did you follow your heart? Stuck here for all those years."

"Stuck? Oh, Harper, never. I chose this place. Chose your father, too. I know that behind my back you all think I'm some downtrodden, unfulfilled ranch widow, but it's not true. Your father was a wonderful husband—romantic in his own way. A good lover."

"Ma!" Harper formed a cross with her two index fingers and held it up to ward off further mom-sex anecdotes. Her mother laughed.

"Well, he was. And I wasn't stupid all those years. While he was off building his family empire, I was building mine. I raised six of the strongest women in Wyoming and encouraged them in whatever they wanted to do. Now each of them is a fabulous success. I served my country. I have credit cards in my own name and a small bank account. I have insurance that will take care of expenses at the end of my life. I kept the books for the ranch and understood all the nuances. I was never forced to stay—but I did and loved it. I don't want to do it anymore."

If there were more shocks to come from her mother's mouth, Harper didn't think she could handle them. And if she felt guilty about how she'd thought of her father or treated Cole, she was thoroughly shamed by how she'd always looked at her mother.

How could she have missed what an amazing woman she'd grown up with?

Because she was just like her father.

She launched herself into her mother's arms, remorseful as a scolded child. Except she didn't feel scolded, just loved and overwhelmed.

"I'm sorry, Mama."

"Nonsense. These are things you didn't need to know until you were a grown woman, in love for yourself."

"What do I do now?"

"I can't tell you that." Her mother squeezed more tightly. "I loved a man. I miss him every minute of every day, but it was a great love. If you can say that someday, I'll be happier than I can say for you. But it's not a requirement for a happy life. You simply have to do what will leave you with no regrets."

COLE WAITED IN the ICU family area, staring at the elevator bank waiting for Harper in a funk of anticipation and depression. Even after the body-and-soul-melding start to a new life together, he couldn't convince Harper to stay in Wyoming. Her loyalty to Cecelia and to art seemed to have a hold on her he couldn't break.

Only two hospital visits stood between this moment and the one where she boarded her flights to Chicago to get there an hour before the start of Cecelia Markham's party.

He couldn't go. No matter how desperately he wished to stay by her side, he'd told Harper the truth. He was really a hired hand, and he had his own goals to meet. It was fence-riding time. Repairs on half the ranch's machinery awaited his skill. Hay had to be set in all the winter pastures. The horses would soon start staying inside at night, and that meant barn chores. If the ranch was to be functional and in good shape by the time Joely and Bella were ready to take over, then he, Leif, Bjorn, Rico, and Neil had boatloads of work ahead of them. Chicago had to wait for a quieter weekend.

She stepped off the elevator with a smile he couldn't quite read, and he stood, his body leaping to attention.

"How's your mom?"

The enigmatic smile broadened. "Better than I ever knew. Utterly amazing."

He hadn't expected that. Visits with her mother usually left her subdued. "I'm…glad?"

She laughed at that and kissed him. "I'll tell you about it," she said without further elaboration. "When I've figured it out myself."

He had to settle for the cryptic offering because Mia appeared before he could ask anything more.

"You're here, I'm glad," she said, taking them both in with tired eyes. "Joely has been asking for both of you. She wouldn't let me leave until we all talked to her."

"That's a good sign, isn't it?" Harper asked. "She's been pretty uninterested in everyone and everything until now."

"I'm not sure," Mia said. "Something's up."

They entered Joely's room quietly out of habit, but now that she was awake, she actually needed stimulation more than peace and quiet. They found her staring blankly at the wall, her head elevated five inches and swathed in bandages, one arm in a cast. The rest of her battered body, including the nerve-damaged leg, was hidden beneath stark white sheets and blankets.

"Hey, sis," Harper said. "I hear you summoned your minions." She reached Joely's side and took her hand. "We're here. What can we do for you?"

It would take a long time before Joely's face looked anything like it had two weeks earlier. Scrapes and rough scabs cover most of her forehead and cheeks. One eye still opened only half way, and the hazel of both irises paled behind swollen purple, red, and yellow skin. Her jaw had been wired back into place, and when she spoke it was sibilantly through partially clenched teeth. Her hair had been carefully washed, but the honeyed tresses that hung below the skull cap of bandaging held none of its normal luster and lay against the hospital linen as limp and drained of fire as the rest of her body.

She turned her head slowly toward them.

"Thank you for watching over me, all of you." She'd learned to form her consonants behind her teeth, and they were stiff and slow.

"Don't be ridiculous." Harper kissed her cheek. "What else would we do?"

"I don't want you to think you have to come all the time. I don't really need minions."

"Yeah? Well too bad." Harper grinned. "We live to serve."

"That's what I need to talk to you about," Joely closed her eyes. "I've had a lot of time to think and to ask questions, and I've accepted the fact that I'm never going to be fully whole and functional like I was before."

"Don't be silly! It's only been a couple of weeks. You're going to be perfectly fine. Tell her, Mia."

"I know I'll be *fine*." Joely opened her eyes again. "But I won't walk normally or have full coordination. There may even be some brain injury that leaves motor skills impaired."

Harper searched for Mia's assurance, but her smile was faint.

"I don't blow smoke up peoples' butts," she said. "That doesn't help anything."

"A little wouldn't hurt," Harper murmured.

Mia firmed her lips and shot her a don't-be-a-child look. "I won't sugarcoat things for you, Joely. The nerve damage to your leg is serious, and a traumatic brain injury diagnosis is far from an exact science. It is possible you won't gain full use of your leg. It's possible you'll have to relearn some motor skills. But. It is also possible, with all the new techniques and therapies they're pioneering here at this very hospital, you'll recover almost a hundred percent. I'd say the odds are not that bad. You'll just have to work hard."

"And I intend to. But in the meantime I've made a decision. I think we need to go back to your plan for Paradise Ranch. We need to sell it and all move on. I can't handle running it. I don't want to. I refuse to require others to do the work for me."

Cole's breath caught in his throat.

He'd spent enough time looking over the ranch finances with Joely to know that, with some sacrifices, good planning, and little help from above, they had a shot at keeping Paradise afloat. And if they did work with Mountain Pacific, within a year things could be looking downright positive. In his head, he'd already put his plan into action. He'd only been waiting for Joely to recover enough that she could start talking shop in the hospital.

She couldn't pull the plug now.

"Joely, honey," he said. "Being in a place like this, after what happened and with the kinds of injuries you have, is bound to be depressing. Don't you think it's the situation talking? You love the ranch."

Her green-brown eyes filled with sadness. "I know all that. I even know I'm depressed. But that's the key—I *know*. I'm not talking through anger or despair; I'm talking reality. I know I can't run Paradise; I think I knew that even when I first offered to try. Of course I don't want it to leave the family, but sometimes reality slaps you in the face and tells you to use your head instead of your heart."

"Oh, Joely." Harper pulled a chair next to the bed and sat as close to her sister as she could, holding Joely's hand in both of hers. "Don't make this decision now. Give it until you're out of the hospital."

"You don't really have that much time. There are bills coming due in November and December that creditors won't wait for. The lumber yard, the balloon payment on the barn that's now ten years old—they've already extended that three times. You know all this, Cole."

"I do. And the beef shipment looks good this time— better than our estimate. I've got a little bit saved I can lend the ranch until spring."

Now where had *that* come from? His savings were sacrosanct. His living expenses—and two recent trips to Chicago—were all he'd taken from it. He'd never considered using his money to pay someone else to hang onto the property he wanted to buy with his money.

It made a backward kind of sense. He supposed.

"I wish it were enough for you to just buy the place outright." Joely sighed and closed her eyes again. This was the most talking she'd done since the accident. "You've got the vision for Paradise Ranch, Cole. I saw that in those weeks we worked on books. But I don't have vision or strength."

"I wish I could buy it, too." Cole's words tangled surprisingly with a tide of emotion. The very real possibility that the ranch was slipping away was like having a noose draped over his neck. He'd never had this suffocating despair over Paradise before—he'd always seen an option for saving it. But with Joely's pronouncement, his brain froze. Not a single solution came to him. The Crocket girls had ordained this moment the day each of them had walked away.

"There's a lot for all of us to talk about." Mia broke the silence that had fallen. "I believe you don't want to take on the ranch, Jo-Jo, and I do understand. We'll tell the triplets and see what they think."

"But you're the one who insisted we should sell." Joely made the reminder in a flat, uncaring tone.

"I did. Maybe it would be best. But..." Mia shrugged. "We've come this far. It feels like we owe Paradise at least another family meeting."

MIA STAYED WITH Joely when Harper and Cole said good-bye so they could get to Skylar.

"Thank you," Harper whispered to Amelia when they hugged. "You said everything right."

"It's the truth, that's all. Say hello to Skylar. Tell her to get better."

"Thanks, I will."

"So what do you think is the next step?" Cole asked when they were out of the room. "We've come this far. I hate seeing Joely give up."

"We'll talk to the rest of the girls." Harper shrugged.

"You still think you have to go back tonight?" he asked.

"I do."

He looked askance. "Even in light of this? Don't you think it's time to finally work out the ranch's future? We..." He stopped to correct himself. "*You* keep kicking the can down the road."

"I have a commitment to fulfill," she said, letting his arm go. "And the reason for not fulfilling it no longer exists. Since nobody is going to buy Paradise Ranch in the seven weeks left to Christmas, I say we keep kicking until then."

Cole felt a little like he was the embodiment of that can.

"Look." He tried one more tactic. "Cecelia doesn't have to know everything's finished here. At least not yet. What if I'm not ready to let you go?"

She smiled. "I'm not thrilled about leaving you, either, but if I'm not honest about my promises, then I'm not much of a role model for the kid I'm about to go see. I made a big arrogant speech about respect to her mother. I have to learn to keep my priorities straight."

"I agree. But don't you feel like the emergency with Paradise is just as big a deal as the one with Skylar?"

"No."

The one word cut him to the quick. "Wait. Let me understand. You're on the 'we should sell' side now?"

She place both hands on his chest. "I'm not. But I don't know what to think either. This is all like a freak storm—it roared in out of nowhere, and it's blowing everything around so hard and so fast that I'm lost. We all are. I don't want to talk about the ranch right now. Let the storm pass first."

Reluctantly he opened the car door for her and watched her slip in. All he knew was somebody had to start talking about the ranch pretty damn soon.

"You know," she said, once he was behind the wheel. "There could be a silver lining in all of this. If we sold the ranch, you could come to Chicago with no strings. Easy-peasy happily ever after."

"That's your idea of a solution?"

"Why so shocked? In a way, it's perfect."

"Oh really?" A huge block of anger broke free inside him, like an ice floe after a ship had hit an iceberg. "And what about the work I've put into this the past few weeks? No, years actually. What about my dreams for the future?"

"I'm sorry," she said. "I must be remembering incorrectly. What happened to you deciding you'd follow me anywhere?"

He stopped, his anger refreshed at her attempt to call him on his own words. "Don't turn that around. Of course I'll follow you, but I didn't think you'd truly ask me to give up my legacy. Is it okay for one person to sacrifice everything?"

He felt like that was honestly what she was suggesting he do. It seemed unbelievable, after all the emotion she'd expended on oil, back-to-the-past cattle roundups, and figuring things out with Mia. Now they'd flipped positions like two politicians, and he was caught in the fallout. He loved her stubborn hide, but the stones in his gut felt like betrayal.

"And if I stay here, I'm not sacrificing everything?" she asked.

"You can't bring your brushes and paints here?"

She looked like he'd struck her, and he resented that, too. Wasn't it the truth? Couldn't she paint anywhere?

"Look," she said before he could say more. "Nobody should have to sacrifice everything, but it seems like both people should be willing to and neither of us is willing.

Clearly. This is precisely why I've said all along a relationship like this doesn't work. It sorts out priorities pretty fast, doesn't it?"

"Clearly yours is Chicago."

"Clearly yours is getting the Double Diamond back."

"What do you really want, Harper? I've asked you before."

"I want to be who I am. Not who my father wanted me to be."

"And have you gotten anywhere close to that independence?"

"I'm getting *dang* close."

"Then by God you'd better stay the course until you're all the way there. Nothing more to say." He turned the ignition key, feeling for the first time since the death of his mother that he could weep for something about to be irrevocably lost. He headed out of the parking lot a little too fast.

Chapter Twenty-Five

"You came!"

Skylar's bullfrog voice and follow-up cough didn't stop her from sounding like she'd won the lottery when Harper walked into her hospital room, with a mask over her nose and mouth and worry zipping through her veins. Only when she bent to the sick girl and got a forceful bear hug did she believe the child was going to be all right.

"I am so glad to see you," Harper said.

"Yeah, me too," Skylar replied. "Mom said you came all the way from Chicago."

"We all do crazy things when we're upset."

"I'm supposed to say I'm sorry." Skylar stared up at Harper, and Cole behind her, with wide eyes in a pale face that sported two brightly flushed cheek spots. "I'm sorry I got sick and made everyone worry."

"Well, that's something." Harper wanted to be angry with Skylar, but she identified too strongly with her anger. The whole world was frustrating at the moment. Harper would have run off to a pup tent in the wilderness if she could have."

"I know everyone's mad at me, but I don't care," Skylar croaked. "I knew I would get in trouble for this, and I already told my dad he could punish me however he wants. I only wanted them to be mad enough to listen to me."

"I actually know that, Skylar. I ran away for the very same reasons you did. Truth be told, you did it a little smarter than I did. I ran away for years instead of days."

"But you came back."

"Not to stay."

"You're going away again?"

"I have to go back to Chicago tonight."

"Tonight? But I won't get to see you. I wanted to show you some sketches."

"I'd love to see them. I'll plan to stay longer next time."

"Sure. Okay."

Skylar covered her eyes with the backs of both hands and held them there until it was clear she was hiding. To Harper's dismay, a tiny rivulet of water dripped past the barrier and coursed across Skylar's temple.

"Sweetie, sweetie, don't cry. You'll only feel worse."

"That's not possible."

"But that's why things seem so bad and sad right now. You feel lousy. And just because you did kind of what you set out to do, doesn't mean you forgive your mom for taking away the prize for your painting. You will forgive her, but it still feels bad right now."

She uncovered her wet eyes. "See. You're the only one who gets it. Nobody else does."

"Lots of people get it. They do. But I remember feeling exactly like this when I was your age."

"Really?"

"My dad used to hide my sketchbooks so I'd focus on what he thought were the right things."

"Am I, like, your long lost kid or something?"

Harper laughed. "No. An adopted sister, maybe. This just means there are a lot of misunderstood people in the world. So, we have to learn not to run away but to stand up for ourselves and still be respectful. I wasn't very good at it. Your mom has reasons for what she decided. Talk to her about them."

"But that's the thing. I did. She already changed her mind."

Harper sat upright, confused. "She did?"

"She said they can hang the picture, but there have to be rules. They can put my name with it and say I'm a local artist. But I can't have my picture or my age with it."

Harper's immediate instinct was to rant that while Melanie had come close, she'd missed the mark. But she waited for her pulse to calm and reason to kick in.

"What do you think?" she asked.

"It's a big change for her. She still doesn't get it. She doesn't get that I wasn't thinking about sex or something stupid when I was painting the picture. She thinks the worst all the time. But, I guess I kind of won my point."

"You did," Harper conceded. "But don't you go thinking you can do stupid stuff every time you want your way.

This was a pretty dangerous thing you did. If Nate hadn't remembered what you said about wanting to climb the mountain on your own, we might not have found you in time."

"I know." Her voice got small and tired. "I was scared. I couldn't make myself walk or anything. And Asta came and found me, too. I left her at home, but she didn't stay."

"Really? That's pretty incredible."

"Yeah," she whispered.

"From now on promise me you'll talk to your mom. Show her why she should respect you. Do what I never did while my dad was alive."

"Okay."

"And." Harper winked over her mask. "There's Nate. He likes you in case you haven't figured it out."

"He was here already." The fever spots on her cheeks deepened.

"Having a trustworthy boyfriend and showing how you can be trustworthy, too, will help your mom a lot in the, you know, worrying-about-sex department."

"I can't date until I'm sixteen."

"I'll bet they'd let him come and visit. Or paint with you sometime."

The thoughtfulness in her face proved how much she liked the idea. She glanced at Cole.

"Are you going back with her to Chicago?"

Harper swore Cole grimaced. "Not this time," he said. "It wouldn't be a good idea to leave right now. Lots of things are happening here, and Harper has too much work to do."

She read his tone and wanted to smack him.

"Are you painting lots?" Skylar asked.

"I am. And meeting lots of people who want to share what I paint. I'm lucky to have the chance to visit with them. That's where I'm going tonight—to a gathering I promised to attend."

"You should go with her," Skylar said to Cole.

"No. We learned that Joely is going to be away from working at the ranch for quite a long time. That means somebody has to help figure things out here."

"Are you going to sell the ranch?"

Cole took a step back. "Why would you ask that?"

"Everyone thinks I'm a kid, but I'm not. I understand what my grandpa is talking about with my dad. I know what's happening with the money and the bills. Kind of. Everyone is worried."

"Yeah they are," he agreed. "But it's more complicated than deciding to sell the ranch. Nobody thinks about that lightly. There might not..." He hesitated and then shrugged. "You'll hear sooner or later. There might not be any other way."

"There's always a way." Skylar's croaking was deepening, but she struggled to a partial sit and studied the two of them as if she were the only adult in the room.

"Are you two mad at each other?"

Harper tried to find last ditch camaraderie in Cole's eyes, but he only gave her a helpless look. Skylar's eyes darkened as she waited.

"We have some differences of opinion," she said. "That's not really being mad."

"I don't know. I think you're pretty mad at me," Cole said.

"That's not appropriate here."

"That's what I mean." Skylar's voice was now a squeak. "You think I'm too dumb to be honest with. You forgot that I saw you kiss each other. Do you think I can't tell when you're mad?"

"Sometimes money makes people very upset, because it's so important," Harper said. "It takes time to work things out."

"Why is everyone freaked out about money all the time?"

"Skylar, you know why." Cole admonished her gently.

"I know the ranch needs it. Everybody needs it. But so what? My parents are always telling me life is about doing things the best I can. Maybe you guys should stop worrying about money and work with what's here."

Good Lord, had the child aged ten years up on that mountain? Harper couldn't reconcile the wisdom, idealistically naïve as it was, with the usually pouty fourteen-year-old who'd run away from home.

"Maybe you're a little bit right, sweetheart," she said. "But it really is more complicated than that. It's not only about money. It's about obligations and agreements grownups have to meet. We can't always live the way we want to."

"Like the agreement you made with that lady in Chicago?"

"Exactly."

"Seems like ever since you told me about her, she's been telling you how to be a painter. But you said nobody could tell us how to make our art. That the kind of artist we are comes from inside. Is your deal with that lady about money?"

Once again Harper wanted to be furious at the child. But her words slammed home like bullets with pinpoint accuracy.

"That's not quite fair," Cole said.

Skylar set her fevered little jaw. "But you care about money, too. You want the old ranch back. I know because Dad and Grandpa know. Everybody does. But I think who cares if you buy it back? It's here. You have it. We used it. Just stay on the ranch and it's yours."

If she hadn't been stricken herself, Harper would have laughed at the traumatized shock on Cole's face. Skylar was possessed by some kind of holy fire of righteousness, and the weaker her voice got, the more pointed her arguments became.

"What if I told you you've given me a lot to think about?" she asked.

"Whatever. You probably won't."

Ah, good. There was still a familiar Skylar in there.

"I will."

"You know, it was cool having you teach us. You get it. You should keep teaching people. Plus, you could paint here some more. I bet if you brought that bossy old bat here, she'd want a thousand paintings of the views."

"Skylar!" This time Harper did cover her mouth to hold in laughter. "She's not a bossy old bat."

"I don't know." Cole's eyes shone with fun for the first time since their angry argument. "Maybe she is. A bossy bat in sheep's clothing."

Harper wasn't amused by him—he knew better than Skylar. But her brain and her heart were on fire with an agitation she couldn't name. Some idea, some truth just beyond where she could wrap her mind around it, drained her of energy to waste on any more anger with Cole.

"Everybody's worried all the time." Skylar's voice was nothing but a whispered scratch now.

"It's all right," Harper soothed. "You need to rest that voice. You got a lot off your chest."

"I wasn't getting it off my chest for me. It's because grown-ups can be too stupid to live sometimes. They worry, worry, worry. My mom worries about me. You worry about money. Even a kid learns fast there will never be enough money. But you could do a hundred different things on this ranch besides what you do. Sell your paintings here. Or let people go fishing in the stream. Or raise sheep or something."

"Or look for oil," Cole said quietly.

"Or talk to the wind power people..." Harper murmured.

Clarity struck like a thunderbolt from the Good Lord Himself—and out of the mouths of runaway babes. The answers were obvious. One whole big package of solution stared her in the face as solid and real as Wolf Paw Peak. It would take more concentrated effort in the next few days than she'd given anything but a painting in her life.

And it would take all her diplomatic skill and salesmanship. But she knew it would work. Harper literally leaped so quickly from the chair that it crashed to the floor.

"What the…Harpo?" Cole cried out in alarm.

She planted a kiss through her mask onto Skylar's forehead. She straightened and spun toward Cole. "Go home," she said. "I'm going to Chicago. Don't wait for me or worry about me or follow me."

She might be certain, but she wasn't going to promise anyone anything until it happened. She'd let adversity steamroller her for six weeks now without using her brain. It was time to change that. If everyone thought she was so much like her father, then she'd by gosh show them all how right they were.

"Harper, stop," Cole said. "How are you going to get to the airport?"

"Let me worry about that. Skylar? Thank you, sweetheart. Thank you more than you'll ever know. Now swear to me you won't speak again unless you have to answer a question for a doctor or nurse. Your poor voice did its job and then some. I love you, kiddo. See you soon."

She righted the chair and shot Cole a warning look to stay put as she picked up her purse and jacket and headed for the door.

Still he caught her out in the hall. "Come on, Harpo, don't leave like this. I'm sorry. I spoke without thinking. I…Hell! That crazy kid completely blew me away in there. We need to talk—"

Harper held up her hand. "She's not crazy. She's a genius. And I'm not angry at you anymore. I don't think.

But I definitely will be if you follow me. I don't want your help with this one."

It killed her to ignore his look of desolation, but she couldn't afford to get soft and mushy—which she'd surely do if she gave him one more second. Instead, she practically jogged down the hall toward the elevator.

"So you'll do it?" Harper asked Mia as they pulled up to the terminal at Jackson Hole International. "You're okay with this for sure?"

"I am totally okay. I'll make the follow-up call tomorrow."

"I can't believe how stupid I've been. I spent all that time hearing Cole tell me he was gathering information, and arguing with every single piece of it he got, that I never did my own. Like a dang hound dog sitting on a tack, too ornery to get up."

Mia laughed. "One of Dad's favorite sayings."

"Laura Nestrud at Wind Power Solutions. She's awesome. Be nice to her." Harper smiled.

"Go." Mia pointed toward the entry door to the terminal. "I'll use my mix of bedside charm and bitch on her. Promise."

"Great."

Harper hesitated before opening the door. Impulsively she reached across the console and hugged Mia with all her strength. "Thank you. I'm scared to death—this is a lot in a few days. But I'll be back Tuesday or Wednesday. I'll call."

"Go get 'er, Harpo."

Mia hadn't called her that in fifteen years.

CECELIA'S PARTY WAS a huge success. Harper, who'd returned on time, and her newest unveiled painting were even greater successes, and after all the guests had gone, Cecelia herself was beyond ecstatic. It was personally and professionally satisfying and, more importantly, it was deviously helpful to her plan, Harper thought, as she waited for Cecelia to bring late night coffee into her parlor where Harper had asked to meet.

When it arrived, the hot, cream-drenched Columbian brew shored up the nerves jangling in Harper's stomach. "Thank you for staying up with me," she began. "I know it's late."

"It's fine. Harper, dear, I'm concerned that you're still upset about our conversation the other day."

"No, you said all is forgiven."

"I said there was nothing to forgive." She cocked her head and smiled. "We both had stressful mornings at the same time."

"I was a bit rude," Harper said.

"I prefer forthright." Cecelia laughed. "With the exception of your talent, of which I have none, you remind me of myself. I'm vain enough to like that. Plus, I got my way and you came back anyway. How could I be angry?"

"Don't tell me I can't bribe somebody with the best of them. And that's really why I'm here. I have another...forthright...proposal."

"Oh?"

Harper reached into the pocket of the shimmery black oversweater she'd worn and pulled out a set of four pictures. "This is Double Diamond Ranch. It's a part of my family's fifty-thousand acre Paradise Ranch, and it's the place where I'd like to set up a community arts guild, an education facility for arts training, and a studio. Our little town and the surrounding counties are facing the possibility of having all school arts programs cut. I want to make sure there's something to take their place. And you can help."

Half an hour later Cecelia sat back in her chair and released a gently whistling breath.

"And that's it?" she asked.

"*It* is a lot. Goodness I'm asking for the moon."

"It's a rough proposal. It would take some more in-depth planning."

"I have no doubt of that. I suspect lawyers and business planners will need to be involved."

"I'm sure they have those people in Wyoming. Perfectly fine lawyers willing to work with mine."

"Oh, Cecelia, really? You'd consider this? Letting us move my base of operation for you to Wyoming and using my stipend to fund the center?"

"Don't you know by now that I'm not in this for the money, I'm in it for the pure vanity?"

"Not even a little true," Harper said.

Cecelia shook her head as if seeing a wonder for the first time. "Helping fund an arts guild. In Wyoming. Named after me? I couldn't get any more egotistical."

"Art classes. Guest artists. Retreats. Event hosting. It wouldn't be about ego."

"Well I'm in, at least as far as checking out the ranch and talking to planners."

Harper had hoped she'd have the tact to talk Cecelia into this plan. She hadn't foreseen such enthusiasm, even from art-obsessed Cecelia Markham.

"You are much too good to be true."

"One stipulation. Your stipend doesn't get touched. Let's keep the guild separate and see what we can come up with for financing. When do you want to leave? Wednesday you said?"

Her final generous offer was almost one kindness too many to absorb at the end of such a long, emotional day. Harper covered her face with her hands and started to weep for joy.

THREE DAYS LATER, she stepped off a commuter plane for the fourth time in five days. She raised her chin toward the sky and drew in healthy lungfuls of sweet Wyoming air. Her air. The air she wanted to breathe forever. She'd been catching the fever for weeks, and it had finally caught hold. She was terminal. She'd be here, as Cole said, until they buried her. He'd been right and so had Skylar—Harper belonged here, in jeans and boots. Her skirts and bohemian dress code had been a disguise for a woman who didn't believe in herself and had tried to create a persona.

Her head still spun with all the people who had brought the true Harper back to life. Skylar with her end-less spout of idealistic-kid wisdom: grown-ups are some-times too stupid to live; there are a hundred things you could do with this ranch; the bossy bat's been telling you what kind of artist to be.

Betty Hodges with her predictions of doom—that it might be the last time for the art competition.

And Cole with his unintentional reminder that she'd never stopped whining about the oil drilling she really didn't want long enough to do something about it.

No longer. If this was going to be home, it was going to be home on her terms. And she had Skylar to thank for reminding her with that verbal sledgehammer to the head that she had the brains and the right to name those terms.

She'd named them all right. People were scurrying all over to meet them.

The last step of her hurricane-strength plan was all that remained. It hinged on the prayer that all of Cole Wainwright's romantic compliments and declarations of love had come honestly from his heart and weren't just pretty cowboy poetry. Because he was the biggest reason of all she was coming home to stay.

His spate of texts made her fairly confident.

Harpo—Please. Call me or you know I'll hound you.

Harpo—Remember, I've been known to show up without warning.

Harpo—Three time's the charm. Please talk to me.

She'd texted back one mean, misleading message. "Don't come. I won't be here."

It was cruel to make a cowboy beg—but it was also cuter than heck.

"My word, this is beautiful." Cecelia stepped out of the plane behind her.

"I promise you haven't seen anything yet."

They walked through the door at Rosecroft forty minutes later. Without greeting or preamble, Mia grabbed her into a bear hug, letting her go only to pass her to Grace who was the last triplet to take her turn at home. Finally, Grandma Sadie got in the last huge squeeze.

"Thank heavens you're back," Mia said. "We've had to manufacture disasters for Cole to stay and handle around here. He was bound and determined to haul his jumpy ass off to find you."

"I know. He's texted countless times. But he doesn't know I'm here?"

"I don't think so. And there's other news. Mom is coming home day after tomorrow. Skylar came home yesterday, although she has no voice and looks terrible."

"She'll be fine." Harper's heart swelled at the thought of the teen. "I have absolutely no doubt."

"And the reps from Wyoming Wind will be here with their report in two hours."

"Are we crazy?" Harper asked.

"Certifiable," Grace said. "But since it includes every one of us Crockett women, if we end up being committed, we'll have a very happy rubber room at the asylum."

Harper laughed. With a deep breath she took in her sisters, standing united for the first time in their lives. "Before we spring this on poor Mr. Wainwright, I need to tell you all how much I love you. I can't thank you enough."

"We've never had a plan to rally behind," Grace said. "This includes us all and gives Paradise Ranch the potential to be reborn. We've been waiting for this and didn't know it."

"Then let's get underway. I want to start by introducing my wonderful friend Cecelia Markham."

SHE THOUGHT SHE'D prepared herself for seeing Cole again. It had only been three days, for crying out loud. But when he stood in the doorway, his cheeks slapped red from the wind and his hair sexily mussed from his hat, Harper's pulse started a conga beat that led the rest of her vital parts off on a wild line dance, as if she hadn't seen in him a year.

He stepped slowly into the room, rolling the brim of his Stetson with his long deft fingers. She swallowed, remembering exactly how deft they could be.

"Harpo?" His uncertain surprise gave away nothing about what he felt after their strained, strange parting three days earlier. "What are you doing here?"

Nervousness added its beat to the crazy rhythm of her heart. "Turns out I live here. And I came to find you."

"Funny thing," he said, still without expression. "I've been looking for *you* for three days."

"I know." She took one step toward him. "I'm sorry, Cole. I've been working on something, and I really wanted to surprise you. Forgive me?"

"I don't know." He let a lazy smile slip onto his lips. "Maybe. But since you ignored almost all my messages. I get to talk first. Then I'll decide."

"In front of everybody?"

"You brought them to the party."

She looked around and caught winks and thumbs-up from every woman who flanked her. "Fair enough."

"I thought hard about what you said—nobody should have to give up everything in a relationship, but I did ask you to do exactly that. I've been so focused on "my" ranch that I forgot to think about what it is that makes someplace home. Home is where the love is. Here's my idea. What if I give up the Double Diamond, and you give up half the year in Chicago?

"Cole…Give up your land? You can't."

Her plan had him buying back the Double Diamond for a pittance and leasing the house and its immediate yard to Cecelia for the arts guild.

"Yes, I can. I want to take my savings—which, as you know, is nearly enough for the down payment—and invest it here in Paradise. Jump start it. Get it going full strength again so it can be run by you girls and the Thorsons even when we're gone. I'll summer in Chicago with you. You winter with me here."

"But your legacy—this will destroy it. At least for a while. What about your dad?"

"Turns out, he wanted the old dream because I did. He thought he'd disappointed me. I don't need the Double Diamond name. It's just a name. I'll build a new legacy."

She was blown away. All the time she thought she'd been solving the problem—he'd been planning his own changes.

"So? What do you say?" he asked. "Can we start there?"

"Nah," she said, biting her lip at the utter shock in his eyes. "I say let's stay here year 'round?"

"Damn, Harper. I can't keep up." He smiled, still confused.

"I'm coming back to Paradise Ranch, and I have a plan, too. But what I still need before it will work is a full partner. Someone who can be here every day with me to, you know, see to the care of the place. If you're interested, you'd be the only candidate I'd interview for the position."

Suspicion burned in his eyes.

"There are five women surrounding me like the warriors of Amazon. What's the catch?"

"The catch is, that my full partner, aka you, hears what my new business model is, and is okay with it. If he's not, I'll discuss other options because my heart is set on him being part of this."

Cole shook his head, cast a glance at each watching woman and then grabbed Harper into a feet-off-the-floor hug and a twirl.

"I accept."

"You don't know the idea yet."

"Raise pink pandas and sell 'em. I'm all in if you're the boss lady."

"Not the boss. Just the opinionated partner. I want to turn Paradise green. My one and only executive decision will be no oil. It's not a political statement, it's our philosophical one. It was Skylar who said we should focus on what's already here. I want to make this a unique old-fashioned, modern ranch. I have other ideas, too, but they can be discussed later. As can the finances. Your offer is generous, Cole. Maybe too generous."

"Nope. That's part of the package or I'll mutiny."

She laughed. "Okay. You won't be upset if I tell you I've all but made a unilateral decision to have the wind power people come in, oh, say, this afternoon?"

He shook his head in resignation and laughed again. "I don't care about the oil," he said. "I just wanted you to grab some mane on whatever horse you chose and ride like hell to save this place. Oil, wind, solar, hell, five thousand trained monkeys blowing on pinwheels. I want to be with you. Having the ranch is a dream bonus."

"Pinwheels?" Her smile stretched wide. "I vote for them!"

He kissed her silly, right in front of her Amazon posse, and suddenly the room was filled with cheers. She pulled away.

"Now. I have someone I want you to meet."

DARKNESS HAD FALLEN like a heavy velvet blanket over Paradise. The stars above the Henhouse Hilton put Chicago's neon show to shame. Cole leaned against the side of the chicken coop, and pulled Harper to him torso to torso.

"Heck, we should shove all these chickens into a normal pen and live here. Your daddy was nuts."

"Yeah. I think that's where I got it."

He laughed and sighed, looking up into the stars.

"So this is how you think it's going to work: We turn the Double Di into an arts guild with Joely as a live-in caretaker for people who pay to use it as retreat center. You set up regular art classes for the community, and people pay to attend. A volunteer board also lines up visiting artists, and people pay to learn from them. Cecelia will start an endowment to fund the infrastructure. We rake in the dough."

"You added that last part. We work to make a profit. Over time."

"Yeah, yeah. In addition, we build a small wind turbine farm on the far outskirts of the property—fifty miles from the house, in sight of only the freeway and the cattle."

"And we become some of the first in this area to hook into the new power grid. We get paid for adding to that grid, and we get free electricity. Oh," she added, "we also buy a small flock of sheep."

"What? That wasn't in the original business plan."

She rubbed his chest, running her palms across the broad planes of his pecs, and he shivered deeply when she squeezed his shoulder and skimmed up his neck with her fingers, exploring what felt like every sinew and every inch of skin.

"I know," she said. "I only recently talked about it with the local border collie owner. She needs maybe ten. Sheep not border collies. For Asta to herd and for herself to paint. An experiment. And the yarn shop's co-op of knitters and spinners will buy the wool."

"I see. You really figured all this out in two days?"

"No. In two months and then two minutes. When Skylar said grown-ups sometimes acted too stupid to live, she was right, and in that instant I knew I didn't want to be that grown-up in her eyes. But especially not in yours. I spent all this time fighting you every step of the way but never coming up with alternative solutions. When I realized I was waiting for someone else to contact the wind energy company, and I needed to find my own answers, the rest of what I needed to do kind of fell into place."

He adopted a rigid stance and locked his gaze on her, making it as stern as he could fake it. "I am amazed, and I didn't think you could amaze me any more than you already had, but I have one stipulation before I sign onto this craziness. I didn't want to say anything in front of the others. This is a private request."

"What?"

He couldn't keep his face straight at the sight of her big, round, melted chocolate eyes. "I can't say yes unless you first agree to marry me and make this partnership permanently official. I refuse to live in sin with you in Paradise."

She burst out laughing. She laughed so hard she had to hold it back with both hands.

"That's a fine blow to a guy's ego," he said.

"Good." Her breath came in wheezes through her tears of laughter. "Then you won't be expecting my answer."

"Oh?"

"Yes, cowboy. I'll marry you. Gimme a day to find a white dress and you're on. Right here by the Henhouse Hilton if you want."

"You don't need a white dress, Harpo. Wear pajamas. Wear a bath towel. Wear your jeans—that's how I love you best. Cowgirl."

He lowered his head and met her in a long, hard, insanely deep and dangerous kiss. He only stopped to check her eyes. They rested on his, thoughtful and suddenly serious.

"I would."

"Would what?"

"Marry you the day after tomorrow."

"Deal."

"But I'd like to wait for Joely. I want her here."

"Of course," he said. "She needs to be here."

"Is it too fast? Are we being foolish?"

"No, sweetheart. This is not a new love. I've loved you a long time. Ever since you were the wannabe pirate captive princess."

"Oh my gosh! You knew?"

"Of course. I just wasn't very smart in those early days. I didn't know how to take what I really wanted."

"You didn't want me." She scoffed at the idea, sure he was teasing.

"Hey," he said firmly. "Don't argue with a pirate."

He scooped her into his arms and gave two bangs on the side of the henhouse with his boot heel. "Listen up, chickens," he said. "Get ready. Next event around here is a big old Wyoming wedding."

"Hey," she said, stopping the advance of his mouth with a finger. "One more thing I need to say."

"Oh?"

"I love you."

His smile was bright and wide as the Wyoming sky. "And I love you. More than any buried treasure from the past," he said.

Then he bent his head and plundered her mouth until the past was excised, and the only treasure they cared about was the future.

Epilogue

SKYLAR STARED AT the gallery-like wall of beautiful paintings in the community events room of the VA hospital in speechless awe. It was the first time she'd seen it— her painting. The big room was super classy, with wood planks half up the walls and giant floral bouquets on every side table. This was the space where all the winners of the art competition were permanently displayed, and when she'd looked at some of the past winners, Skylar was pretty blown away that her painting was now among them.

"Nothing like that feeling, is there? Seeing your work in public."

Two light, delicate hands floated onto her shoulders and squeezed gently. Skylar craned her neck to find Harper smiling at her, more beautiful than any of the paintings.

"It's cool," she said, trying not to sound too excited or vain. Her mother had warned her about vanity.

Harper laughed. "You can be a little more excited. It's okay."

Skylar couldn't stop her grin then. "Okay, it's the coolest thing ever."

"Yup. I think it is."

"Oh, well, not really. You and Cole being engaged—that's the coolest thing."

"You know? Under that cowgirl cool exterior of yours, you're a pretty awesome kid," Harper said. "Thank you. But we reserved this room to serve double duty—a chance for everyone to see your painting, too. Believe me, I don't mind sharing the night."

Skylar gave the picture one more long look, then she turned to face the room. It was an awesome sight. Fifty people milled around. Denim blue and white streamers swooped along the ceiling in twisted loops. Joely's wheelchair and a rolling hospital bed took up a spot in the middle of the action. She couldn't stand or even sit for long yet, but Harper had insisted the engagement party had to include her. At the moment she greeted people from the chair, and she was actually laughing at something.

The party was like magic.

"Hey, you two!"

Skylar met her mom's smile with a tentative one of her own. Things had been a little better since she'd agreed to let the painting hang. Even though it wasn't labeled with her whole name or age—it was okay.

"Hey, Mel," Harper said.

"Nate just got here," her mom said. "I told him I'd come get you."

That was a miracle, too. She was actually allowed to see Nate as long as there were other people around. The miracle would probably burst like a bubble if her mother knew that they'd sneaked kisses, once in the corner of the basement at, gasp, church, and once behind the park gazebo at a co-op picnic. But they'd been plain, ordinary kisses. Fun, but not as fun as heading out riding with Marcus or going to a movie. Or talking. Nate was hyper-smart. And who was going to tell about plain simple kisses? Not her.

"I'll go find him," Skylar said. "Thanks."

As she walked away she heard her mother's voice as it faded, "Thank you for this, Harper. For knocking a little sense into..."

Skylar didn't know the whole story, but she knew Harper had somehow convinced her mom to let the hospital hang her painting. She didn't even know how to say thank you for that.

She found Nate, and he greeted her with a fist bump. "You look pretty," he said.

"I guess you have to wear dresses to an engagement party," she said, secretly pleased that he liked the jean skirt and boots. The skirt wasn't as short as she wanted, but at least it was above her knees.

They ate until they were stuffed with chicken wings and mini cheesecakes. They got sodas at the bar for free, and she showed him where her painting was hung.

"Next year yours will be here," she promised.

"Maybe," he said. "I'm glad yours is here now."

Music from the hired DJ filled the room with a sudden burst of rich, mellow sound and Tim McGraw and Faith Hill sang out "It's Your Love." A moment later Harper and Cole were on the dance floor, and the room went still. Skylar stared. Harper wore a fluffy layered white skirt on the bottom with a fitted denim shirt on top and beautiful blue cowboy boots. Cole had on jeans and a shirt to match Harper's, with a super-hot, long, leather sports coat. They held each other and danced almost like they'd practiced, with slow, intricately swaying steps. They were so close, Skylar didn't think they could get a feather between them.

Nate put his arm absently around her shoulders, and she snuggled next to him. For a long, nice moment she rested her head against his side.

"Aren't they a sweet couple?" Her mother crept up from behind and budged herself totally between them until she had one arm draped over each of their shoulders.

Skylar started to protest, but Nate caught her eye. He was laughing. Suddenly she couldn't be mad either. Her mom was weird. But she was there for her. All the time.

Skylar watched until the dance ended, and Cole bent Harper backward like she was a fairy princess. He bent over her and kissed her until his mouth melded with hers, and Skylar's heart went a little funny and mushy. They straightened, but the kiss continued, and pretty soon all the people in the room were clapping and stomping their feet and the whistles drowned out the applause.

Skylar laughed and clapped, too. Her mother might still be holding her apart from Nate to keep her safe, but Skylar knew one thing for sure. Nobody was ever going to pull Harper and Cole apart—not for a hundred years.

Keep reading for a sneak peek at the next book in
Lizbeth Selvig's
Seven Brides for Seven Cowboys series,

THE BRIDE WORE RED BOOTS

Available September 2015
From Avon Impulse!

An Excerpt from

THE BRIDE WORE RED BOOTS

DR. AMELIA CROCKETT adored the kids. She just hated clowns. Standing resignedly beside Bitsy Blueberry, Amelia scanned the group of twenty or so young patients gathered for a Halloween party in the pediatric playroom at NYC General Hospital. She didn't see the one child she was looking for, however.

Some children wore super-hero-themed hospital gowns and colorful robes that served as costumes. Others dressed up more traditionally—including three fairies, two princesses, a Harry Potter, and a Darth Vader. Gauze bandage helmets had been decorated like everything from a baseball to a mummy's head. More than one bald scalp was adorned with alien-green paint or a yellow smiley face. Mixed in with casts, wheelchairs, and IV poles on castors, there were also miles of smiles. The kids didn't hate the clown.

Amelia adjusted the stethoscope around her neck, more a prop than necessary at this event, and glared—her sisters would call it the hairy eyeball—at Bitsy Blueberry's wild blue wig. Bitsy thrust one hand forward, aimed one of those obnoxious, old-fashioned, bicycle horns–with-a-bulb that were as requisite to clowning as giant shoes and red noses, at Amelia's face and honked at her rudely. Three times.

Amelia smiled at Bitsy through gritted teeth. "I detest impertinent clowns," she whispered. "I can have you fired."

She wasn't *afraid* of clowns. She simply found them unnecessary and a waste of talent, and Bitsy Blueberry was a perfect example. Beneath the white grease paint, red nose, hideous blue wig, and pinafore-and-pantaloons costume that looked like Raggedy Ann on psychedelic drugs was one of the smartest, most dedicated pediatric nurses in the world—Amelia's best friend Brooke Squires.

"Look who's here, boys and girls." Bitsy grabbed her by the elbow and pulled her unceremoniously to the front of the room, honking in time with Amelia's steps all the way. "It's Dr. Mia Crockett!"

She might as well have said Justin Bieber or One Direction for the cheer that went up from the kids. It was the effect Bitsy's squeaky falsetto voice had on them. Then again, they'd cheer a stinky skunk wrangler if it meant forgetting, for even a short time, the real reasons they were in the hospital. That understanding was all that kept Mia from cuffing her friend upside the head to knock some sense into her. She waved—a tiny rocking motion of her wrist—at the assemblage of sick children.

"Dr. Mia doesn't look very party ready, do you think?" Bitsy/Brooke asked. "Isn't that sad?"

"Not funny," Amelia said through the side of her mouth, her smile plastered in place.

Bitsy pulled a black balloon from her pinafore pocket and blew it into a long tube. Great. Balloon animals.

"I know a secret about Dr. Mia," Bitsy said. "Would you like to know what it is?"

Unsurprisingly, a chorus of yeses filled the room.

"She…" Bitsy dragged the word out suggestively, "is related to Davy Crockett. Do you know who Davy Crockett was?"

The relationship was true thanks to a backwoods ninth cousin somewhere in the 1800s, but Mia rolled her eyes again while a cacophony of shouts followed the question. As Bitsy explained about Davy and hunting and the Alamo, she tied off the black balloon and blew up a brown one. She twisted them intricately until she had a braided circle with a tail.

"You're kidding me," Mia said when she saw the finished product.

"That's pretty cool about Davy Crockett, right?" Bitsy asked "But what isn't cool is that Dr. Mia has no costume. So I made her something. What did I tell you Davy Crockett wore?"

"Coonskin cap!" One little boy shouted the answer from his seat on the floor at the front of the group.

Mia smiled at him, one of a handful of nonsurgical patients she knew from her rounds here on the pediatric floor. Most of her time these days was spent in surgery and following up on those patients. Her work toward fulfilling the requirements needed to take her pediatric surgical boards left little time for meeting all the patients on the floor, but a few kids you only had to meet once, and they wormed their ways into your heart. She looked around again for Rory.

"That's right," Bitsy was saying. "And this is a bal*loon*-skin cap!"

She set it on Mia's head, where it perched like a bird on a treetop. The children clapped and squealed. Bitsy did a chicken flap and waggled one foot in the air before bowing to her audience.

"I want a boon-skin cap!"

A tiny girl, perhaps four, shuffled forward with the aid of the smallest walker possibly in existence. She managed it deftly for one so little, even though her knees knocked together, her feet turned inward, and the patch over one eye obscured half her vision. She wore a hot-pink tutu over frosting-pink footie pajamas, and a tiara topped her black curls. To her own surprise, Mia's throat tightened.

"But, Megan, you have a beautiful crown already," Bitsy said gently.

Megan pulled the little tiara off her head and held it out. "I can twade."

Mia lost it, and she never lost it. She squatted and pulled the balloon cap off her head then held it out, her eyes hot. "I would love to trade with you," she said.

Megan beamed. Mia placed the crazy black-and-brown balloon concoction on the child, where it slipped over her hair and settled to her eyebrows.

"Here," Megan said, pronouncing it "hee-oh." "I put it on you."

She reached over the top of her walker and pressed on Mia's nose to tilt her face downward. She placed the tiara in Mia's hair and patted her head gently. It might as well have been a coronation by the Archduke of Canterbury. Megan had spina bifida and had come through surgery only four days earlier. No child this happy and tender and tough should have such a poor prognosis and uncertain future.

"You can be Davy Cwockett's pincess." Megan smiled, clearly pleased with herself.

"I think you gave me the best costume ever," Mia replied. "Could I have a hug?"

Megan opened her arms wide and squeezed Mia's neck with all her might. She smelled of chocolate bars, apple-cinnamon, and a whiff of the strawberry body lotion they used in this department. A delicious little waif.

She let the child go and stood. A young woman with the same black hair as Megan, arrived at her side. It could only be the girl's mom. She bent and whispered something in her daughter's ear. The child nodded enthusiastically. "Thank you, Doc-toh Mia."

"You're welcome. And thank *you*."

The young mother's eyes met Mia's, gratitude shining in their depths. "Thanks from me, too. This is a wonderful party. So much effort by the whole staff."

"I wish I'd had more to do with it."

"You just did a great deal."

Megan had already started on her way back to the audience. Mia watched her slow progress, forgetting about the crowd until a powerful shove against her upper arm nearly knocked her off her feet. She turned to Bitsy and saw Brooke—grinning through the white make-up.

"What the heck? Clown attack. Go away you maniac."

A few kids in the front row twittered. *Bitsy* honked at her, but it was *Brooke* who leaned close to her ear. "That was awesome, Crockett," she whispered. "It's the kind of thing they need to see you do more of around here."

"They" referred to the medical staff. It was true she didn't have the most warm-hearted reputation—but that was by design. She grabbed Bitsy's ugly horn.

"*They* can kiss my—" *Honk. Honk.*

All the kids heard and saw was Davy Cwockett's pincess stealing a clown's horn. Bitsy capitalized, placing her hands on her knees and exaggerating an enormous laugh.

"Hey! I think I have a new apprentice clown. What do you all say?"

Bitsy pulled off her red nose and popped it on Mia's. The kids screeched their approval.

"I'm going to murder you," Mia whispered, smiling pleasantly.

"Our newest clown needs a name. Any ideas?"

Princess! Clowny! Clown Doctor! Sillypants! Stefoscope!

Names flew from the young mouths like hailstones, pelting Mia with ridiculousness.

"Stethoscope the Clown, I like it." Bitsy laughed. "How about Mercy?"

"Princess Goodheart." That came quietly from Megan's mother, standing against the side wall, certainty in her demeanor.

"Oh, don't you dare," Mia hissed at her friend the clown.

"Perfect!" Bitsy called, her falsetto ringing through the room. "Now, how about we get Princess Goodheart to help with a magic trick?"

Mia's sentimentality of moments before dissipated fully. This was why she couldn't afford such soppy silliness, even over children. If she was going to turn to syrup at the first sign of a child with a walker and a patched eye, perhaps pediatrics wasn't the place for her.

On the other hand, Megan represented the very reason Mia wanted to add pediatric surgery to her resume. She had skill—a special gift according to teachers and some colleagues—and she could use it to help patients like Megan.

"Pick a card, Princess Goodheart." Bitsy nudged her arm.

Mia sighed. She'd have thought a party featuring simple games, fine motor skill-building, and prizes would have been more worthwhile. The mindlessness of magicians and the potential for scaring children with clowns seemed riskier. Indeed there were a few uncomplicated, arcade-type games at little stations around the room, but the magic and clown aficionados had prevailed. Mia grunted and picked a six of clubs.

"Don't show me," said Bitsy.

"I wouldn't dream of it."

"Now, put the card back in the deck. Who wants to wave their hand over the deck and say the magic words?" Bitsy asked.

"Oh God, help! Oh, help, help please. Something's happening to him!"

Bitsy dropped the card deck. In the back of the room, next to a table full of food and treats, a woman stood over the crumpled body of a boy, twitching and flailing his arms. Mia heard his gasps for breath, ripped the ridiculous nose off her face, and pressed into the crowd of kids.

"Keep them all back." She gave the order to Brooke, right beside her and already shushing children in a calm Bitsy voice.

The fact that she continued acting like a clown in the face of an emergency made Mia angry, but there was no time now to call her out for unprofessionalism. In the minute it took Mia to reach the child on the floor, five nurses had surrounded him, and the woman who'd called for help stood by, her face ashen.

"Are you the boy's mother?" Mia asked.

"No. I was standing here when he started choking."

"Out of the way, please." Mia shouldered her way between two nurses, spreading her arms to clear space. They'd turned the boy on his side. "Is he actually choking?"

"He's not. It looks like he's reacting to something he ate," a male nurse replied.

She knelt and rolled the child to his back and froze. "Rory?"

"A patient of yours?" the nurse asked.

"The son of a friend." Mia had missed his arrival. She forced back her shock and set a mental wall around her sudden emotions. "Is there anything on his chart?"

She'd known Rory Beltane and his mother for three years and didn't remember ever hearing about an allergy this life-threatening.

"I don't believe there were any allergies listed," the nurse said. "We're checking his information now. He's a foster kid."

"Yes, I know," she replied with defensive sharpness. "His mother is incapacitated and temporarily can't care for him. Is the foster mother here?"

"No. At work." The male nurse said. "Poor kid. He was just starting to feel better after having his appendix out. This isn't fair."

She had no time to tell him exactly how unfair Rory Beltane's life had been recently. "I need a blood pressure cuff stat. Get him on IV epinephrine, methylpred, and Benadryl, plus IV fluids wide open."

"Right away, Doctor." Nurses scattered.

The male nurse calmly read from a chart. "Excuse me, nurse, are you getting me that cuff?"

"It's on the way," he said, and smiled. "Just checking his chart for you. No notations about allergies. I'll go get the gurney."

Mia blew out her breath. She couldn't fault him for being cool under pressure. Another nurse, this one an older woman with a tone as curt as Mia's, knelt on Rory's far side holding his wrist. "Heart rate is one-forty."

Mia held her stethoscope to the boy's chest. His lips looked slightly swollen. His breathing labored from his tiny chest.

"Here, Dr. Crockett. They're bringing a gurney and the electronic monitor, but this was at the nurse's station if you'd like to start with it."

Mia grabbed the pediatric-sized cuff, its bulb pump reminding her of Brooke's obnoxious horn. With efficient speed, she wrapped the gray material around Rory's arm, placed her stethoscope beneath it, and took the reading.

She'd always been struck by what a stunning child he was. His mother was black and his father white, and his skin was the perfect blend, like the color of a beautiful sand beach after a rain. His head was adorned with a thick shock of dark curly hair, and when they were open, his eyes were a laughing, precocious liquid brown.

"Seventy-five over fifty. Don't like that," she said.

The male nurse appeared with a gurney bed. "I can lift him if you're ready. We have the IV catheter and epinephrine ready."

"Go," Mia ordered.

Moments later Rory had been placed gently on the gurney, and three nurses, like choreographed dancers, had the IV in place, all the meds Mia had ordered running, and were rolling him toward the elevators to get him to intensive care.

"We've called Dr. Wilson, the pediatric hospitalist on duty this week who's seen Rory a couple of times. He'll meet you downstairs," said the male nurse, who'd just begun to be her favorite.

She frowned. "It wasn't necessary to bring him in yet. I think we have this well in hand. We need fewer bodies not more."

"I'll let him know."

The epinephrine began to work slowly but surely, and most of the staff, at Mia's instruction, returned to the party to help the remaining kids. The older nurse and the male nurse remained.

They reached the ICU in mere minutes, and twenty minutes after he'd first passed out, Rory opened his eyes, gasping as the adrenaline coursed through him and staring wild-eyed as if he didn't believe air was reaching his lungs. They'd caught his reaction quickly. Thank God.

"Slow breaths, Rory." Mia placed her hand on his. "Don't be afraid. You have plenty of air now, I promise. Lots of medicine is helping it get better and better. Breath out, nice and slow. I'm going to listen to your heart again, okay?"

Mia found his heart rate slowing. A new automatic blood pressure cuff buzzed and Rory winced as the cuff squeezed. Tears beaded in his eyes. Mia stared at the monitor, while the same male nurse calmed the boy again.

"That's a little better," Mia said. "But, I think we need to keep you away from the party for a while. That was scary, huh?"

"Dr. Mia?" He finally recognized her.

"Hi," she said. "This is a surprise, isn't it?"

"You saved me." He whispered in a thick, hoarse rasp. "Nobody ever saves me."

For the first time Mia truly looked at the nurse who still stood with her. His eyes reflected the stunned surprise she felt.

"Of course I saved you," she said. "Anybody would save you, Rory. You probably haven't needed saving very often, that's all."

"Once. I ate some peanut butter when my mom wasn't at home. I couldn't breathe but Mrs. Anderson next door didn't believe me. " His voice strengthened as he spoke. "I can't eat peanut butter."

"What did you eat today? Do you remember? Right before you couldn't breathe?"

He shook his head vehemently. "A cupcake. A chocolate one. I can eat chocolate."

"Anything else?"

"I had one little Three Musketeer. Bitsy gave it to me. She said the nurses said it was okay to have one because my stomach feels better."

Bitsy again.

"And you don't remember any other food?" Mia asked.

"I didn't eat nothing else. I swear."

"It's all right. It really is. All I care about is finding what made you sick. Look, I'm going to go back to your floor for a few minutes and talk to some more nurses—"

"No! Stay here." He stretched out his arm, his fingers spread beseechingly.

"All right." She let him grab her hand and looked at him quizzically. "But you're fine now."

"No."

He was so certain of his answer. Mia couldn't bear to ignore his wish, although it made no logical sense. At that moment a white-coated man with a Lincoln-esque figure appeared in the doorway.

"My, my, what's going on here? Is that you Rory?"

Rory clung to Mia's hand and didn't answer. Mia looked over the newcomer, not recognizing him, although his badge identified him as Frederick Wilson, MD.

His eyes brushed over Mia, and he dismissed her with a quick "Good afternoon." No questions, no request for an update from her, the medical expert already on the case. She bristled but stayed quietly beside Rory, squeezing his hand.

"How's our man?" Dr. Wilson asked. You doing okay, Champ?" He oozed the schmoozy bedside manner Mia found obsequious, and the child who'd been talkative up to now merely stared at the ceiling.

Dr. Wilson chuckled. "That's our Rory. Not great talk show material, but he plays a mean game of chess from what I hear. A silent, brilliant kind of man. I'm Fred Wilson." He held out a hand. "You must be one of the techs or NAs?"

She stared at him in disbelief. A nursing assistant? Who was this idiot? She looked down and remembered her badge was in her pocket. She fished it out and shoved it at him. "I'm *Dr.* Amelia Crockett, and I've been handling Rory's case since the incident about half an hour ago.

"Crockett. Crockett." He stared off as if accessing information in space somewhere. "The young general surgeon who's working toward a second certification in pediatric surgery. Sorry, I've been here two weeks and have tried to brush up on all the staff resumes. I'm the new chief of staff up in peds. From Johns Hopkins."

She had heard his name and that he was a mover and shaker.

"Dr. Wilson," she acknowledged.

"So, since you're a surgeon and not familiar with Rory's whole case, maybe I'll trouble you to get me up to speed on the anaphylaxis, and then I'll take over so you can get back to what I'm sure is a busy schedule." Dr. Wilson crossed his arms and smiled.

She glared at him again. He may as well have called her *just* a surgeon. And to presume she hadn't familiarized herself with Rory's case before prescribing any course of action...

"I'm sorry, Dr. Wilson," she said. "But with all due respect, I happen to know this child personally, and I'm also well aware of the details of his case. I, too, can read a patient history. I believe I can follow up on this episode and make the report in his chart for you, his regular pediatrician, and the other docs on staff who will treat him."

"It really isn't necessary," he replied, and his smile left his eyes.

Unprofessional as it was, she disliked him on the spot, as if she'd met him somewhere else and hadn't liked him then either.

"I was here to help with the Halloween party," she said. "My afternoon is free and clear."

"That explains much. So that isn't your normal, everyday head ornamentation?"

For a moment she met his gaze, perplexed. *Oh crap.* Her hand flew to her head, and in mortification she pulled off the tiara still stuck there with its little side combs.

"I didn't mean you needed to take it off. It was fetching." Dr. Wilson said. He winked with a condescending kind of flirtatiousness—as if he were testing her.

She flicked an unobtrusive glance at his left hand. No band, but a bulky gold ring with a sizeable onyx set in the middle. She got the impression he was old school all the way, a little annoyed with female practitioners, and extremely cocky about his own abilities.

"Rory is improving rapidly since the administration of Benadryl and epinephrine. We are uncertain of the allergen although, from what he's told us, he has a sensitivity to peanut butter. As far as we know, he hasn't eaten any nuts."

Dr. Wilson nodded, patting Rory periodically on the shoulder. Rory continued his silence.

"Rory, do you mind if I do a little exam on your tummy?" Dr. Wilson asked.

"Dr. Mia already did it." He turned his head enough to look at her.

Again he smiled, ignoring Mia. "I'm sure she did, but I'm a different kind of doctor, and I'd like to help her make sure you're okay. Maybe if everyone left the room except you and me and Darren, it won't be so embarrassing if I check you out? Dr. Crockett can go and make sure there's nothing at the party that will hurt you again."

Darren, she noted absently. She hadn't taken the time to look at his nametag.

Rory shook his head and squeezed Mia's hand again.

"As you can see," she said, curtly. "The child is still a little traumatized. Perhaps in this case you and I could switch roles? I'll stay with my patient, and you'll make a better sleuth?"

Dr. Wilson's mouth tightened, and he drew his shoulders back as if prepping for a confrontation. In that instant, the sense of recognition she'd had earlier flashed into unexpected clarity.

Gabriel Harrison.

Her stomach flipped crazily. Fiftyish Dr. Fred Wilson didn't look a bit like the arrogant, self-important, patient advocate she'd met six weeks before at the VA medical center in her old home city of Jackson, Wyoming. In truth, nobody who wasn't making seven figures as a big-screen heartthrob looked like Gabriel Harrison. The trouble was, just as Dr. Wilson knew he was good, Lieutenant—retired Lieutenant—Harrison knew he was gorgeous. Both men believed they had the only handle on expertise and information.

She'd met Harrison after a car accident in the middle of September had left her mother and one of her sisters seriously injured, and he'd been assigned as liaison between her family, her mother and sister, and the medical staff. He'd made himself charming—like a medicine show snake oil salesman—and her sisters, all five of them, now adored him. Her mother considered him her personal guardian angel. But he'd treated Mia like she'd gotten her degree from a Cracker Jack box.

He was continuing the practice to this day in all their correspondence—which was frequent considering how he loved ignoring her requests for information.

Mia was glad that at her planned trip home for Christmas, her mother and sister would be home and Gabriel Harrison, patient advocate, would be long gone from their lives. Unfortunately, it wouldn't work quite so easily with Fred Wilson. She was stuck more-or-less permanently with him.

"I want Dr. Mia to stay."

Rory's fingers tightened on her hand, and the last vestiges of memories from Wyoming slipped away.

"That settles it in my opinion. At my patient's request, I will stay with him. Darren, would you be willing to accompany Dr. Wilson upstairs to ask some questions about the food? And maybe you'd be willing on your way to order Mr. Beltane here a glass of juice and maybe some ice?"

"Yes," Darren said. "Sure."

Fred Wilson, on the other hand, looked as if he might need the Heimlich maneuver. "If I might have a word with you outside, Dr. Crockett."

She met his gaze coolly. "Rory, I need to help Dr. Wilson with some things, but I'll be right back. I promise."

"No."

"I promise, honey." She smoothed the child's hair back, and he finally nodded.

Dr. Wilson patted Rory on the shoulder a final time. "I'll see you tomorrow, young man. You may even get to go home. Bet you'd like that."

Rory gave an anemic shrug.

She slipped out of the room with Fred Wilson behind her, took several steps away from the door, and spun to face him.

"Would you care to explain what this is about?" she demanded.

"Dr. Crockett, I have heard your reputation as the wonder child of this medical community," Wilson said. "But in my department you have no seniority, and your fast track to the top is not impressive. No matter how good you are technically, nothing can take the place of years of experience. And just because you wear a stethoscope and have been in this physical location longer than I have, doesn't mean you possess anywhere near the experience I do. You were insubordinate in front of the patient and my staff. I won't have that."

She didn't blink or raise her voice. She put her hands in her lab coat pockets to keep from showing her flexing fingers.

"In point of fact, Dr. Wilson, you treated *me* like a first year intern in there, even though I am the senior medical staff member in this matter. I also have the trust of the patient and you ignored that along with his wishes. I treated you with the respect you commanded. It's not my style to kiss up to anyone or brown nose a superior to make my way. Good medicine is all I care about. You or one of your hospital staff docs will handle his care in regard to his recent appendectomy. At the moment, because he is still in a little bit of shock, that is secondary to aftercare from the anaphylaxis. I didn't appreciate you not bowing to my expertise or asking me to debrief you— even if I didn't just come from Johns Hopkins."

"You take a pretty surly tone."

"I apologize."

For a long moment he assessed her and finally he shook his head. "I don't like your style, Doctor. But the staff thinks highly of your skill. We'll let this slide because the child did request your presence."

"I don't love your style either." She smiled. "But I've heard the staff thinks highly of your bedside manner. I hope we can continue to understand each other better as we are required to work together."

"I hope that's so." He nodded curtly and left.

Why were older doctors so prejudiced when it came to believing surgeons knew their stuff? Mia was tired of dealing with the game playing and politics of staff. What was wrong with being a damn good physician?

She returned to Rory, and he smiled with relief. "How are you, kiddo?" she asked. "Do your stitches or anything inside your tummy hurt?"

"No."

"You didn't want Dr. Wilson to stay and examine you. Do you not like him?"

"He's nice."

That stymied her. "Then why—?"

"He didn't have nothin' to do with making me better." Rory interrupted. "Only you and Dr. Thomas who took out my appendix. And...you..." His huge, dark eyes brimmed with tears that clung to his lashes like diamonds but didn't spill.

"I what, Rory?"

"You saved me. And I want you to save Jack."

"Jack?" A slice of new panic dove through her stomach. She knew Jack. "Your cat?"

"Yeah."

"Why does Jack need saving?"

"Buster has him," he said. "But Mrs. Murray, the foster lady, she said I couldn't bring him with me 'cause she's allergic to cats. And Buster said he'd keep him for a while, but he can't keep him forever because mostly the shelters won't let him have a cat neither."

A slight dizziness started her head spinning. "Who's Buster?"

"I lived with him a while after my mama got taken away."

"Where does Buster live?"

"Everywhere," he said, and Mia's stomach slowly started to sink. "He's my best friend. Sometimes he goes to the shelter by the church in Upper Manhattan. Sometimes he lives under the bridge by the East River. Sometimes he stays in the camp with his friends."

"Rory? Is Buster a homeless man?"

"Buster says he doesn't want a normal house. He says he owns the whole city of New York, and he should 'cause he fought for it. But Jack does need a house 'cause it's going to snow pretty soon, and he'll freeze. So...will you save him like you saved me?"

"Oh, I don't know if..."

She thought about all the animals she'd had growing up on one of the biggest cattle ranches in Wyoming. Until leaving for college she'd never imagined that some kids might not have pets. No dogs, no cats, no horses.

"Please? Jack's the only one left who really loves me."

"That's so not true, Rory. I know it's not true." She sighed and sat next to him on the mattress. "I love you. I'm your friend, right? And your mom loves you so much."

"Mrs. Murray the foster lady said she was too sick to be a good mother. 'Cause she's in the hospital, too."

"Again?" Mia stared at him, heartbroken. "Rory, since when? What happened?"

"I don't know when. Before I came here. I tried to call her to tell her I was sick, but she wasn't at the jail."

For the past three months, Monique Beltane had resided in a women's prison in upstate New York where she was serving one year for theft and possession of a narcotic. She was also living through treatment for breast cancer.

"That's not true, Rory. Your mom will never be too sick to love you. And she's a good mom, too. She's just been sick for such a long time."

Mia knew Monique's story well. She'd become addicted to prescription opioids after botched hernia surgery four years before. Almost a year after that operation, Mia had been the one to operate again, and had managed to relieve some of Monique's chronic pain. During the three years that had followed, she'd kept in touch with Monique and her son Rory, even seeing them socially. She liked the woman, plain and simple. Monique wanted to get well. She was just weak when it came to pain. Still, she'd gotten herself clean, and Mia believed she might have made a success of it. Then, six months ago, she'd been diagnosed with breast cancer.

She'd managed the chemo, but the mastectomy and the oxycodone to which she was so highly addicted had pushed her back over the edge. Three months ago, she'd purchased oxycodone from an undercover agent and that had been the end.

But she'd just gone back into the hospital. Mia didn't know yet what was wrong, but her intuition didn't offer much hope. At this stage in her recovery, no illness boded well. She had a mental note made to track down Monique's physician.

And now here was Rory.

You couldn't make crap like this up.

"But even if Mom gets better she's in jail for a long time. All I got is Jack."

"But if Jack can't stay with you at the Murrays, where would he go if we find him?"

He shrugged, and his eyes filled with water. Mia sighed. This was so *not* in her job description. How did one even begin to try looking for a homeless cat in New York City?

"Please, Dr. Mia."

She smoothed his thick curls. She'd never find one cat in a city that must have a billion. "All right, listen to me, okay? I will see what I can find out, but you're practically a young man and you're smart. You know I might not have any luck. You promise you won't be angry with me if I don't find him?"

He smiled a watery but genuine true, toothy, ten-year-old's grin. "You will."

About the Author

LIZBETH SELVIG LIVES in Minnesota with her best friend (aka her husband) and a gray Arabian gelding named Jedi. After working as a newspaper journalist and magazine editor, and raising an equine veterinarian daughter and a talented musician son, Lizbeth won RWA's prestigious Golden Heart Contest® in 2010 with her contemporary romance, *The Rancher and the Rock Star*, and was a 2014 nominee for RWA's RITA® Award with her second published novel, *Rescued by a Stranger*. In her spare time, she loves to hike, quilt, read, horseback ride, and spend time with her new granddaughter. She also has many four-legged grandchildren—more than twenty—including a wallaby, two alpacas, a donkey, a pig, a sugar glider, and many dogs, cats, and horses (pics of all appear on her website www.lizbethselvig.com). She loves connecting with readers—contact her any time!

Give in to your Impulses . . .
Continue reading for excerpts from
our newest Avon Impulse books.
Available now wherever e-books are sold.

CHASING JILLIAN
A LOVE AND FOOTBALL NOVEL
By Julie Brannagh

EASY TARGET
AN ELITE OPS NOVEL
By Kay Thomas

DIRTY THOUGHTS
A MECHANICS OF LOVE NOVEL
By Megan Erickson

LAST FIRST KISS
A BRIGHTWATER NOVEL
By Lia Riley

An Excerpt from

CHASING JILLIAN
A Love and Football Novel
by Julie Brannagh

The fifth novel in *USA Today* bestselling
author Julie Brannagh's Love and Football
series! Jillian Miller likes her job working in
the front office for the Seattle Sharks, but
lately she needs a change, which takes her into
foreign territory: the Sharks' workout facility
after hours. The last thing she expects is a hot,
grumbly god among men to be there as witness.

As Jillian discovers that the new her is about
so much more than she sees in the mirror,
can she discover that happiness and love
are oh-so-much better than perfect?

One dance with him and Jillian was pulling herself out of his arms and getting back into the car. She could dance with him and not get emotional about it. He was just another guy. She was not going to let herself get stupid over someone who was clearly only interested in her as a friend.

His hold on her was gentle. He smelled good. She saw the flash of his smile when she peeked up at him. She'd felt shy with Carlos because she didn't know him. She didn't have that problem with Seth. She wanted to move closer, but she shouldn't.

She tried to remind herself of the fact that Seth probably had more than a few friends with benefits, even if he was between girlfriends at the time. He was a guy. He probably wasn't celibate, and they weren't romantic with each other. There was also the tiny fact that anything that happened between them was not going to end well.

She was in more trouble than she knew how to get out of.

At first, Jillian rested her head against his cheek. A minute or so later, she laid her head on his chest. They swayed together, feet barely moving, and he realized his heart was pounding. He'd never experienced anything as romantic as dancing late at night in a deserted city park to a song playing on his car's sound system. The darkness wrapped them in the softest cocoon. He glanced down at her as he felt her slowly relaxing against him.

It's not the pale moon that excites me
That thrills and delights me
Oh, no
It's just the nearness of you

He took a deep breath of the vanilla scent he'd recognize anywhere as hers. His fingers stroked the small of her back, and he heard her sigh. Slow dancing was even better than he remembered. Then again, he wasn't in junior high anymore, and he held a woman in his arms, not a teenage girl. There was a lot to be said for delayed gratification. Dancing with Jillian was all about the smallest movements, and letting things build. He laid his cheek against hers.

"I shouldn't be doing this," she whispered.

"Why not?" he whispered back.

"It's not a good idea."

"We're just dancing, Jill."

And if things got any hotter between them, they'd be naked. She didn't try to step away from him. If she'd resisted him at all, if she'd shown reluctance or fear or hesitation, he would have let her go, and he would walk away. Her fingers tangled in his hair.

They were just friends. He didn't think he had those kinds of feelings for this woman: the sexual, amorous, bow-chicka-bow-bow feelings, despite the fact his pulse was racing, his fingers itched to touch her, and he knew he should let go of her. It didn't matter that he was still having hotter-than-the-invention-of-fire dreams about Jillian most nights, either. He wasn't going to consider what kind of tricks his subconscious played on him. Instead, he pulled her a fraction of an inch closer. He slid one hand up her back, feeling her long, silky-soft blonde hair cascading over his fingers, and she trembled. He cupped her cheek in his hand. He couldn't take his eyes off her mouth. Just a couple of inches more and he'd kiss her. He moved slowly, but purposefully.

He watched her eyelids flutter closed. He felt her quick intake of breath. He wondered how she tasted. He'd know in a few seconds.

"I want to kiss you," he breathed against her mouth.

The silence was broken by the screaming guitars of Guns n' Roses.

That would teach him to use the "shuffle" function.

An Excerpt from

EASY TARGET
An Elite Ops Novel
by Kay Thomas

Award-winning author Kay Thomas continues her thrilling Elite Ops series. Fighting to clear her brother of murder, freelance reporter Sassy Smith is suddenly kidnapped and thrown into a truck with other women who are about to be sold . . . or worse. When she sees an opportunity for escape Sassy takes it, but she may have just jumped from the frying pan into the fire.

"You're thinking too much." She felt his words vibrate against the inside of her thigh as he kissed her there before easing up beside her on the bed. "Stop that."

She smiled, not at all surprised that he seemed to read her mind. He sat up on the edge of the lower bunk next to her and took his own boots and socks off, then his shirt, jeans, and . . .

She closed her eyes.

He was going to be naked soon, and she had to say something first. He slid up beside her on the mattress and pulled her back to his front, with his back toward the wall. She felt the insistence of his erection against her bottom.

She started to turn in his arms, but he held onto her with an arm clamped around her waist. "Slow down. I just want to enjoy holding you a while. I've thought about this for a very long time."

Really? That came as a complete surprise. It was on the tip of her tongue to ask how long, but when he trailed his fingertips back and forth across her rib cage, she quit thinking. Instead, she sighed in relaxed contentment. "I didn't know it could be like that."

Why had she been nervous about this for so long? She could tell him now. It'd be okay.

He kissed the side of her neck and whispered in her ear, "Well, I promise we're just getting started."

She tensed, and he absolutely noticed but misunderstood the reason.

He gathered her more snugly against his chest. "Don't worry, we can take this as slow as you want."

"You'd do that?" The mixture of relief and disappointment she felt was . . . confusing.

"God, Sassy. What sort of men have you—"

The sound of screeching brakes interrupted whatever else he'd been about to say. Sassy felt the momentum shoving her backward into his chest.

"What's happening?" she gasped.

"I don't know." He tugged his arm from under her body to see his watch. "We're not scheduled to stop for several more hours." The stark change from relaxed lover to alert super soldier was dramatic. "Get dressed. Now."

Bryan hauled himself forward out of bed and started shoving clothes toward her while Sassy was still playing catch-up. Her panties were inside out, but she slid them on at his urging without fixing them.

"C'mon, Sassy."

The horrific screeching continued, intensifying as she pulled her jeans, sweater, socks, and boots on. She was lacing up as a rumbling shuddering started.

"Fuck," Bryan mumbled.

"What is it?" She finished with the boots and looked up from her crouched position as the screeching abruptly stopped.

"Hang on!" He grabbed for her.

Easy Target

The rail car shifted, and she felt like she was in a carnival house ride as the compartment swayed wildly from side to side. The car tilted, and the bed she was sitting on flew up in the air. She hit her head on the bunk above, and the world went black.

An Excerpt from

DIRTY THOUGHTS
A Mechanics of Love Novel
by Megan Erickson

Some things are sexier the second time around.

Cal Payton has gruff and grumbly down to an
art . . . all the better for keeping people away. And
it usually works. Until Jenna Macmillan—his
biggest mistake—walks into Payton and Sons
mechanic shop all grown up, looking like sunshine,
and inspiring more than a few dirty thoughts.

An Excerpt from

DIRTY THOUGHTS

A Mechanics of Love Novel

by Megan Erickson

Okay, so admittedly Jenna had known this was a stupid idea. She'd tried to talk herself out of it the whole way, muttering to herself as she sat at a stop light. The elderly man in the car in the lane beside her had been staring at her like she was nuts.

And she was. Totally nuts.

It'd been almost a decade since she'd seen Cal Payton and yet one look at those silvery blue eyes and she was shoved right back to the head-over-heels *in love* eighteen-year-old girl she'd been.

Cal had been hot in high school, but damn, had time been good to him. He'd always been a solid guy, never really hitting that awkward skinny stage some teenage boys went through after a growth spurt.

And now . . . well . . . Cal looked downright sinful standing there in the garage. He'd rolled down the top of his coveralls, revealing a white T-shirt that looked painted on, for God's sake. She could see the ridges of his abs, the outline of his pecs. A large smudge on the sleeve drew her attention to his bulging biceps and muscular, veined forearms. Did he lift these damn cars all day? Thank God it was hot as Hades outside already so she could get by with flushed cheeks.

And he was staring at her, those eyes which hadn't changed one bit. Cal never cared much for social mores. He looked people in the eye and he held it long past comfort. Cal had always needed that, to be able to measure up who he was dealing with before he ever uttered a word.

She wondered how she measured up. It'd been a long time since he'd laid eyes on her, and the last time he had, he'd been furious.

Well, she was the one that came here. She was the one that needed something. She might as well speak up, even though what she needed right now was a drink. A stiff one. "Hi, Cal." She went with a smile that surely looked a little strained.

He stood with his booted feet shoulder-width apart, and at the sound of her voice, he started a bit. He finally stopped doing that staring thing as his gaze shifted to the car by her side, then back to her. "Jenna."

His voice. Well, crap, how could she have forgotten about his voice? It was low and silky with a spicy edge, like Mexican chocolate. It warmed her belly and raised goose bumps on her skin.

She cleared her throat as he began walking toward her, his gaze teetering between her and the car. Brent was off to the side, watching them with his arms crossed over his chest. He winked at her. She hid her grin with pursed lips and rolled her eyes. He was a good-looking bastard, but irritating as hell. Nice to see *some* things never changed. "Hey, Brent."

"Hey there, Jenna. Looking good."

Cal whipped his head toward his brother. "Get back to work."

Brent gave him a sloppy salute and then shot her another

knowing smirk before turning around and retreating back into the garage bay.

When she faced Cal again, she jolted, because he was close now, almost in her personal space. His eyes bored into her. "What're ya doing here, Jenna?"

His question wasn't accusatory. It was conversational, but the intent was in his tone, laying latent until she gave him reason to really put the screws to her. She didn't know if he meant what was she doing here, at his garage, or what he was doing in town. But she went for the easy question first.

She gestured to the car. "I, uh, I think the bearings need to be replaced. I know that I could take it anywhere but . . ." She didn't want to tell him it was Dylan's car, and he was the one who let it go so long that she swore the front tires were going to fall off. As much as her brother loved his car, he was an idiot. An idiot who despised Cal, and she was pretty sure the feeling was vice versa. "I wanted to make sure the job was done right and everyone knows you do the best job here." That part was true. The Paytons had a great reputation in Tory.

But Cal never let anything go. He narrowed his eyes and propped his hands on his hips, drawing attention to the muscles in his arms. "How do you know we still do the best job here if you haven't been back in ten years?"

Well then. Couldn't he just nod and take her keys? She held them in her hand, gripping them so tightly that the edge was digging into her palm. She loosened her grip. "Because when I did live here, your father was the best, and I know *you* don't do anything unless you do it the best." Her voice faded off. Even though the last time she'd seen Cal, his eyes had been snapping in anger, at least they'd been showing some sort of emotion. This steady blank gaze was killing her. Not when she knew how his eyes looked when he smiled, as the skin at the corners crinkled and the silver of his irises flashed.

She thought now that this had been a mistake. She'd offered to get the car fixed for her brother while he was out of town. And while she knew Cal worked with his dad now, she'd still expected to run into Jack. And even though he was a total jerk face, she would have rather dealt with him than endure this uncomfortable situation with Cal right now. "You know, it's fine. Don't worry about it, I'll just—"

He snatched the keys out of her hand. Right. Out. Of. Her. Hand.

"Hey!" She propped a hand on her hip, but he wasn't even looking at her, instead fingering the key ring. "Do you always steal keys from your customers?"

He cocked his head and raised an eyebrow at her. There was the smallest hint of a smile, just a tug at the corner of his lips. "I don't make that a habit, no."

"So I'm special then?" She was flirting. Was this flirting? Oh God, it was. She was flirting with her high school boyfriend, the guy who'd taken her virginity, and the guy whose heart she'd broken when she had to make one of the most difficult decisions of her life.

She'd broken her own heart in the process.

His gaze dropped, just for a second, then snapped back to her face. "Yeah, you're special."

He turned around, checking out the car, while she stood gaping at his back. He'd . . . he'd flirted back, right? Cal wasn't really a flirting kind of guy. He said what he wanted and followed through. But flirting Cal?

She shook her head. It'd been over ten years. Surely he'd lived a lot of life during that time she'd been away, going to college, then grad school, then working in New York. She didn't want to think about what that flirting might mean, now that she was back in Tory for good. Except he didn't know that.

An Excerpt from

LAST FIRST KISS
A Brightwater Novel
by Lia Riley

A kiss is just the beginning . . .

Pinterest Perfect. Or so Annie Carson's life
appears on her popular blog. Reality is . . . messier.
Especially when it lands her back in one-cow
town, Brightwater, California, and back in the
path of the gorgeous six-foot-four reason she left.

"Sawyer?" All she could do was gape, wide-eyed and breathless—too breathless. Could he tell? Hard to say as he maintained his customary faraway expression, the one that made it look as if he'd stepped out of a black and white photograph.

"Annie."

She jumped. Hearing her name on his tongue plucked something deep in her belly, a sweet aching string, the hint of a chord she only ever found in the dark with her own hand. It was impossible not to stare, and suddenly the long years disappeared, until she was that curious seventeen-year-old girl again, seeing a gorgeous boy watching her from the riverbanks, and wondering if the Earth's magnetic poles had quietly flipped.

Stop. Just say no to unwelcome physical reactions. Her body might turn traitor, but her mind wouldn't let her down. She'd fallen for this guy's good looks before, believed they mirrored a goodness inside—a mistake she wouldn't make twice. No man would ever be allowed to stand by and watch her crash again.

Never would she cry in the shower so no one could hear.

Never would she wait for her child to fall asleep so she could fall apart.

Never would she jump and blindly fall.

Sawyer removed his worn tan Stetson and stood. Treacherous hyperawareness raced along her spine and radiated through her hips in a slow, hot electric pulse. He clocked in over six-feet, with steadfast sagebrush green eyes that gave little away. Flecks of ginger gleamed from the scruff roughing his strong jaw and lightened the dark chestnut of his short-cropped hair.

"Hey." Her cheeks warmed as any better words scampered out of reach. The mile-long "to do" list taped to the fridge didn't include squirming in front of the guy she'd nurtured a secret crush on during her teenage years. A guy who, at the sole party Annie attended in high school, abandoned her in a hallway closet during "Seven Minutes in Heaven" to mothballed jackets, old leather shoes, ruthless taunts, and everlasting shame.

He reset his hat. "Did I wake you?" His voice had always appealed to her, but the subtle rough deepening was something else, as if every syllable dragged over a gravel road.

She checked her robe's tie. "Hammering at sunrise kind of has that effect on people."

He gave her a long look. His steadfast perusal didn't waver an inch below her neck, but still, as he lazily scanned each feature, she felt undressed to bare skin. Guess his old confidence hadn't faded, not a cocky manufactured arrogance, but a guy completely comfortable in his own skin.

And what ruggedly handsome, sun-bronzed skin it was, covering all sorts of interesting new muscles he hadn't sported in high school.

"Heard Grandma paid you a visit," he said at last.

Annie doused the unwelcome glow kindling in her chest with a bucket of ice-cold realism. He wasn't here to see her, merely deal with a mess. *Hear that, hormones? Don't be stupid.* She set a hand on her hip, summoning as much dignity as she could muster with a serious case of bedhead. "Visit? Your grandma killed one of our chickens and baked it in a pie. Not exactly the welcome wagon. More like a medieval, craz—"

"Subtlety isn't one of her strong points. We had words last night. It won't happen again." He dusted his hands on his narrow, denim-clad hips and bent down.

Unf.

The hard-working folks at Wrangler deserved a medal for their service. Nothing—NOTHING—else made a male ass look so fine. "Found this, too." He lifted her forgotten bottle of scotch.

"Oh, weird." She plucked it from his grasp. "Wonder how that got out here?" Crap, too saccharine a tone, sweet but clearly false.

He raised his brows as his hooded gaze dropped a fraction. Not enough to be a leer, but definitely a look.

Her threadbare terrycloth hit mid-thigh. Here stood the hottest guy west of the Mississippi and she hadn't shaved since who-the-hell knows and sported a lop-sided bruise on her knee from yesterday's unfortunate encounter with a gopher hole.

Maybe she failed at keeping up appearances, but God as her witness, she'd maintain her posture. "About your Grandma, I was two seconds from calling the cops on her last night."

"That a fact?" The corner of his wide mouth twitched. "Next time, that's exactly what you should do."

"Next time?" She sputtered, waving the bottle for emphasis. "There sure as heck better not be a next time!"

That little burst of sass earned the full-force of his smile. Laugh lines crinkled at the corners of deep-set eyes that belonged nowhere but the bedroom. As a boy, he was a sight, as a man, he'd become a vision. "Why are you back? I mean, after all this time?"